HINGES
MEREDITH MCCLAREN

BOOK 3
MECHANICAL MEN

"MANY THANKS TO ALL THE IMPS AND ODDS, WHO PUSHED, POKED, AND PRODDED ME ALONG."

- MEREDITH MCCLAREN

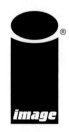

IMAGE COMICS, INC.
ROBERT KIRKMAN — CHIEF OPERATING OFFICER
ERIK LARSEN — CHIEF FINANCIAL OFFICER
TODD MCFARLANE — PRESIDENT
MARC SILVESTRI — CHIEF EXECUTIVE OFFICER
JIM VALENTINO — VICE-PRESIDENT

ERIC STEPHENSON — PUBLISHER
COREY MURPHY — DIRECTOR OF SALES
JEFF BOISON — DIRECTOR OF PUBLISHING PLANNING & BOOK TRADE SALES
CHRIS ROSS — DIRECTOR OF DIGITAL SALES
KAT SALAZAR — DIRECTOR OF PR & MARKETING
BRANWYN BIGGLESTONE — CONTROLLER
SUSAN KORPELA - ACCOUNTS MANAGER
DREW GILL — ART DIRECTOR
BRETT WARNOCK — PRODUCTION MANAGER
MEREDITH WALLACE — PRINT MANAGER
BRIAN SKELLY — PUBLICIST
ALY HOFFMAN — CONVENTIONS & EVENTS COORDINATOR
SASHA HEAD — SALES & MARKETING PRODUCTION DESIGNER
DAVID BROTHERS — BRANDING MANAGER
MELISSA GIFFORD — CONTENT MANAGER
ERIKA SCHNATZ — PRODUCTION ARTIST
RYAN BREWER — PRODUCTION ARTIST
SHANNA MATUSZAK — PRODUCTION ARTIST
TRICIA RAMOS — PRODUCTION ARTIST
VINCENT KUKUA — PRODUCTION ARTIST
JEFF STANG — DIRECT MARKET SALES REPRESENTATIVE
EMILIO BAUTISTA — DIGITAL SALES ASSOCIATE
LEANNA CAUNTER — ACCOUNTING ASSISTANT
IMAGECOMICS.COM

FIRST PRINTING
ISBN: 978-1-5343-0039-2

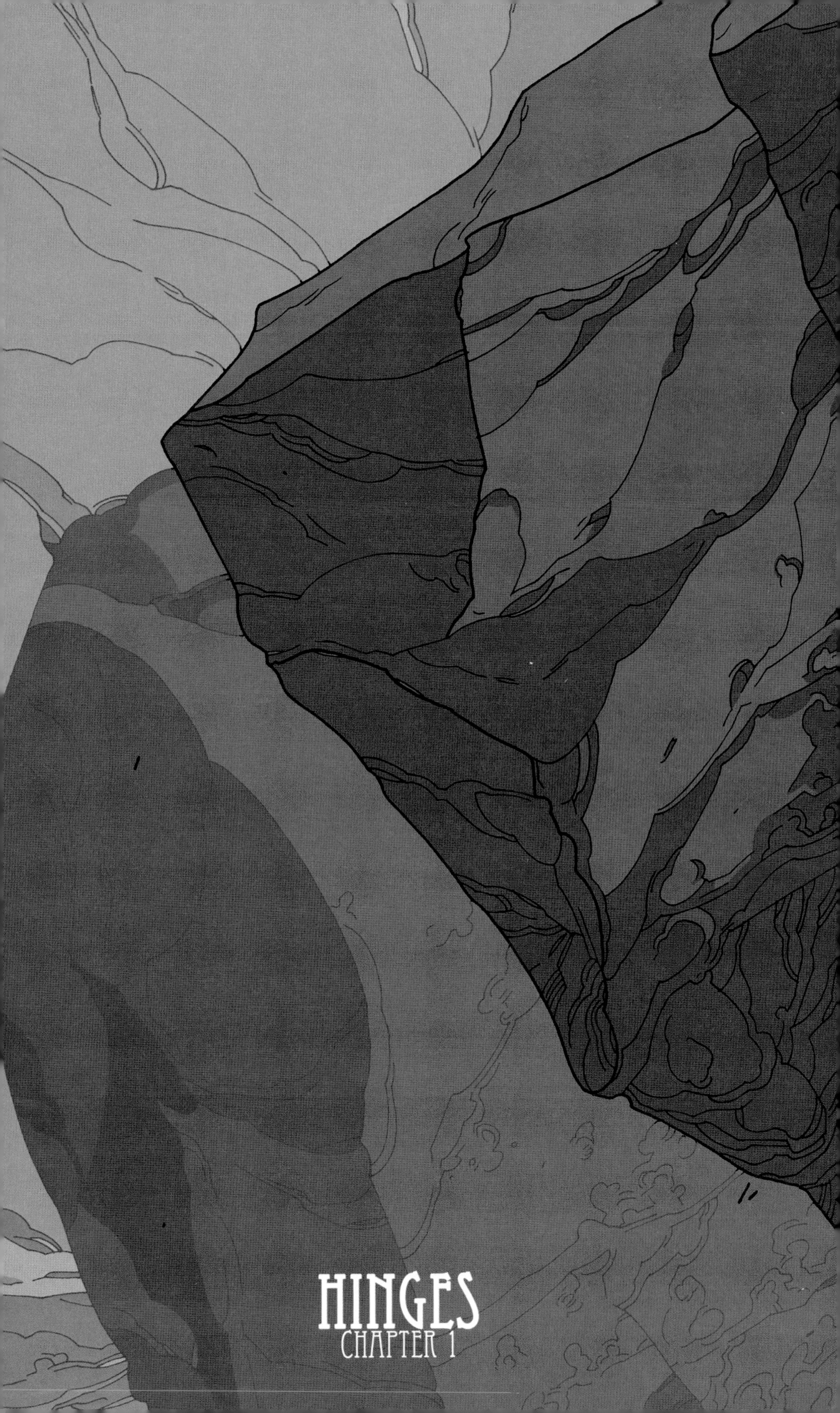
HINGES
CHAPTER 1

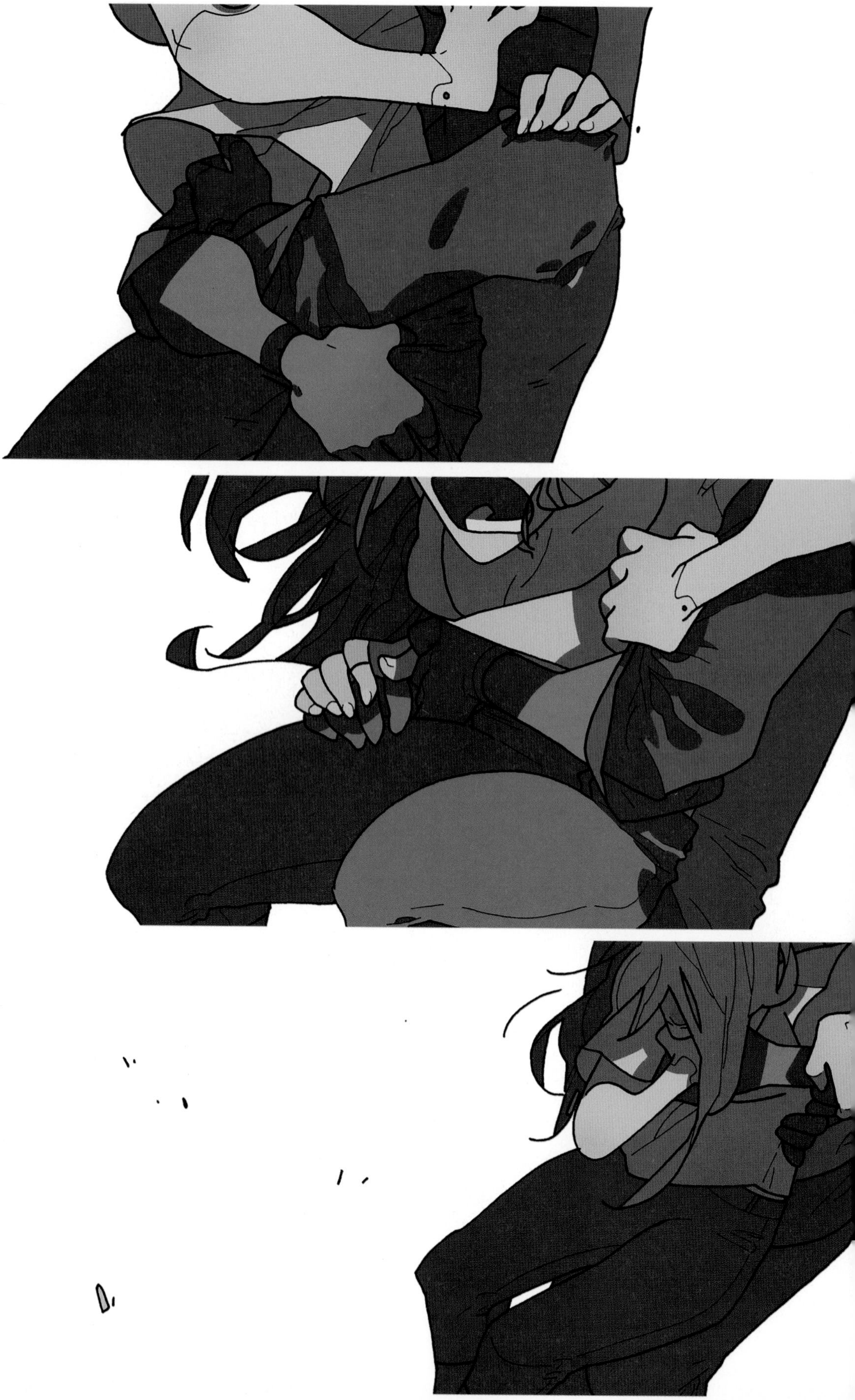

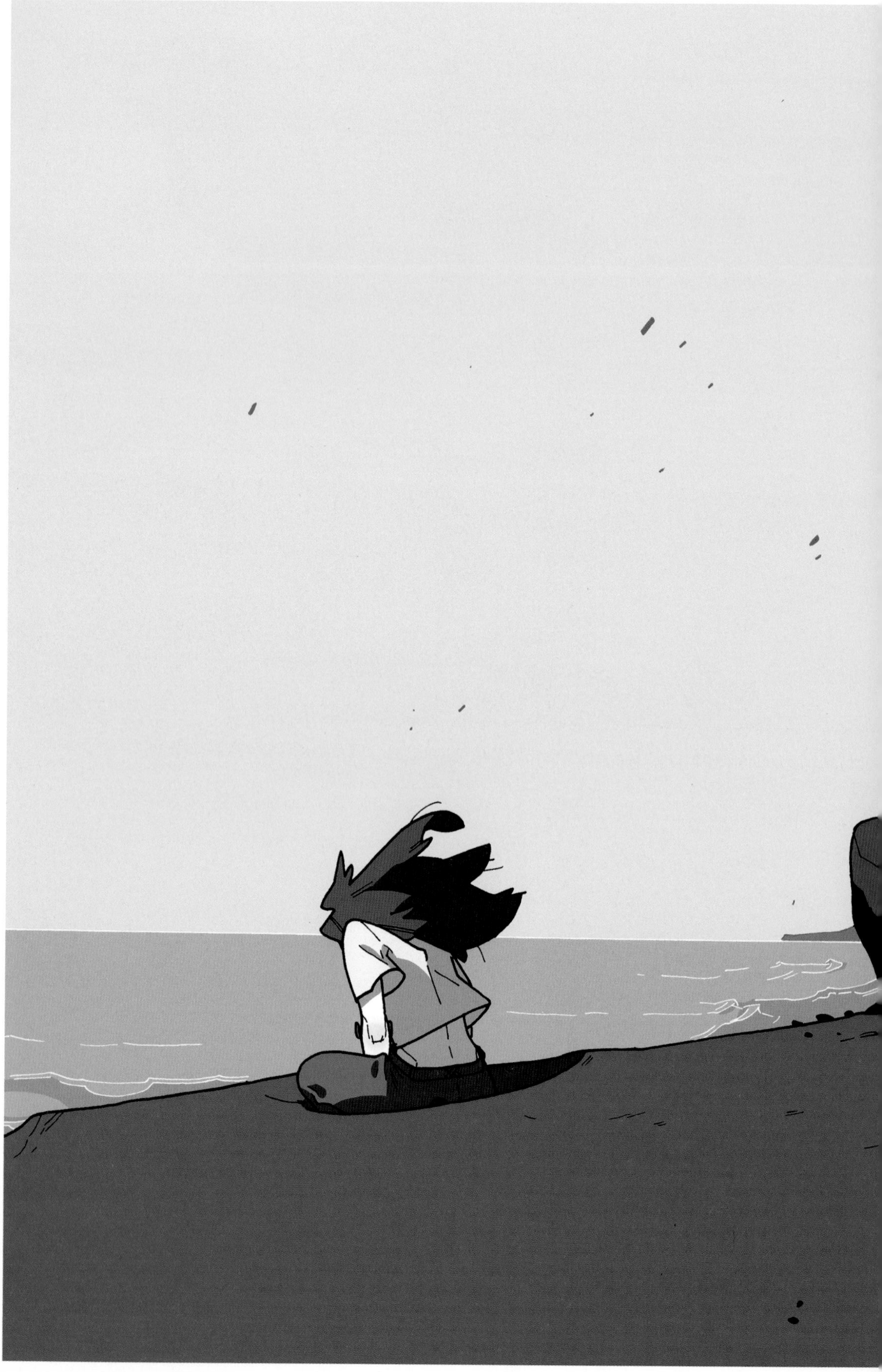

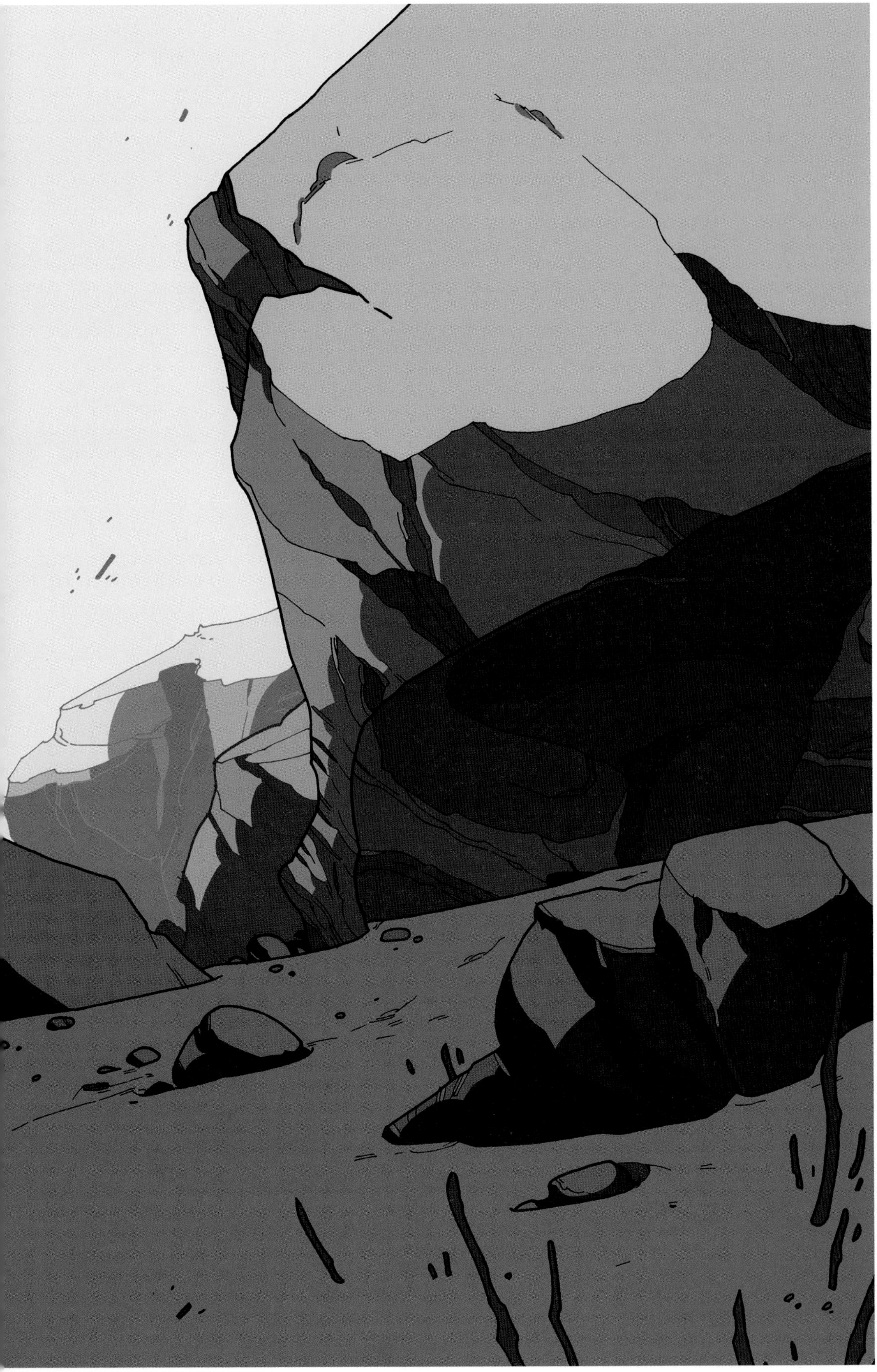

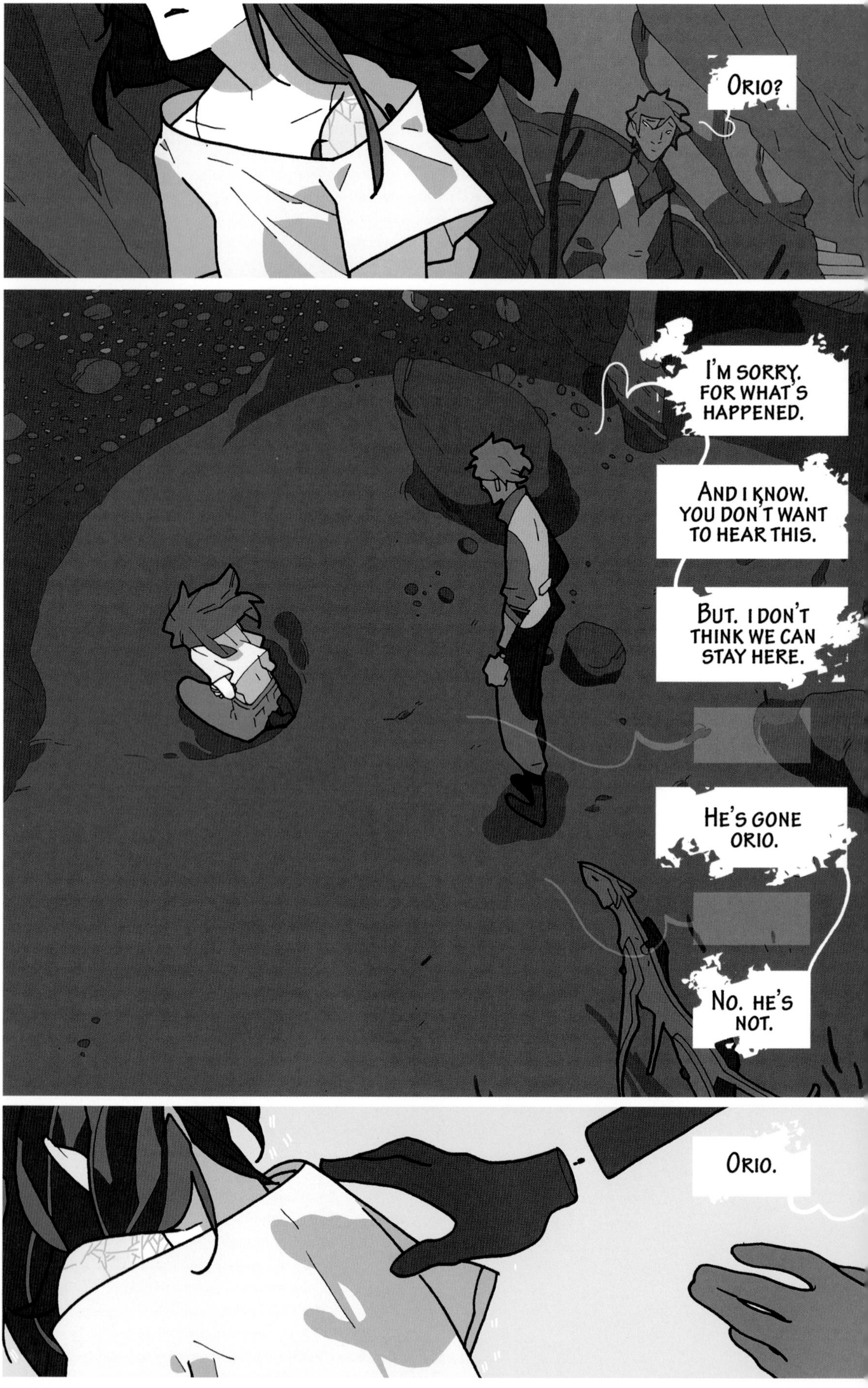
Orio?
I'm sorry. For what's happened.
And I know. You don't want to hear this.
But. I don't think we can stay here.
He's gone Orio.
No. He's not.
Orio.

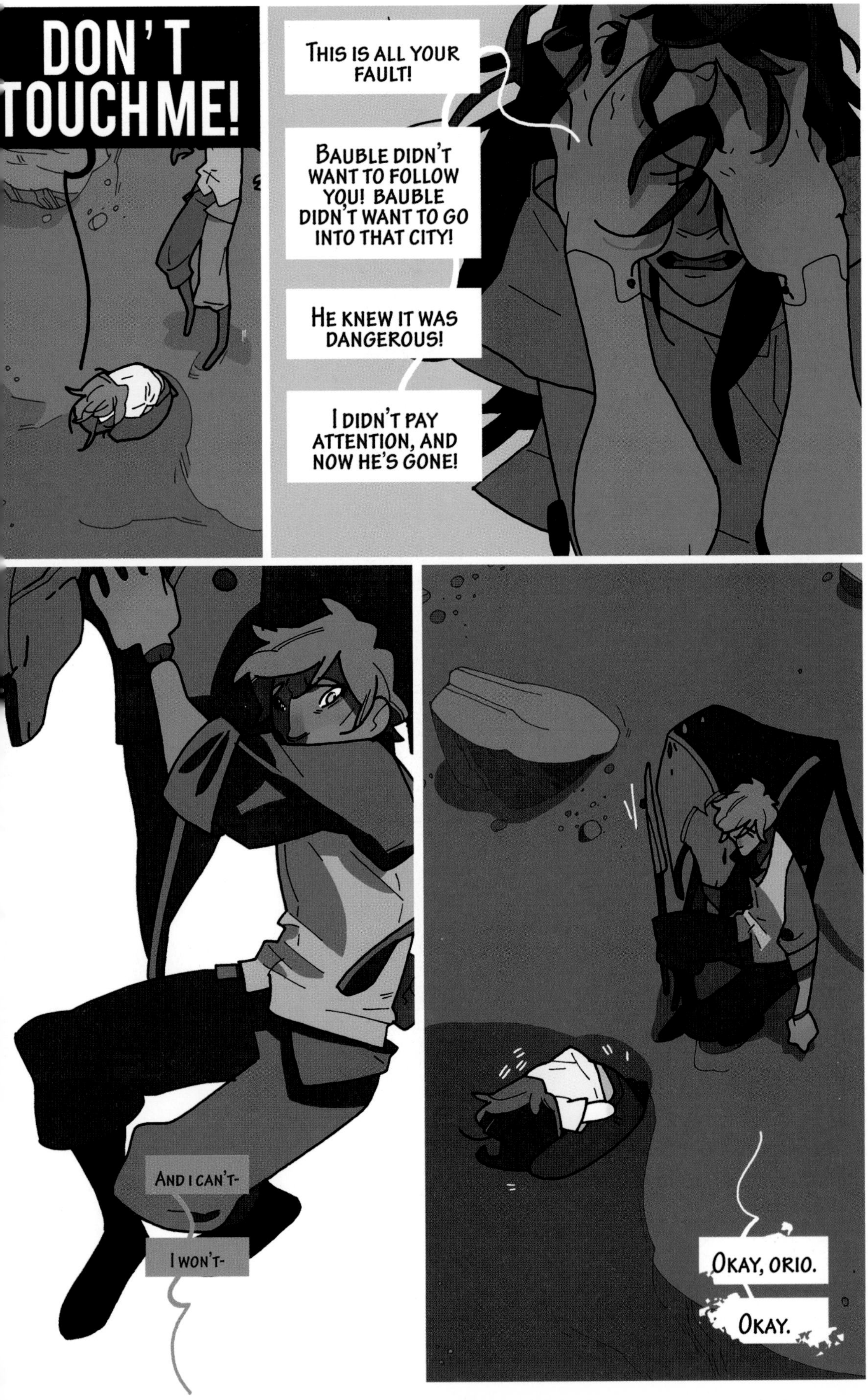
DON'T TOUCH ME!
THIS IS ALL YOUR FAULT!
BAUBLE DIDN'T WANT TO FOLLOW YOU! BAUBLE DIDN'T WANT TO GO INTO THAT CITY!
HE KNEW IT WAS DANGEROUS!
I DIDN'T PAY ATTENTION, AND NOW HE'S GONE!
AND I CAN'T-
I WON'T-
OKAY, ORIO.
OKAY.

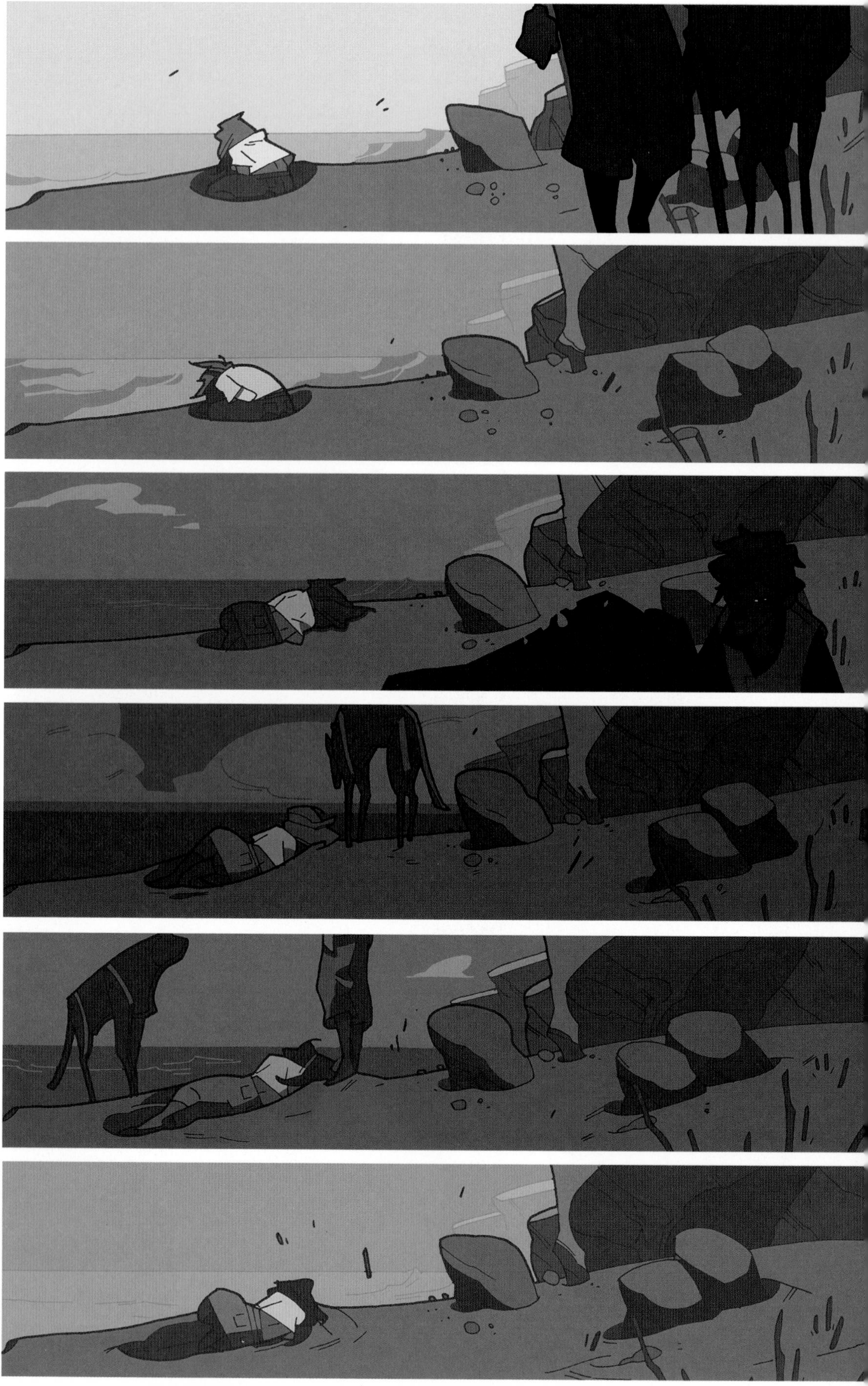

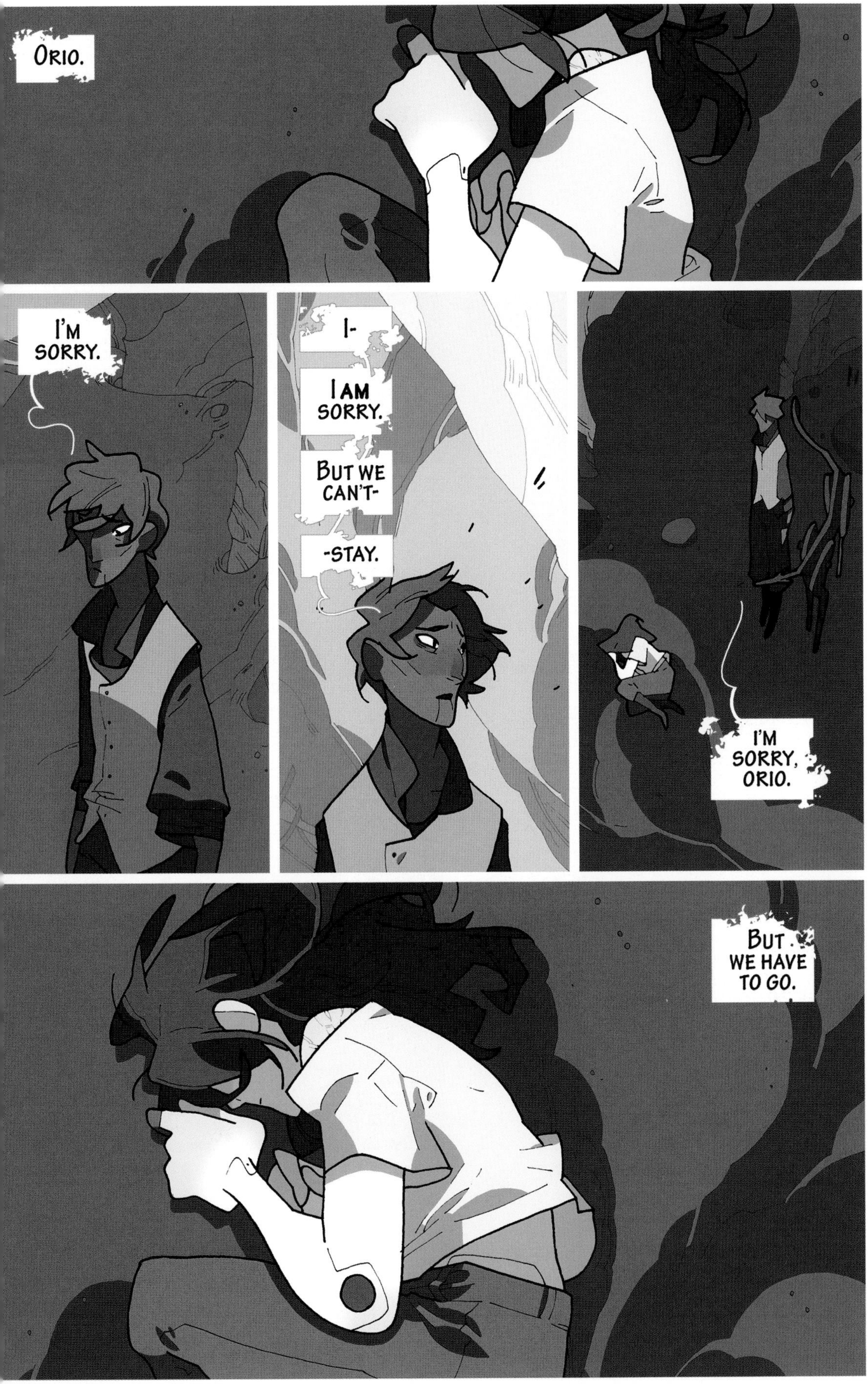
ORIO.
I'M SORRY.
I-
I AM SORRY.
BUT WE CAN'T-
-STAY.
I'M SORRY, ORIO.
BUT WE HAVE TO GO.

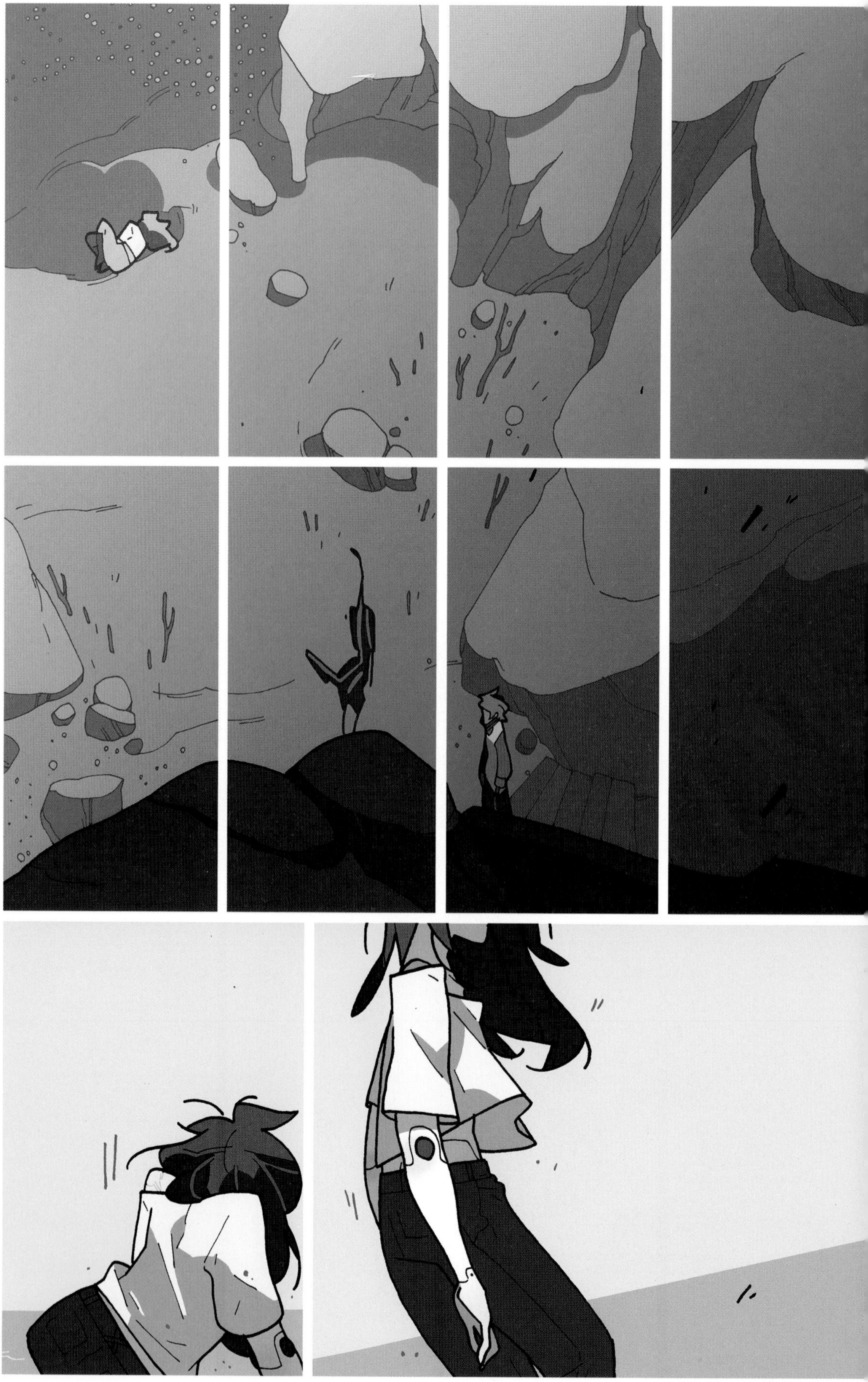

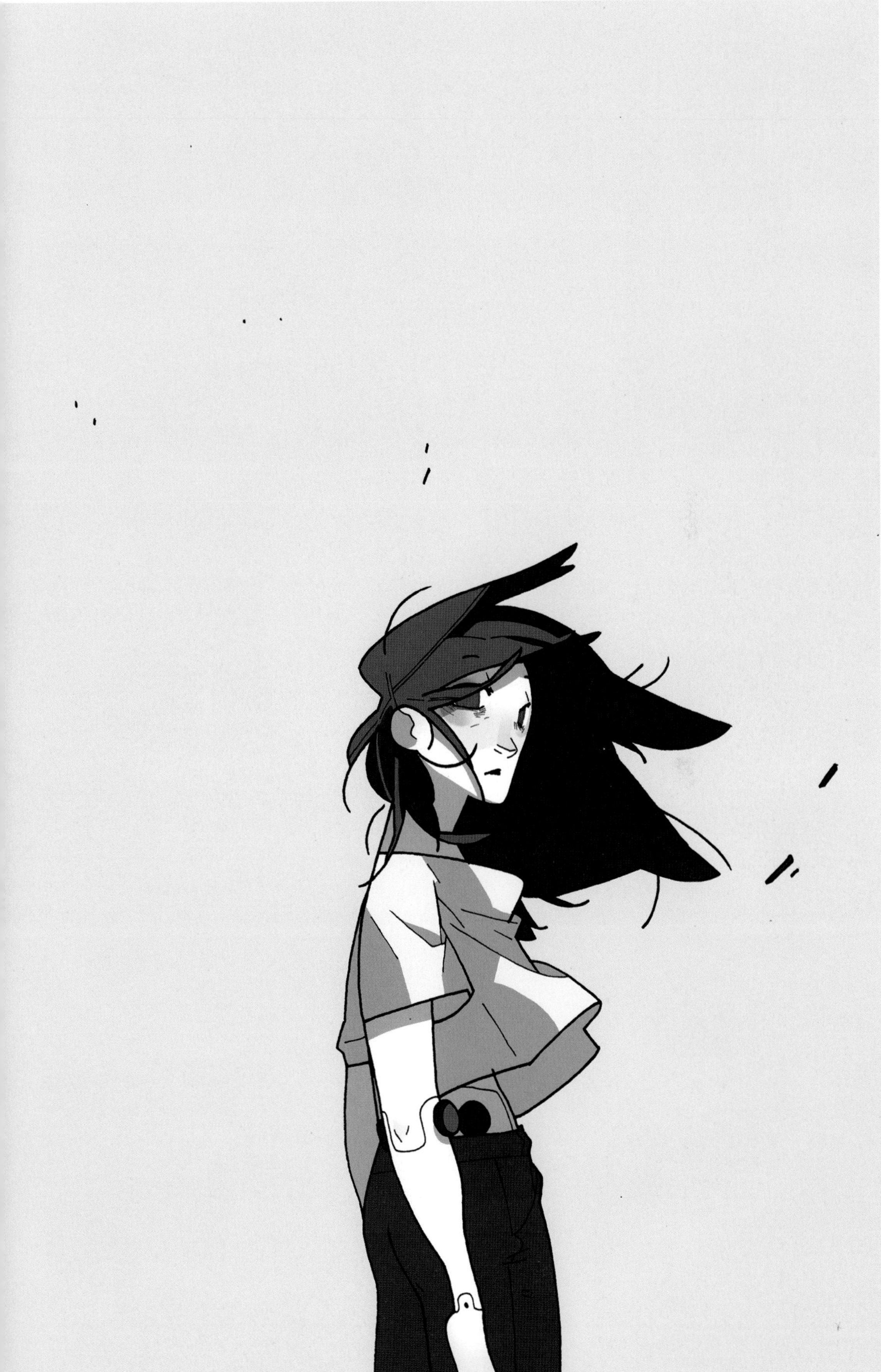

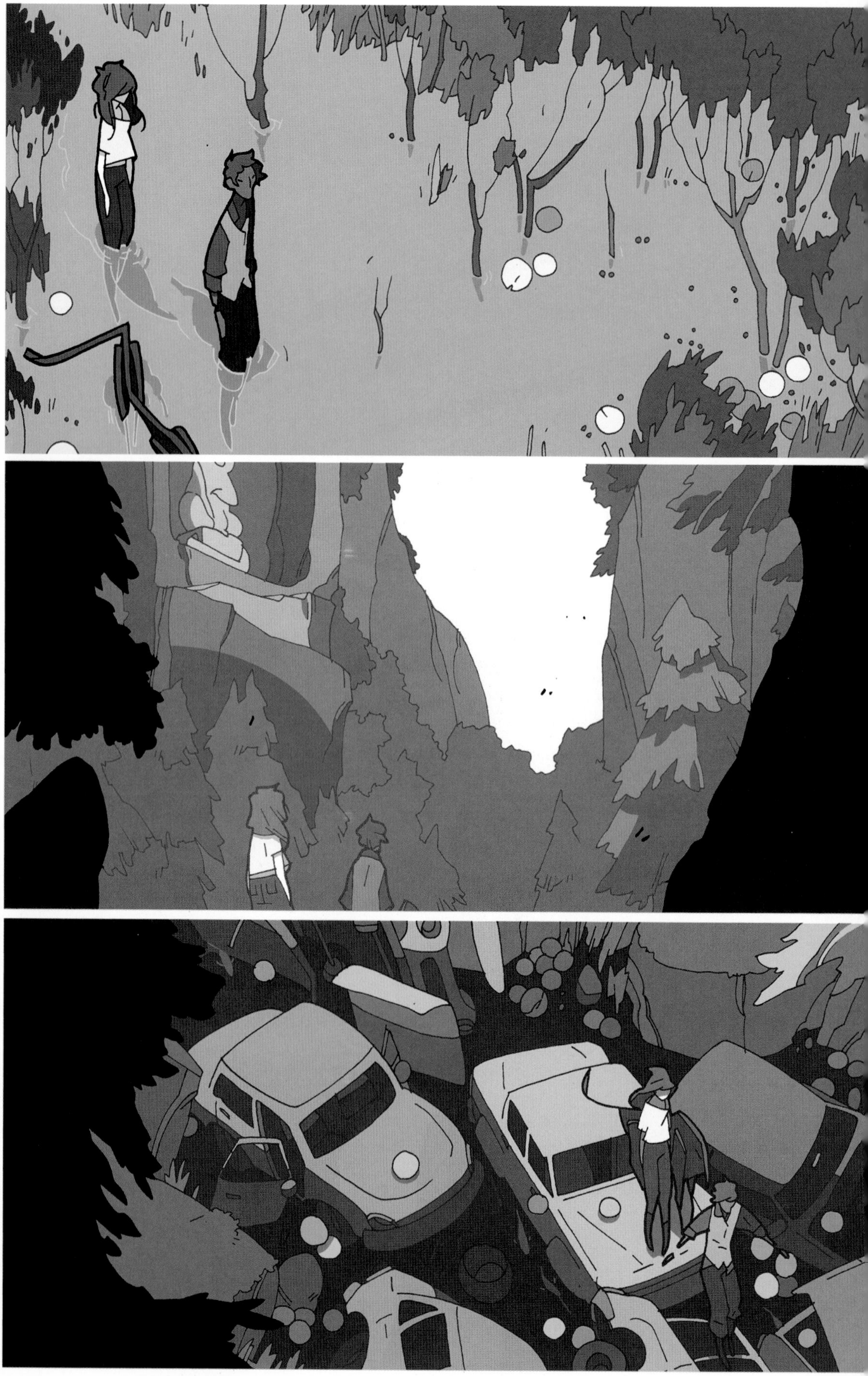

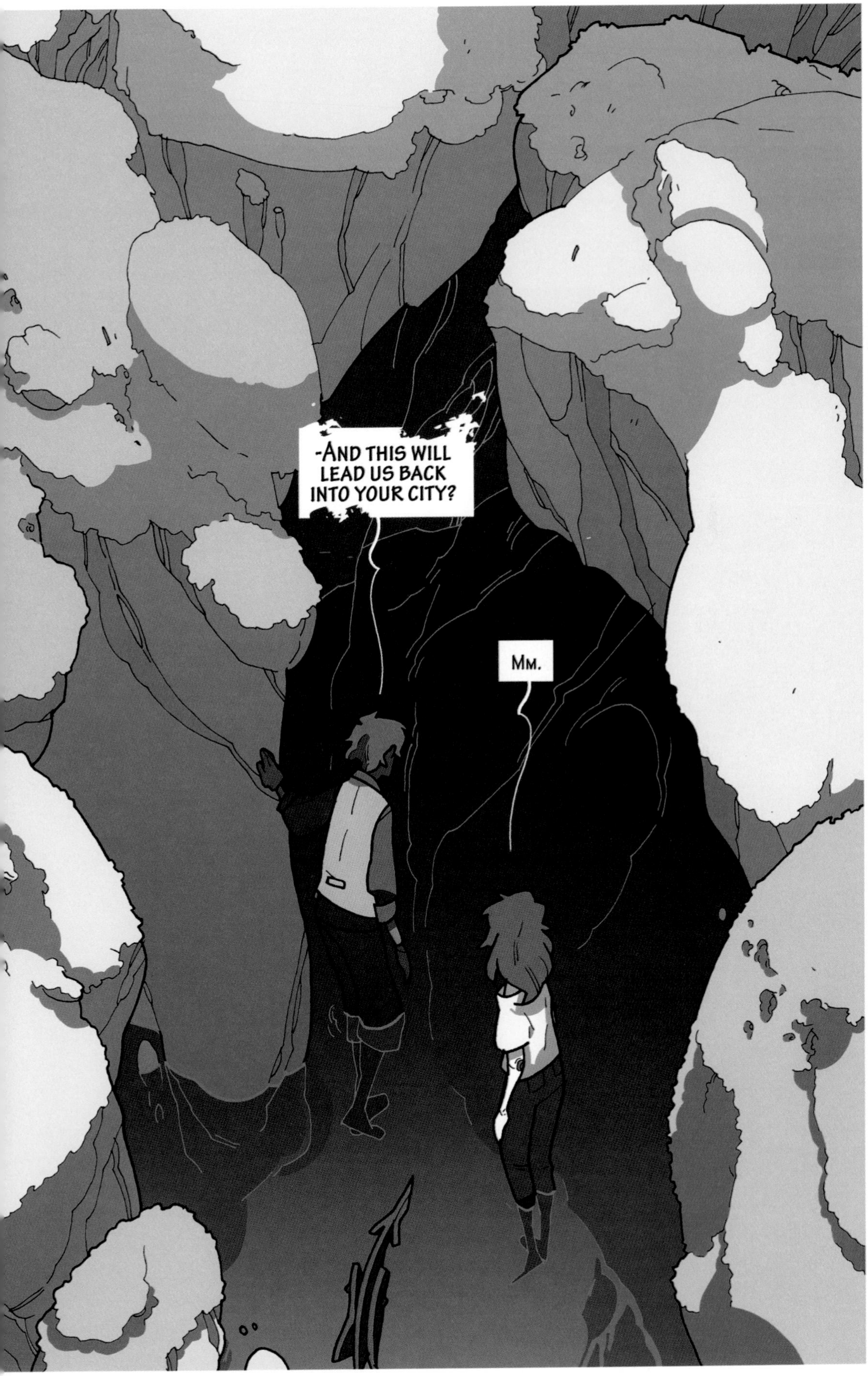
-AND THIS WILL LEAD US BACK INTO YOUR CITY?
MM.

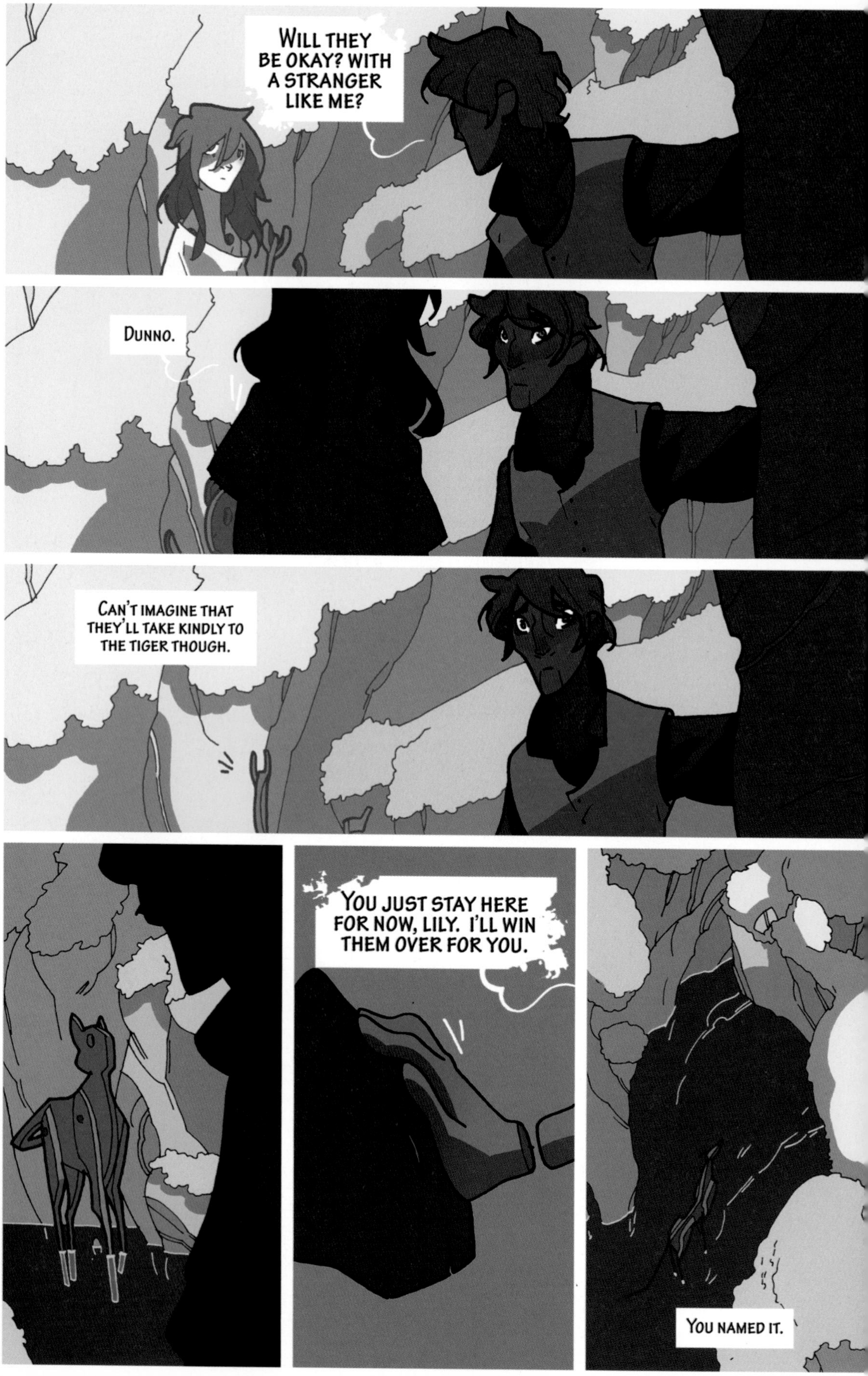
WILL THEY BE OKAY? WITH A STRANGER LIKE ME?
DUNNO.
CAN'T IMAGINE THAT THEY'LL TAKE KINDLY TO THE TIGER THOUGH.
YOU JUST STAY HERE FOR NOW, LILY. I'LL WIN THEM OVER FOR YOU.
YOU NAMED IT.

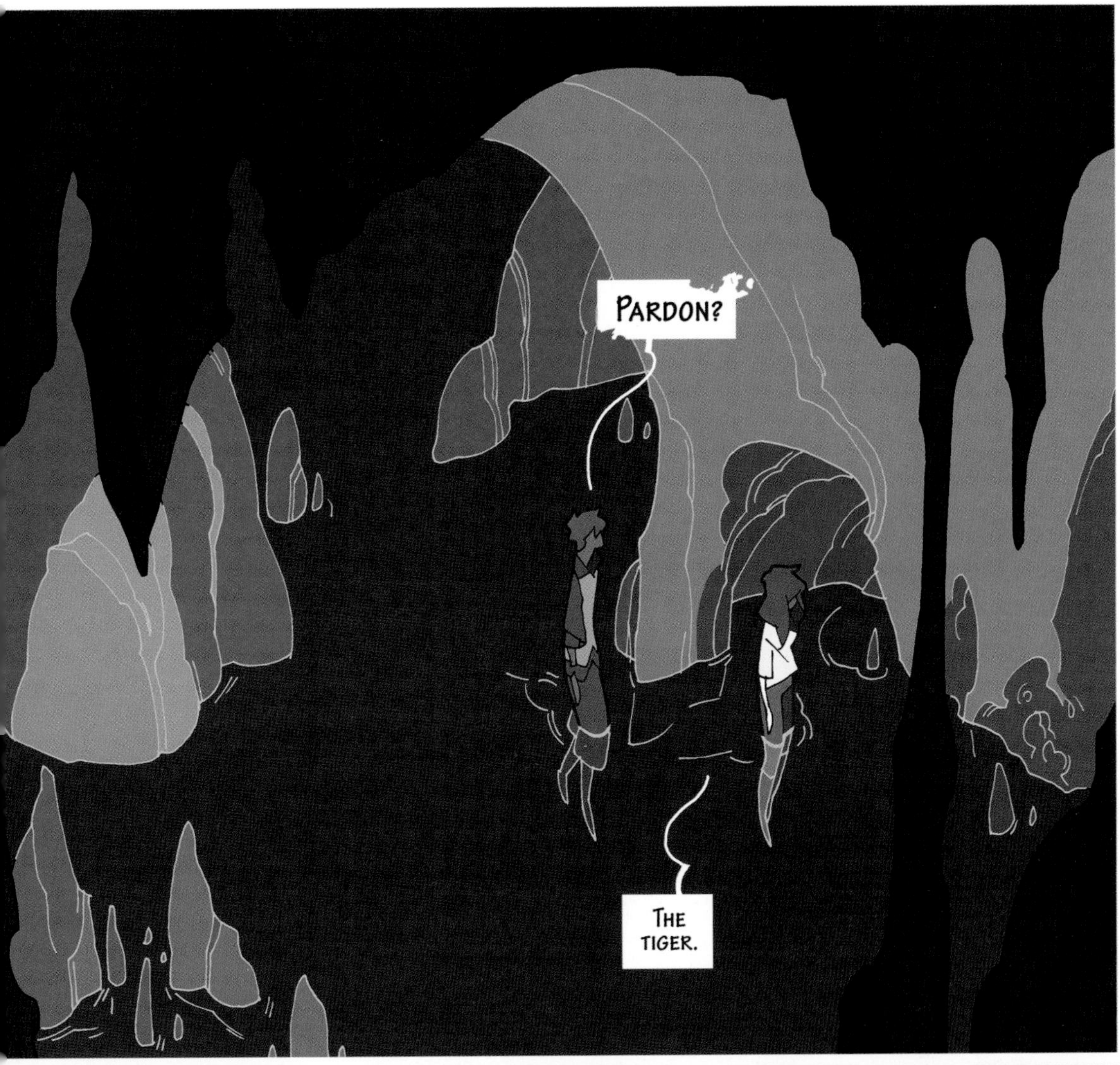
PARDON?
THE TIGER.
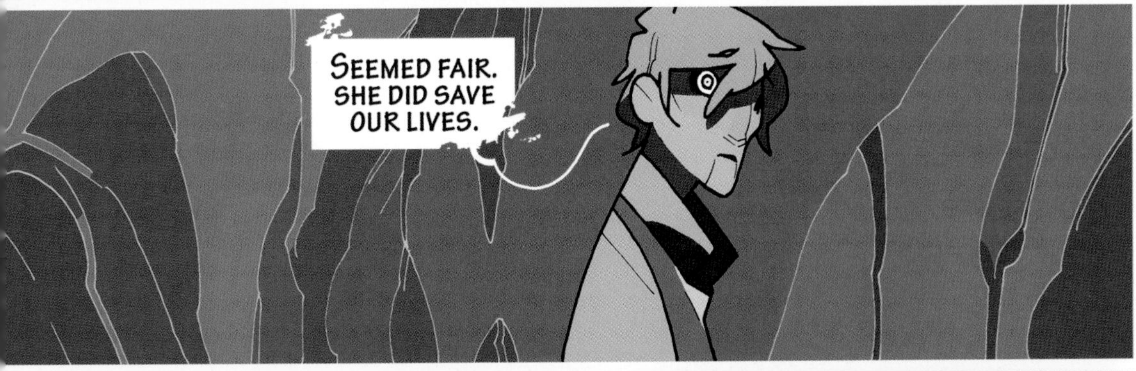
SEEMED FAIR. SHE DID SAVE OUR LIVES.
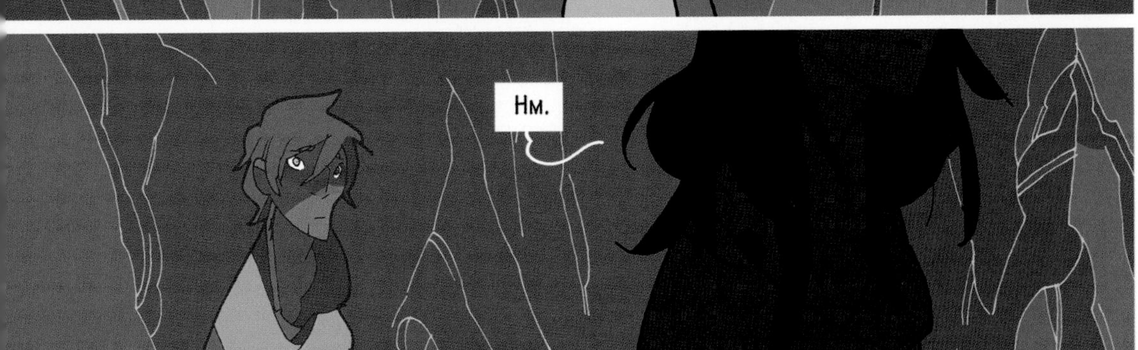
HM.

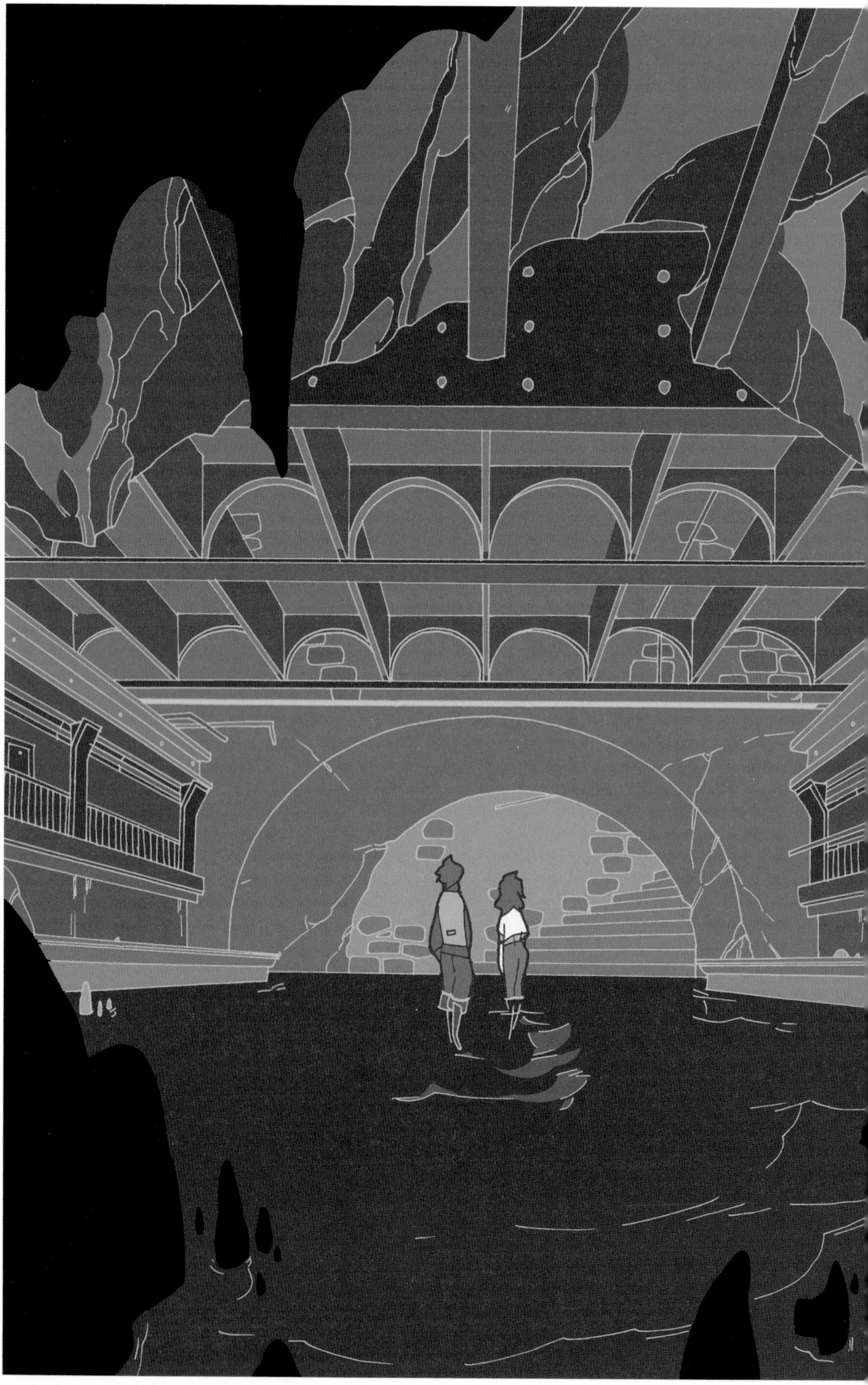

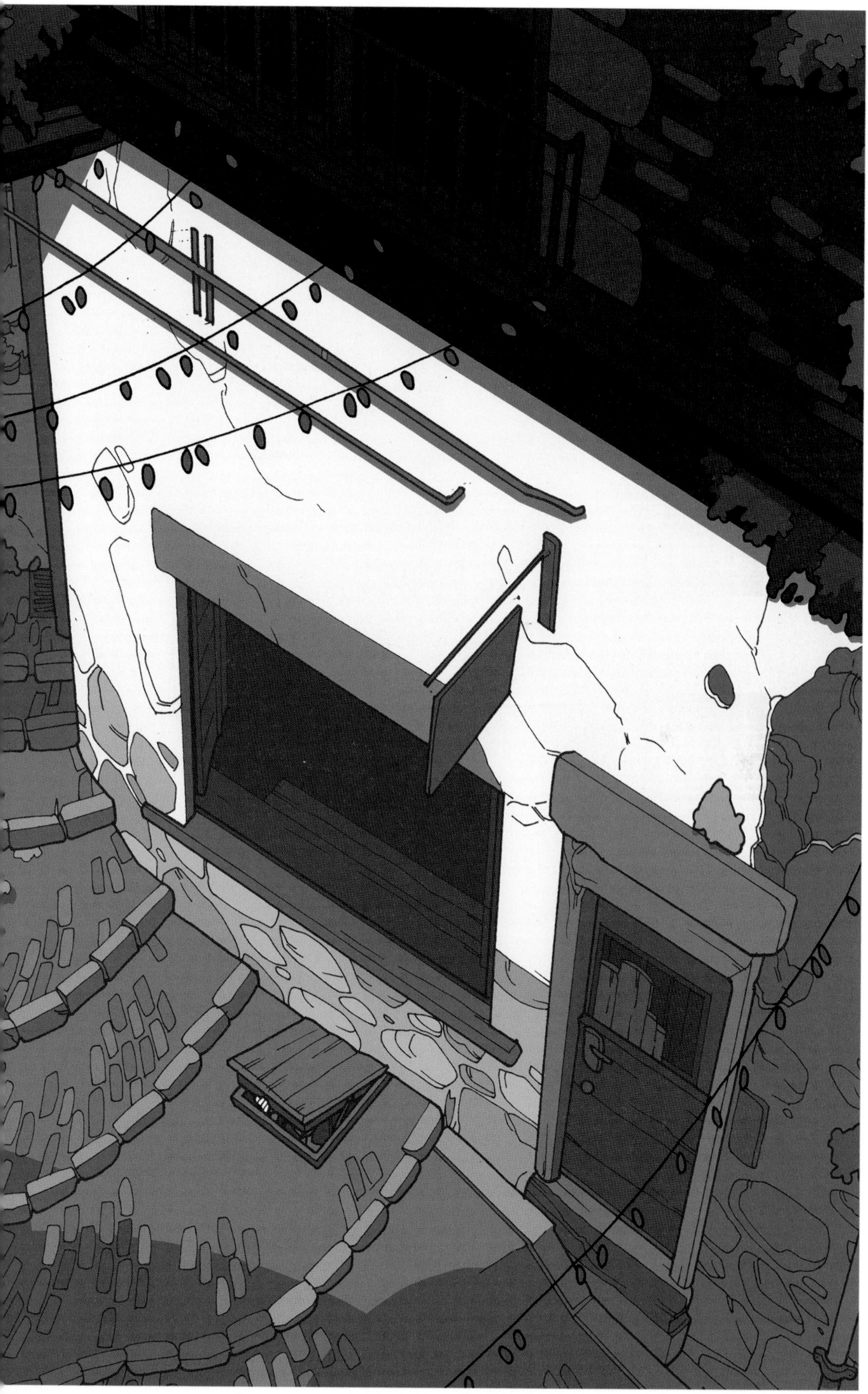

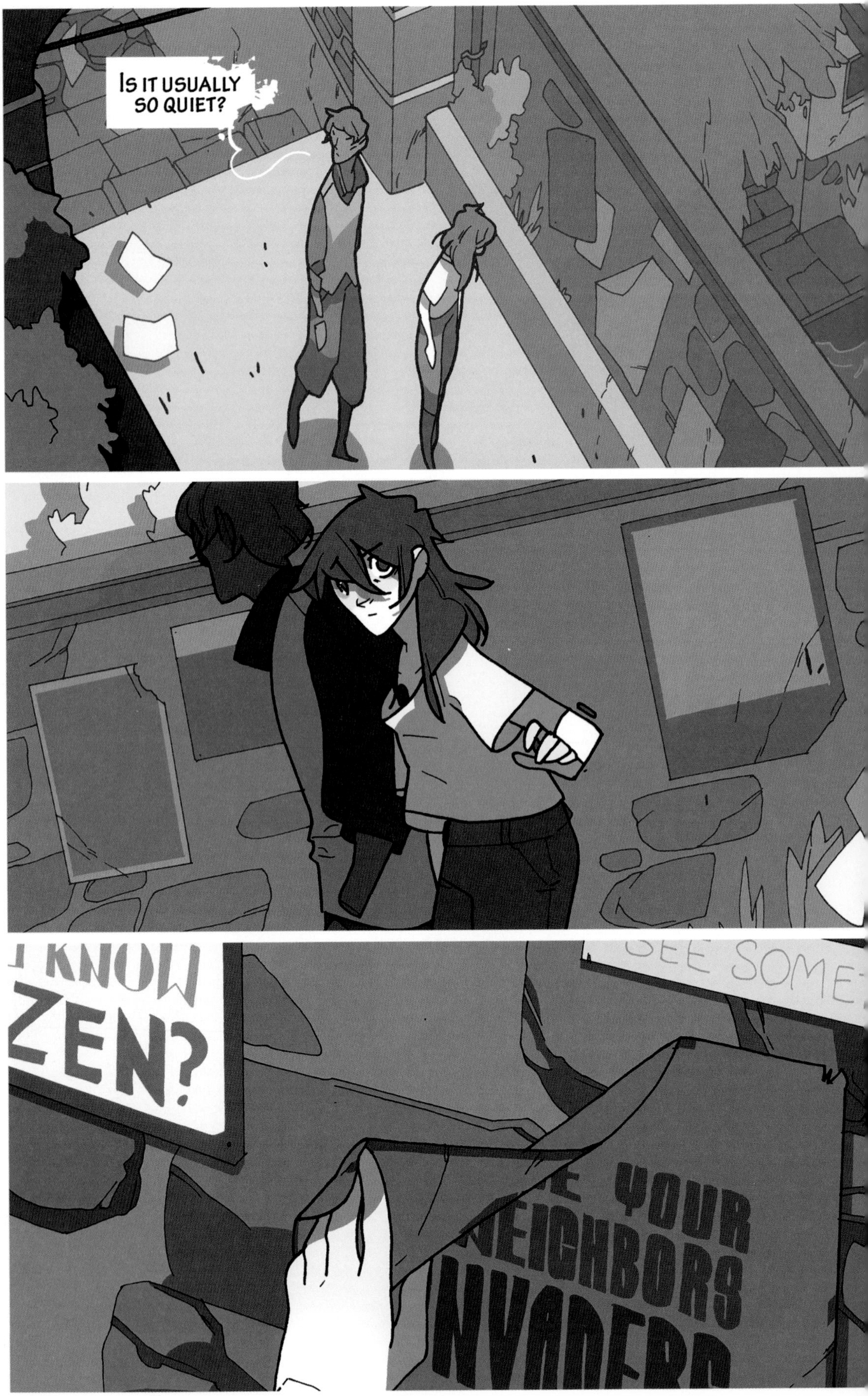
IS IT USUALLY SO QUIET?
ZEN?
SEE SOME-
YOUR
NEIGHBORS

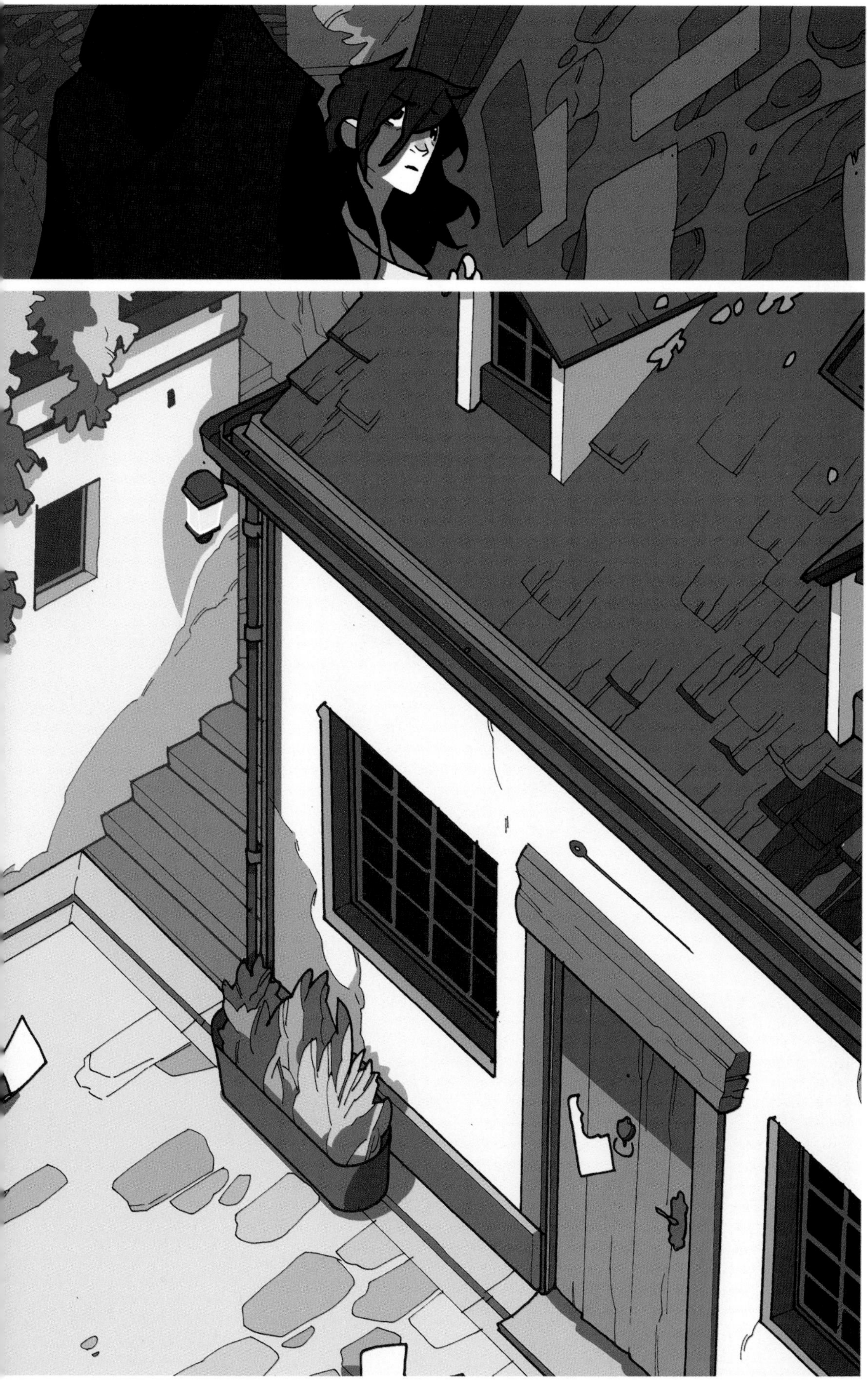

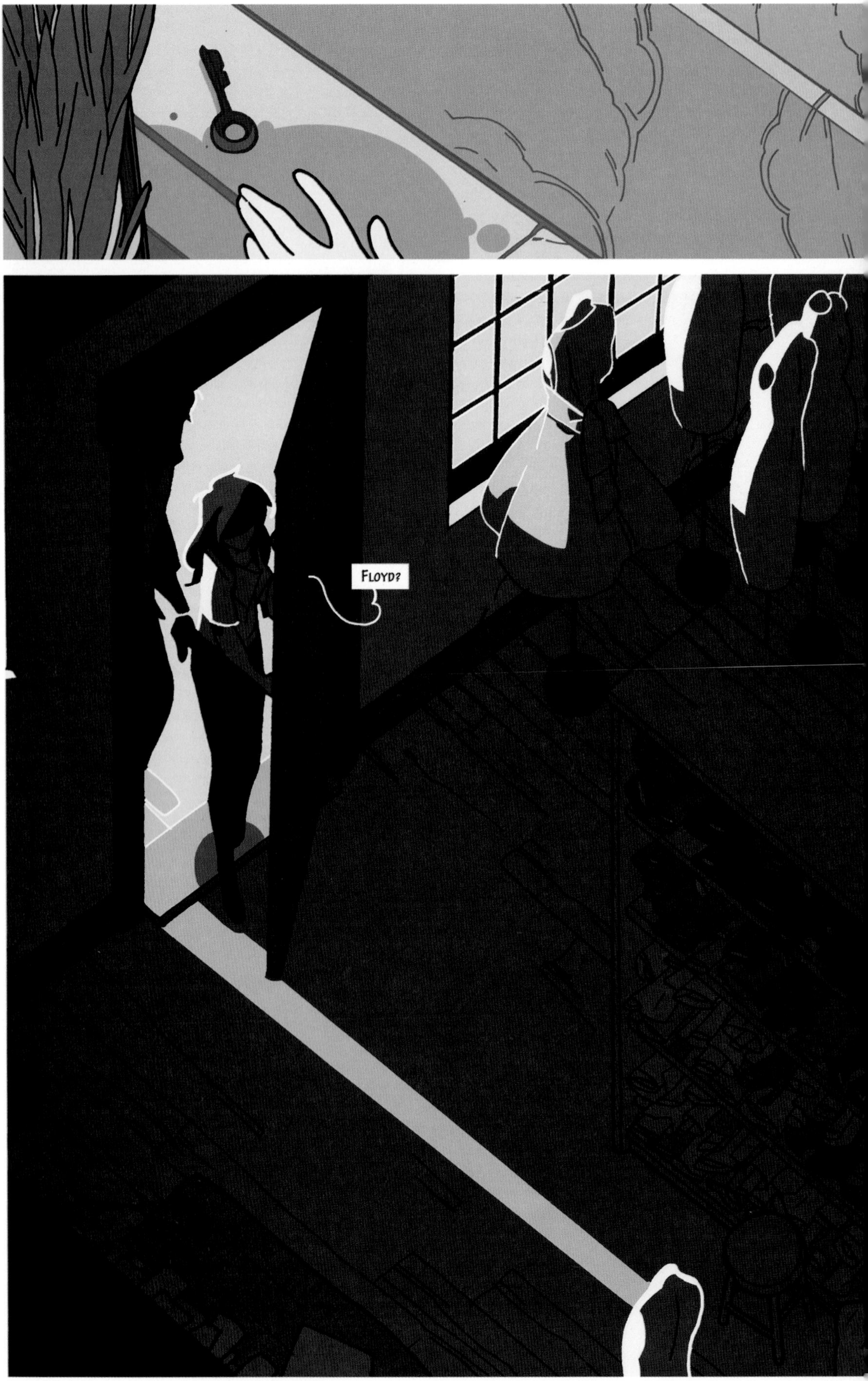
FLOYD?

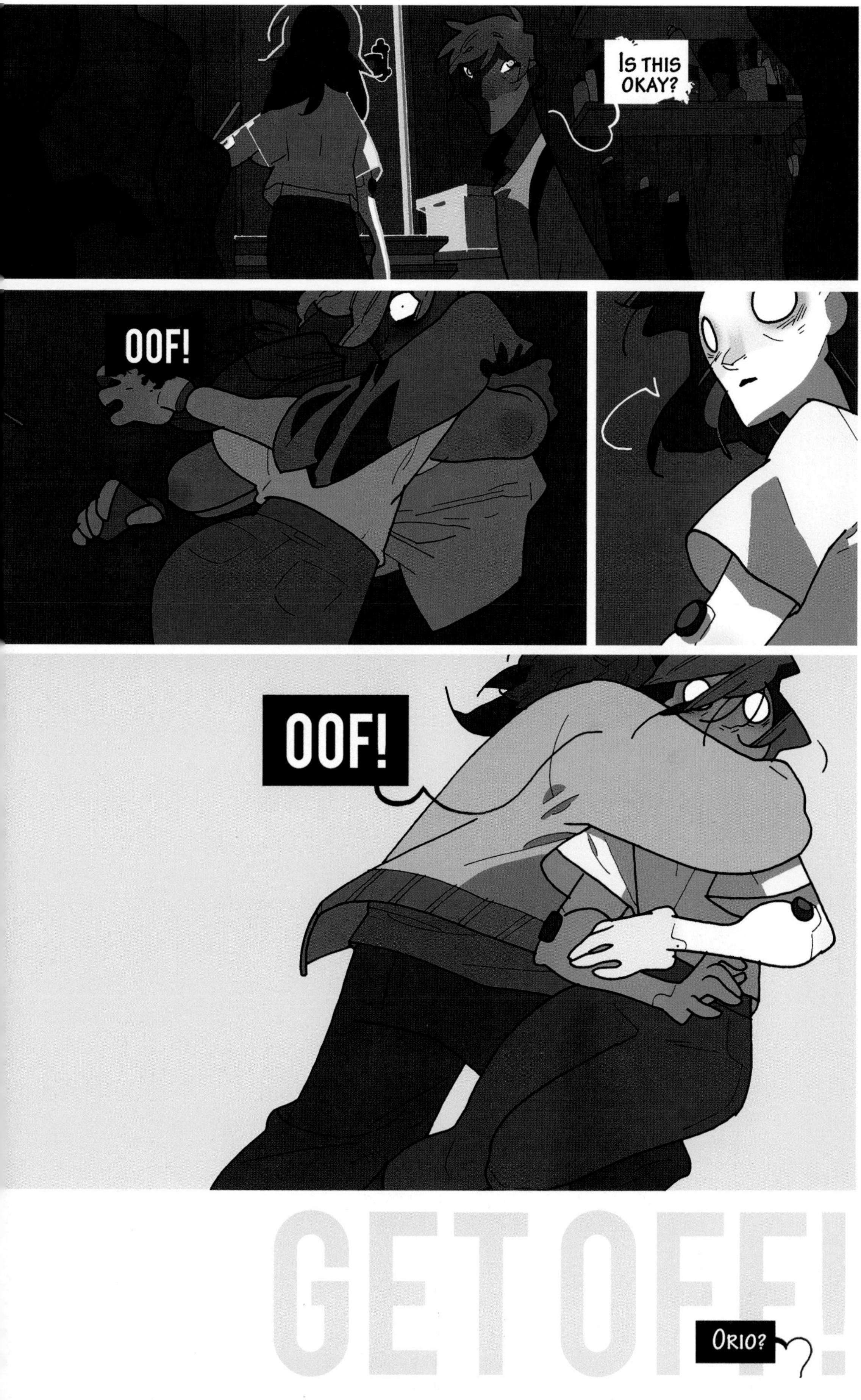
Is this okay?
OOF!
OOF!
GET OFF!
Orio?

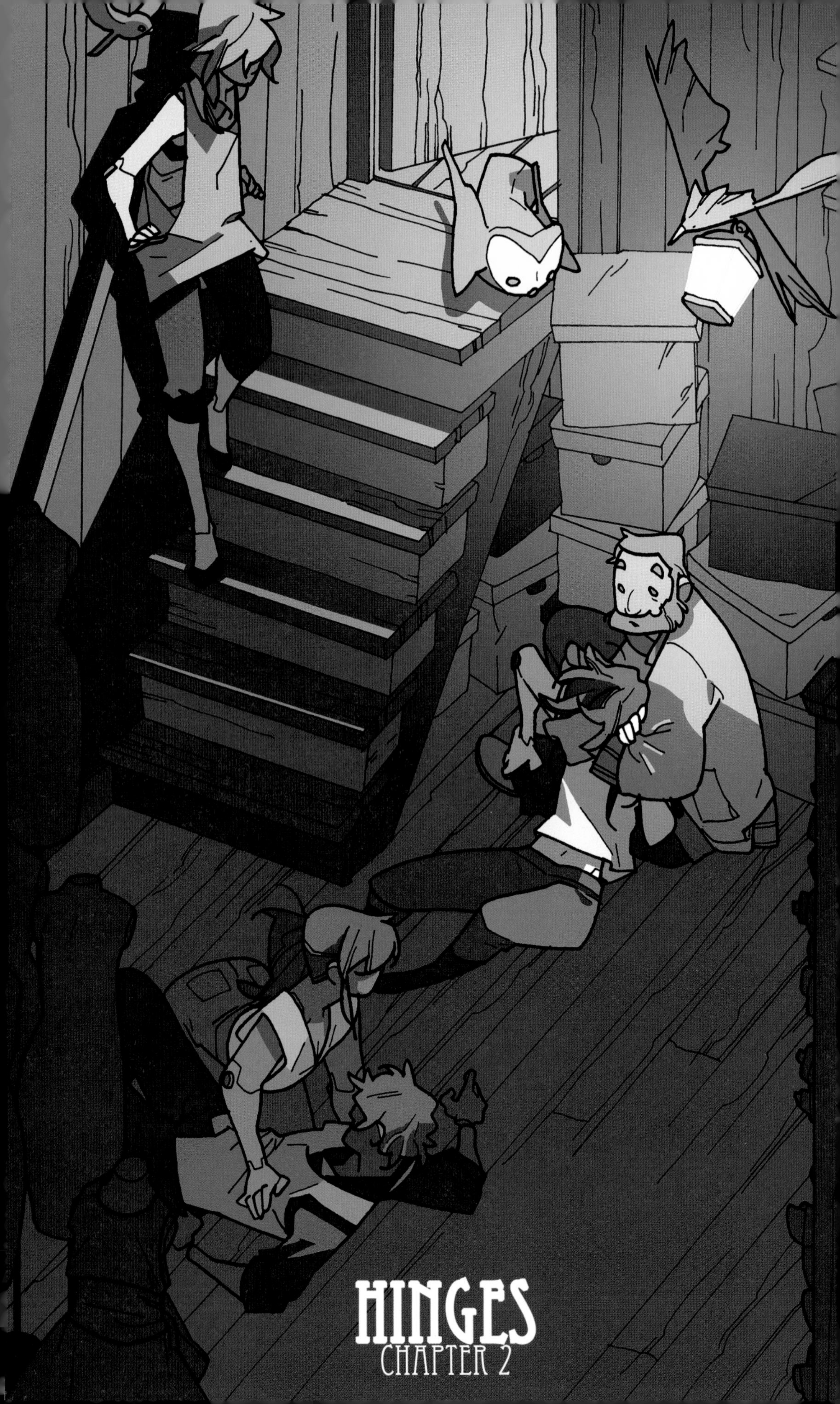
HINGES
CHAPTER 2

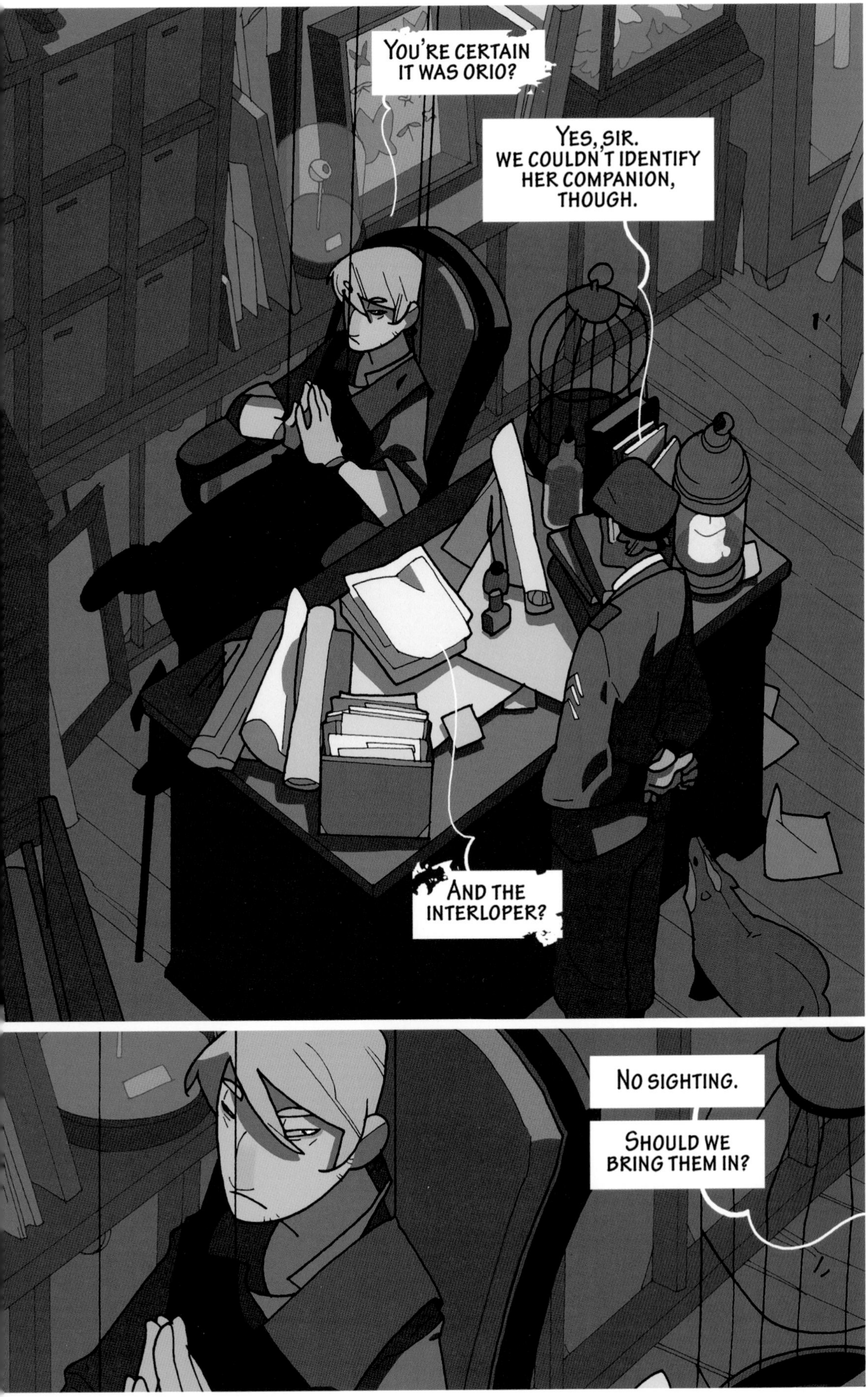
You're certain it was Orio?
Yes, sir. We couldn't identify her companion, though.
And the interloper?
No sighting.
Should we bring them in?

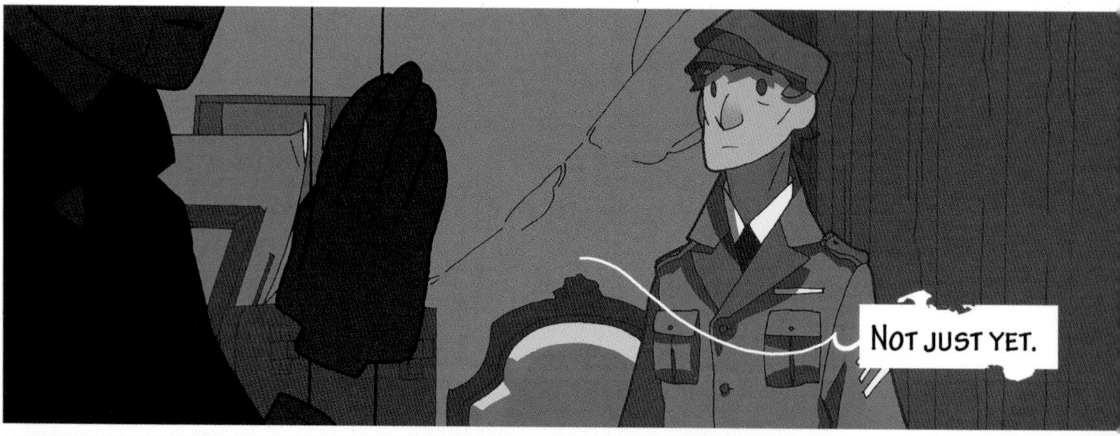
NOT JUST YET.

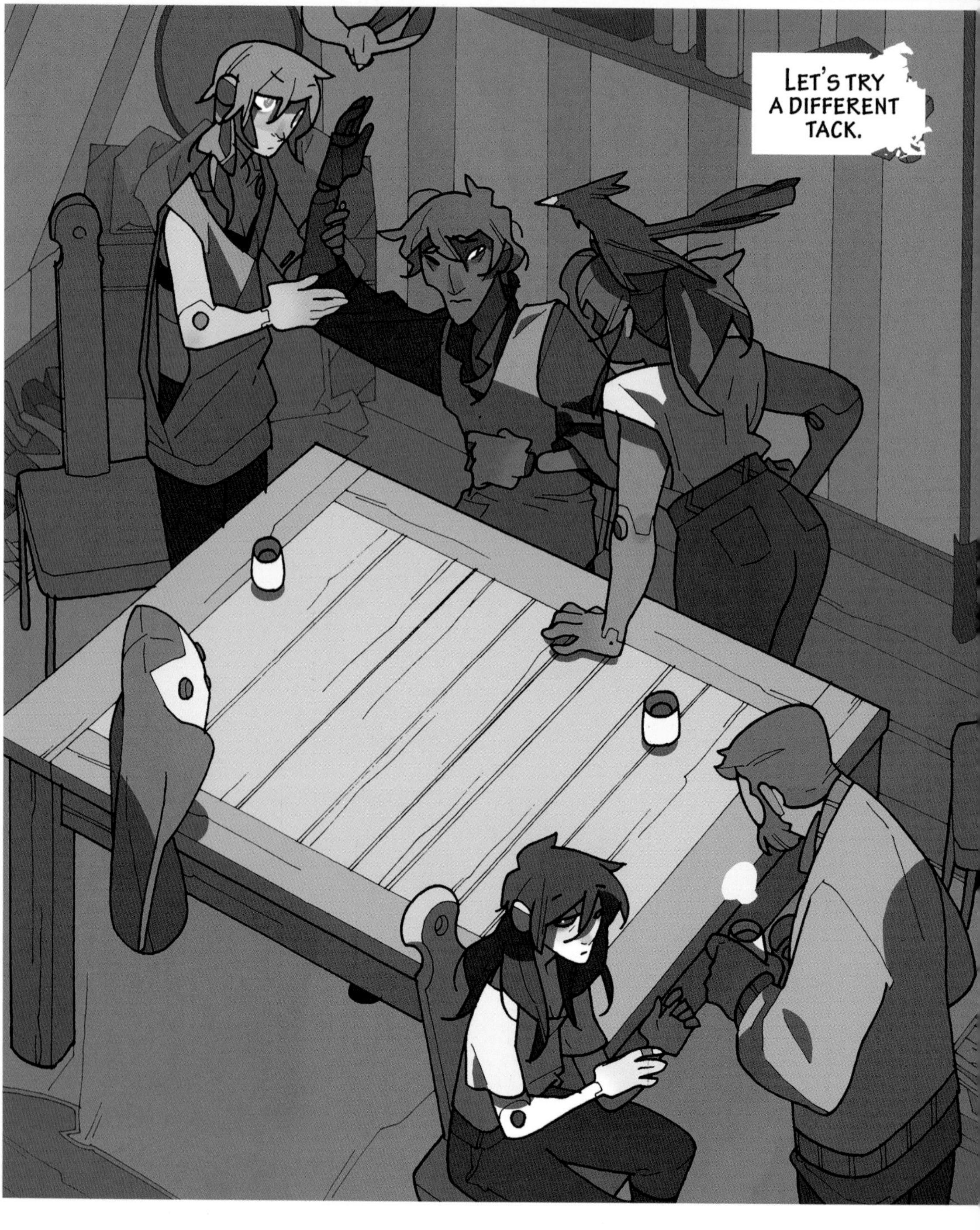
LET'S TRY A DIFFERENT TACK.

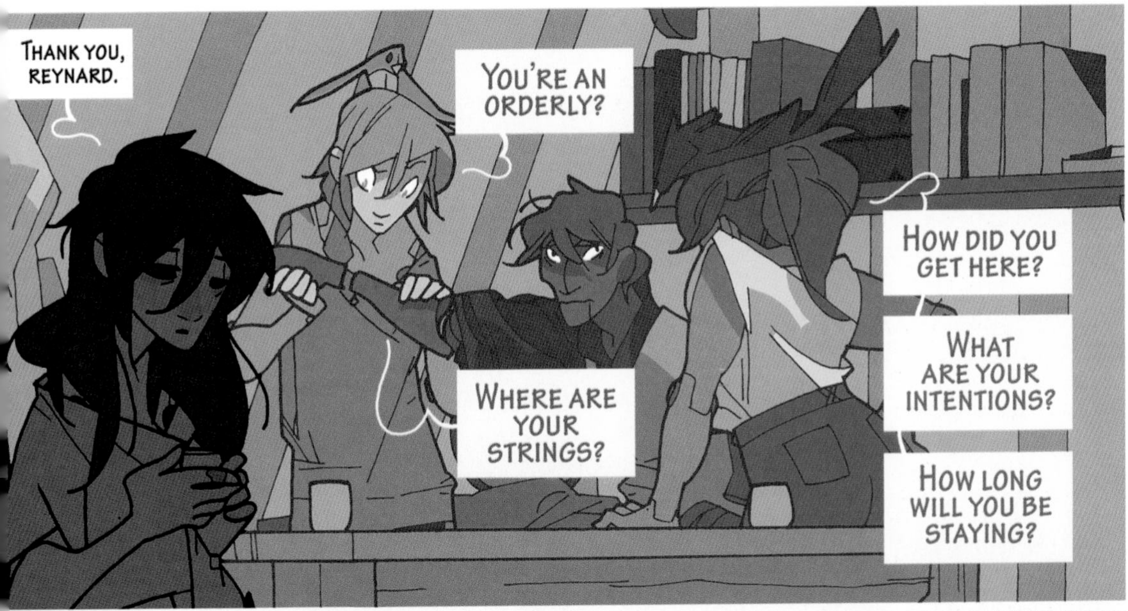

Thank you, Reynard.
You're an orderly?
How did you get here?
What are your intentions?
How long will you be staying?
Where are your strings?

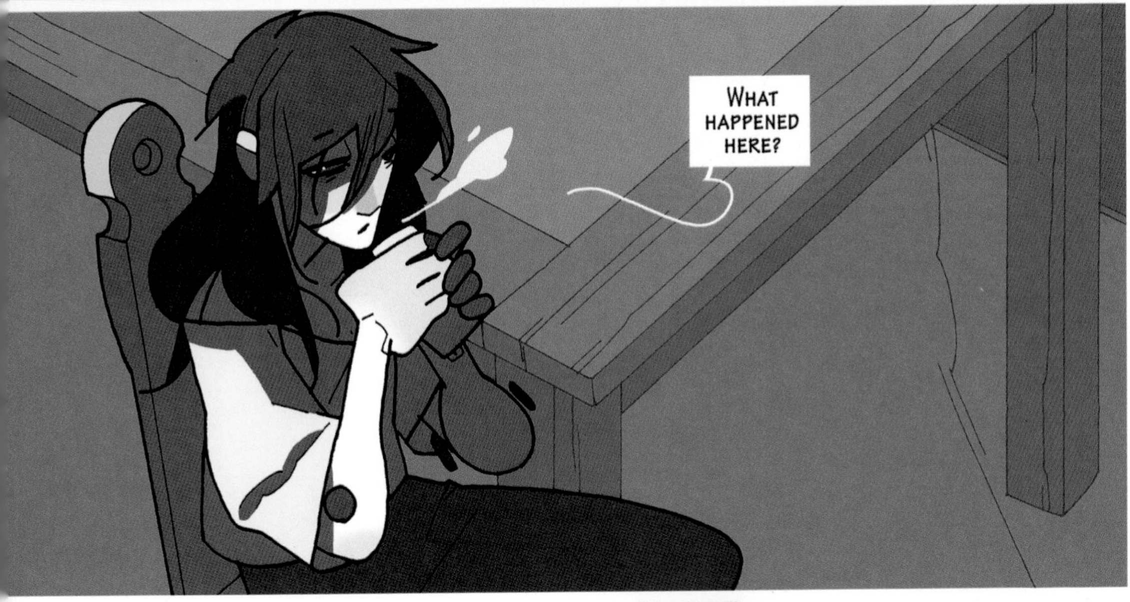

What happened here?

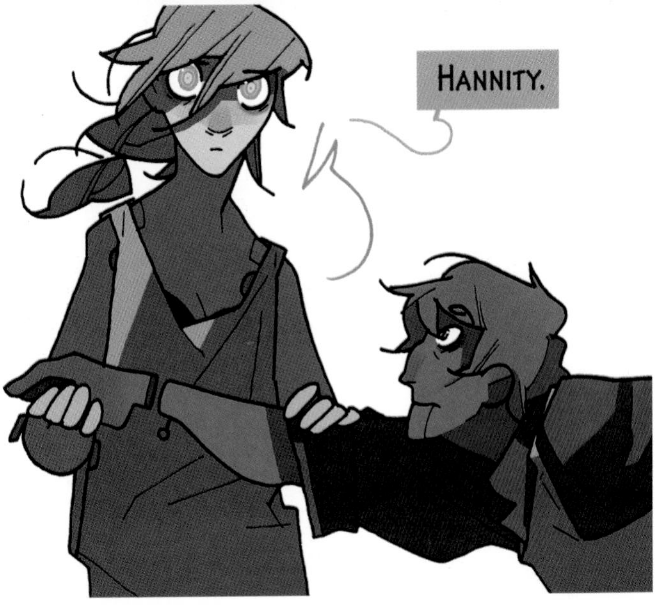

Hannity.

AFTER YOU LEFT

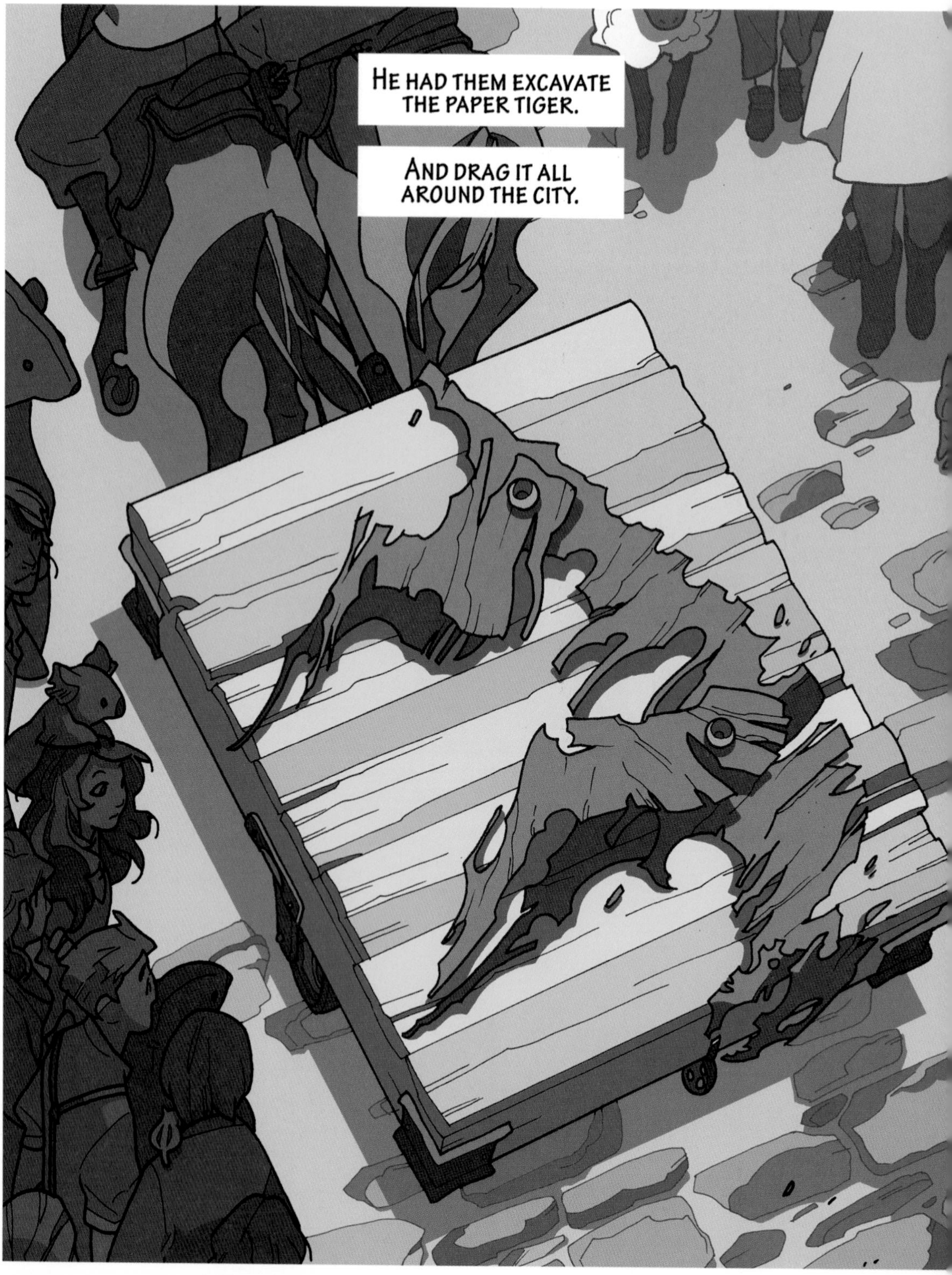
HE HAD THEM EXCAVATE THE PAPER TIGER.
AND DRAG IT ALL AROUND THE CITY.

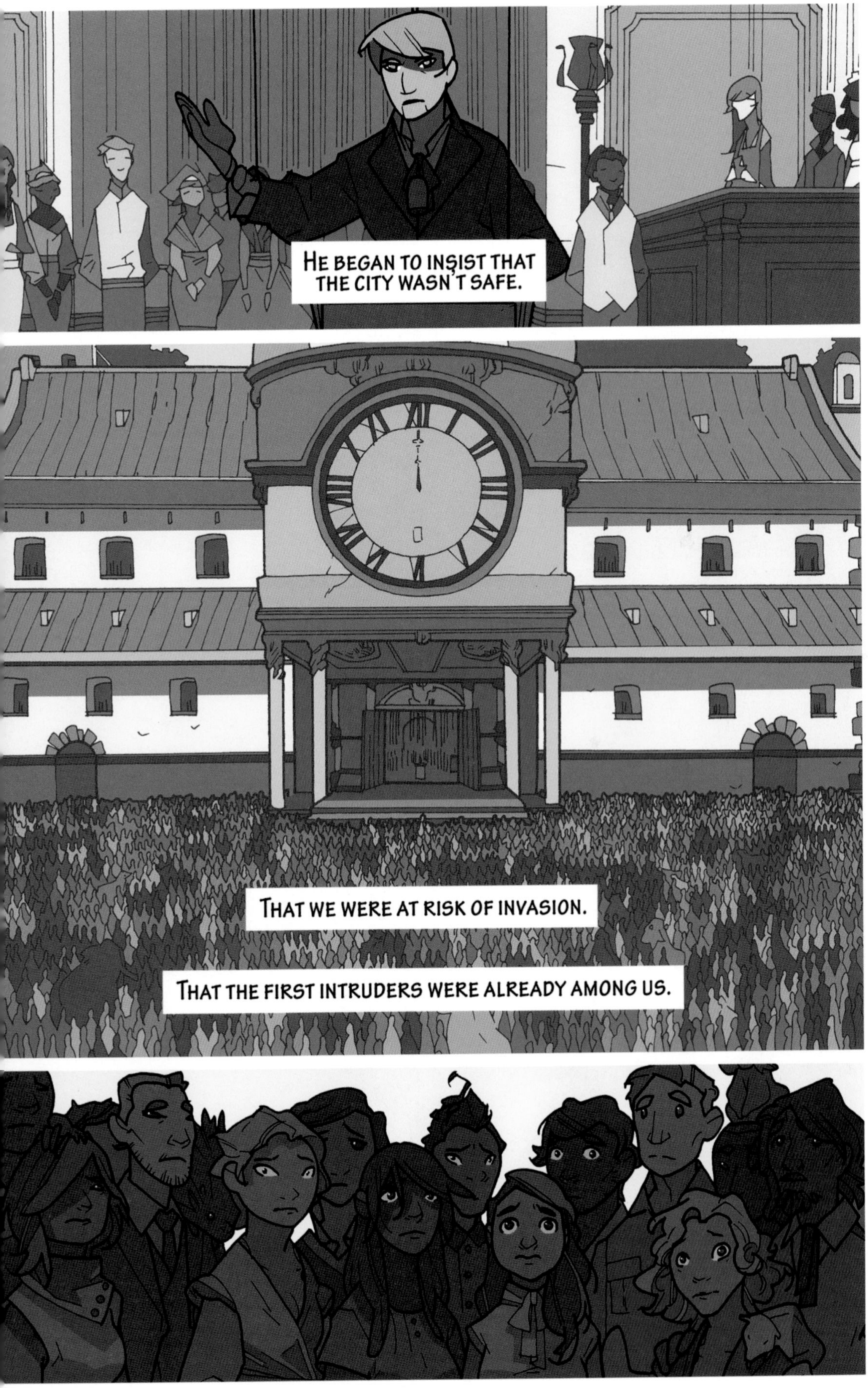
HE BEGAN TO INSIST THAT THE CITY WASN'T SAFE.
THAT WE WERE AT RISK OF INVASION.
THAT THE FIRST INTRUDERS WERE ALREADY AMONG US.

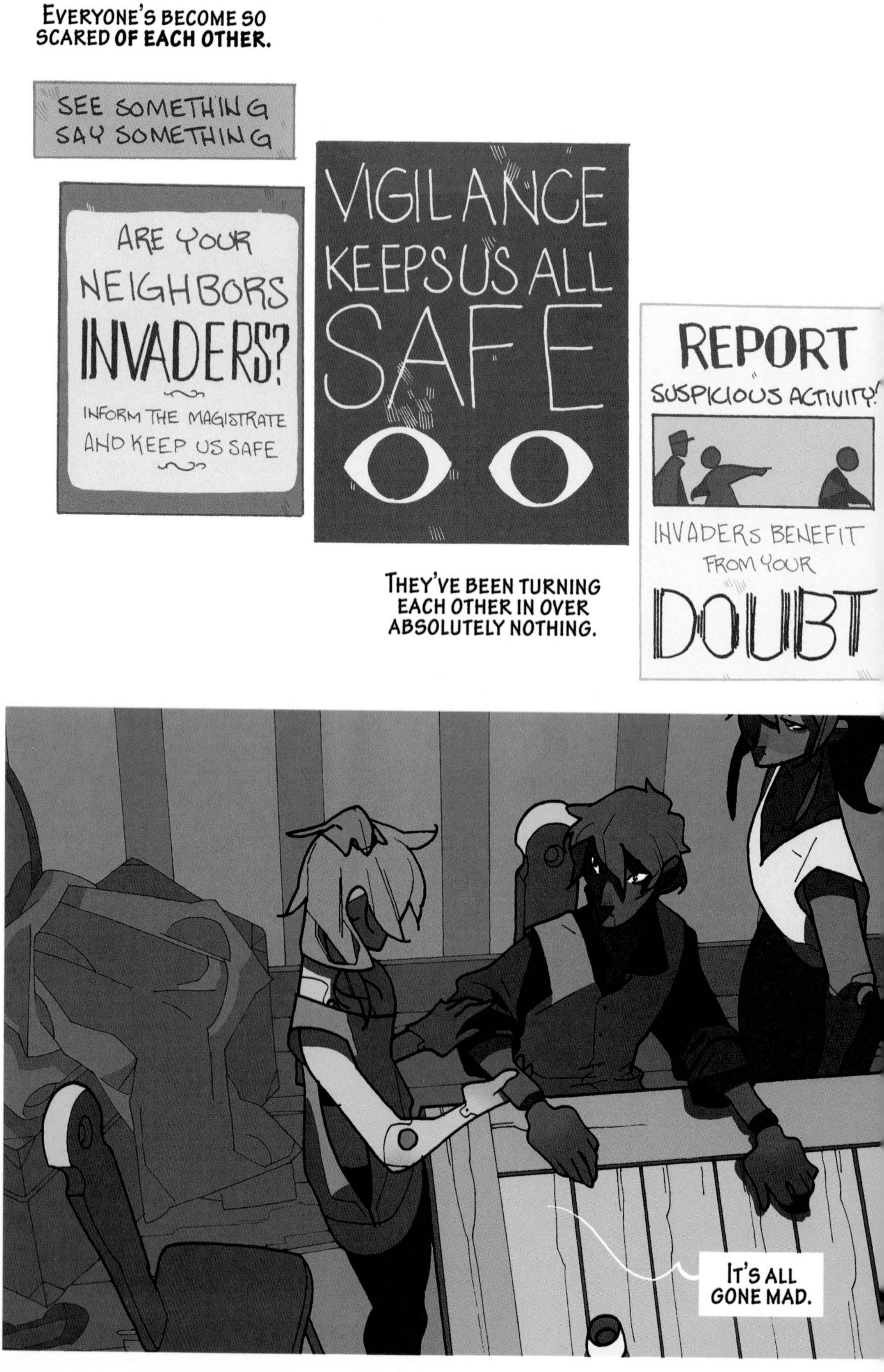
EVERYONE'S BECOME SO SCARED OF EACH OTHER.
SEE SOMETHING SAY SOMETHING
ARE YOUR NEIGHBORS INVADERS?
INFORM THE MAGISTRATE AND KEEP US SAFE
VIGILANCE KEEPS US ALL SAFE
REPORT SUSPICIOUS ACTIVITY!
INVADERS BENEFIT FROM YOUR DOUBT
THEY'VE BEEN TURNING EACH OTHER IN OVER ABSOLUTELY NOTHING.
IT'S ALL GONE MAD.

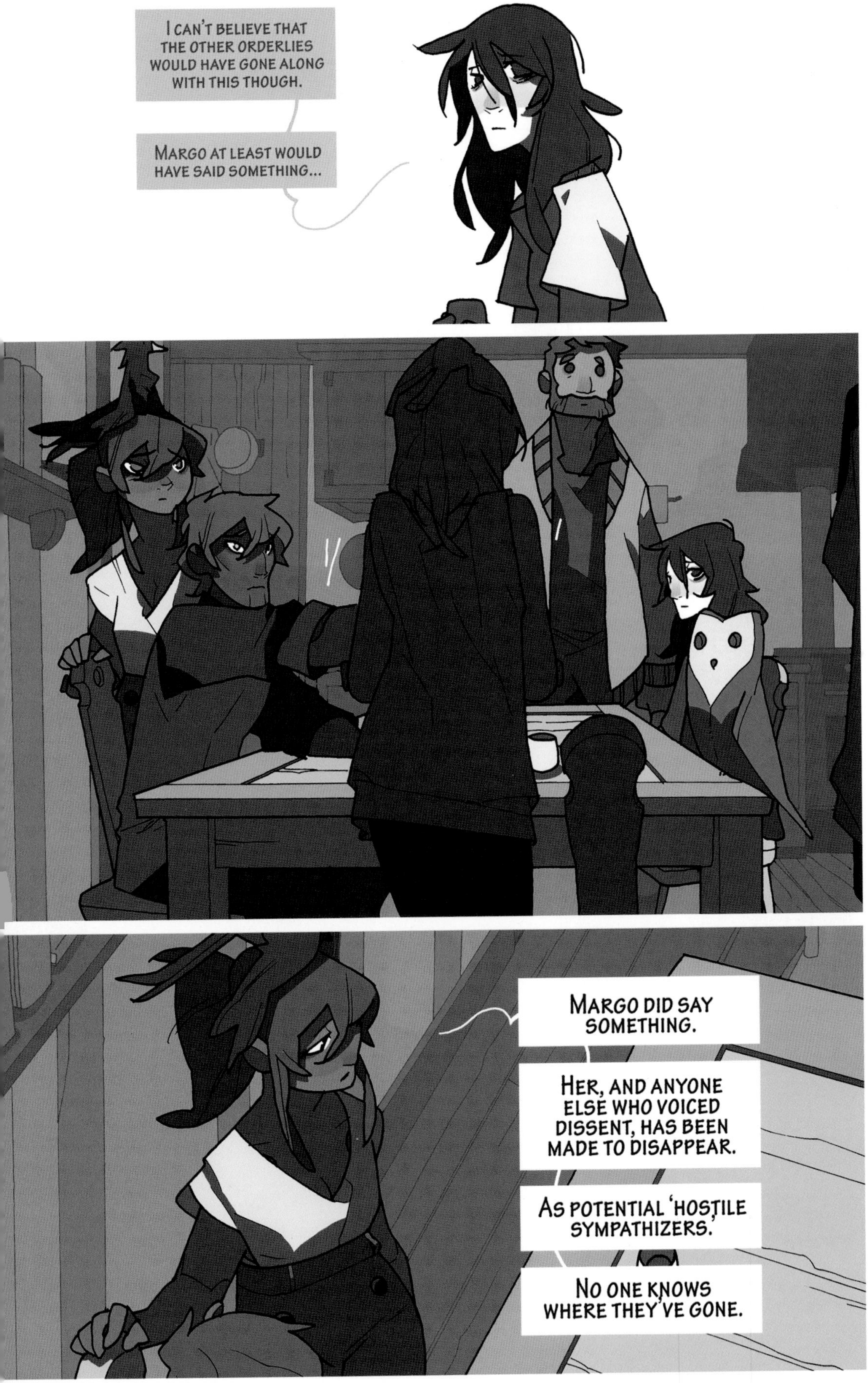
I CAN'T BELIEVE THAT THE OTHER ORDERLIES WOULD HAVE GONE ALONG WITH THIS THOUGH.
MARGO AT LEAST WOULD HAVE SAID SOMETHING...
MARGO DID SAY SOMETHING.
HER, AND ANYONE ELSE WHO VOICED DISSENT, HAS BEEN MADE TO DISAPPEAR.
AS POTENTIAL 'HOSTILE SYMPATHIZERS.'
NO ONE KNOWS WHERE THEY'VE GONE.

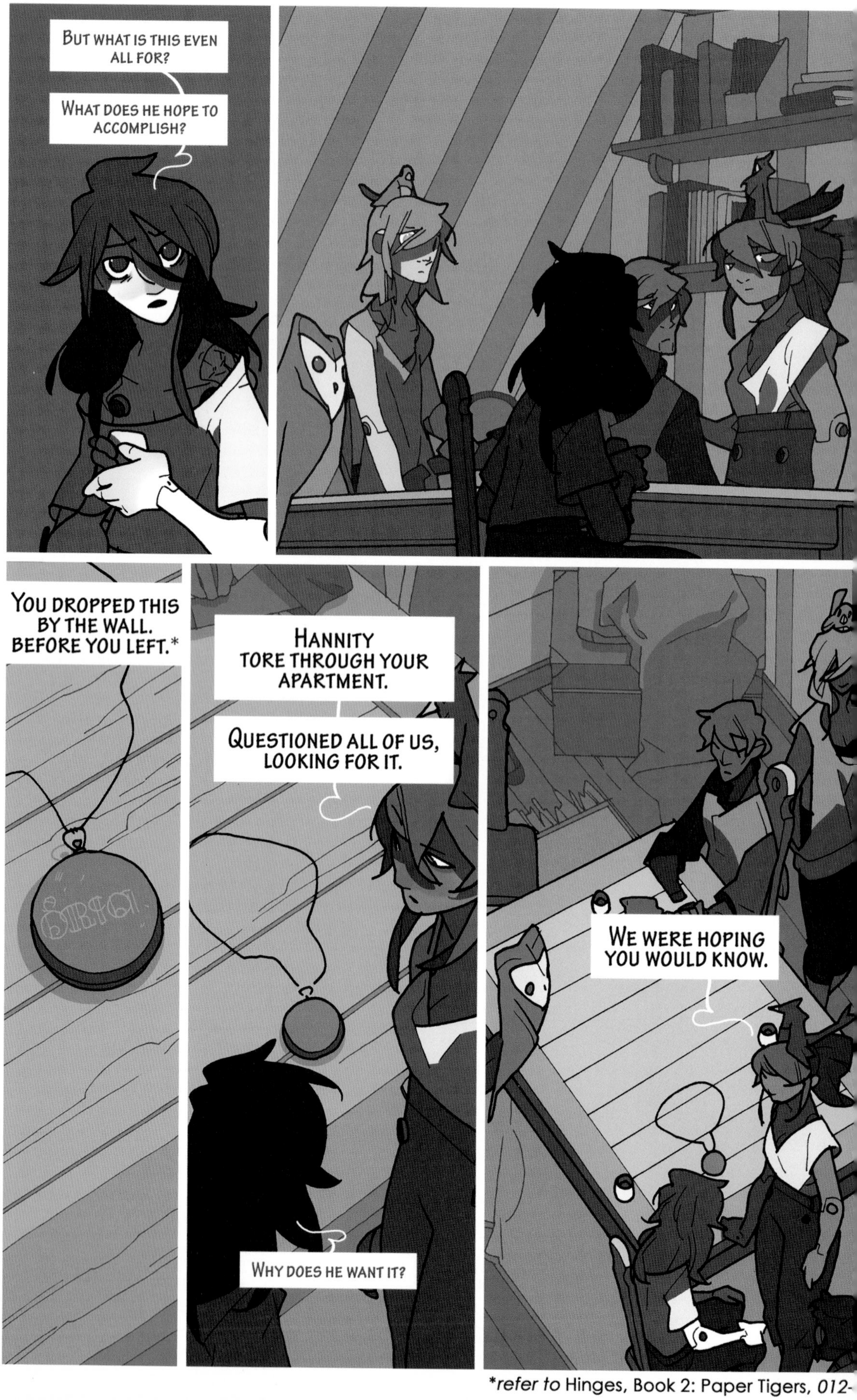
BUT WHAT IS THIS EVEN ALL FOR?
WHAT DOES HE HOPE TO ACCOMPLISH?
YOU DROPPED THIS BY THE WALL. BEFORE YOU LEFT.*
HANNITY TORE THROUGH YOUR APARTMENT.
QUESTIONED ALL OF US, LOOKING FOR IT.
WHY DOES HE WANT IT?
WE WERE HOPING YOU WOULD KNOW.

*refer to Hinges, Book 2: Paper Tigers, 012-

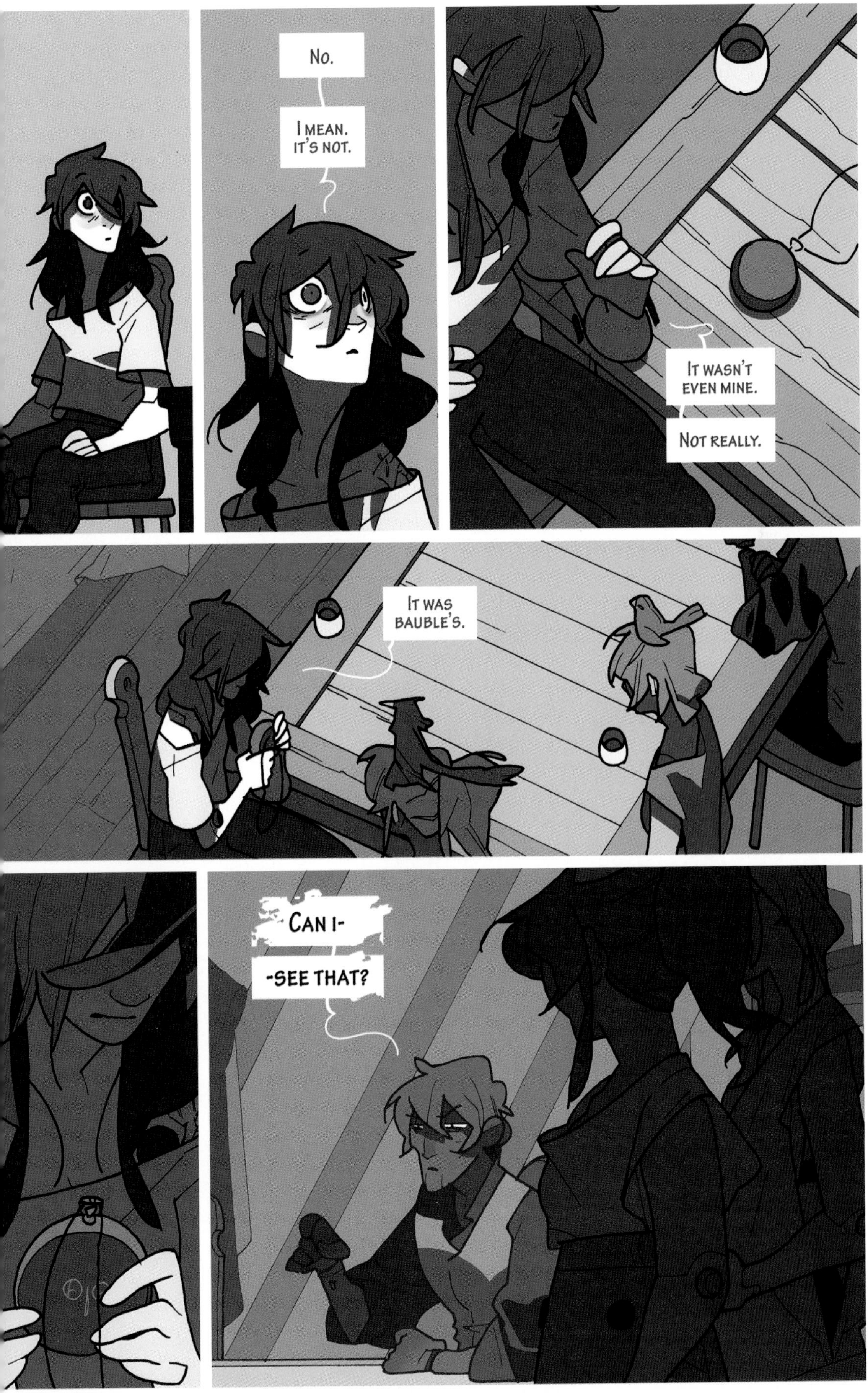
No.
I mean. it's not.
It wasn't even mine.
Not really.
It was bauble's.
Can I-
-see that?

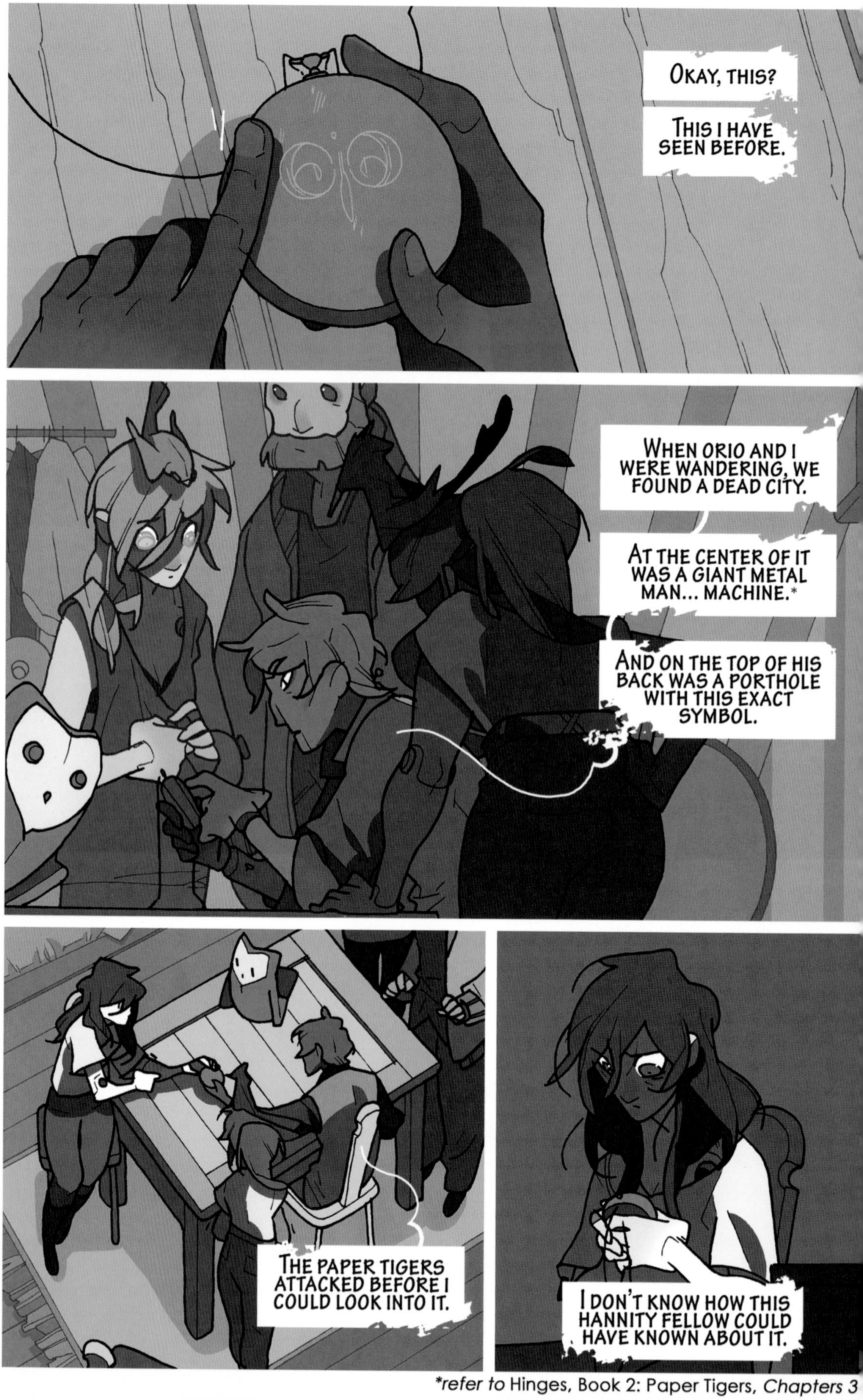
OKAY, THIS?
THIS I HAVE SEEN BEFORE.
WHEN ORIO AND I WERE WANDERING, WE FOUND A DEAD CITY.
AT THE CENTER OF IT WAS A GIANT METAL MAN... MACHINE.*
AND ON THE TOP OF HIS BACK WAS A PORTHOLE WITH THIS EXACT SYMBOL.
THE PAPER TIGERS ATTACKED BEFORE I COULD LOOK INTO IT.
I DON'T KNOW HOW THIS HANNITY FELLOW COULD HAVE KNOWN ABOUT IT.

**refer to* Hinges, Book 2: Paper Tigers, *Chapters 3*

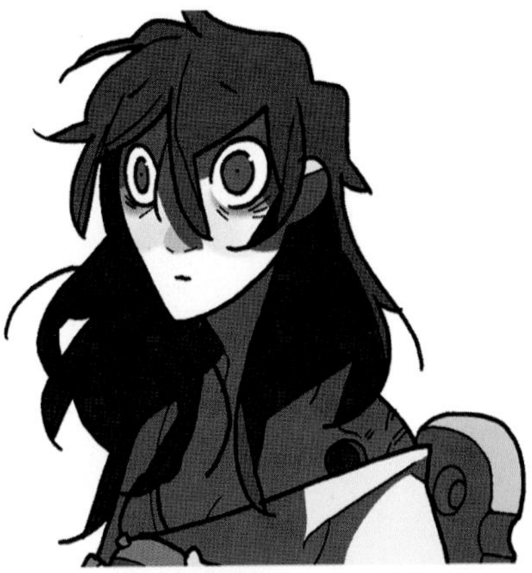

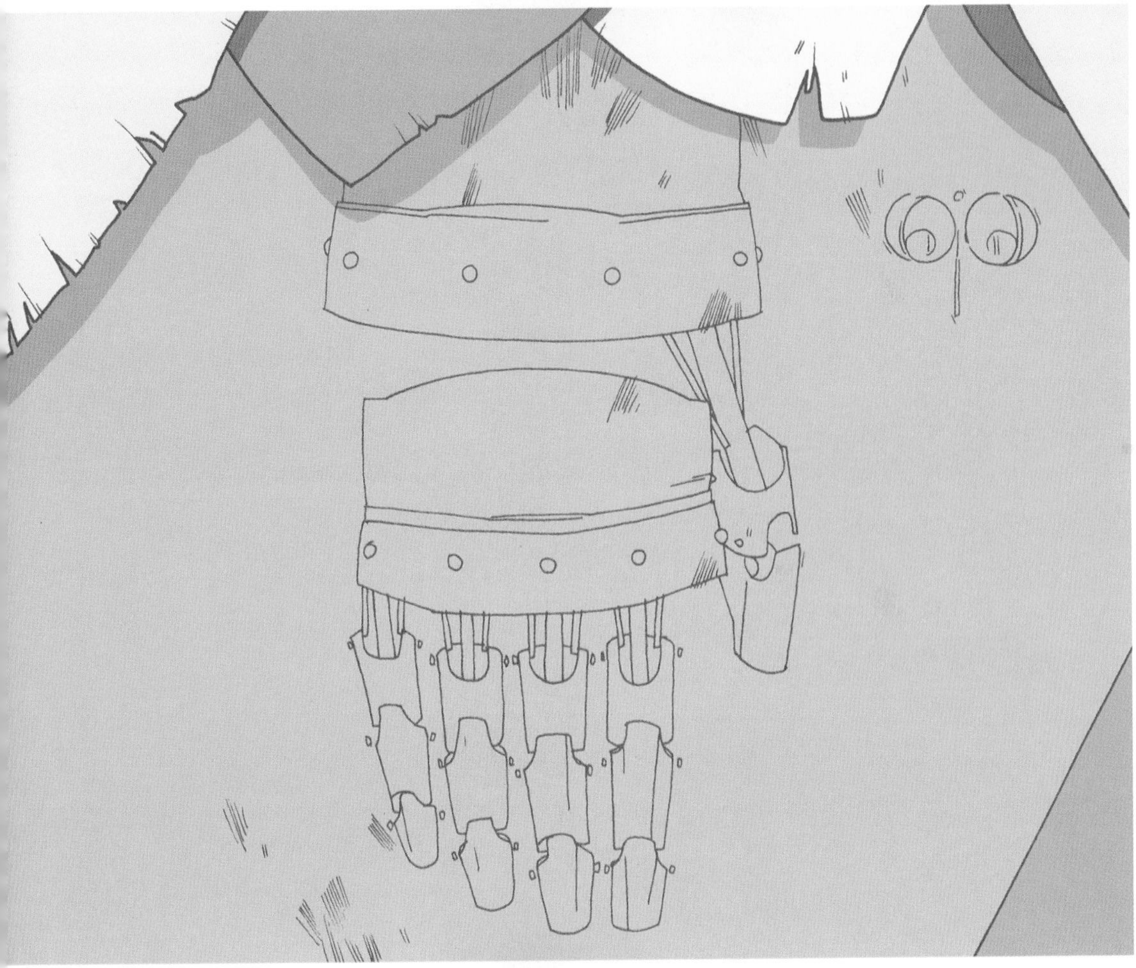

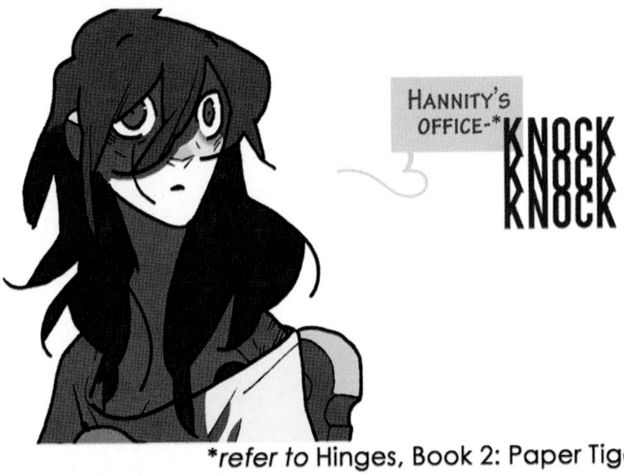
HANNITY'S OFFICE-*
KNOCK
KNOCK
KNOCK

*refer to Hinges, Book 2: Paper Tigers, Chapter 1

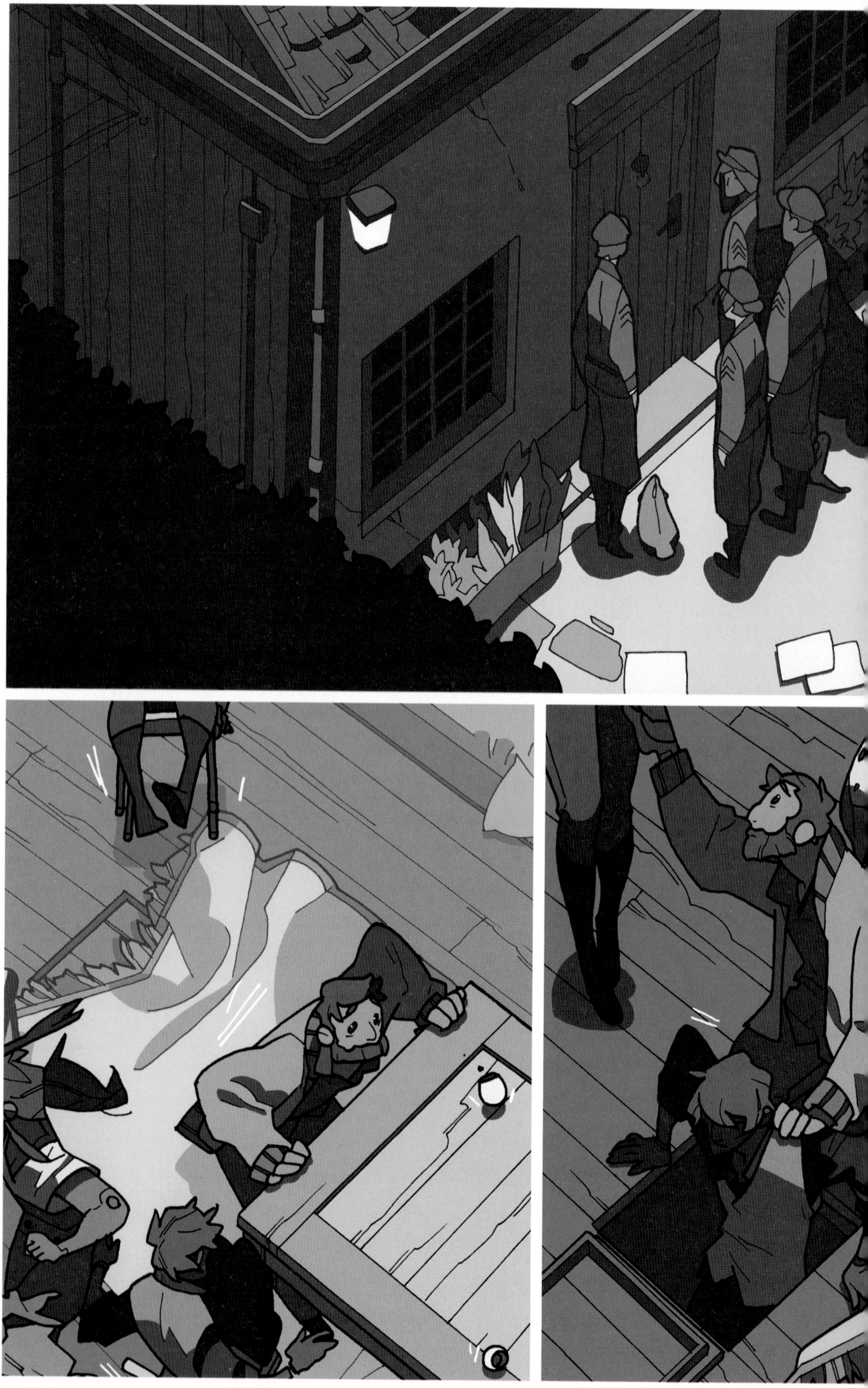

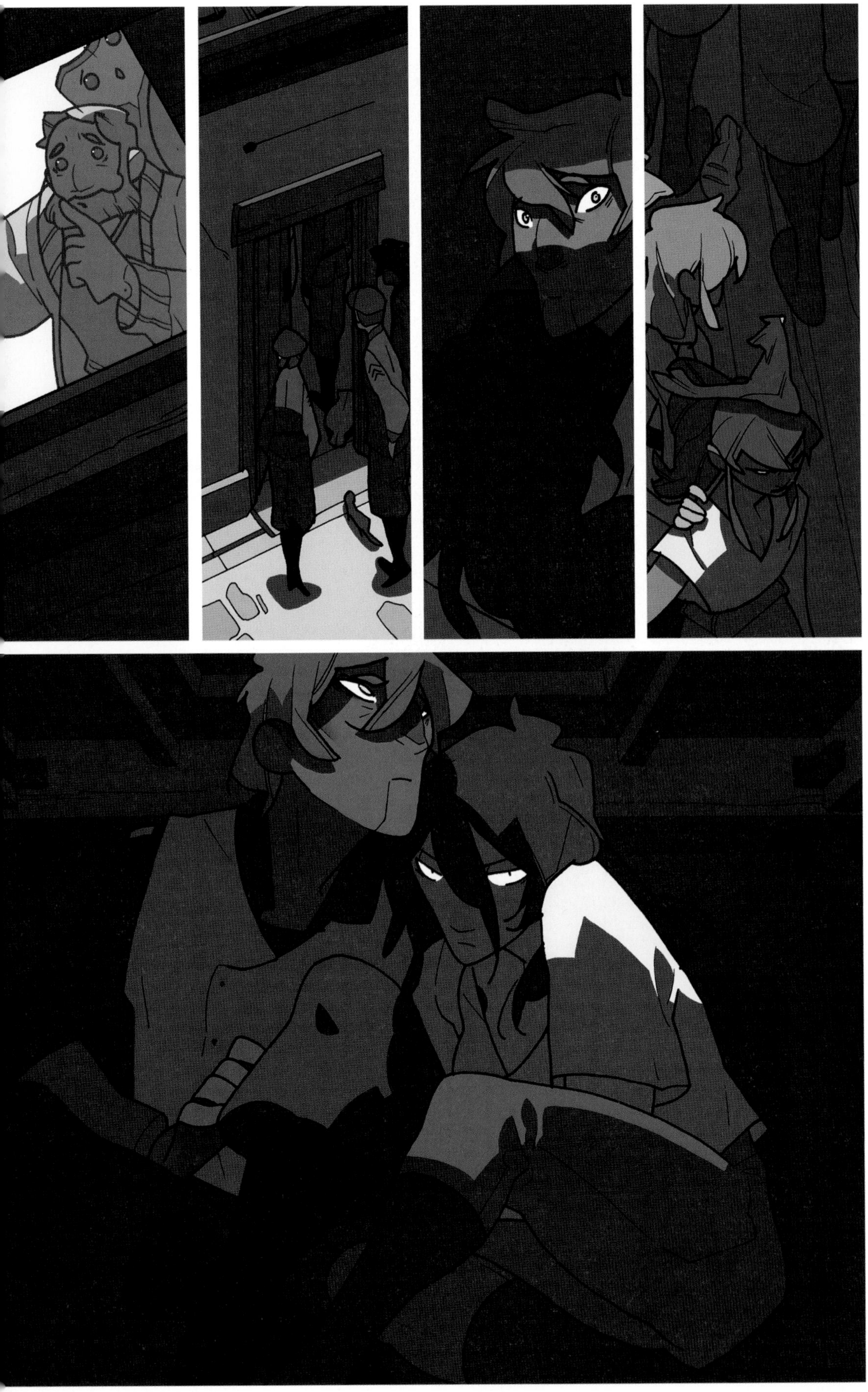

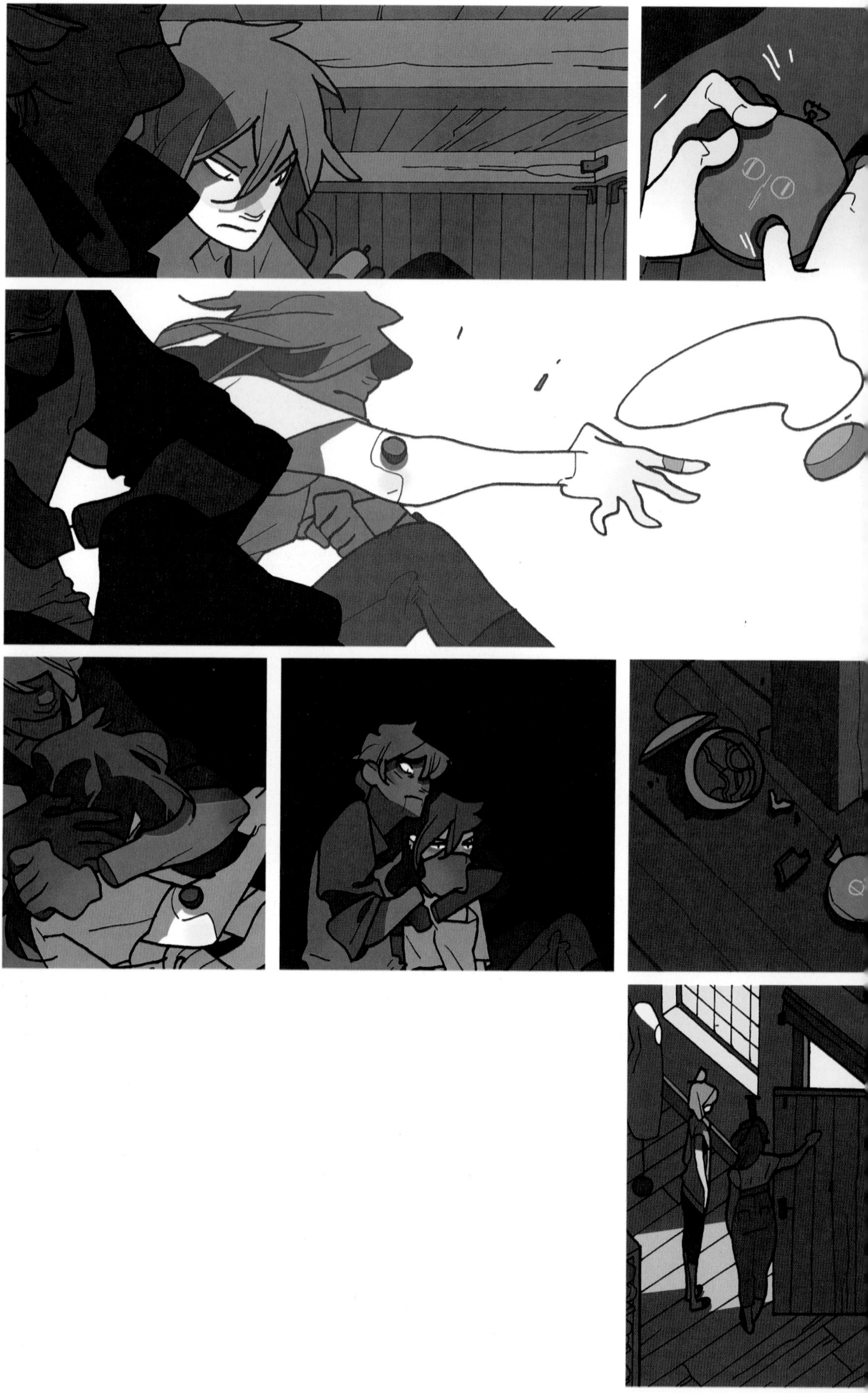

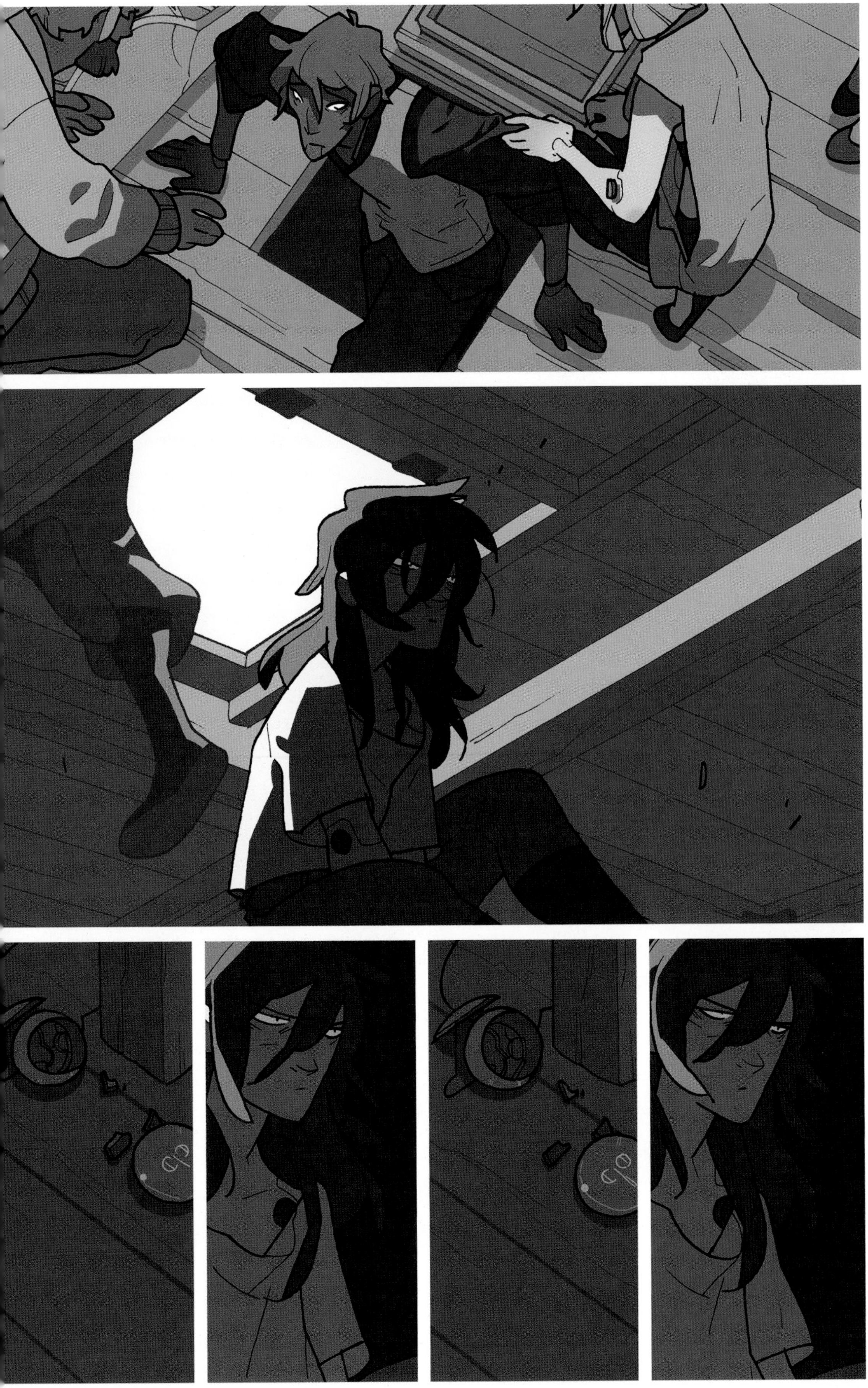

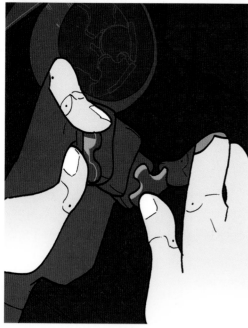

click

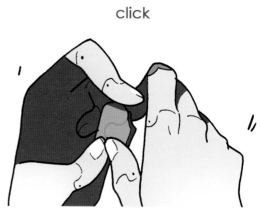

*refer to Hinges, Book 2: Paper Tigers, Chapt

BAUBLE DIDN'T CARE FOR CLOCKS.

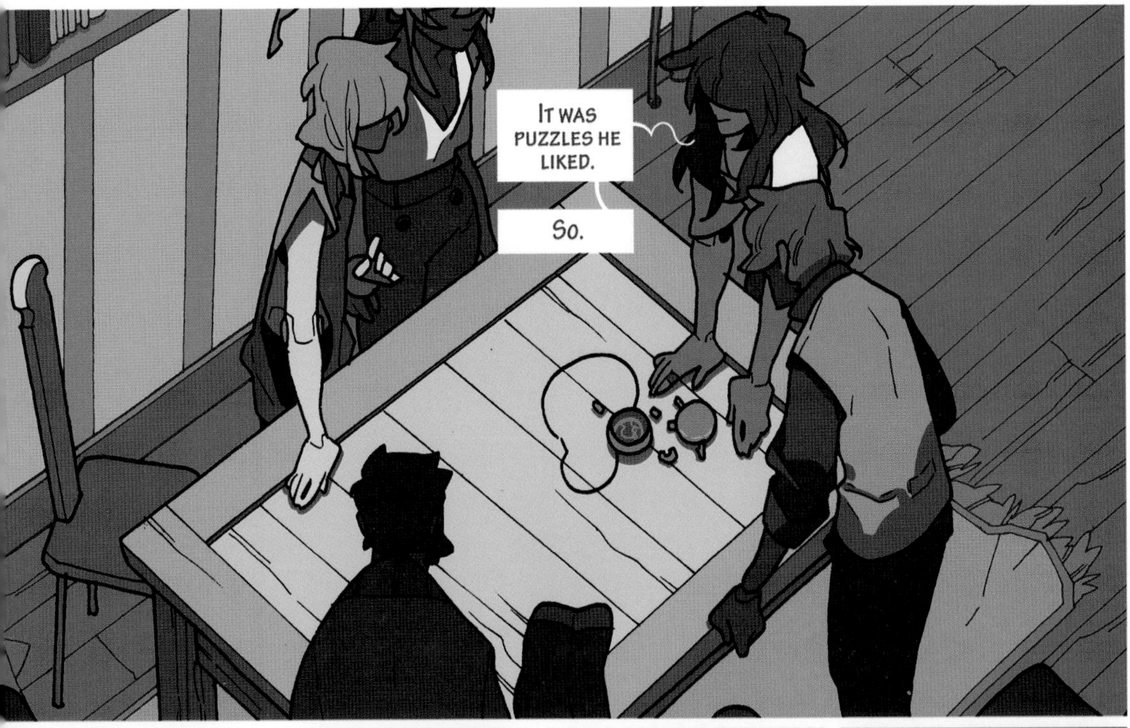
IT WAS PUZZLES HE LIKED.
SO.

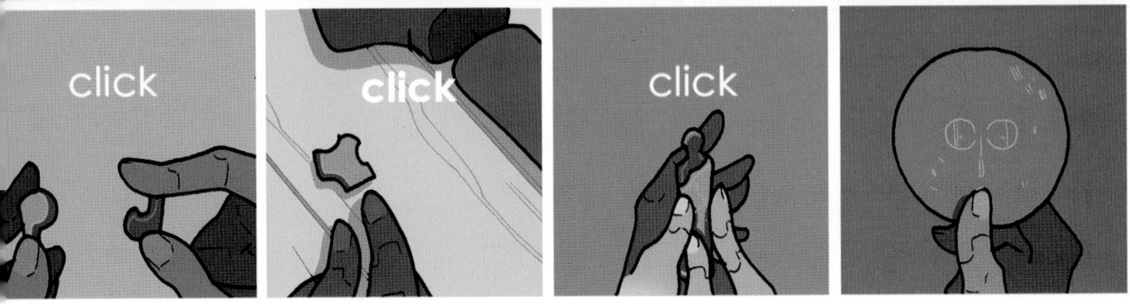
click
click
click

WHAT DO YOU SUPPOSE THIS IS FOR?

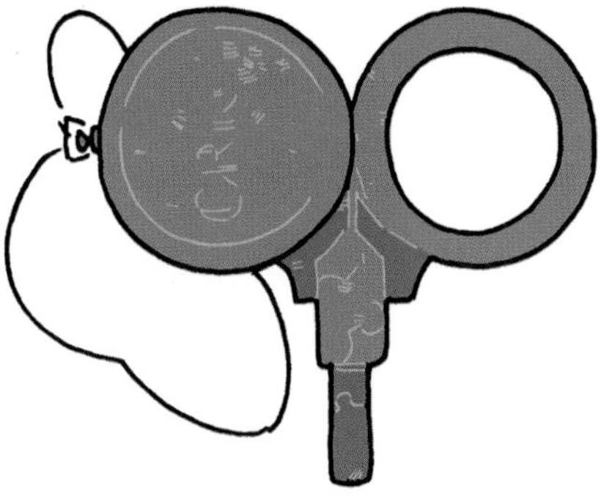

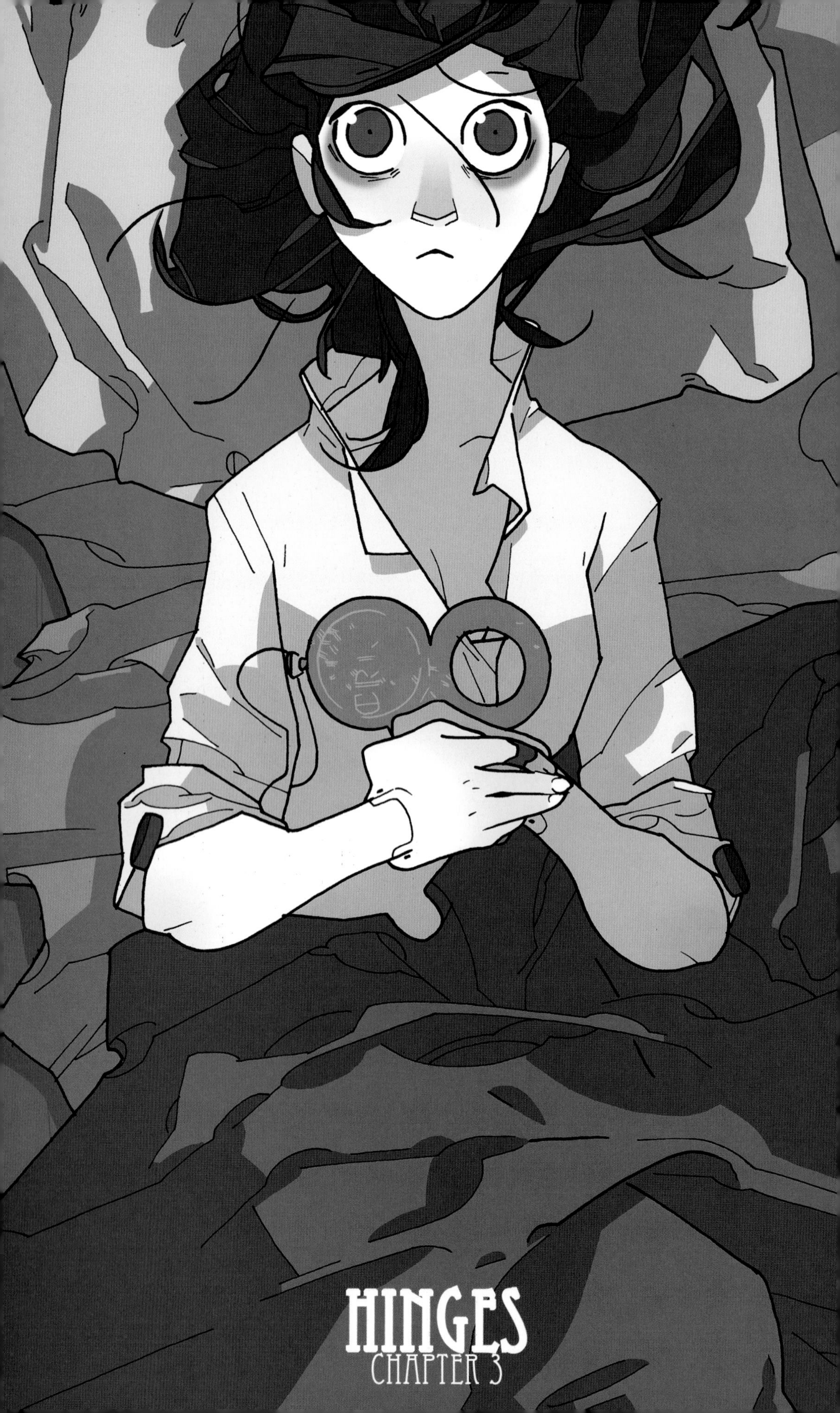
HINGES
CHAPTER 3

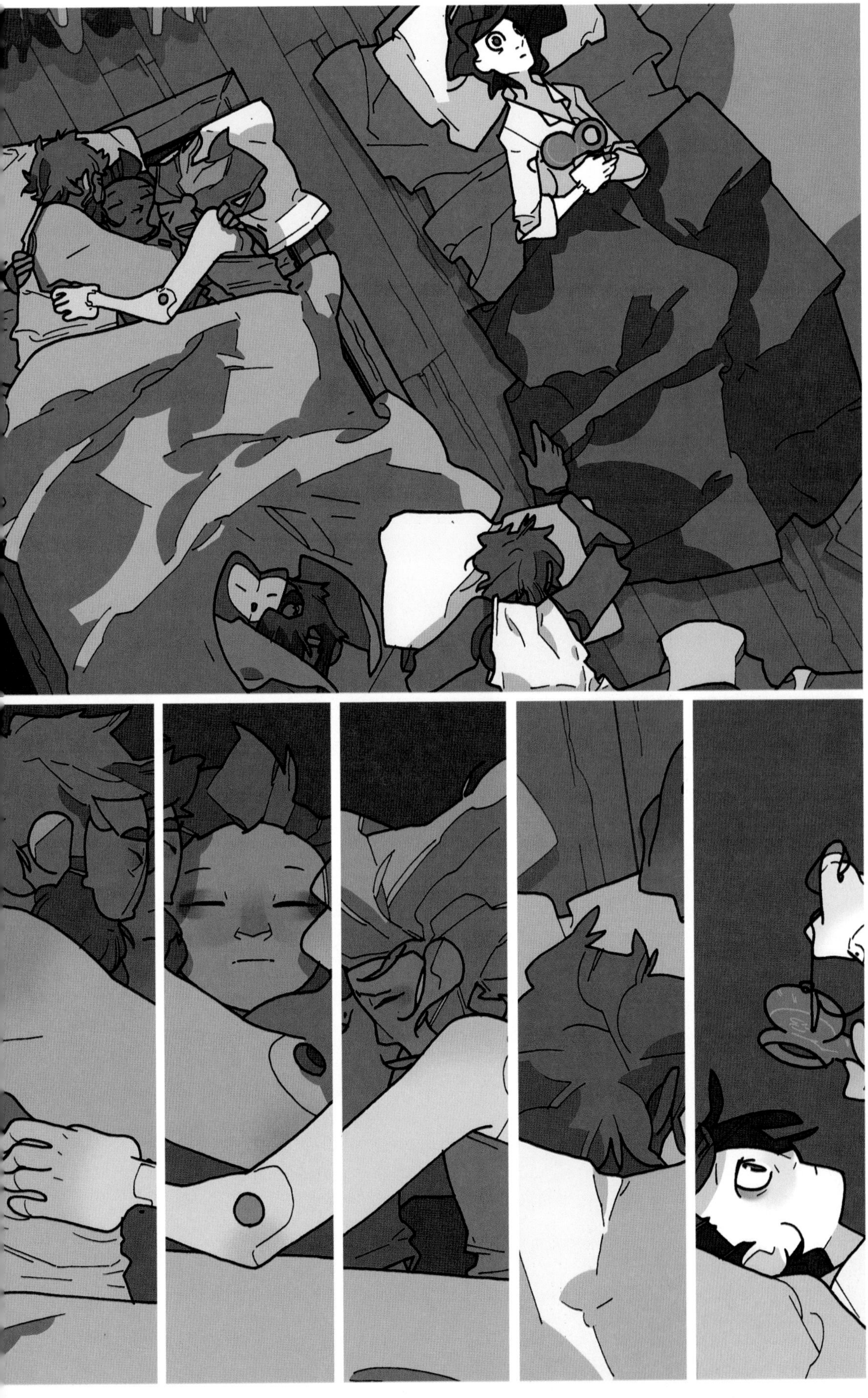

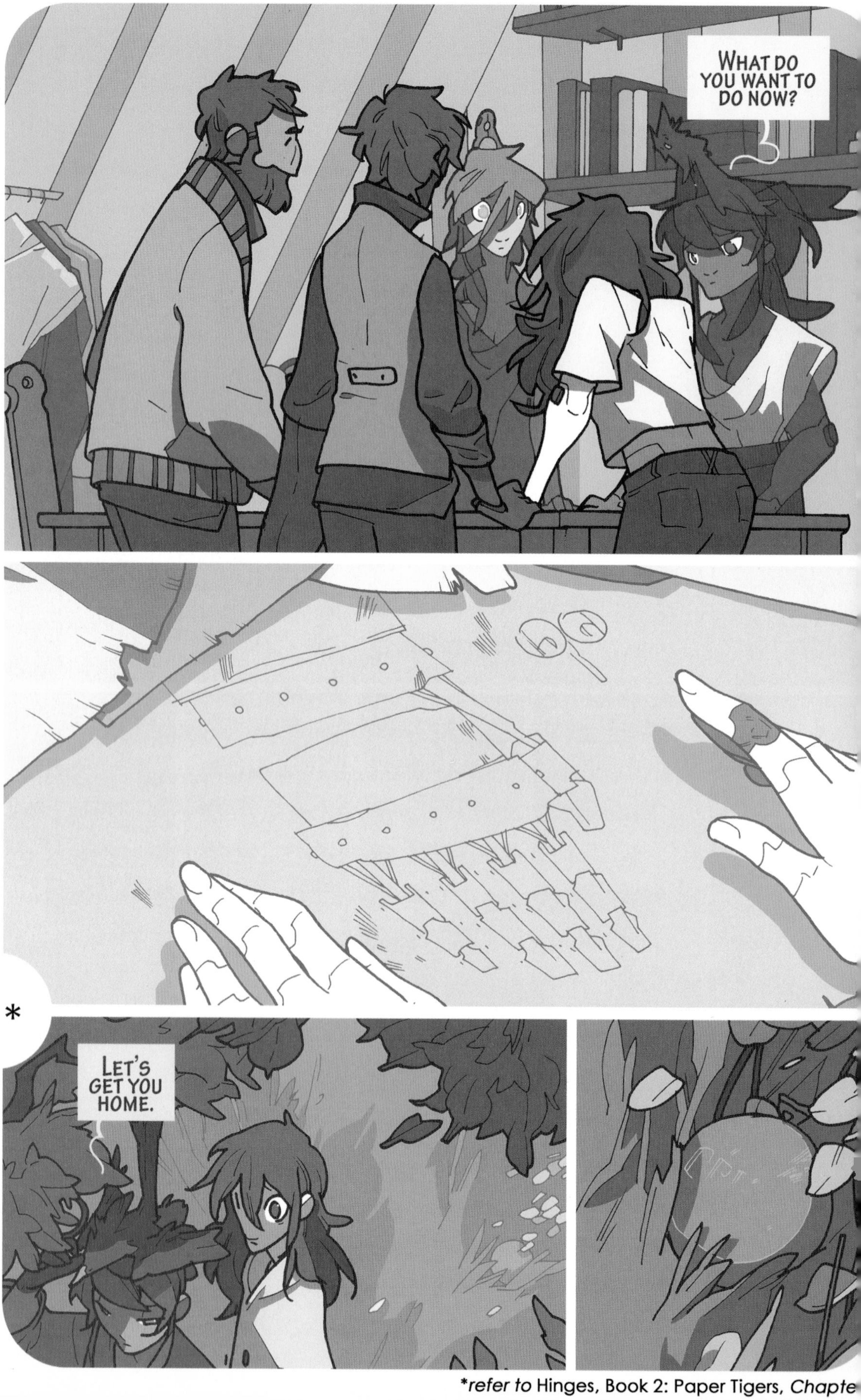
WHAT DO YOU WANT TO DO NOW?
LET'S GET YOU HOME.

**refer to* Hinges, Book 2: Paper Tigers, *Chapte*

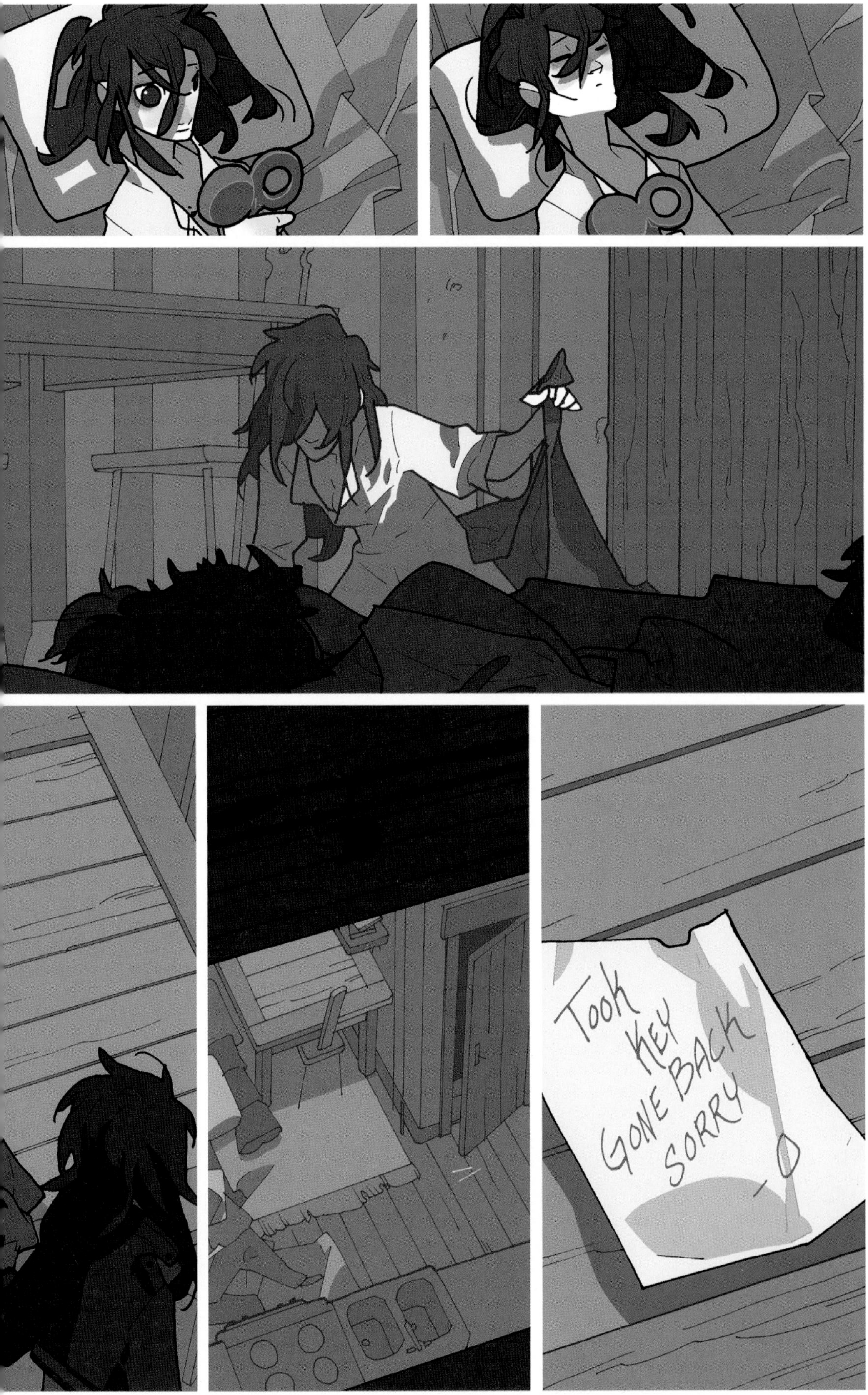
TOOK KEY GONE BACK SORRY
-O

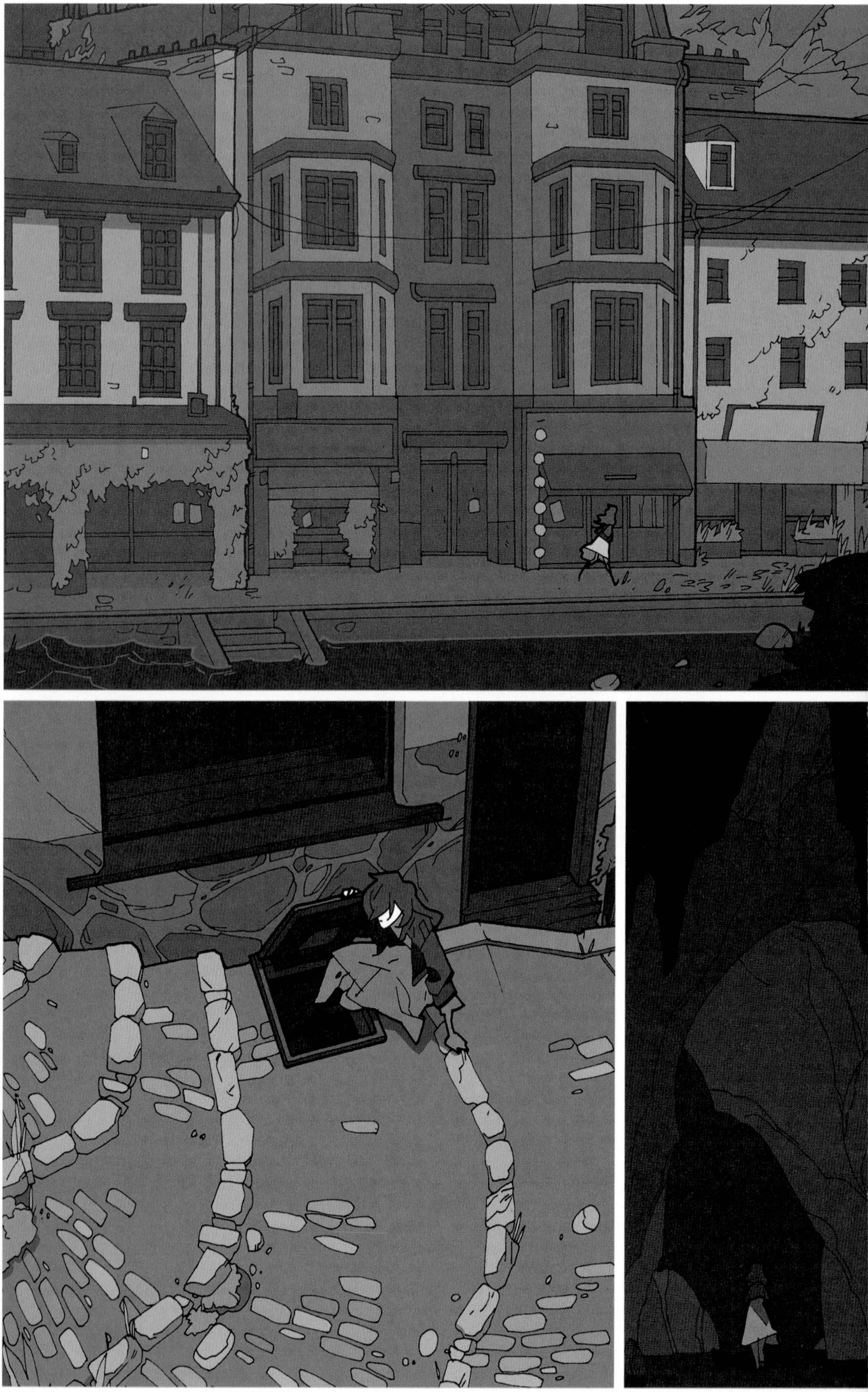

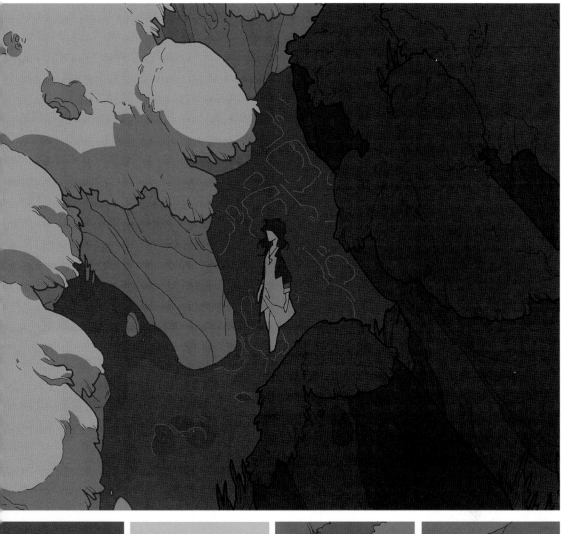

Он.

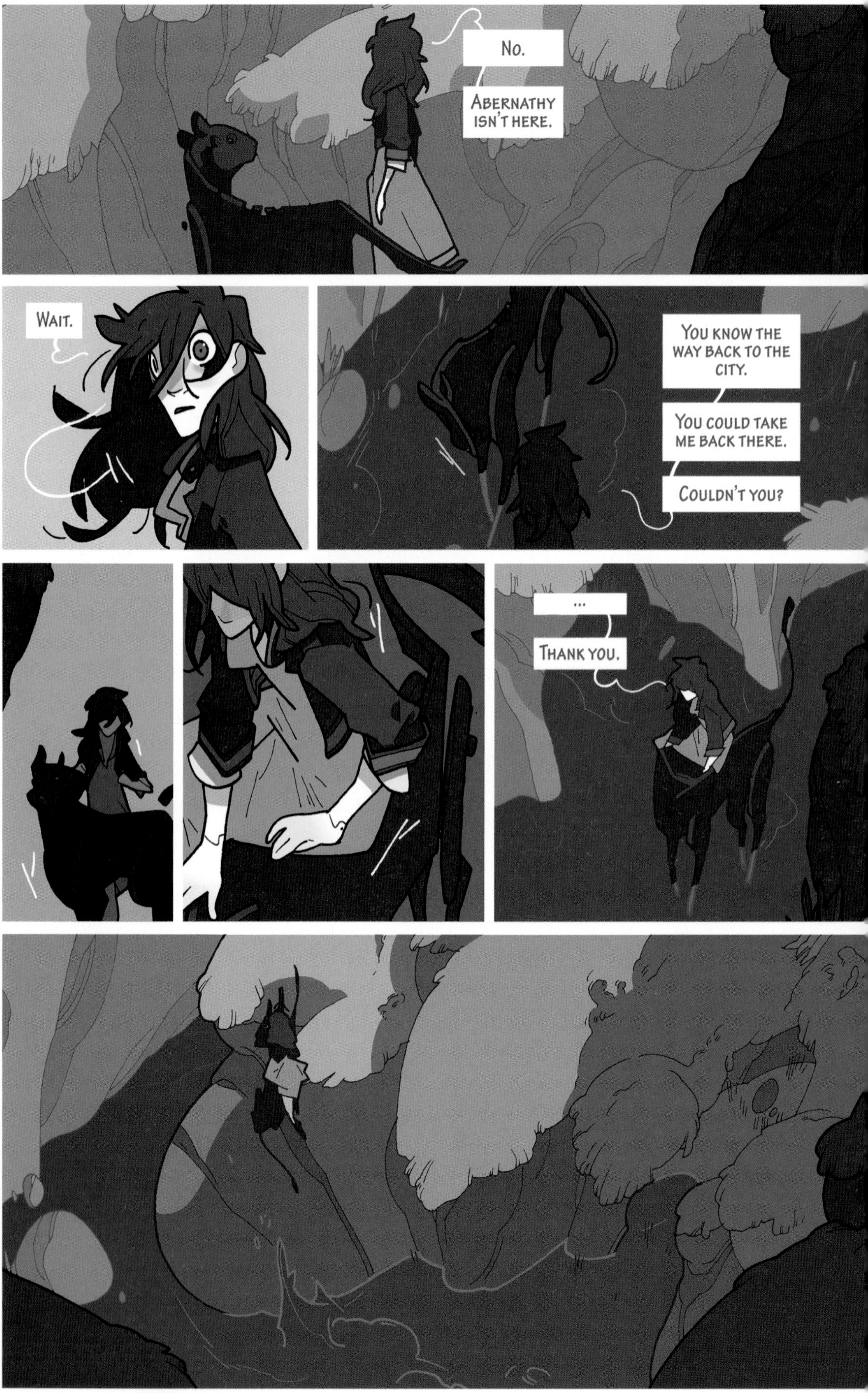
No.
Abernathy isn't here.
Wait.
You know the way back to the city.
You could take me back there.
Couldn't you?
...
Thank you.

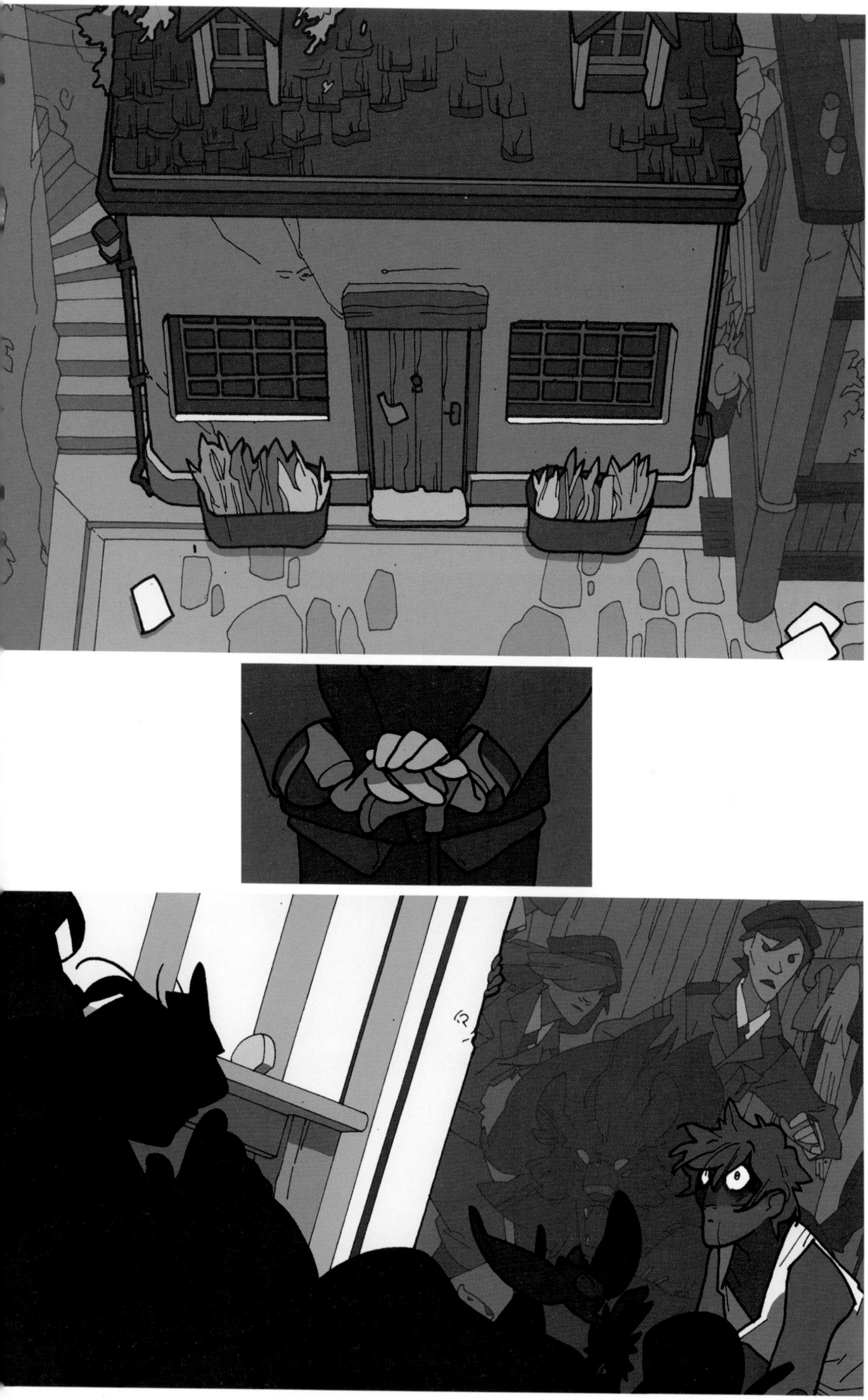

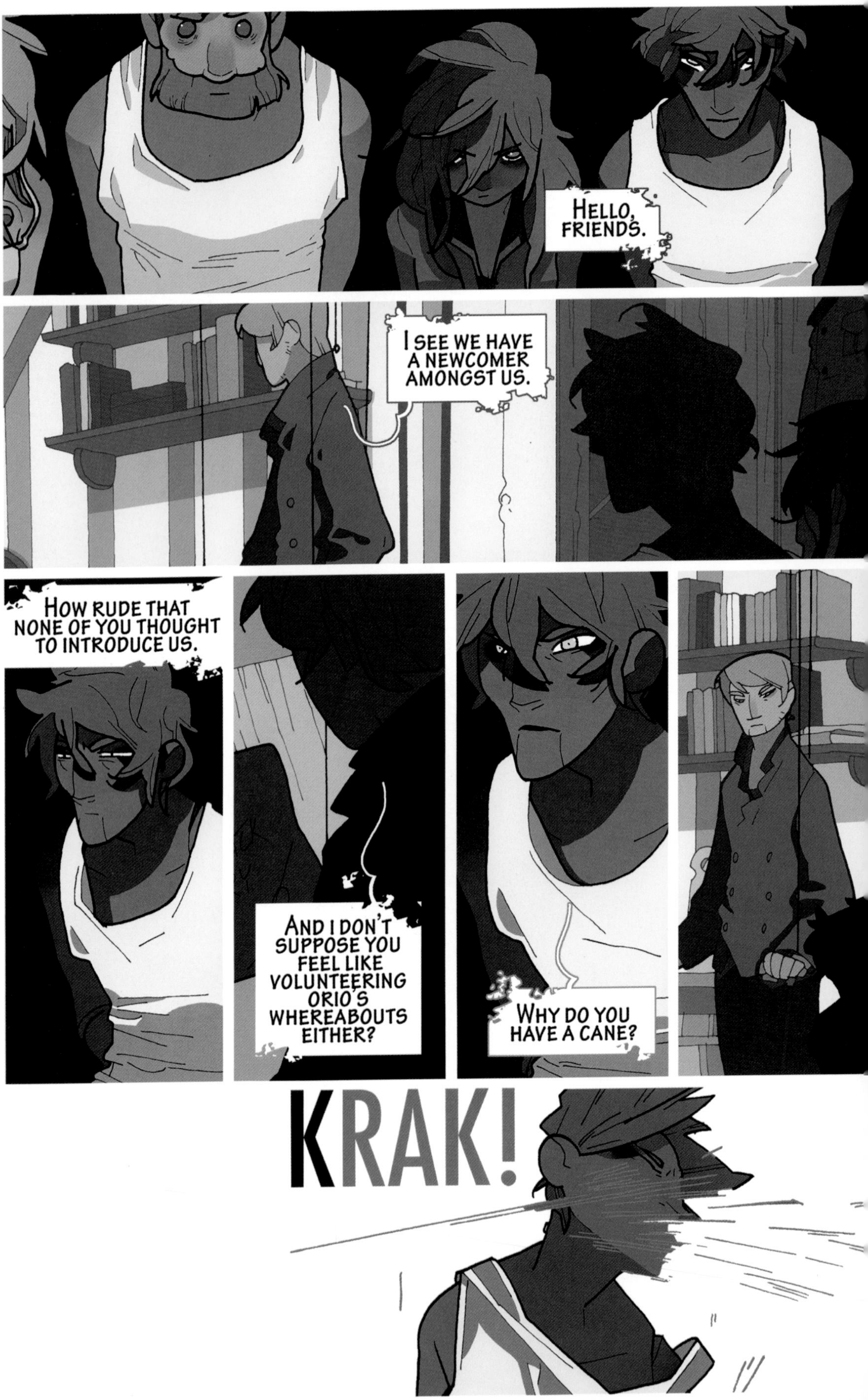
HELLO, FRIENDS.
I SEE WE HAVE A NEWCOMER AMONGST US.
HOW RUDE THAT NONE OF YOU THOUGHT TO INTRODUCE US.
AND I DON'T SUPPOSE YOU FEEL LIKE VOLUNTEERING ORIO'S WHEREABOUTS EITHER?
WHY DO YOU HAVE A CANE?
KRAK!

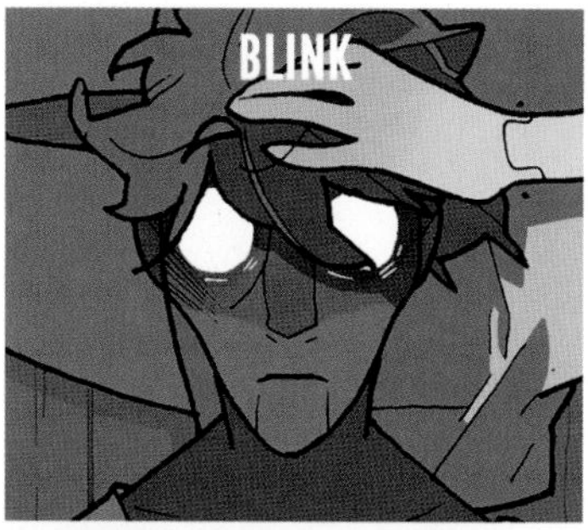
BLINK

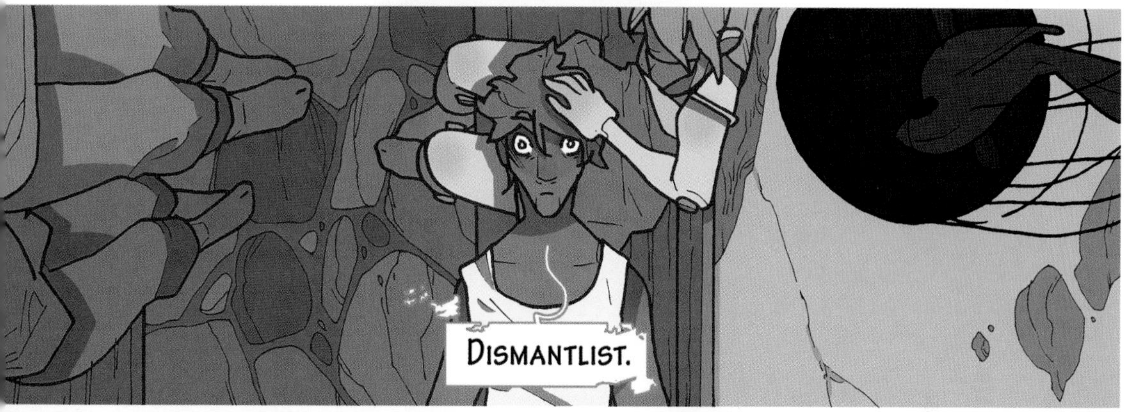
DISMANTLIST.

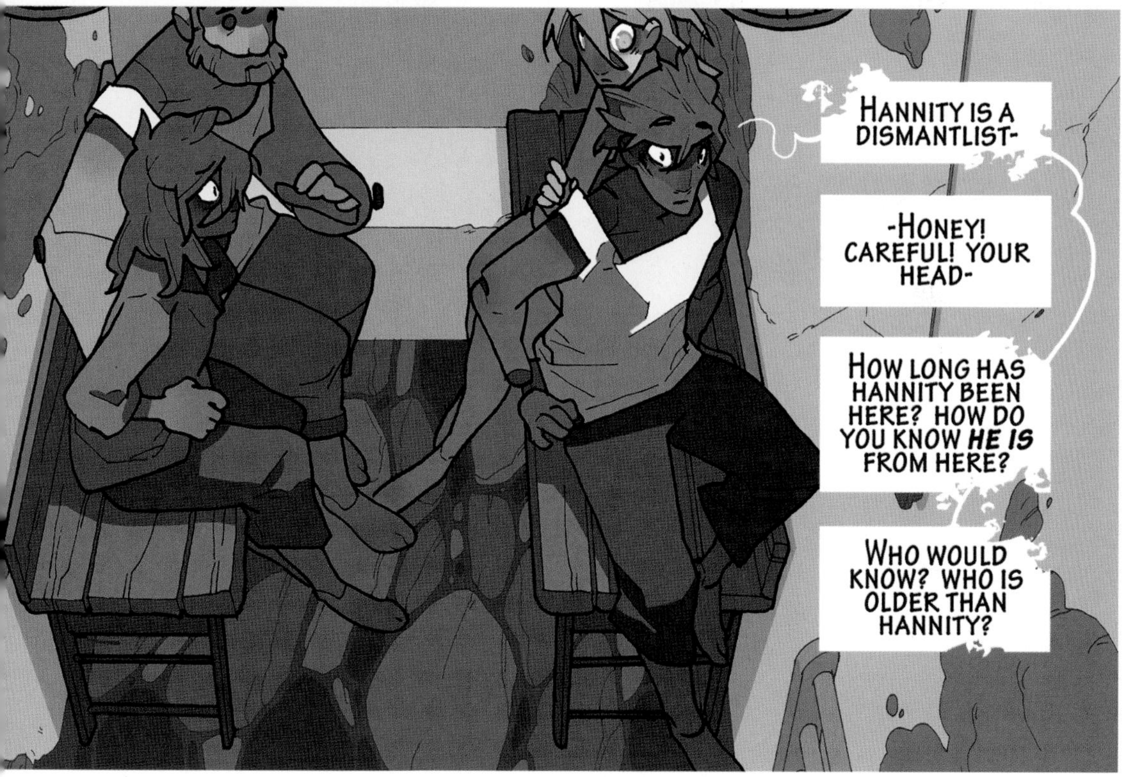
HANNITY IS A DISMANTLIST-
-HONEY! CAREFUL! YOUR HEAD-
HOW LONG HAS HANNITY BEEN HERE? HOW DO YOU KNOW ***HE IS*** FROM HERE?
WHO WOULD KNOW? WHO IS OLDER THAN HANNITY?

NO ONE.

THERE ISN'T ANYONE OLDER THAN HANNITY.

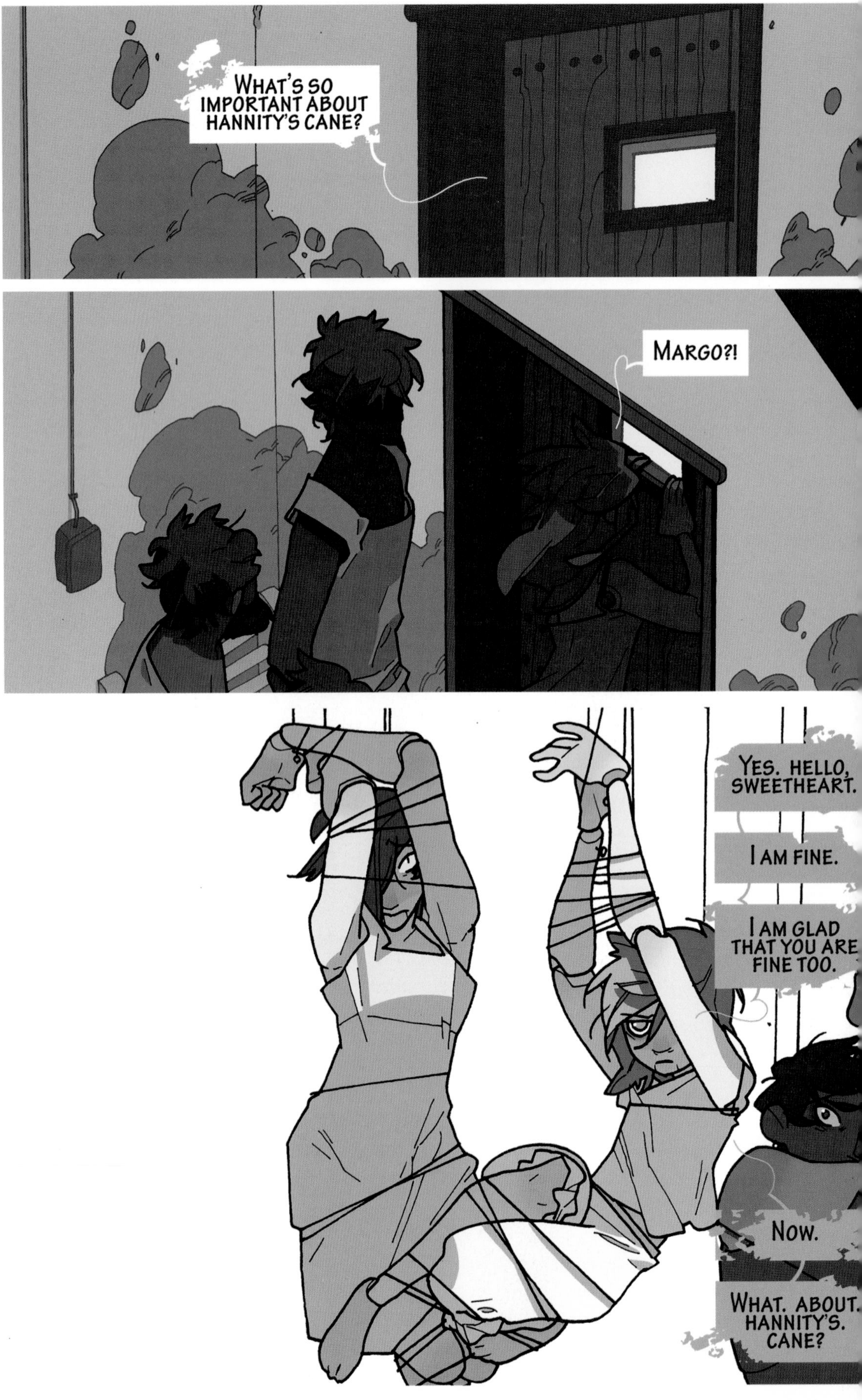
WHAT'S SO IMPORTANT ABOUT HANNITY'S CANE?
MARGO?!
YES. HELLO, SWEETHEART.
I AM FINE.
I AM GLAD THAT YOU ARE FINE TOO.
NOW.
WHAT. ABOUT. HANNITY'S. CANE?

ARE THERE ANY RECORDS OF HANNITY'S ACTIVATION?

THERE MIGHT BE. WE'VE HAD NO REASON TO CHECK.

BUT YOU DON'T KNOW?

NO.

AND HE'S ALWAYS HAD THE CANE?

YES.

YOU DON'T THINK HE NEEDS THE CANE?

NO, MA'AM.

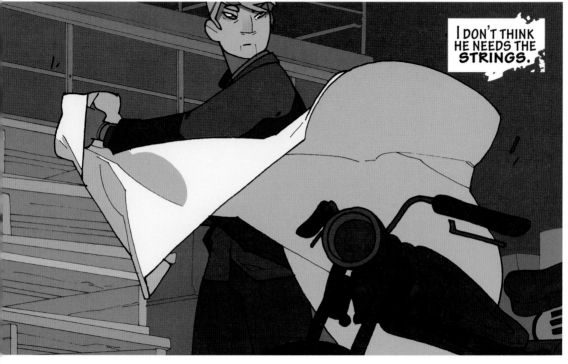

I DON'T THINK HE NEEDS THE STRINGS.

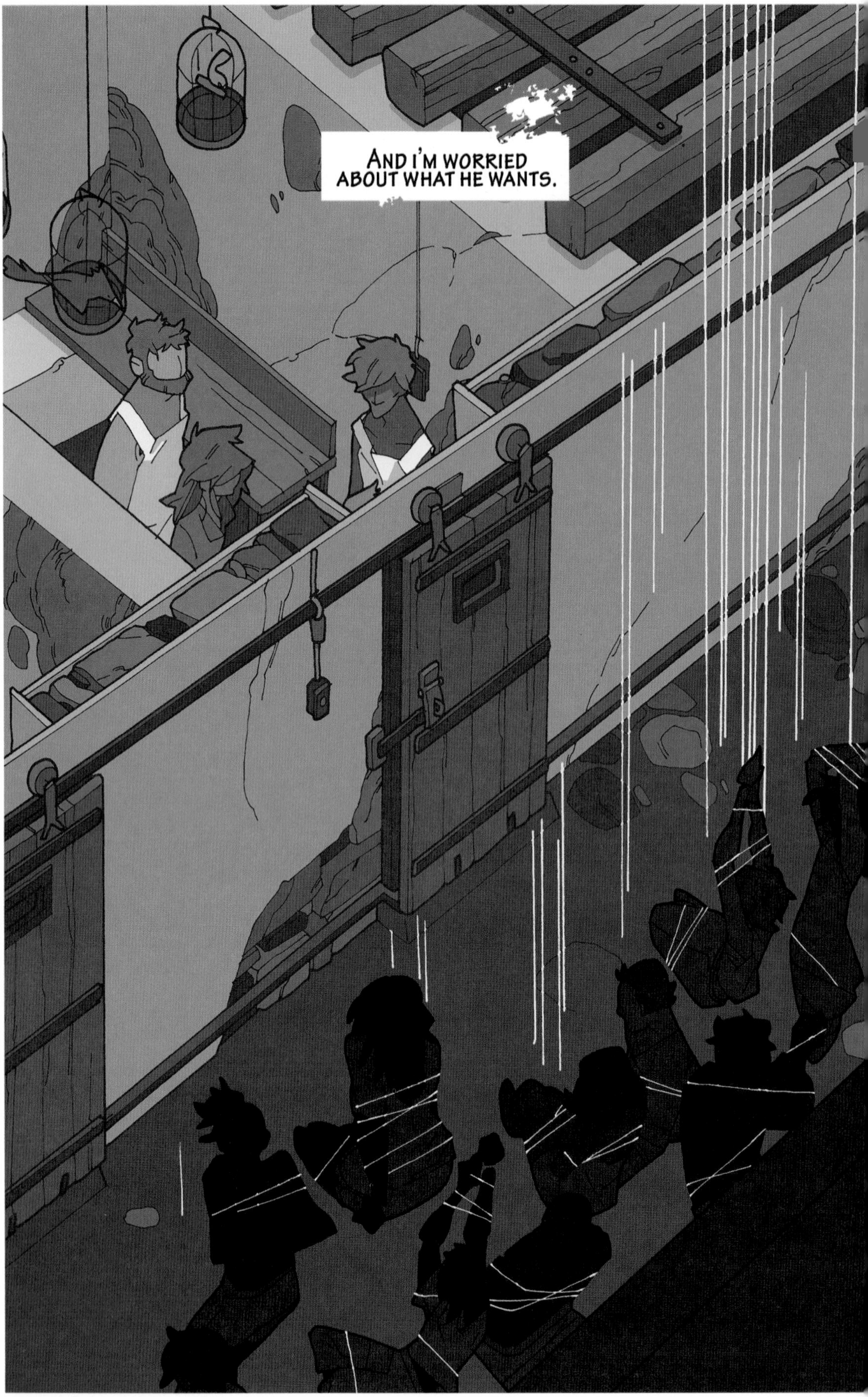
AND I'M WORRIED ABOUT WHAT HE WANTS.

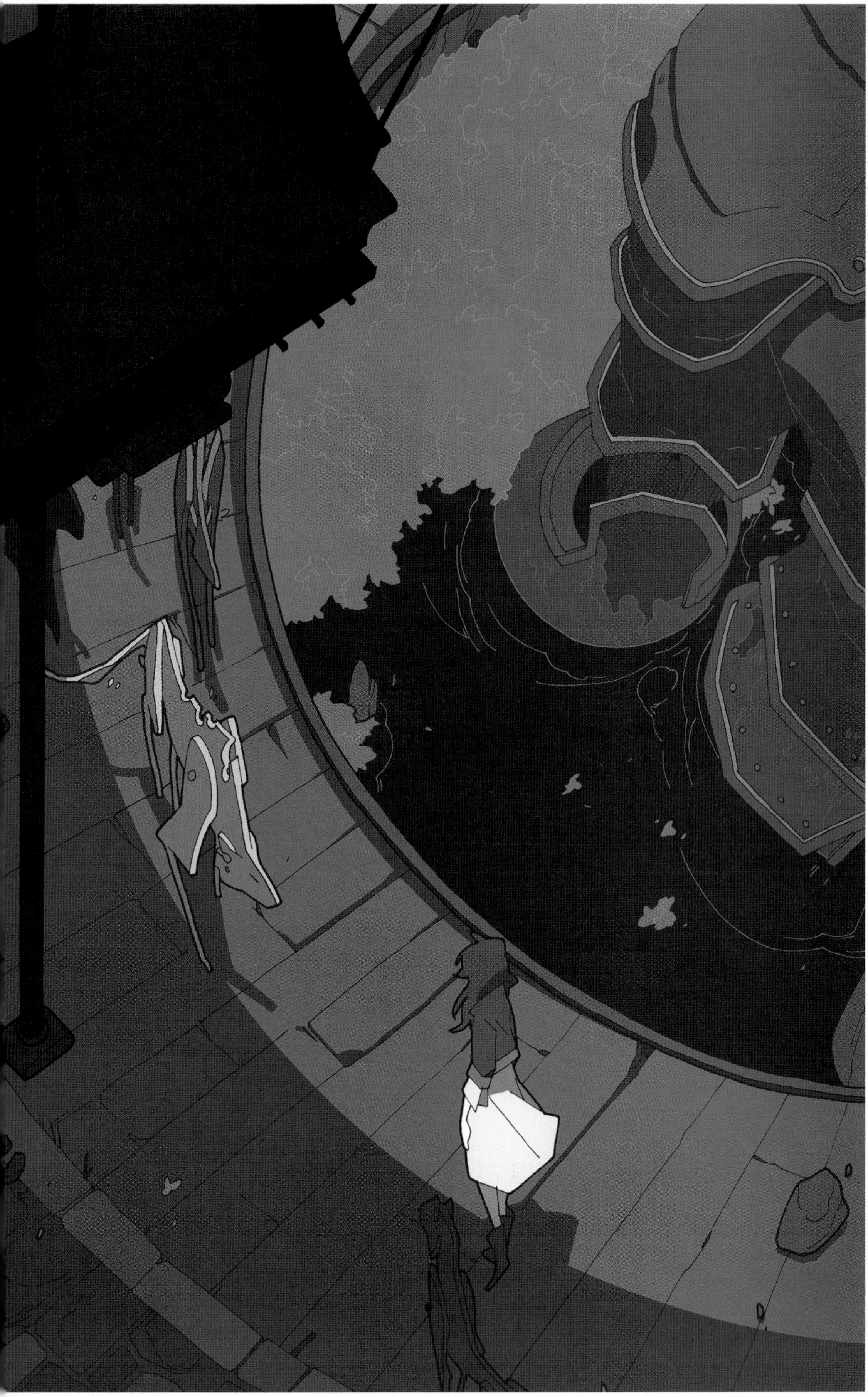

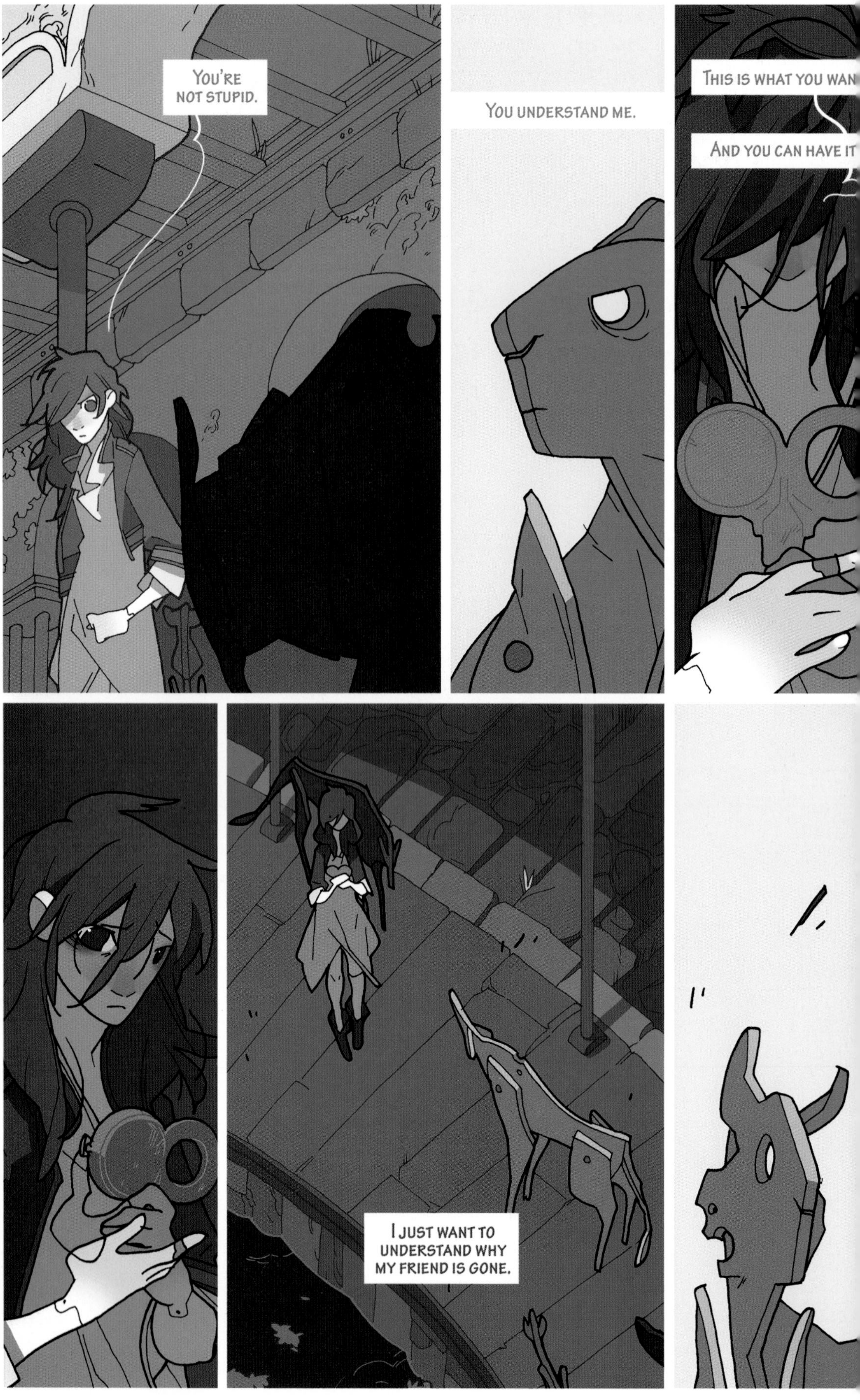
You're not stupid.
You understand me.
This is what you wan
And you can have it
I just want to understand why my friend is gone.

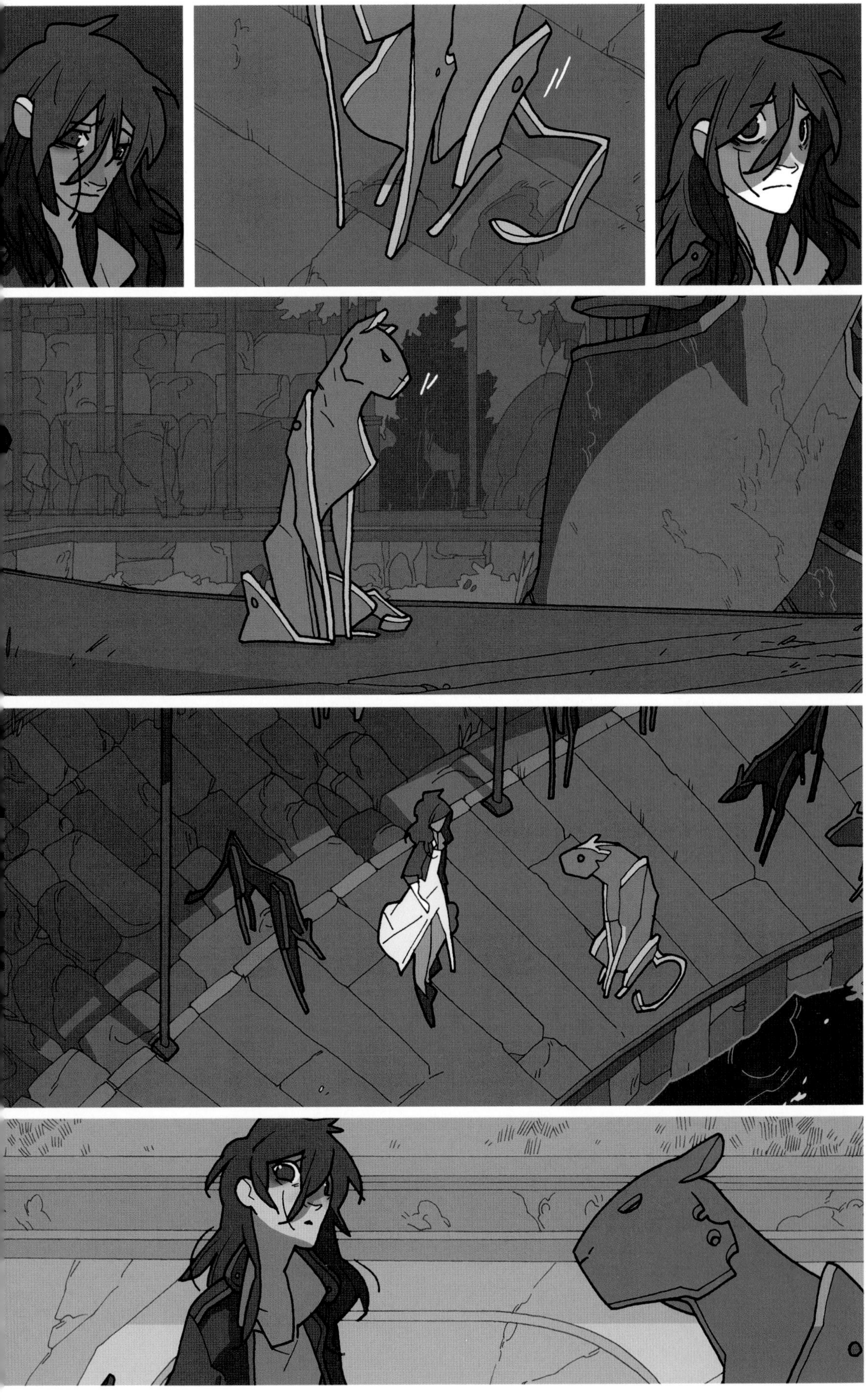

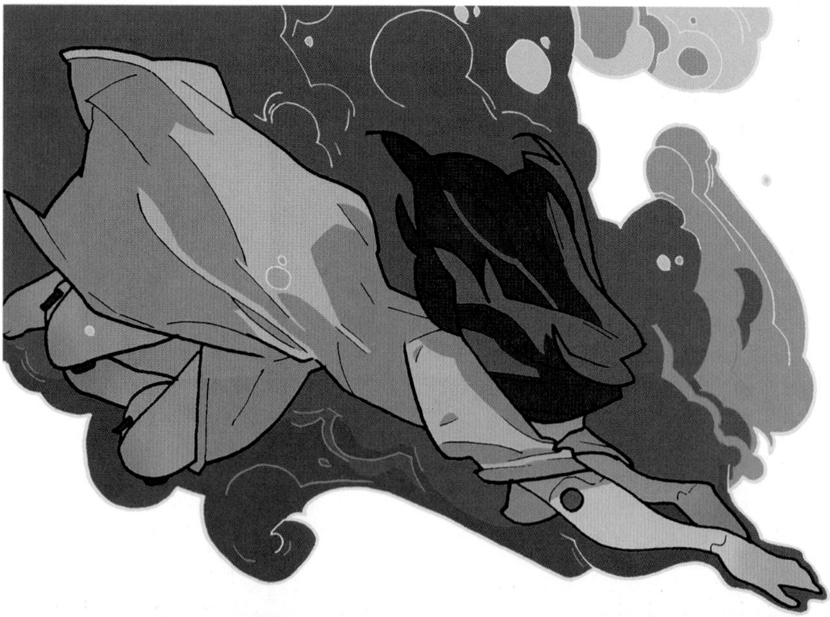

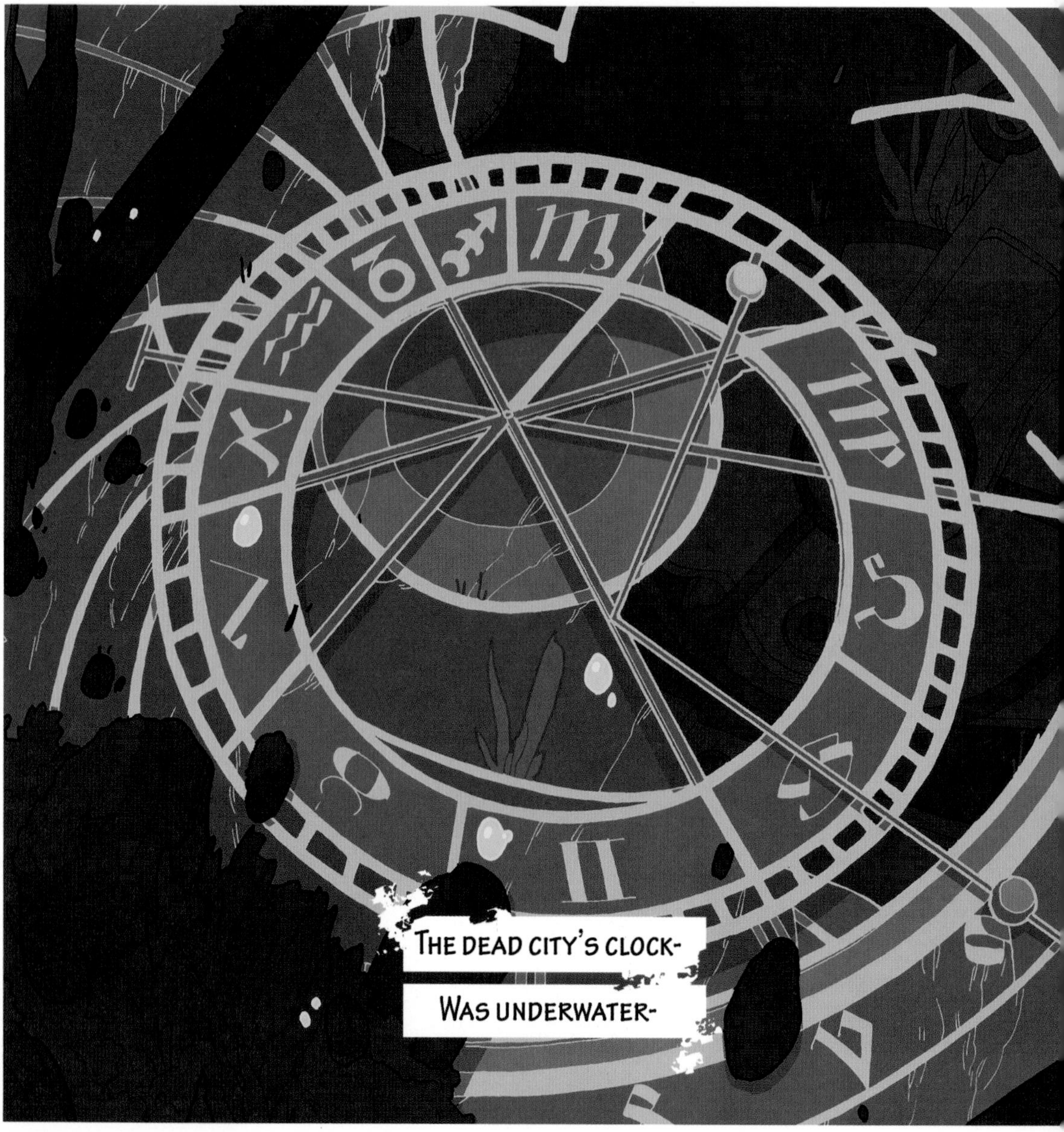
THE DEAD CITY'S CLOCK-
WAS UNDERWATER-

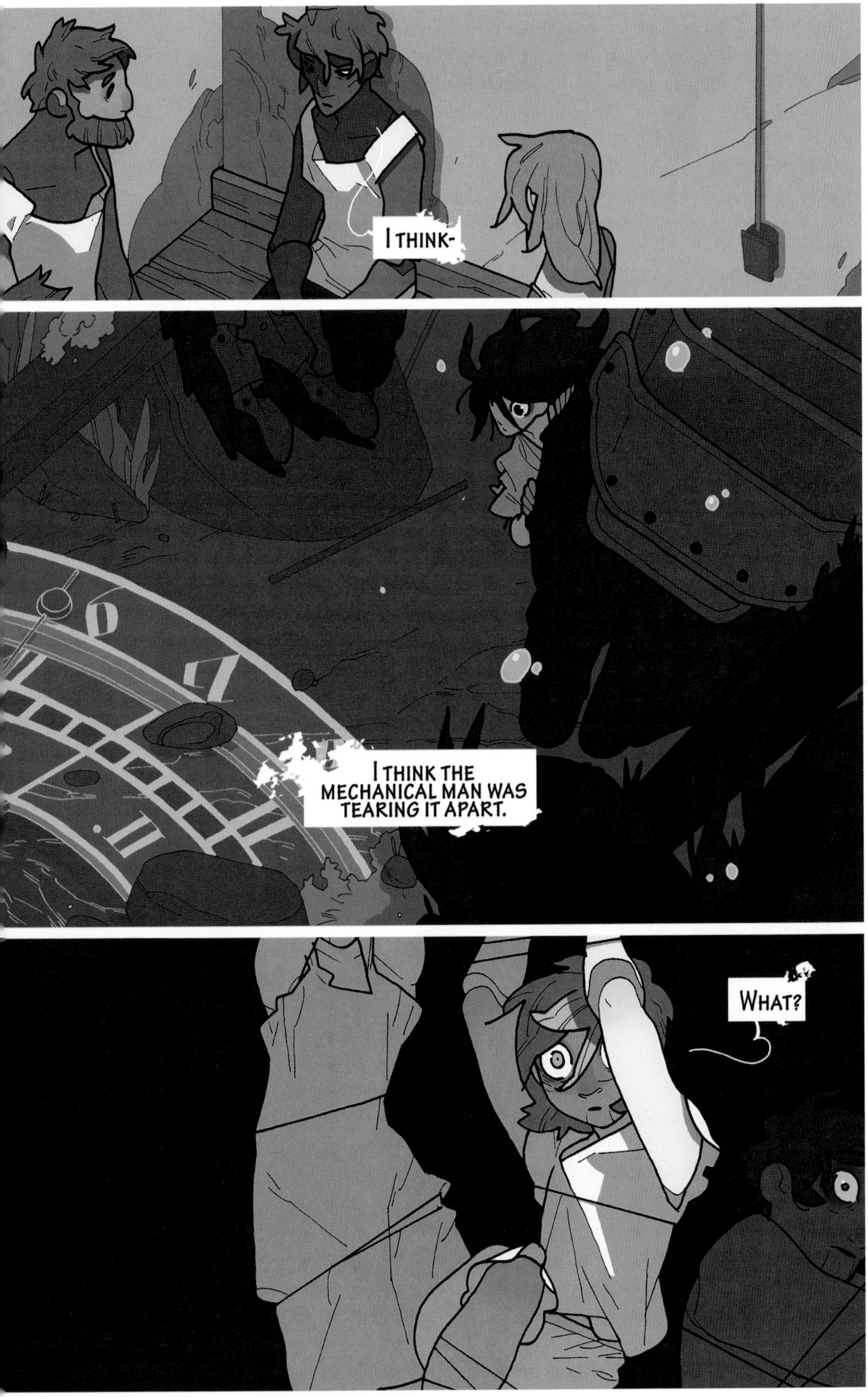
I THINK-
I THINK THE MECHANICAL MAN WAS TEARING IT APART.
WHAT?

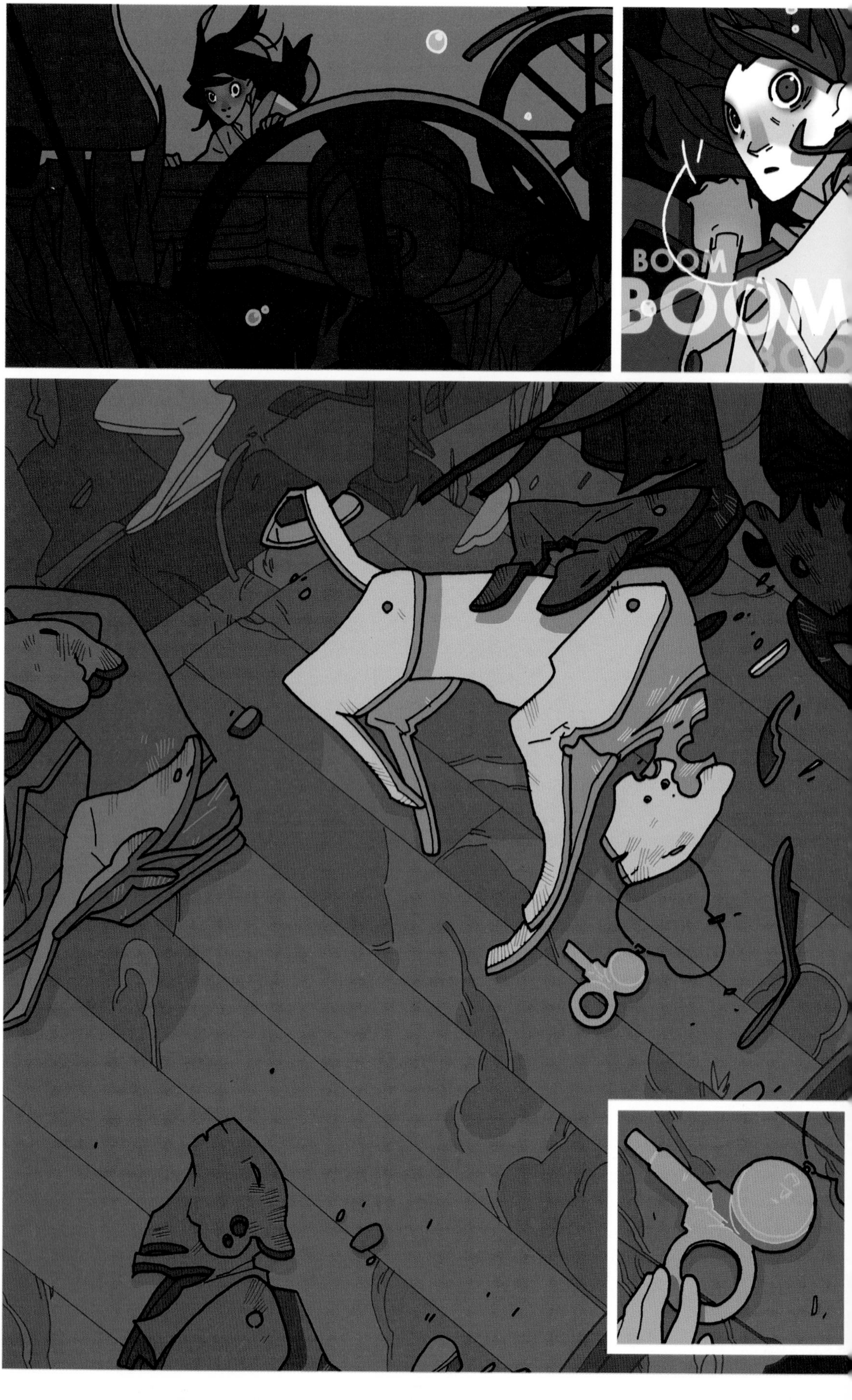
BOOM
BOOM

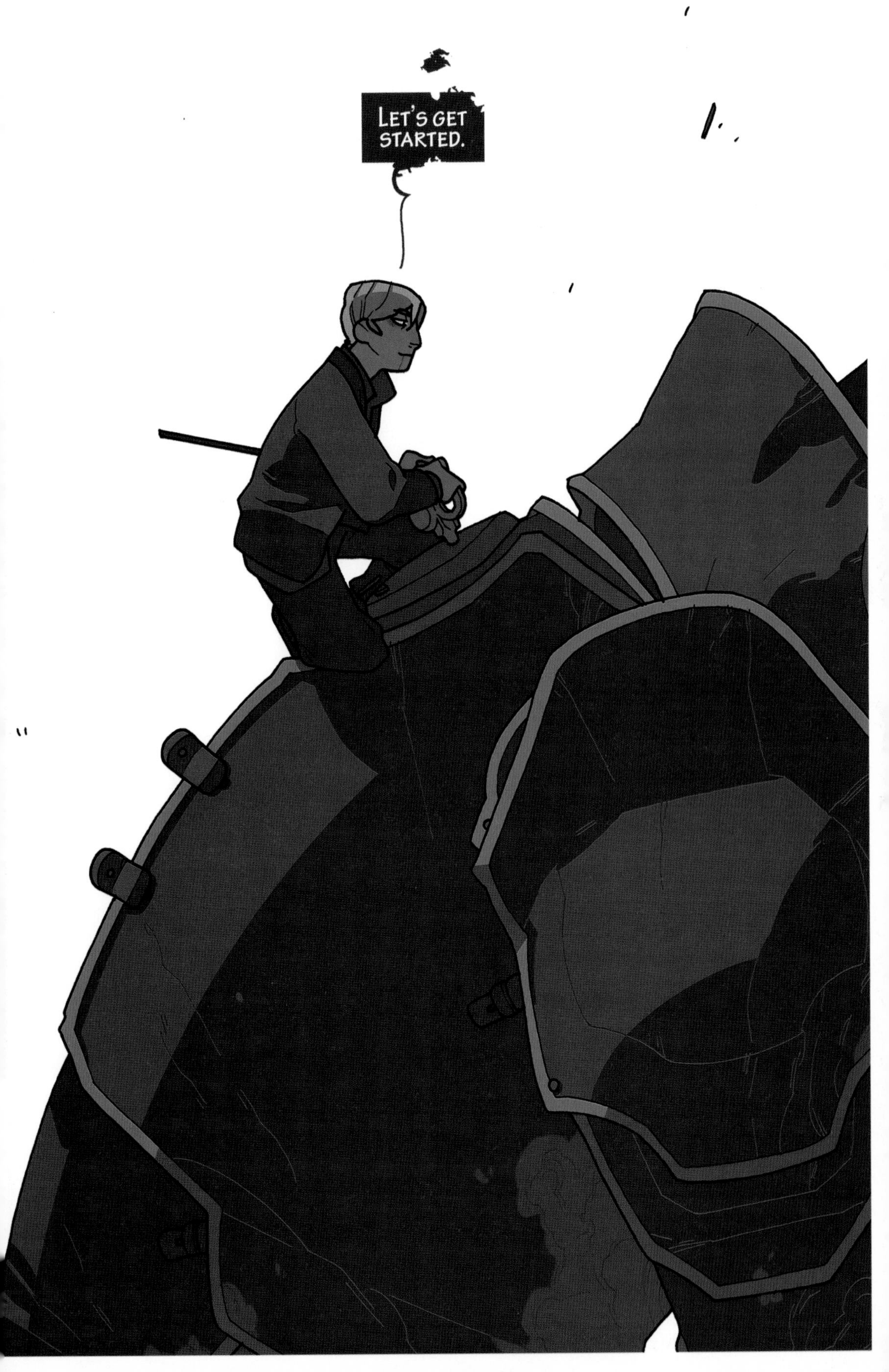
LET'S GET STARTED.

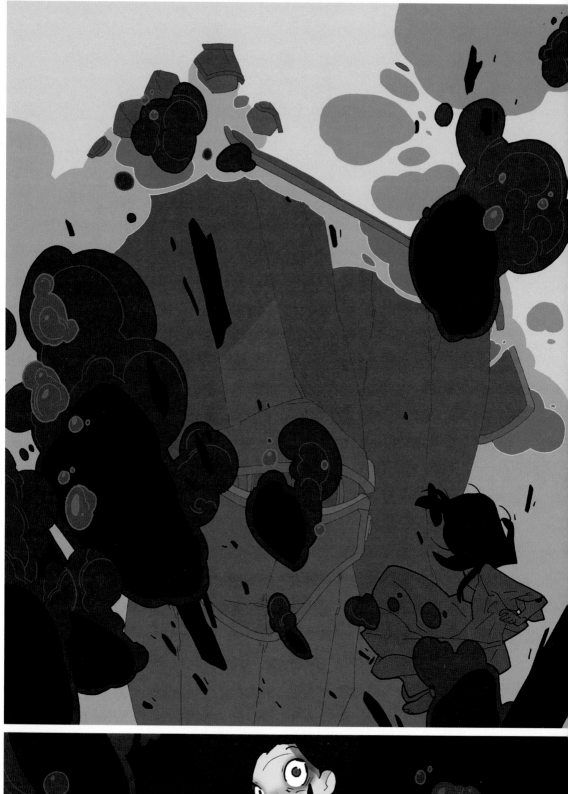

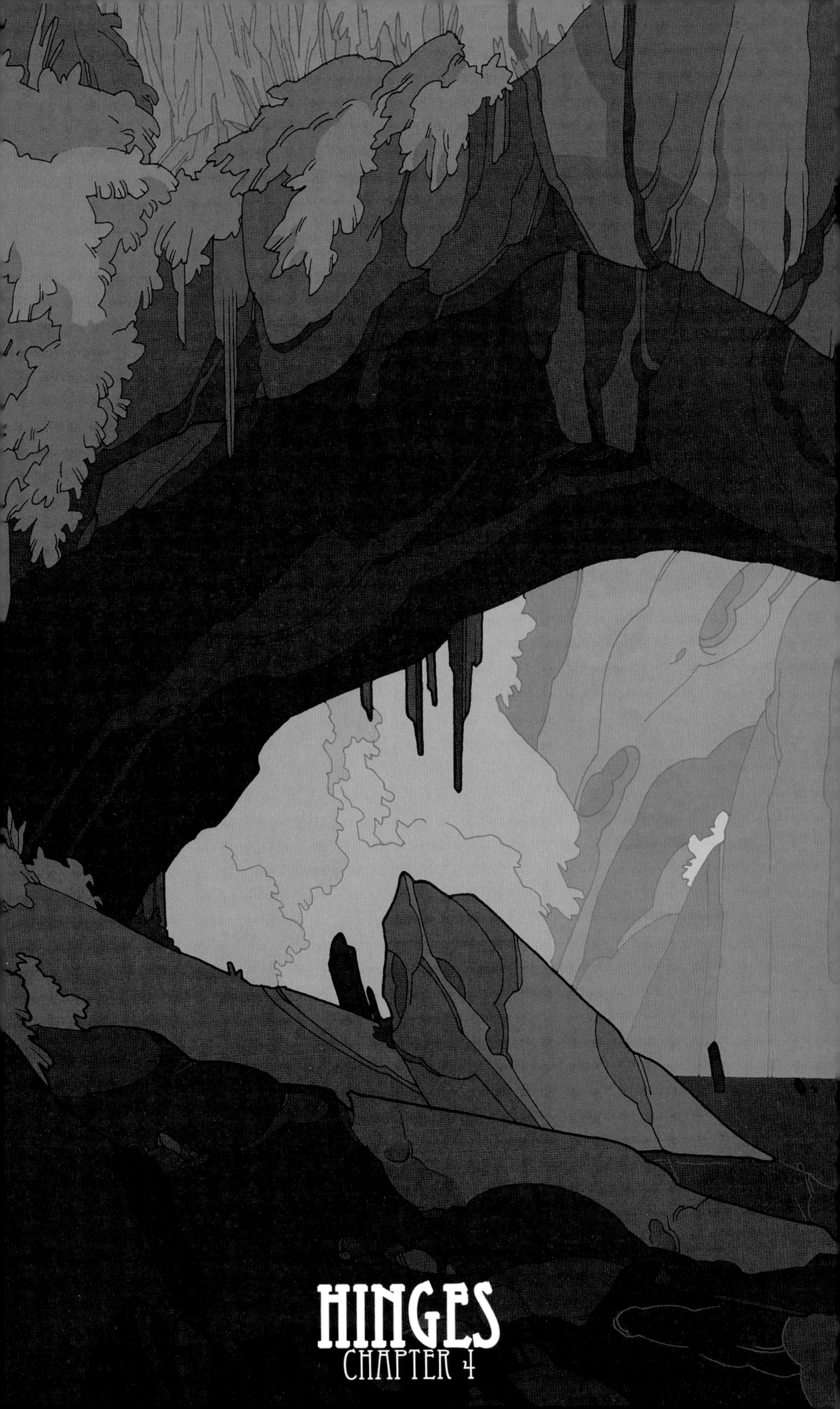
HINGES
CHAPTER 4

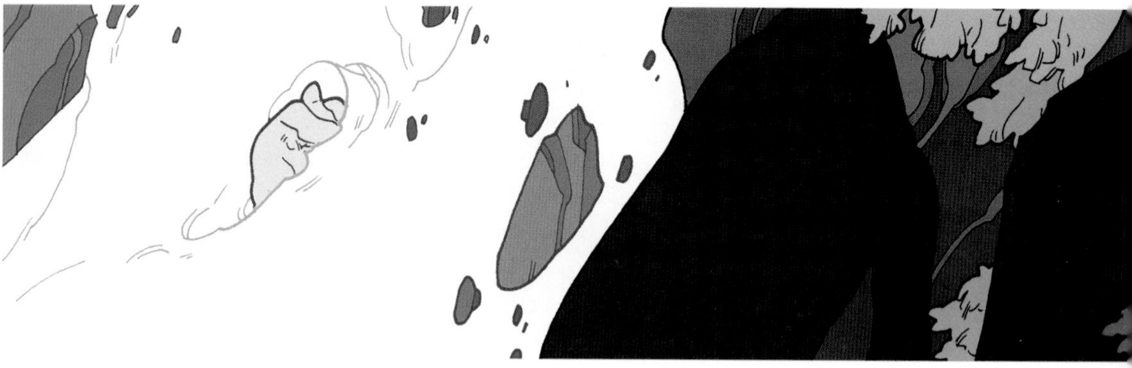
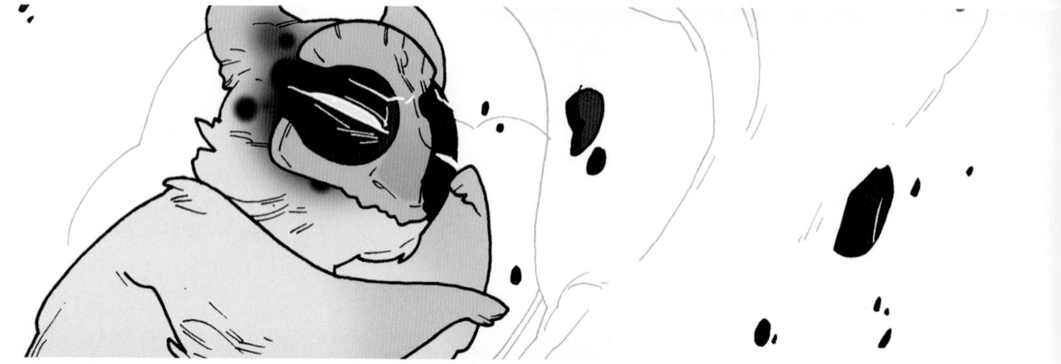
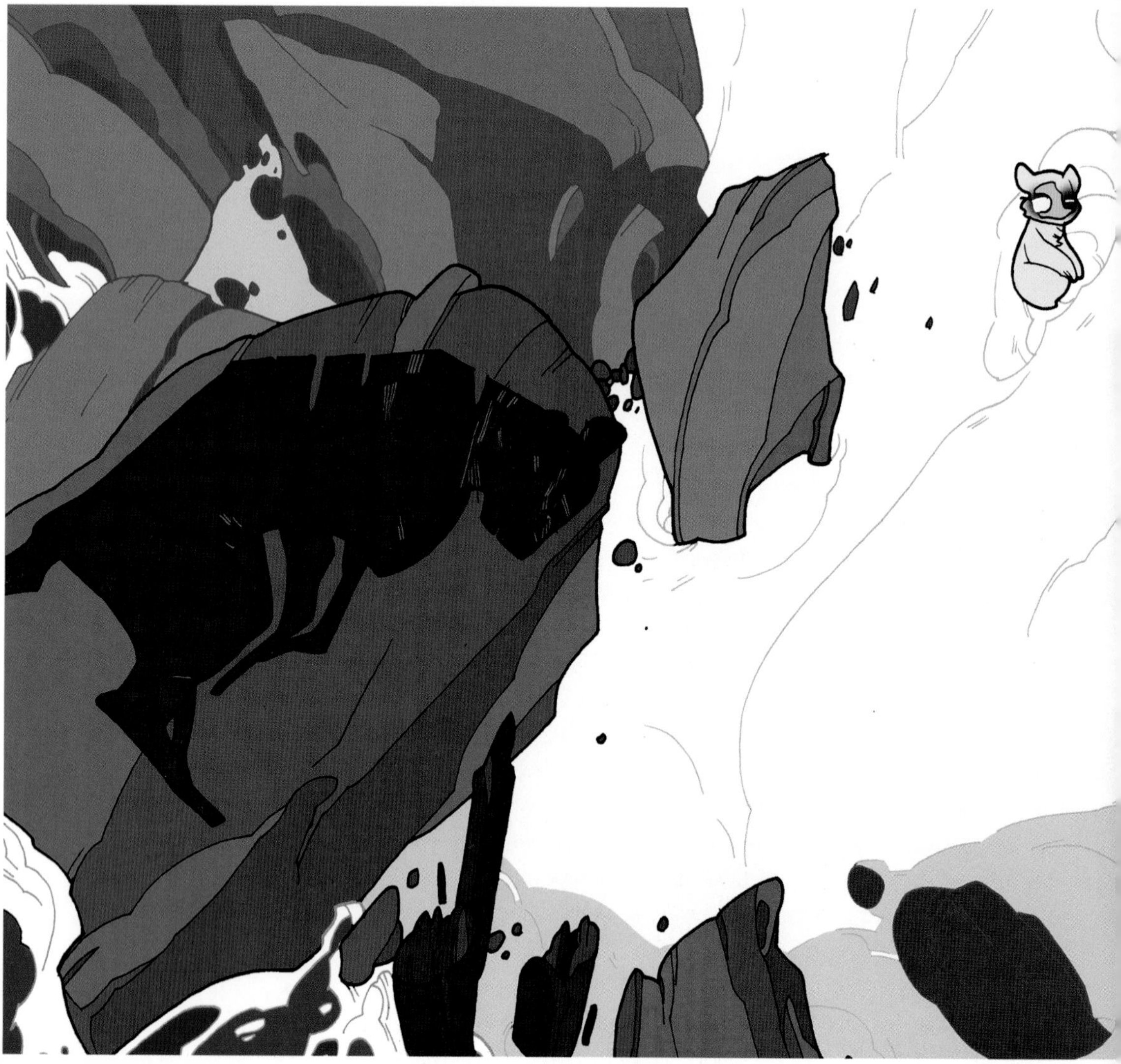

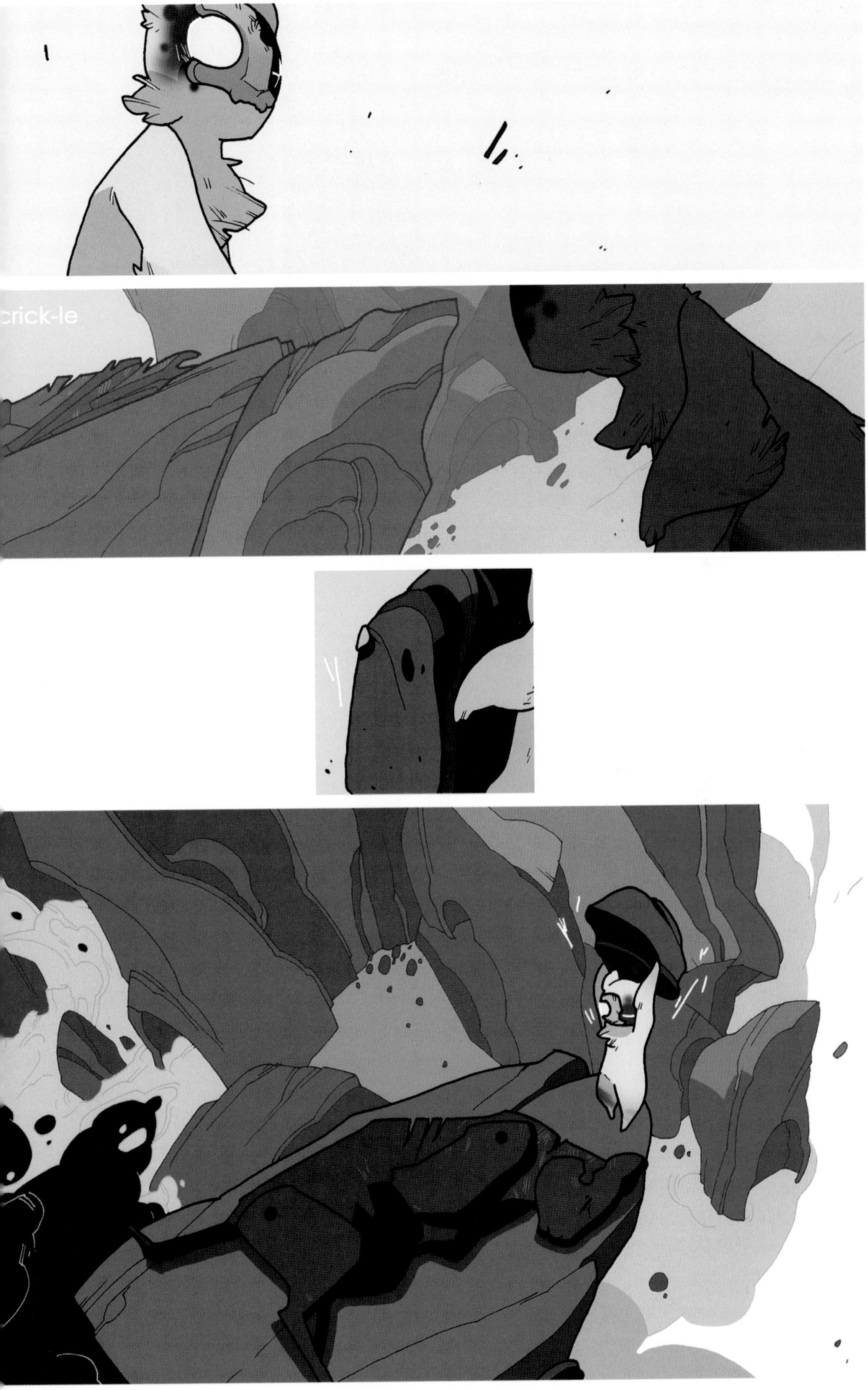
crick-le

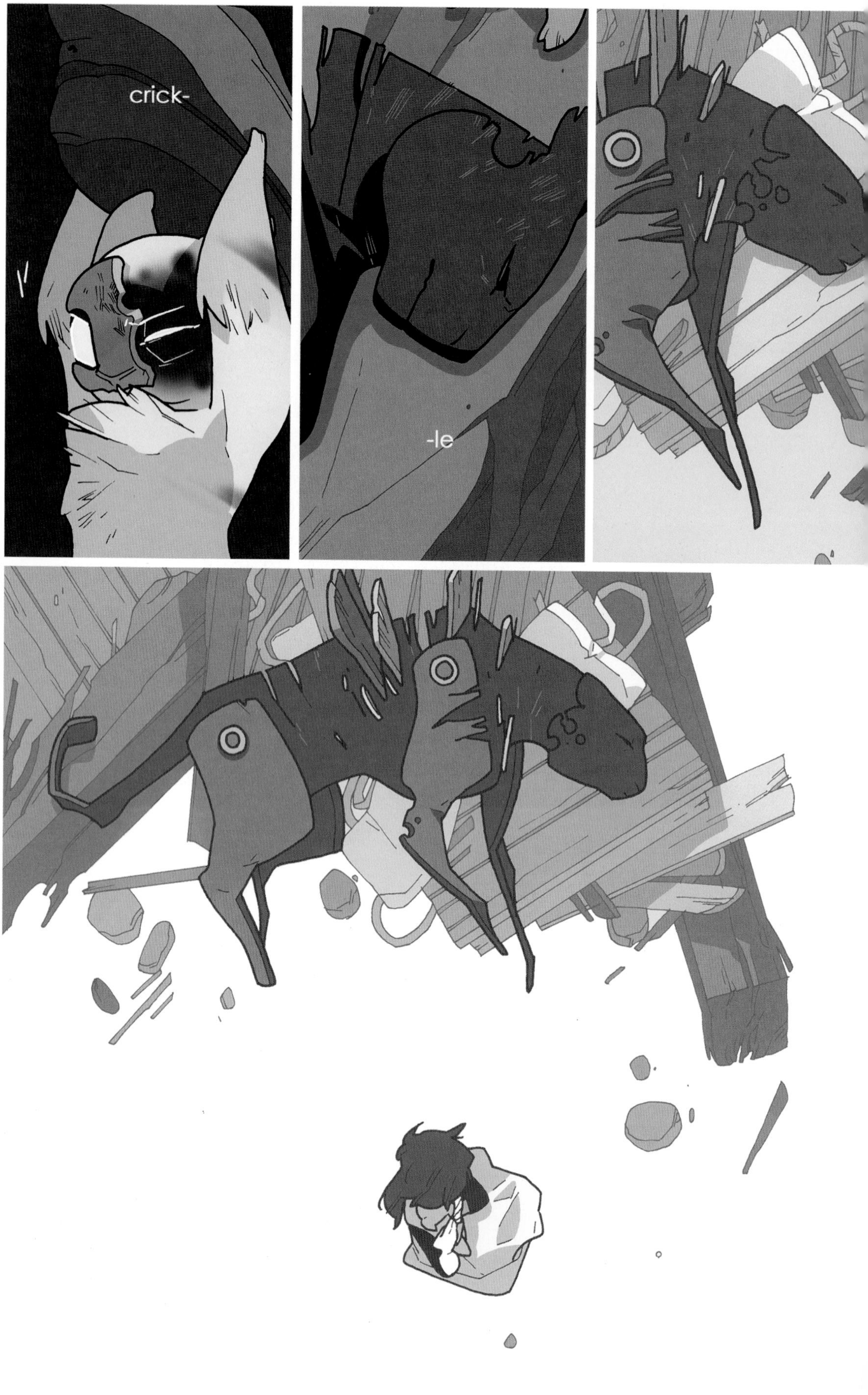

crick-
-le

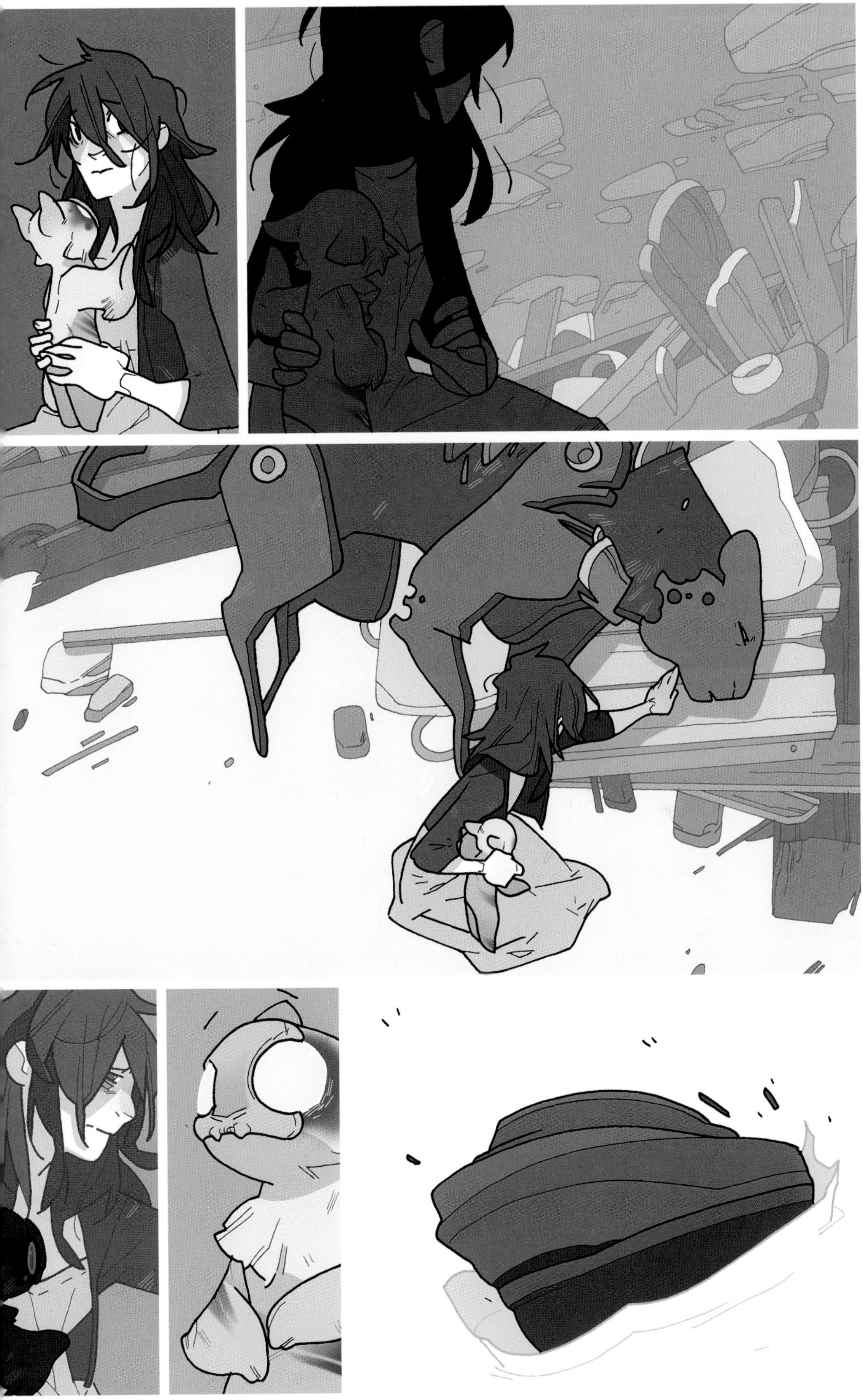

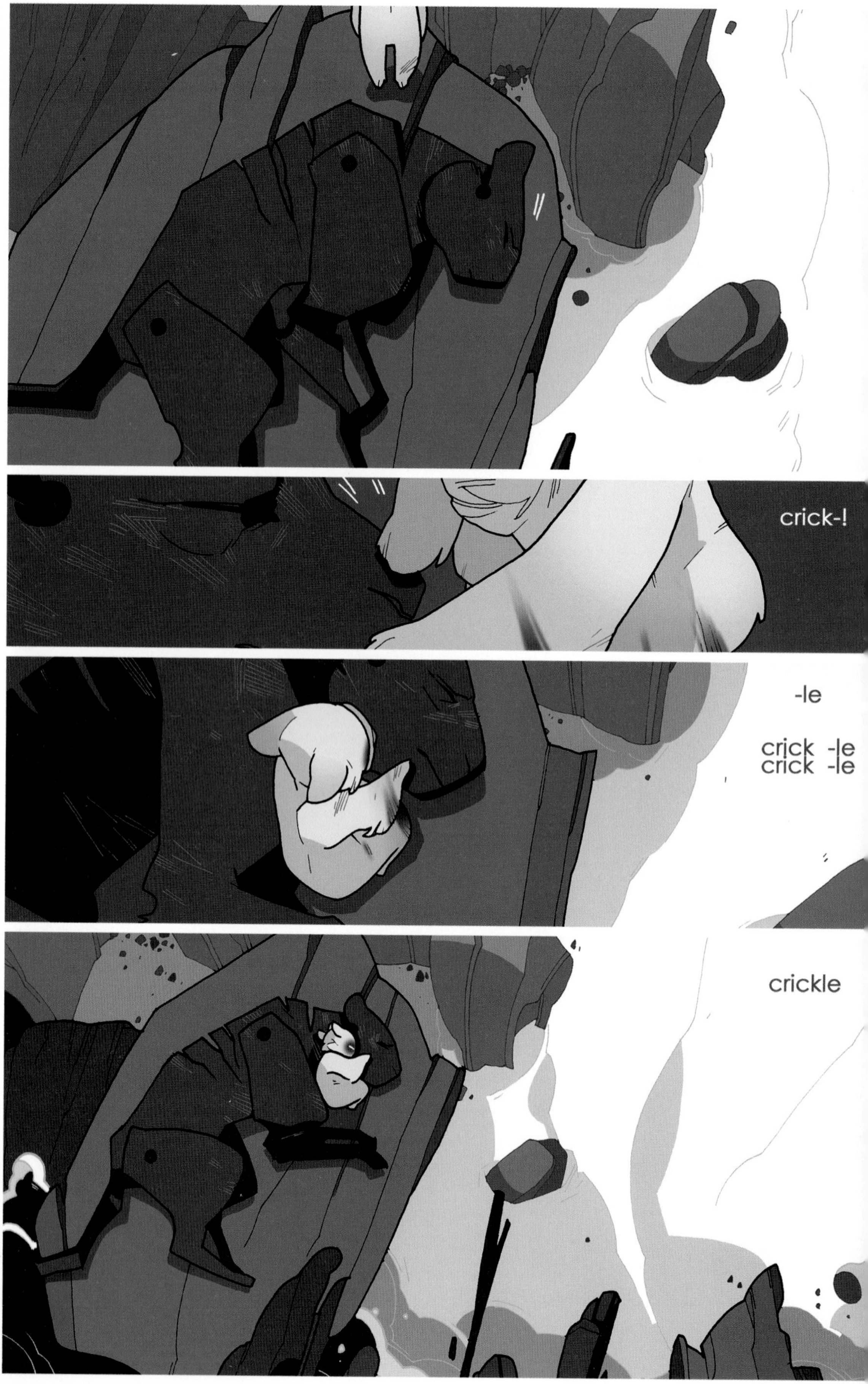
crick-!
-le
crick -le
crick -le
crickle

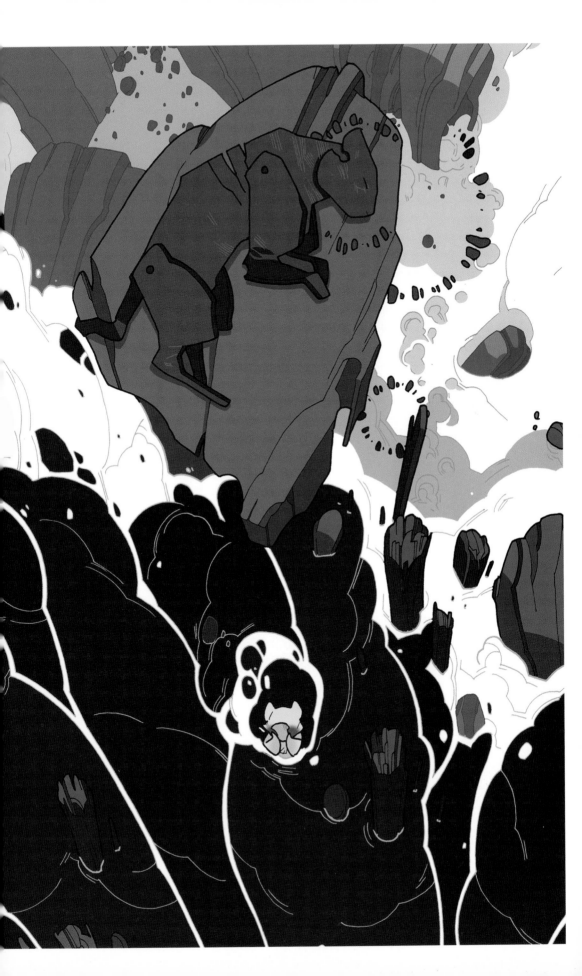

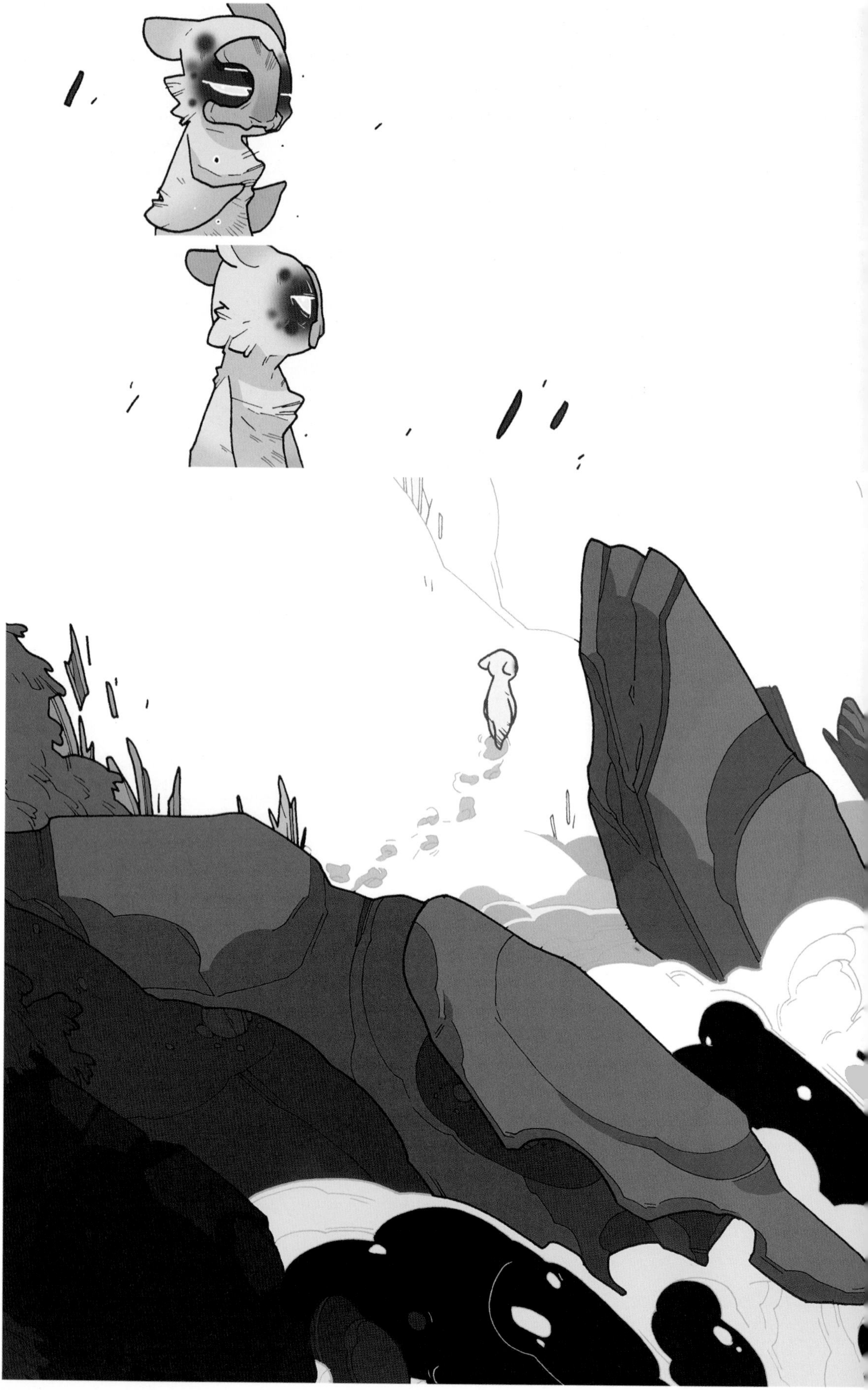

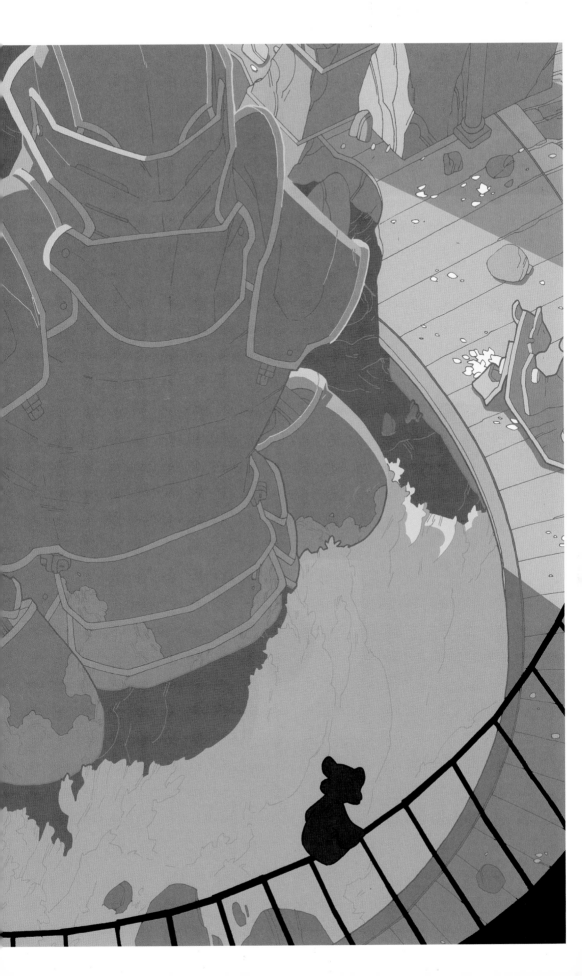

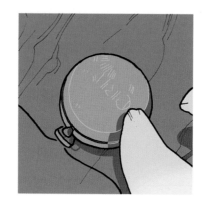

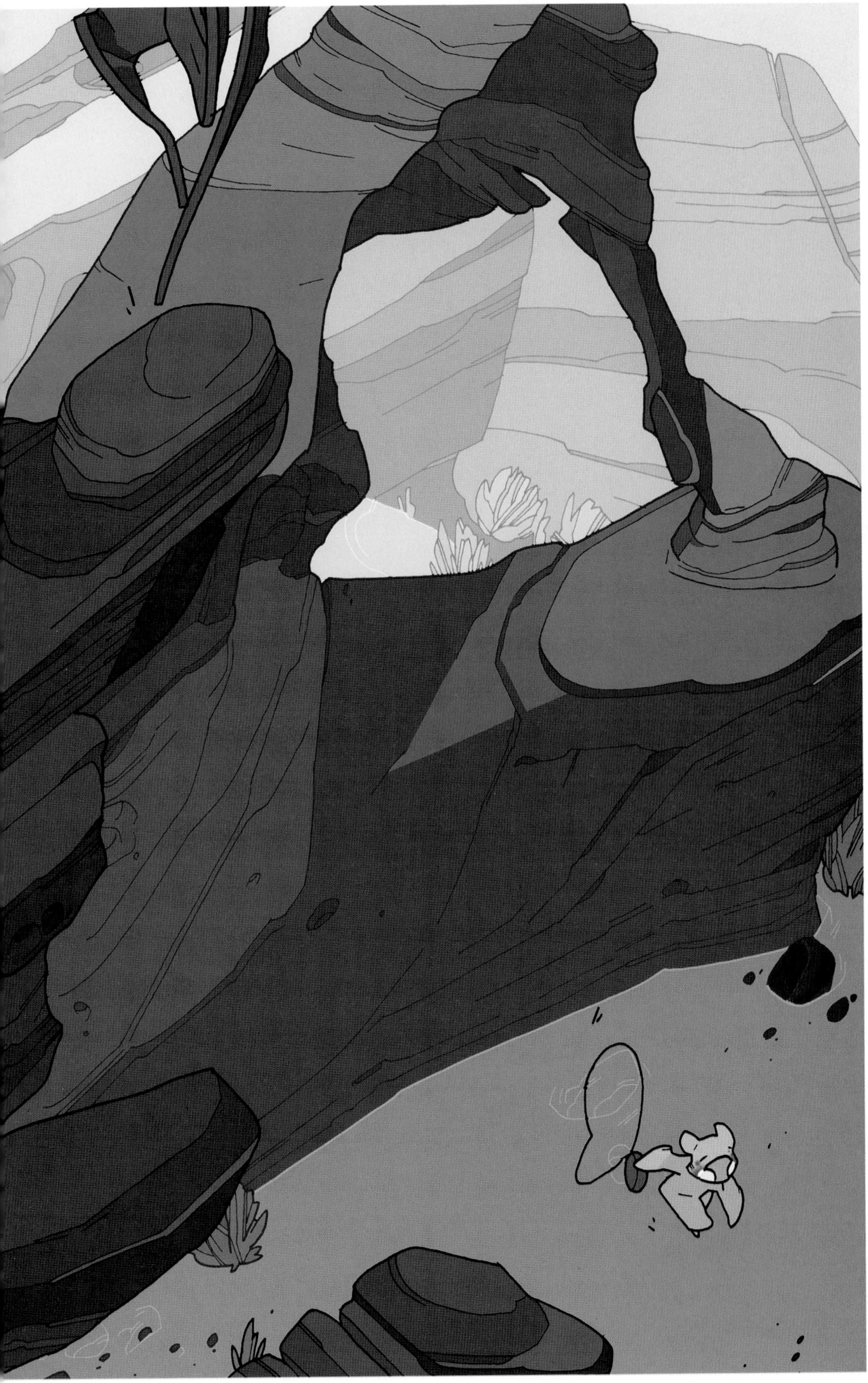

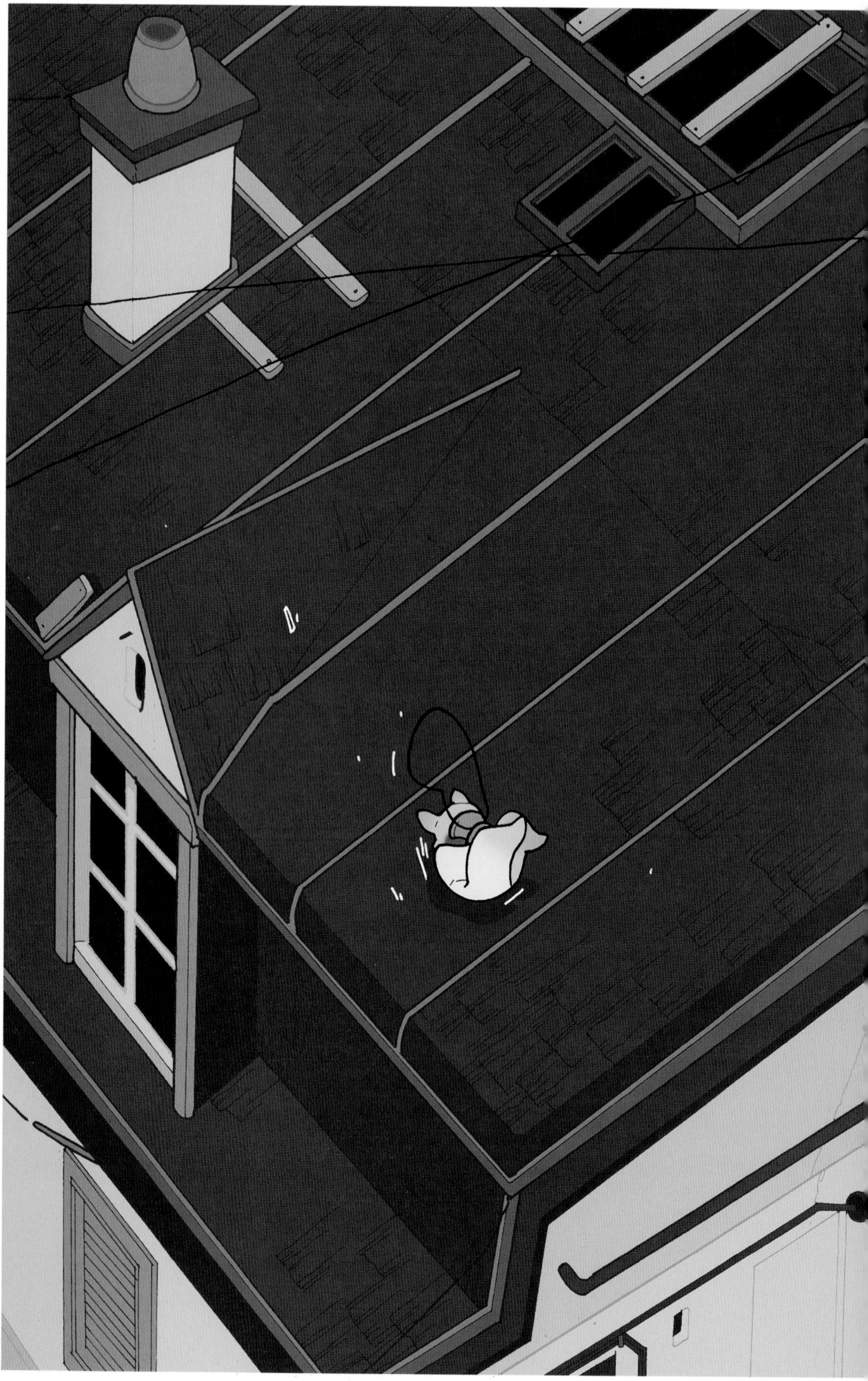

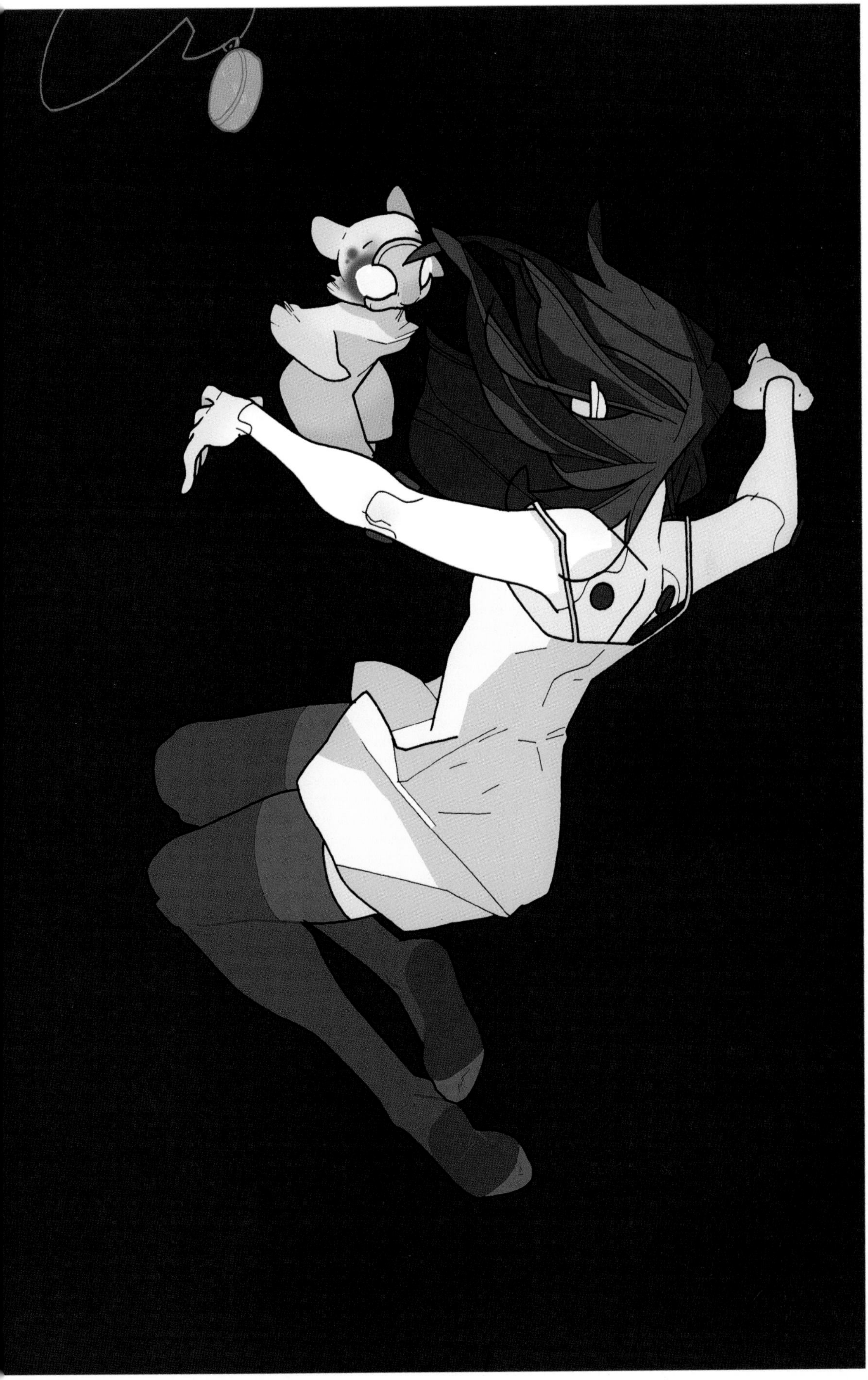

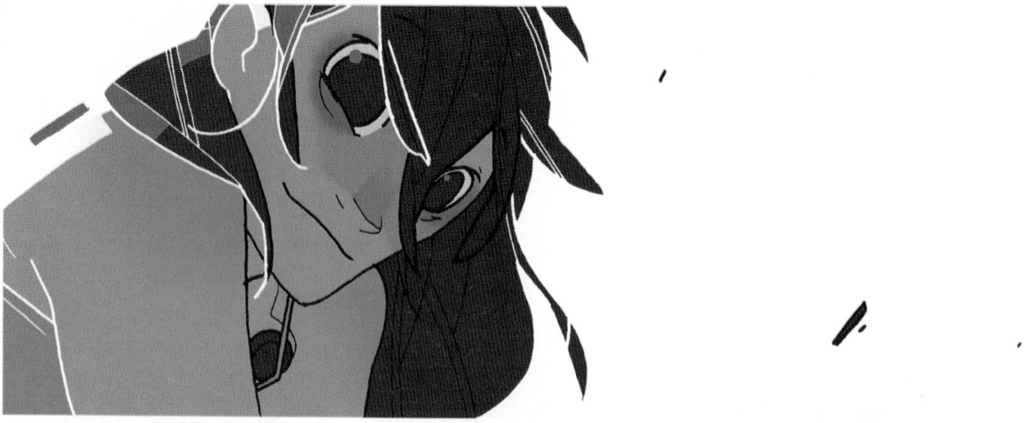

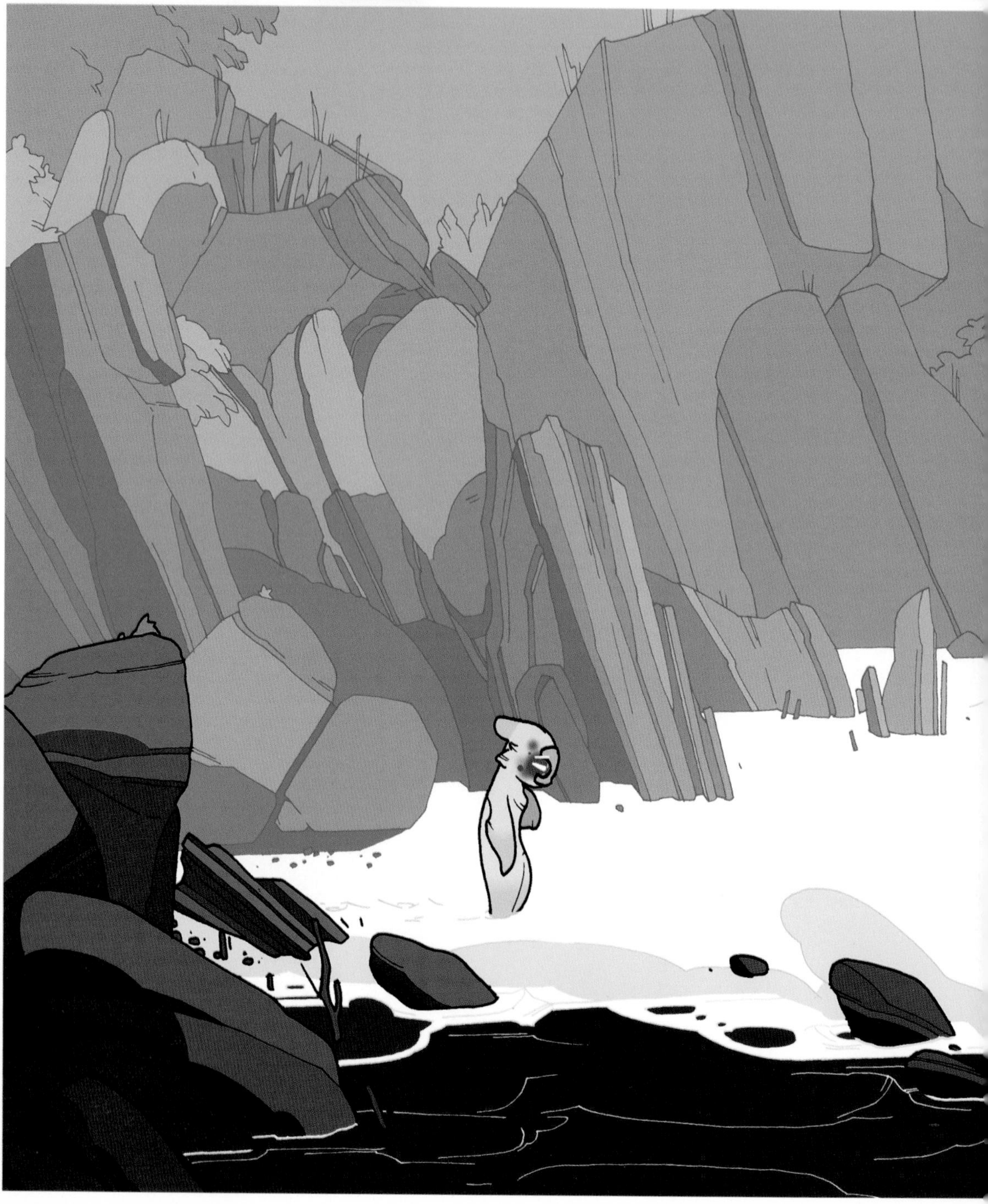

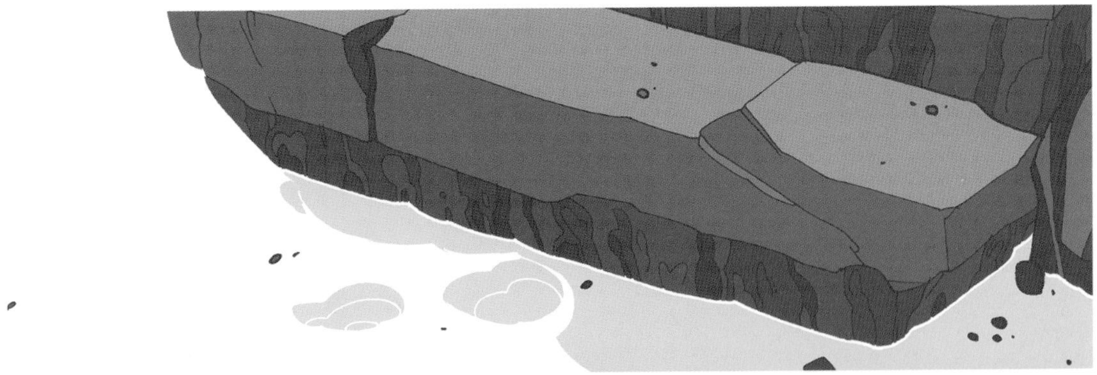

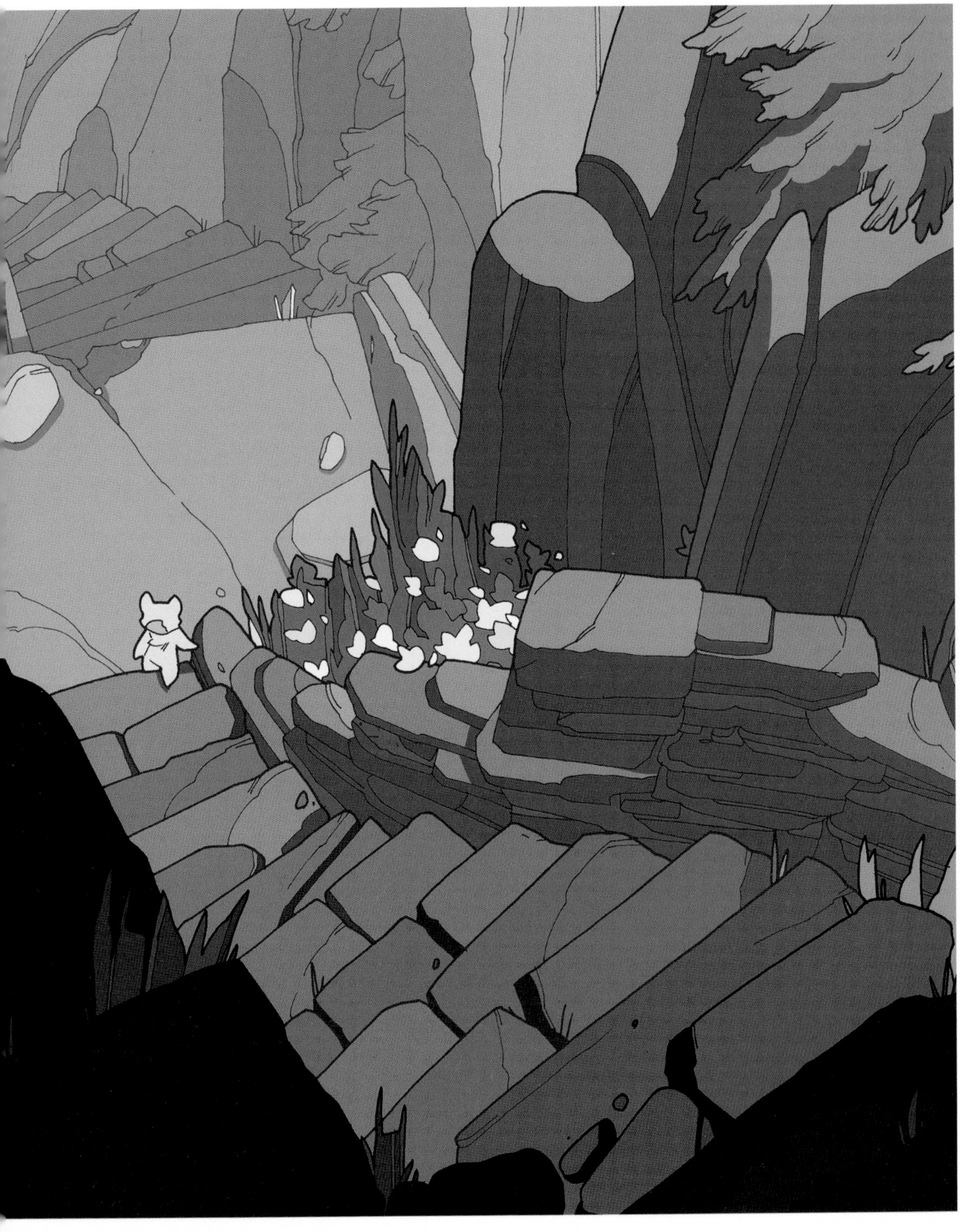

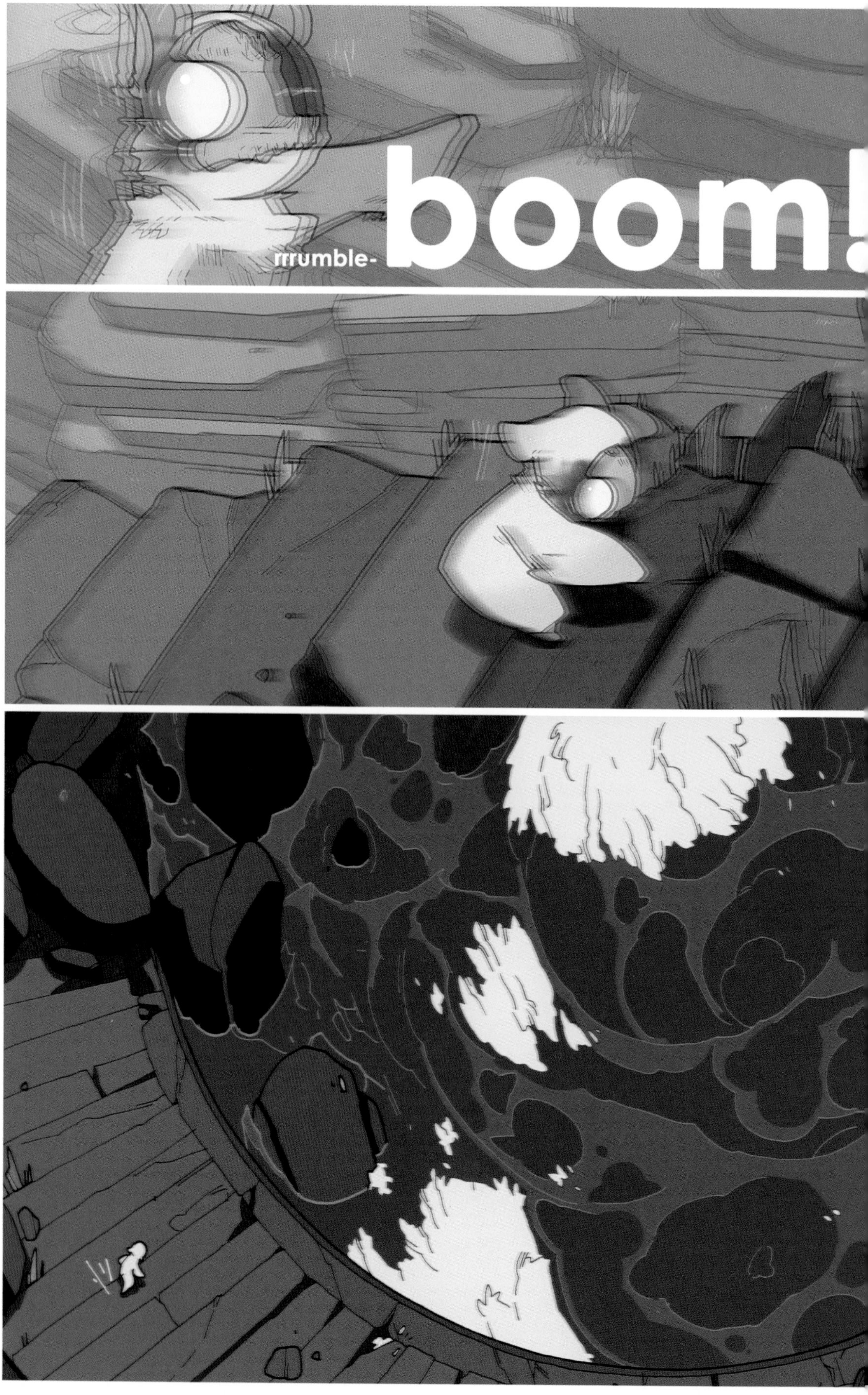
rrrumble-
boom!

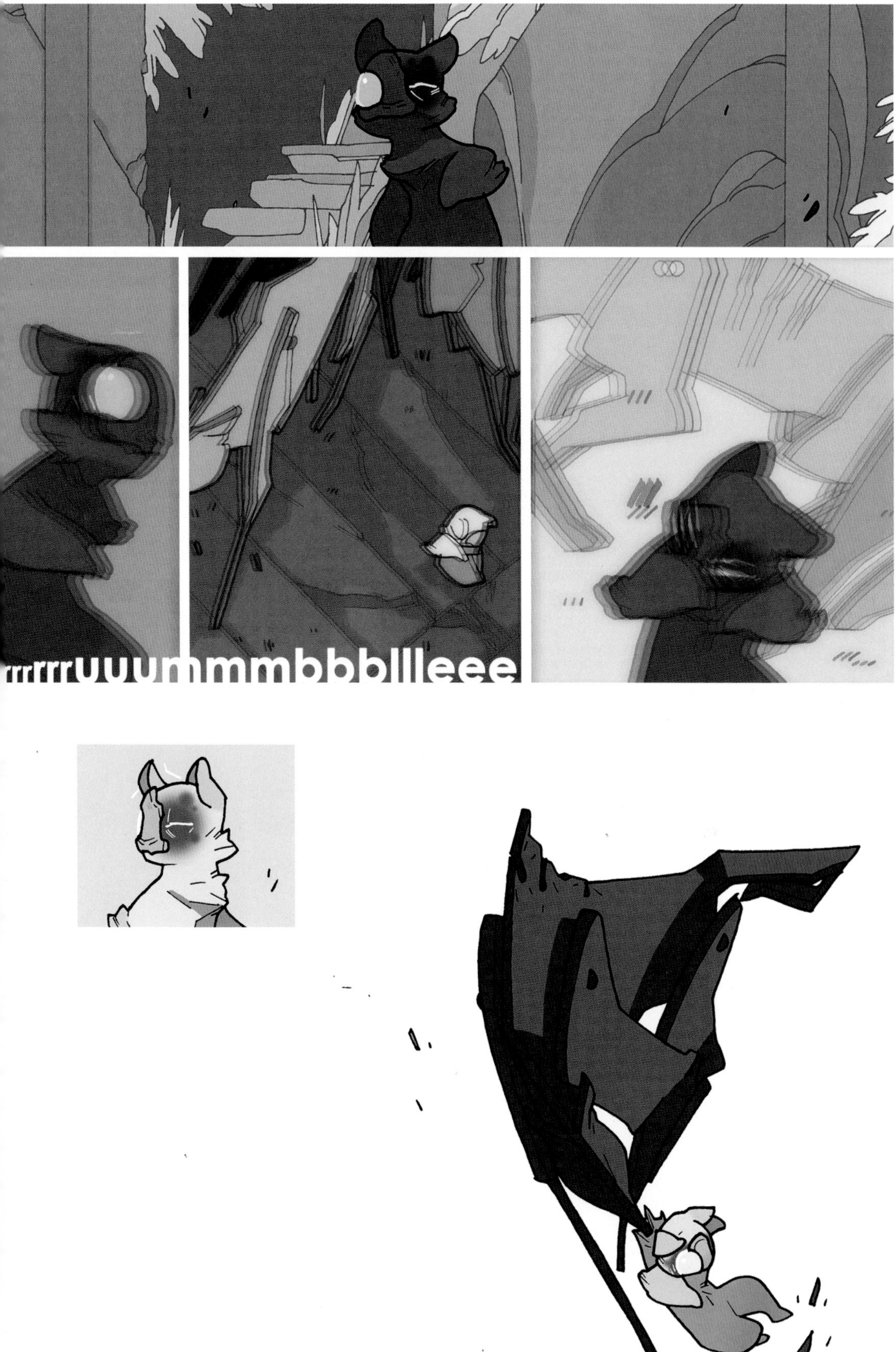
rrrrruuummmbbblllleee

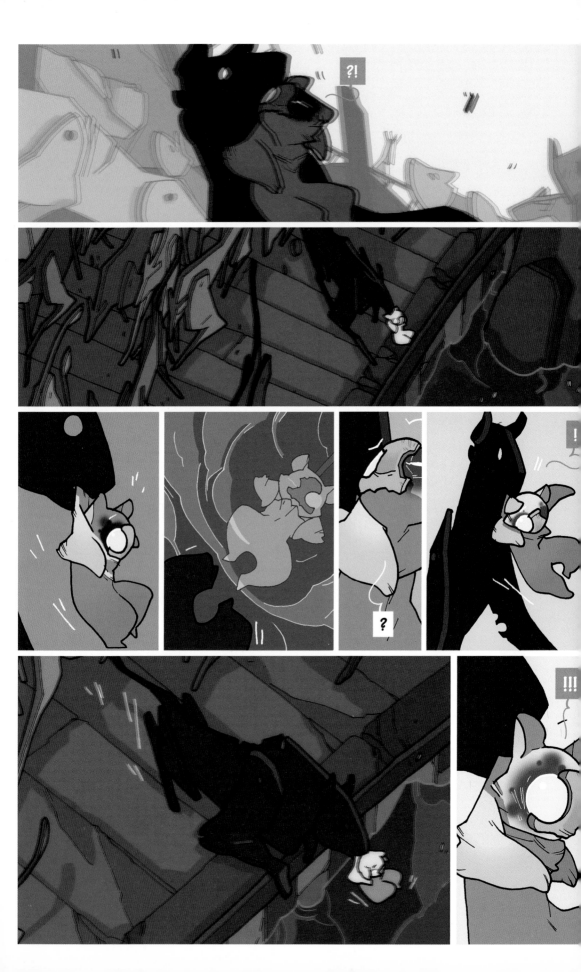

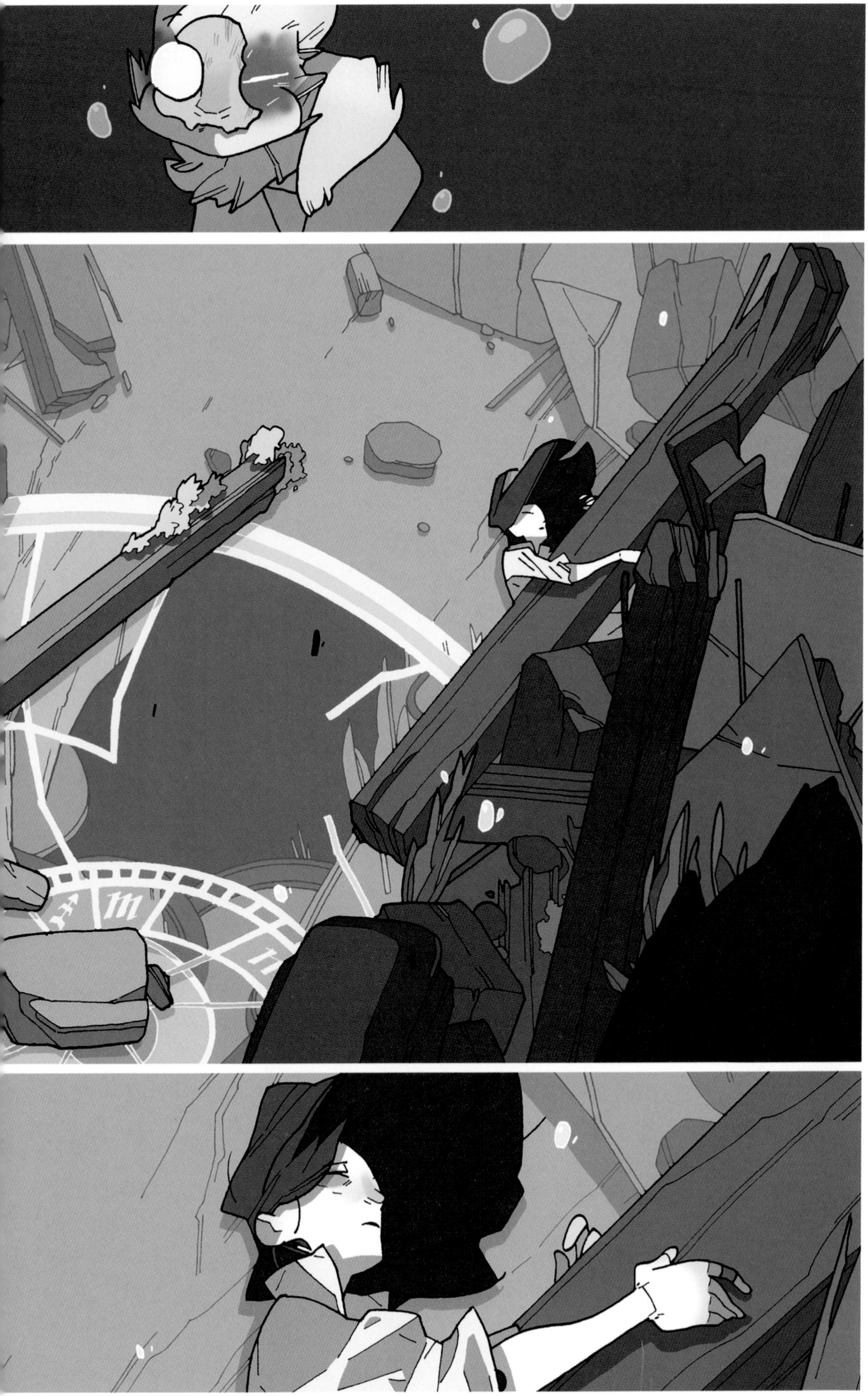

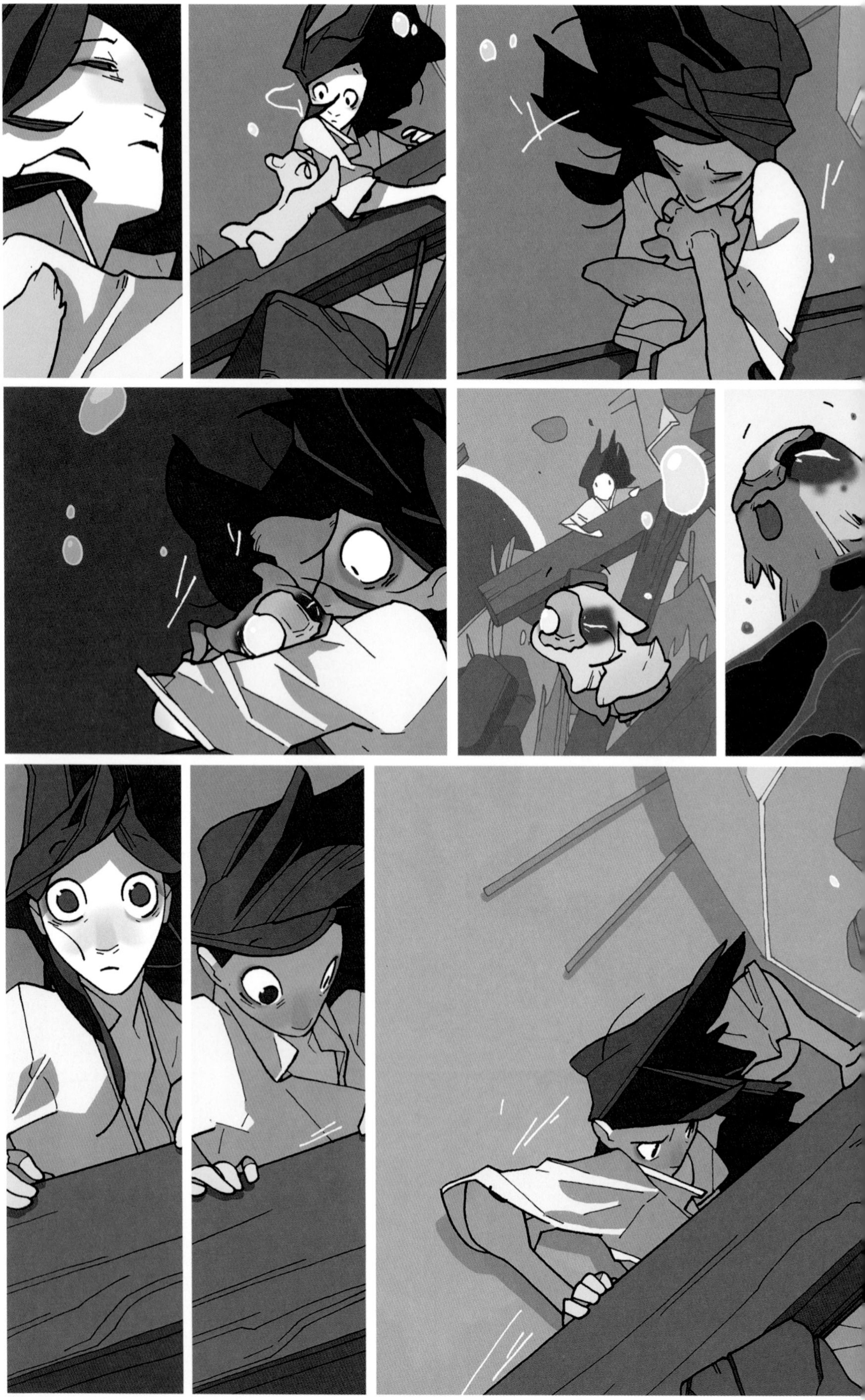

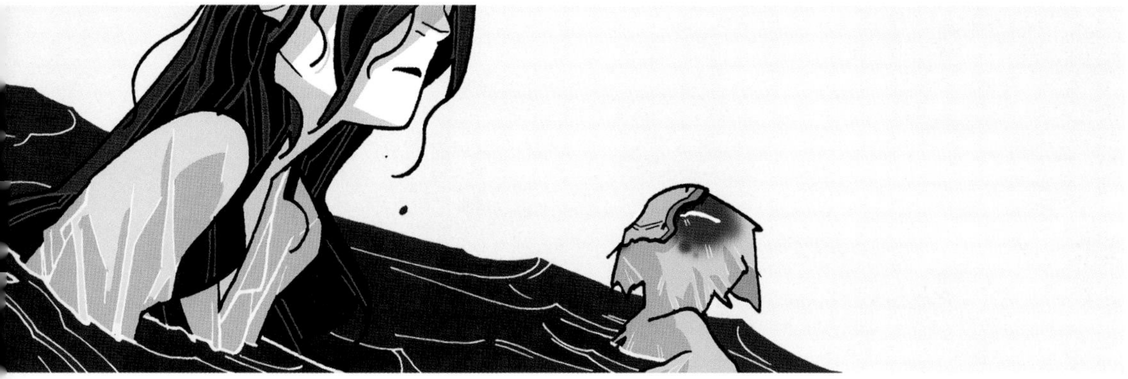

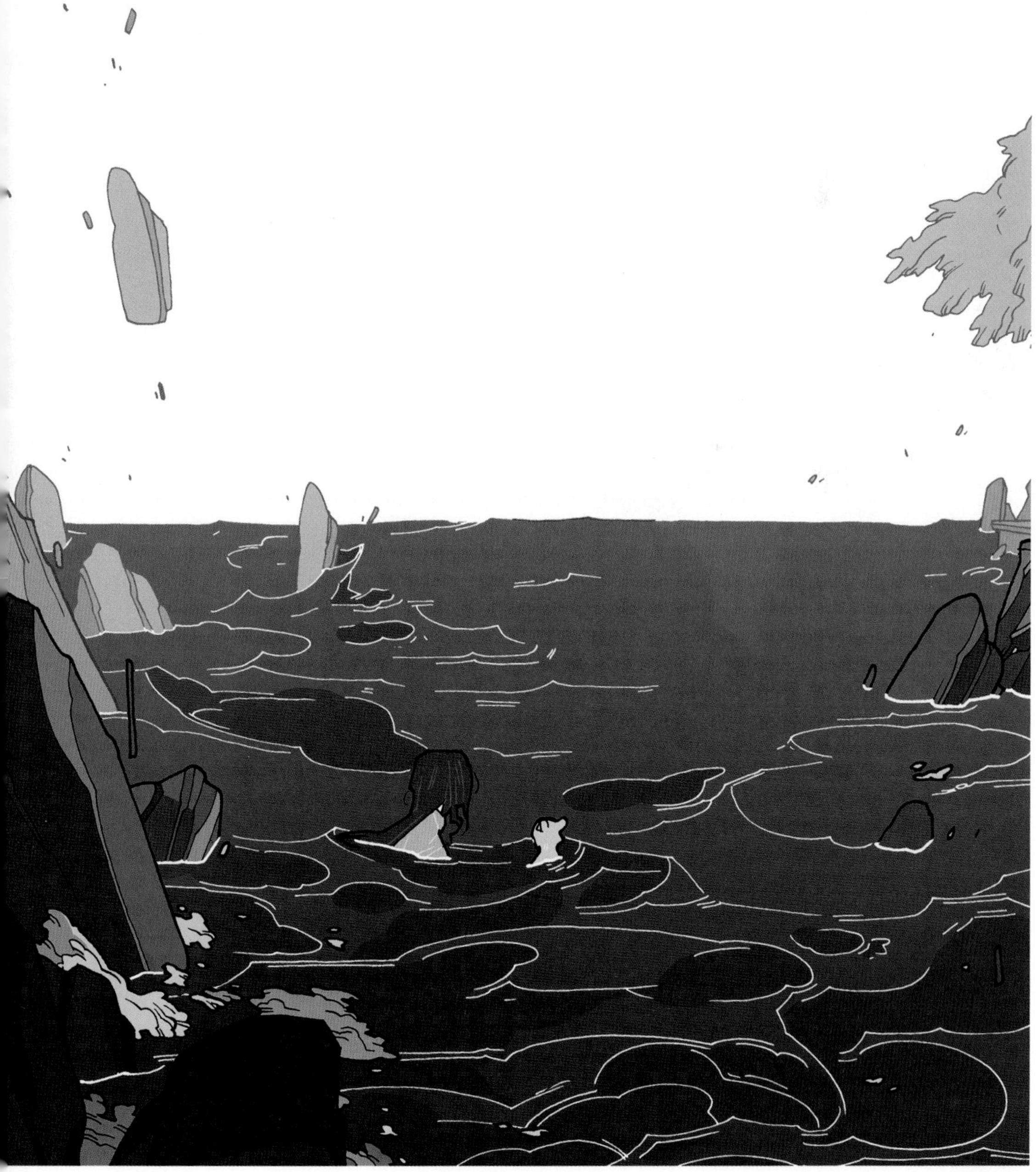

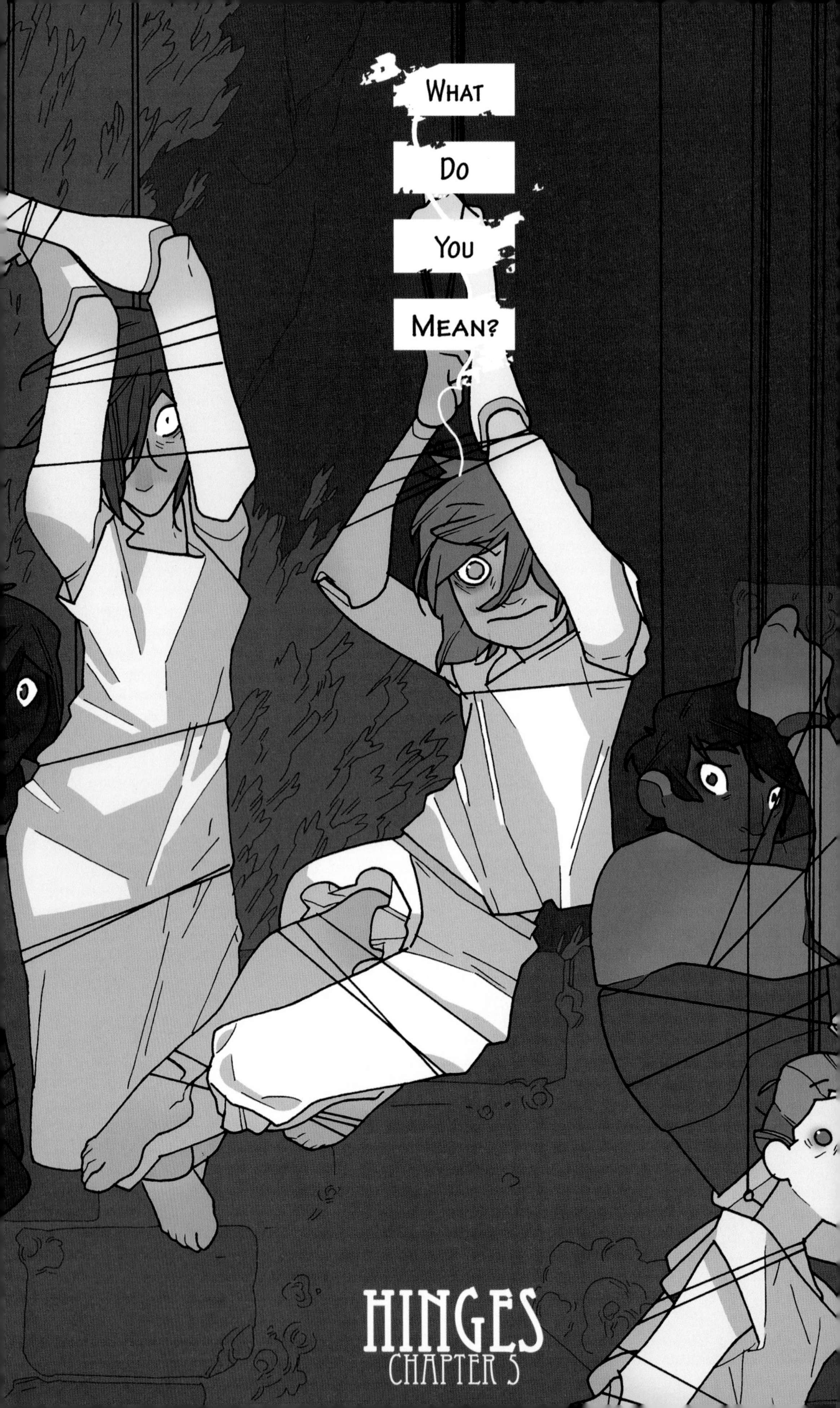
What
Do
You
Mean?
HINGES
CHAPTER 5

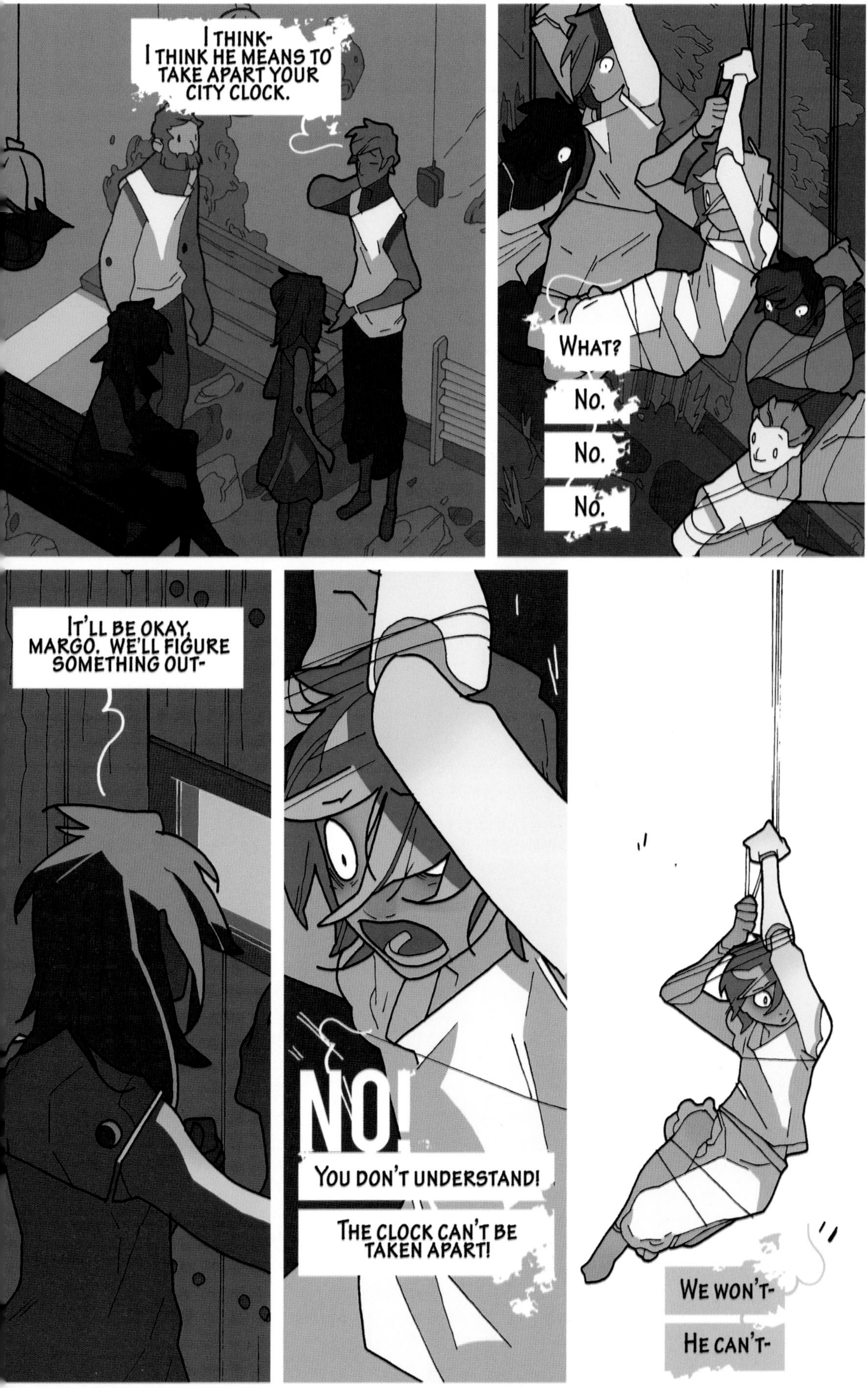
I THINK-
I THINK HE MEANS TO TAKE APART YOUR CITY CLOCK.
WHAT?
NO.
NO.
NO.
IT'LL BE OKAY, MARGO. WE'LL FIGURE SOMETHING OUT-
NO!
YOU DON'T UNDERSTAND!
THE CLOCK CAN'T BE TAKEN APART!
WE WON'T-
HE CAN'T-

HE TRIED.

BEFORE.

TO KNOW HOW THE CLOCK WORKS WOULD BE A HUGE ADVANTAGE SHOULD SOMETHING GO WRONG...

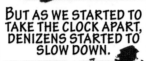

BUT AS WE STARTED TO TAKE THE CLOCK APART, DENIZENS STARTED TO SLOW DOWN.

AND STOP.

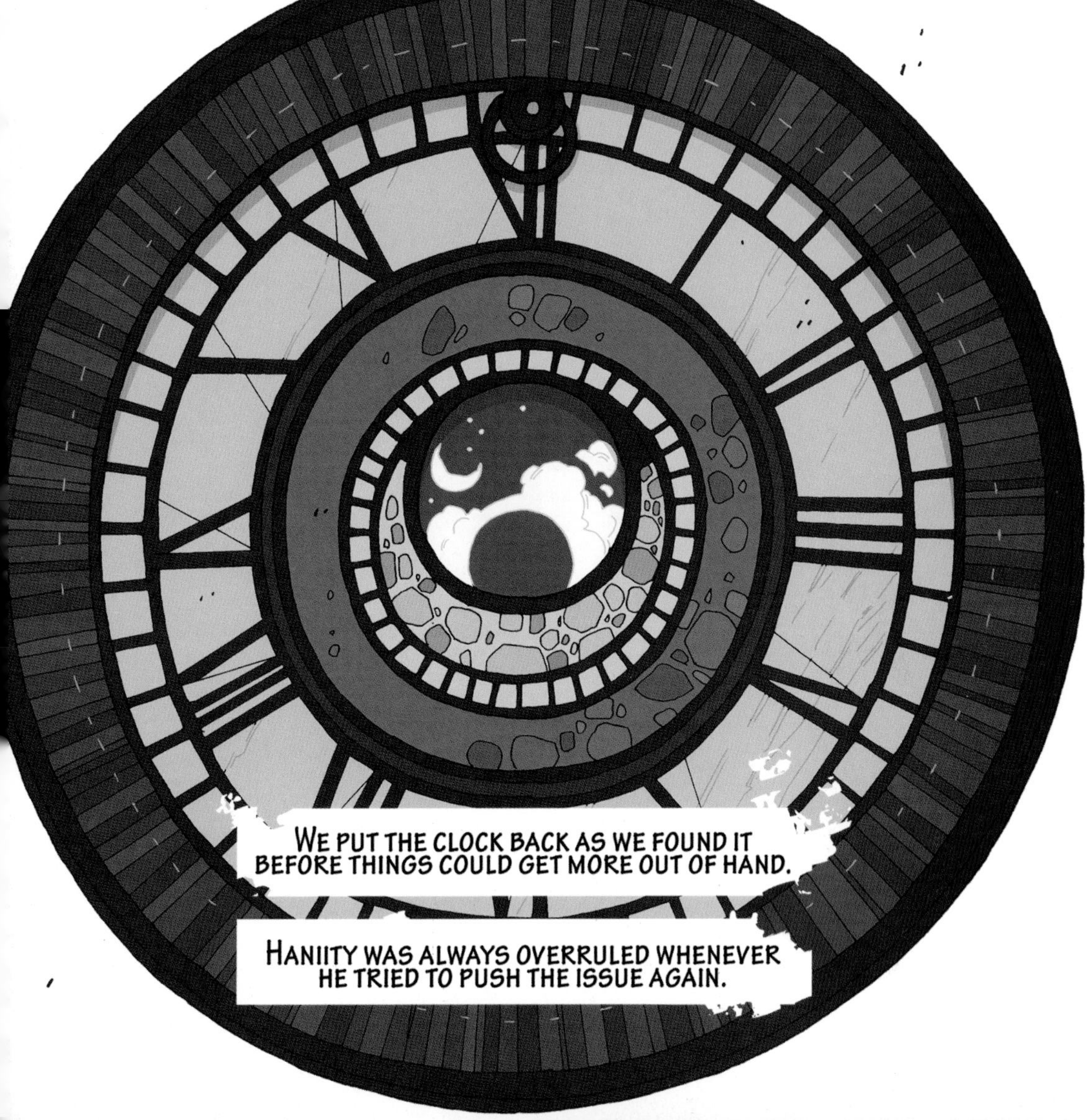
WE PUT THE CLOCK BACK AS WE FOUND IT BEFORE THINGS COULD GET MORE OUT OF HAND.
HANIITY WAS ALWAYS OVERRULED WHENEVER HE TRIED TO PUSH THE ISSUE AGAIN.

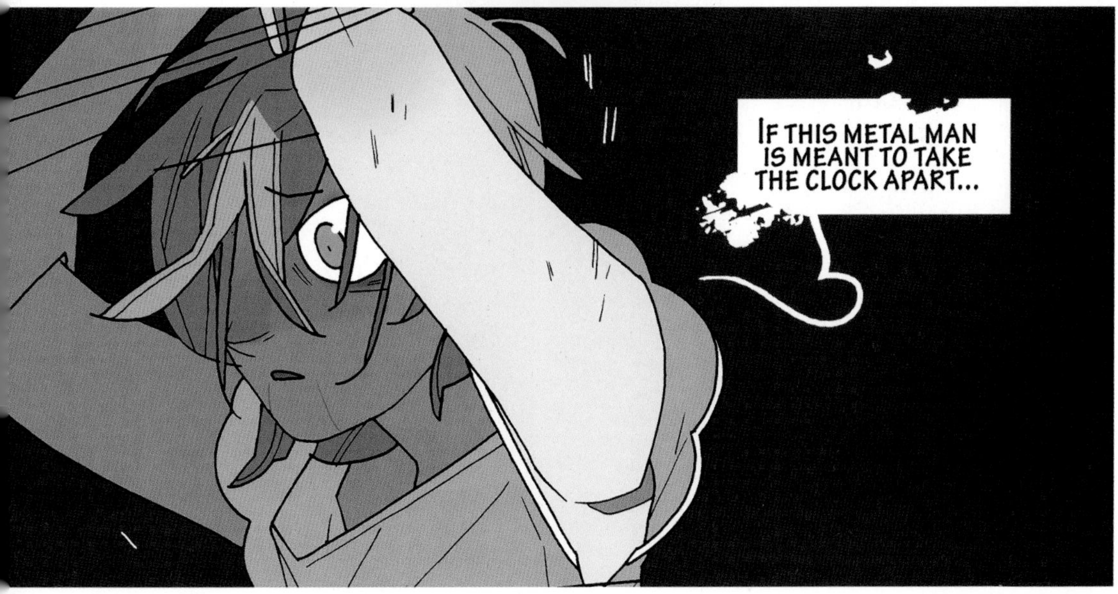
IF THIS METAL MAN IS MEANT TO TAKE THE CLOCK APART...

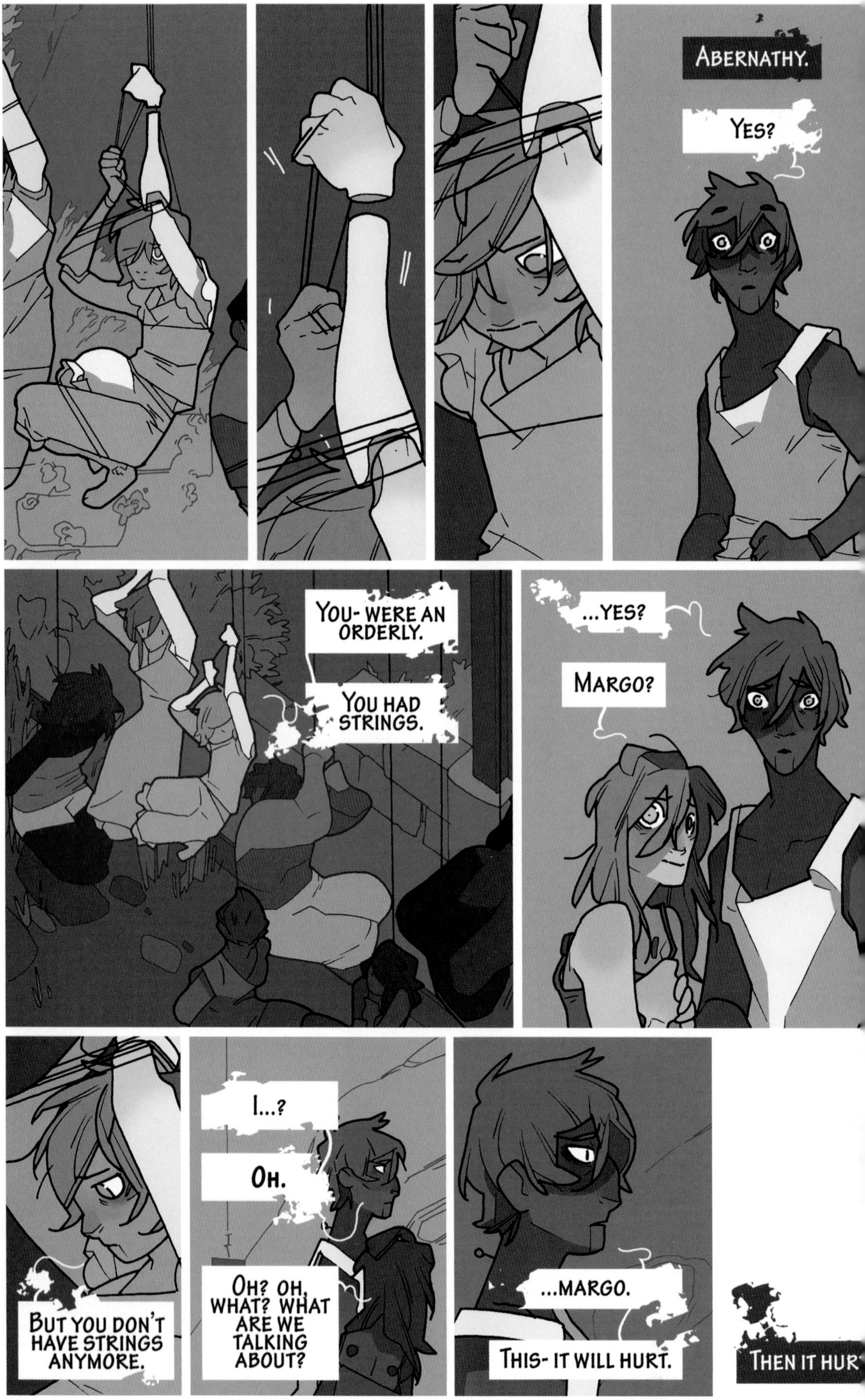
ABERNATHY.
YES?
YOU- WERE AN ORDERLY.
YOU HAD STRINGS.
...YES?
MARGO?
BUT YOU DON'T HAVE STRINGS ANYMORE.
I...?
OH.
OH? OH, WHAT? WHAT ARE WE TALKING ABOUT?
...MARGO.
THIS- IT WILL HURT.
THEN IT HUR

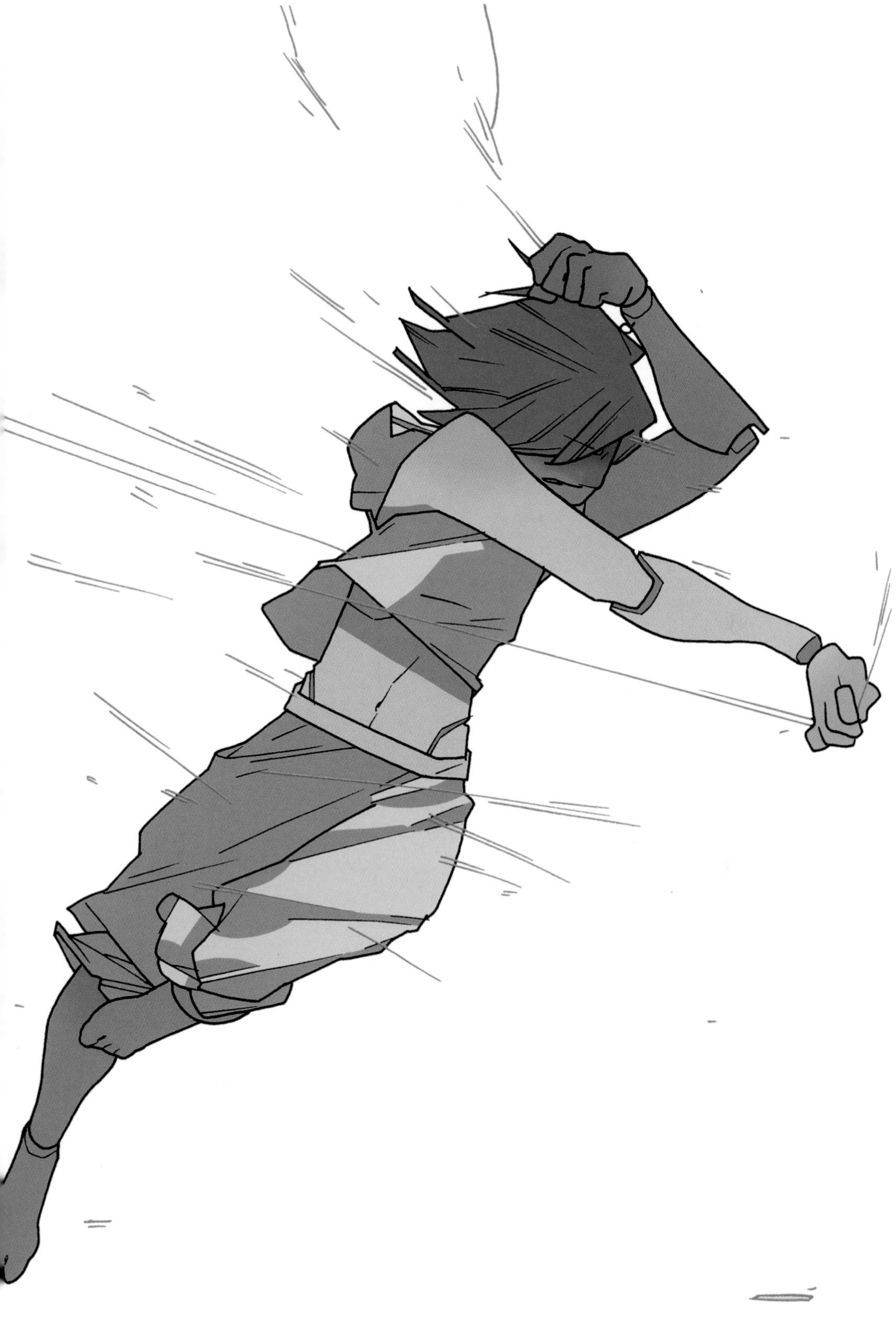

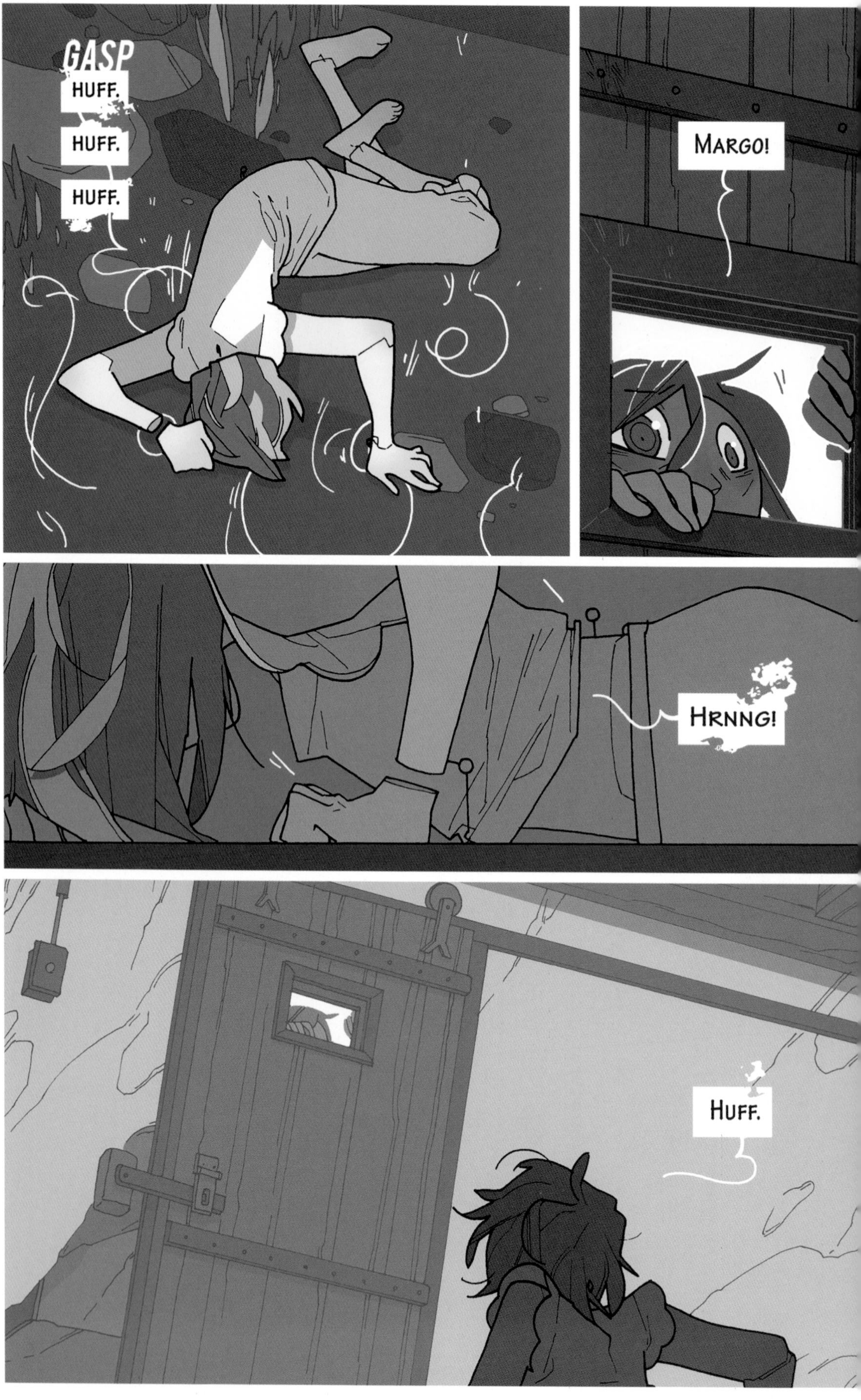
GASP
HUFF.
HUFF.
HUFF.
MARGO!
HRNNG!
HUFF.

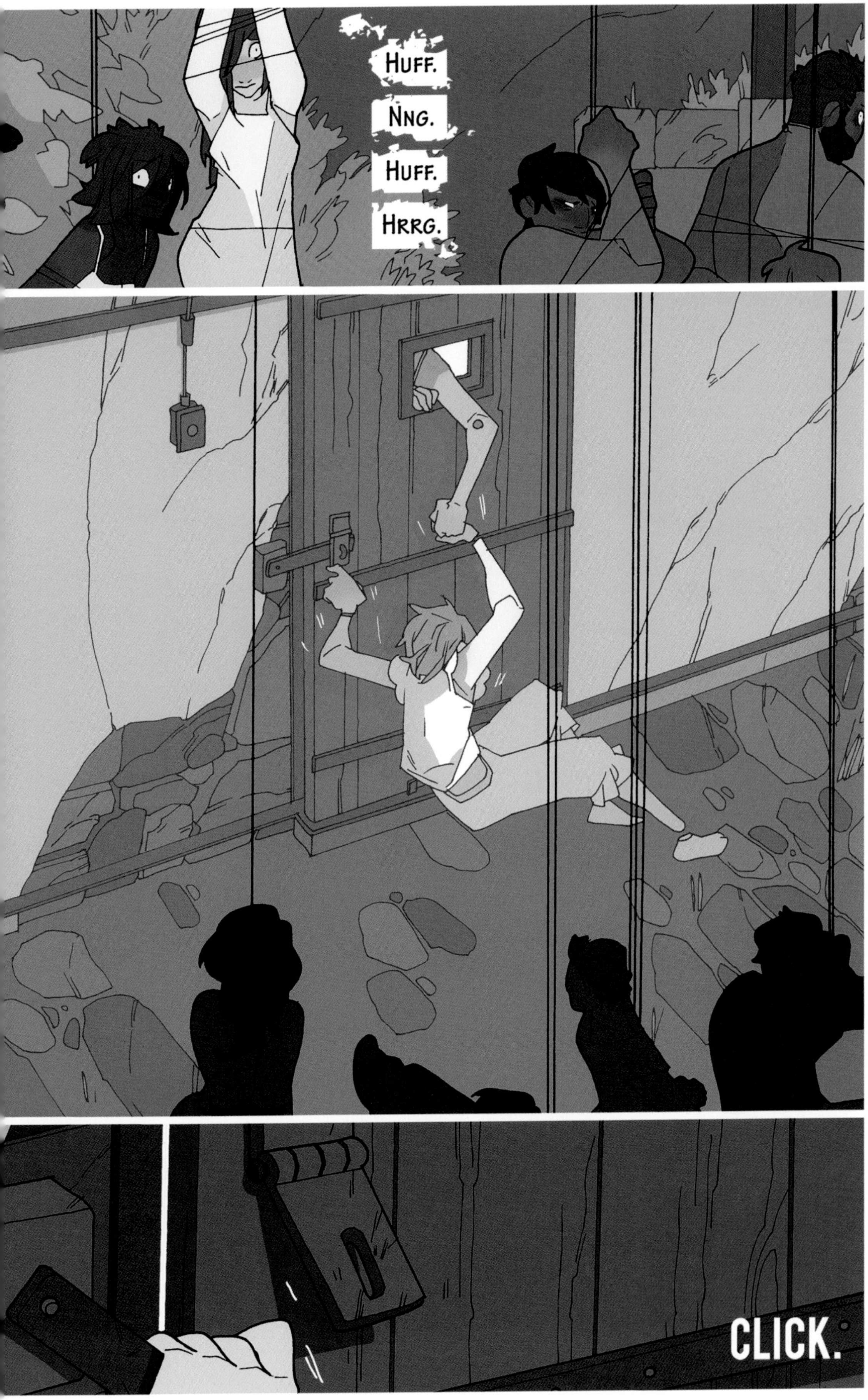
Huff.
Nng.
Huff.
Hrrg.
CLICK.

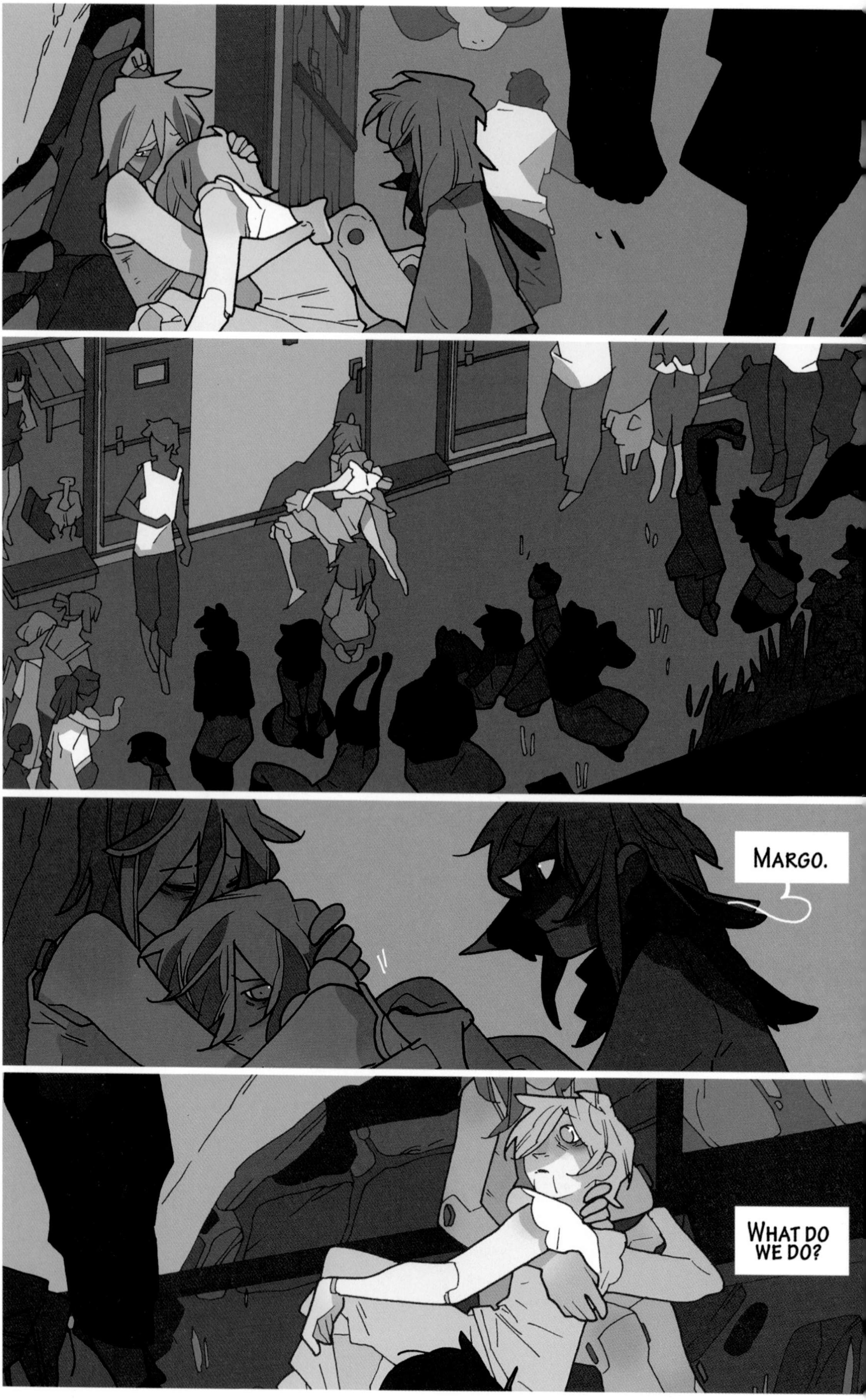
Margo.
What do we do?

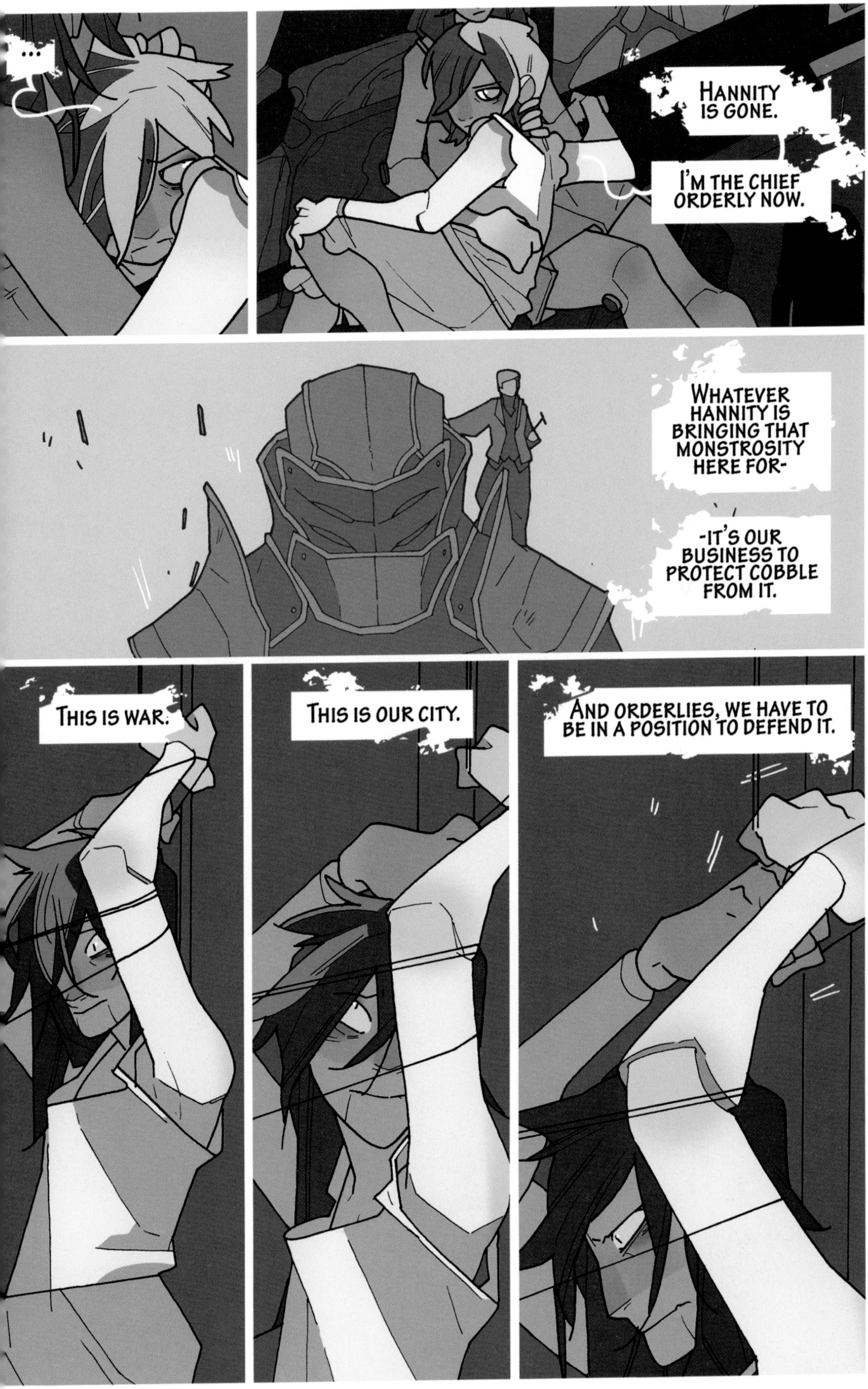
...
Hannity is gone.
I'm the chief orderly now.
Whatever Hannity is bringing that monstrosity here for-
-it's our business to protect Cobble from it.
This is war.
This is our city.
And orderlies, we have to be in a position to defend it.

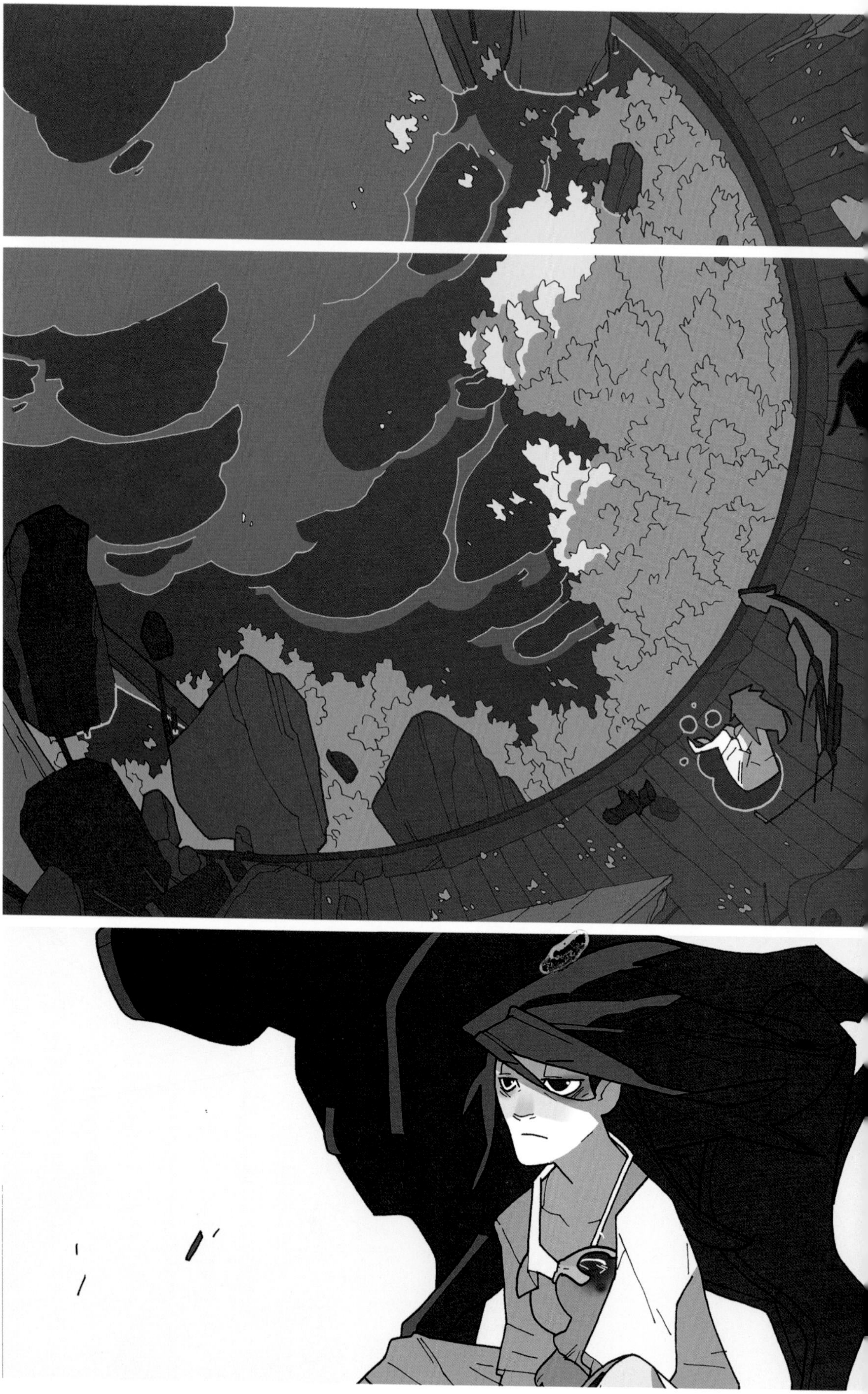

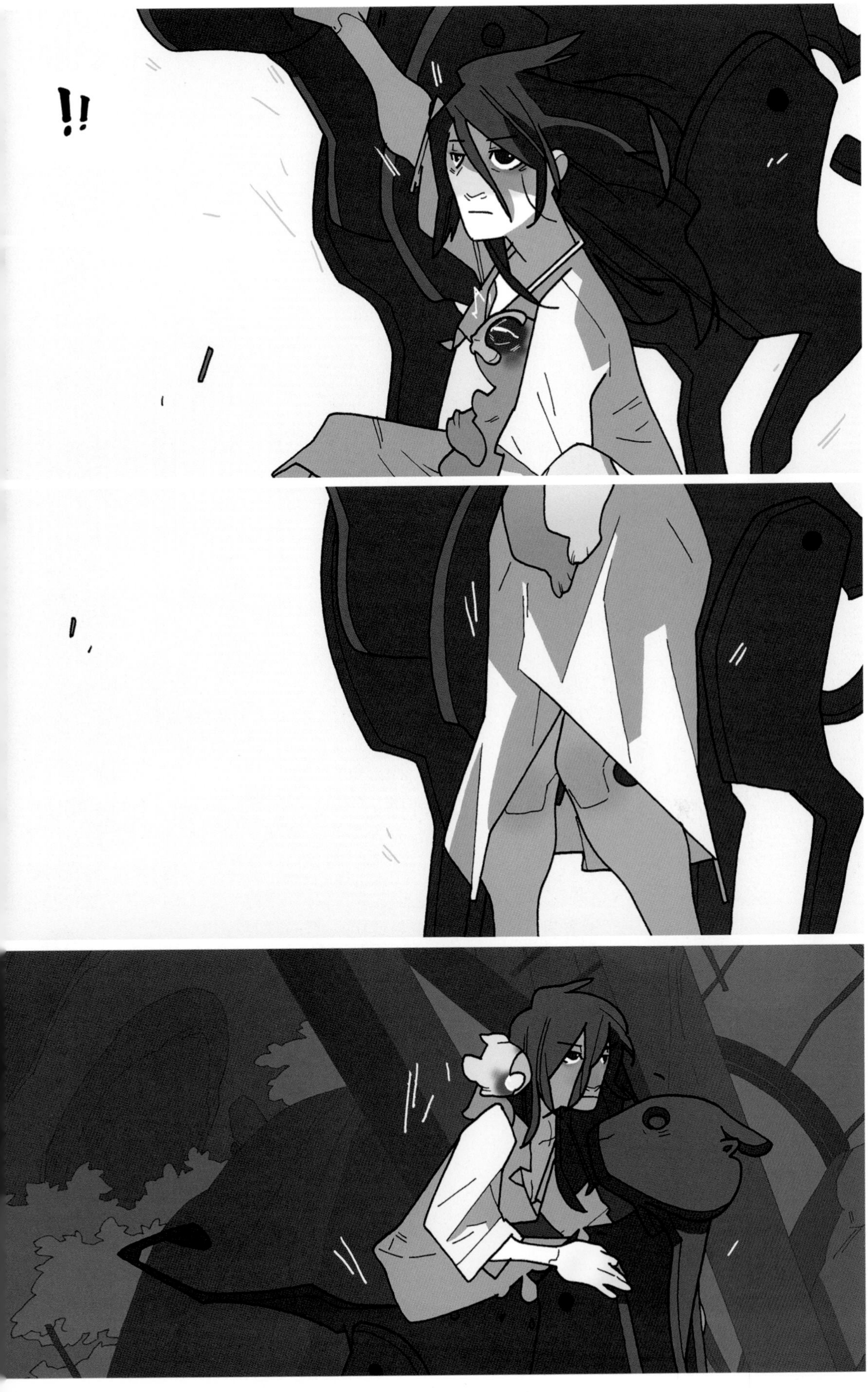
!!

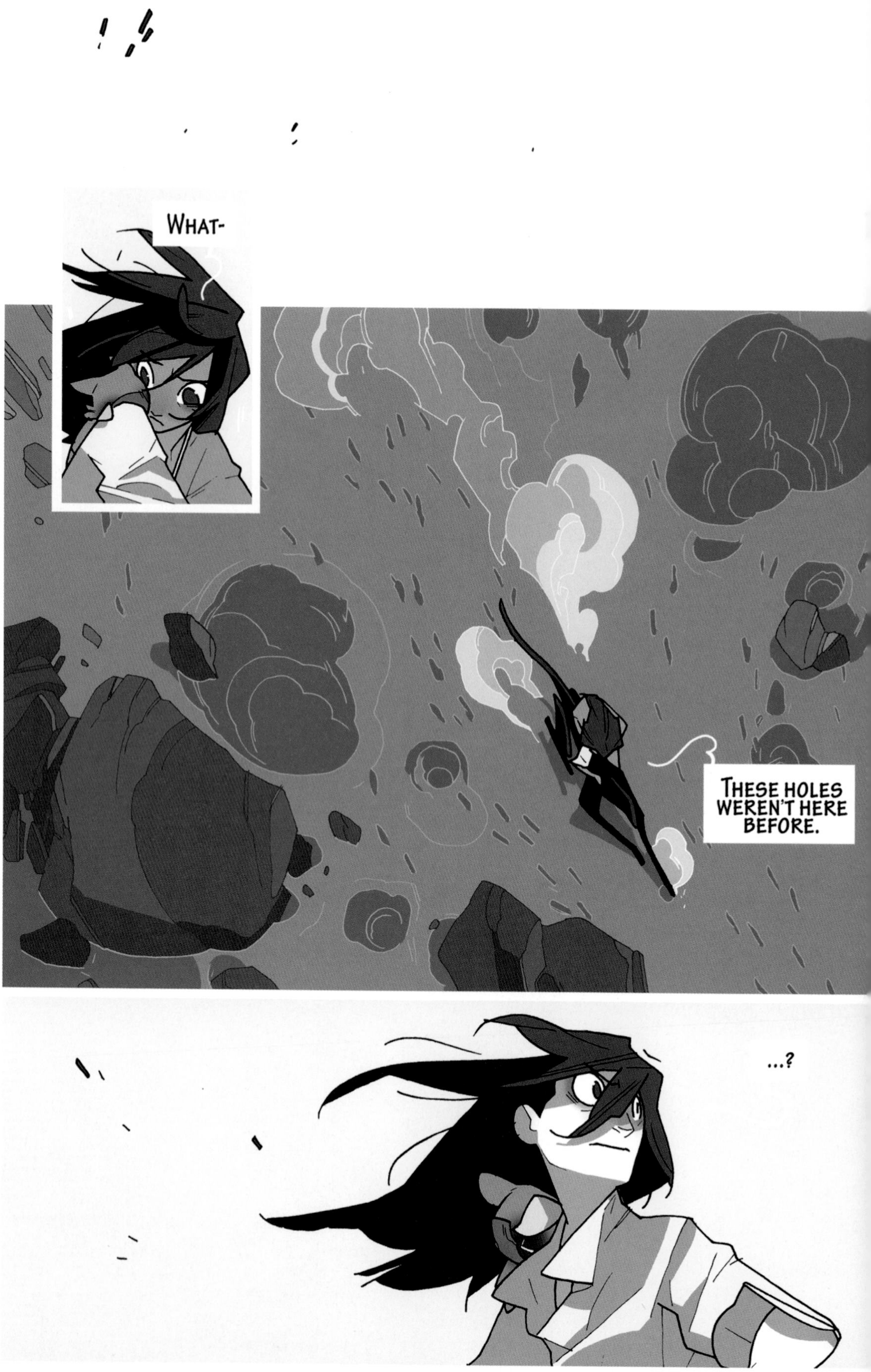
What-
These holes weren't here before.
...?

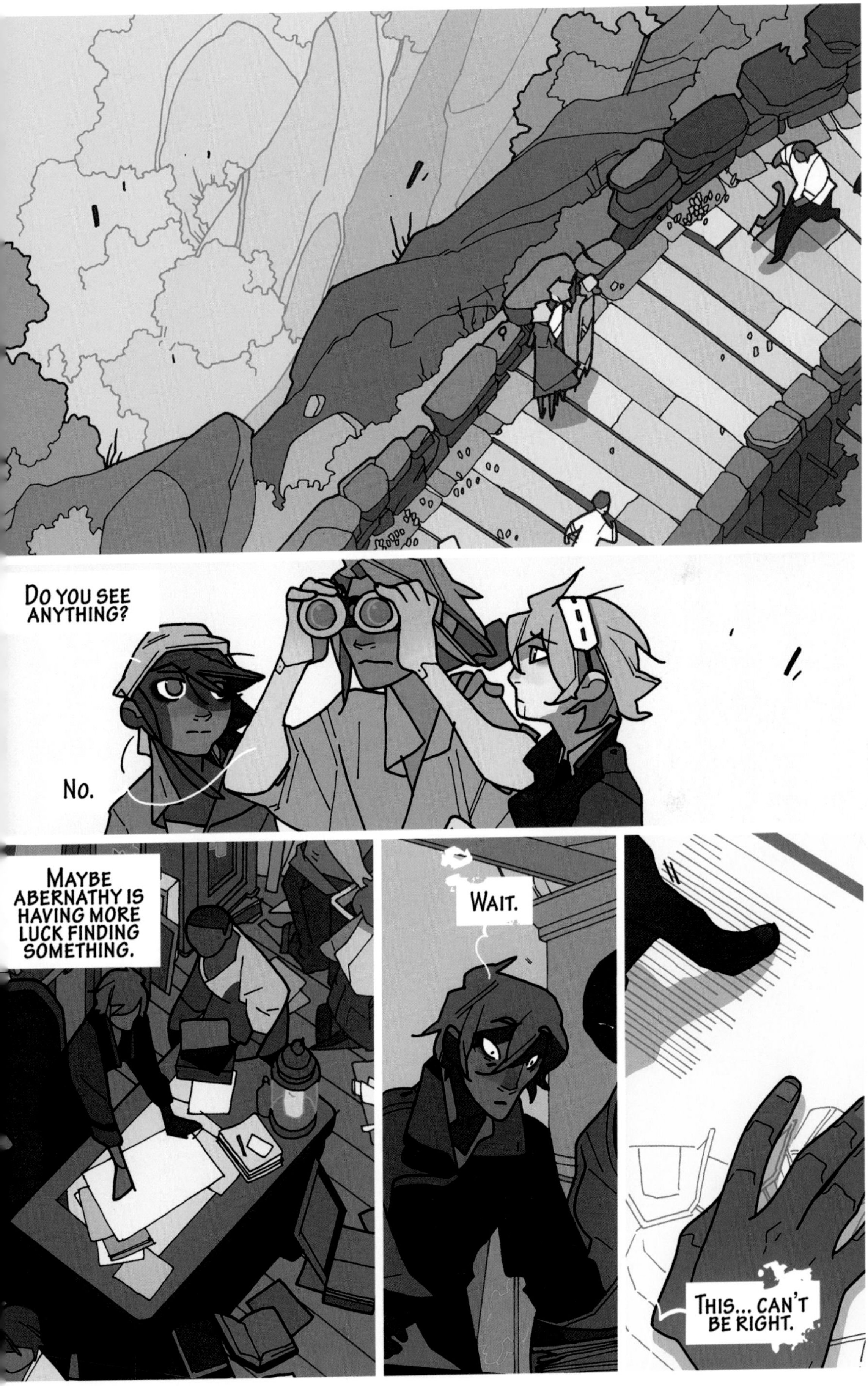

Do you see anything?
No.
Maybe Abernathy is having more luck finding something.
Wait.
This... can't be right.

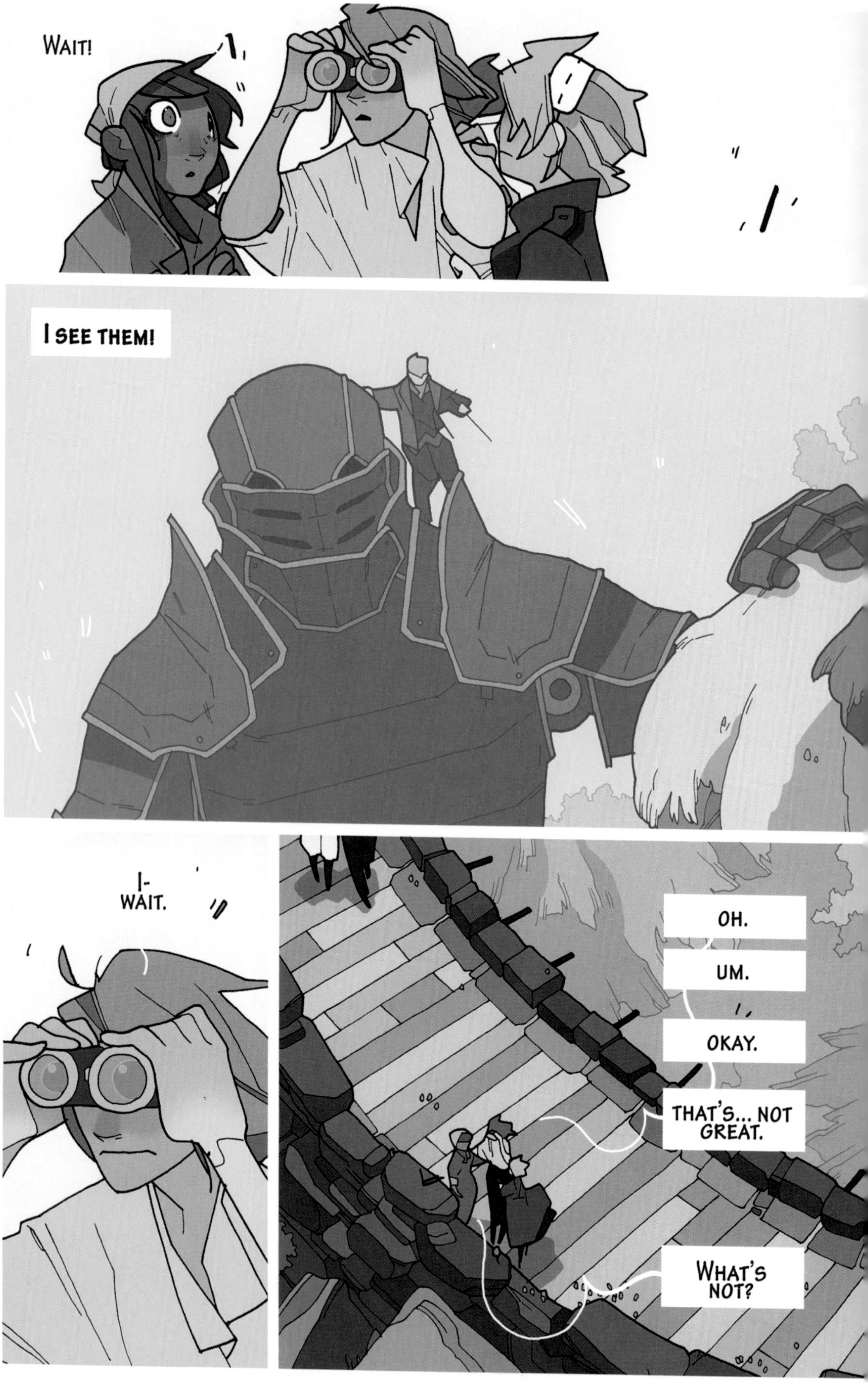
WAIT!
I SEE THEM!
I-
WAIT.
OH.
UM.
OKAY.
THAT'S... NOT GREAT.
WHAT'S NOT?

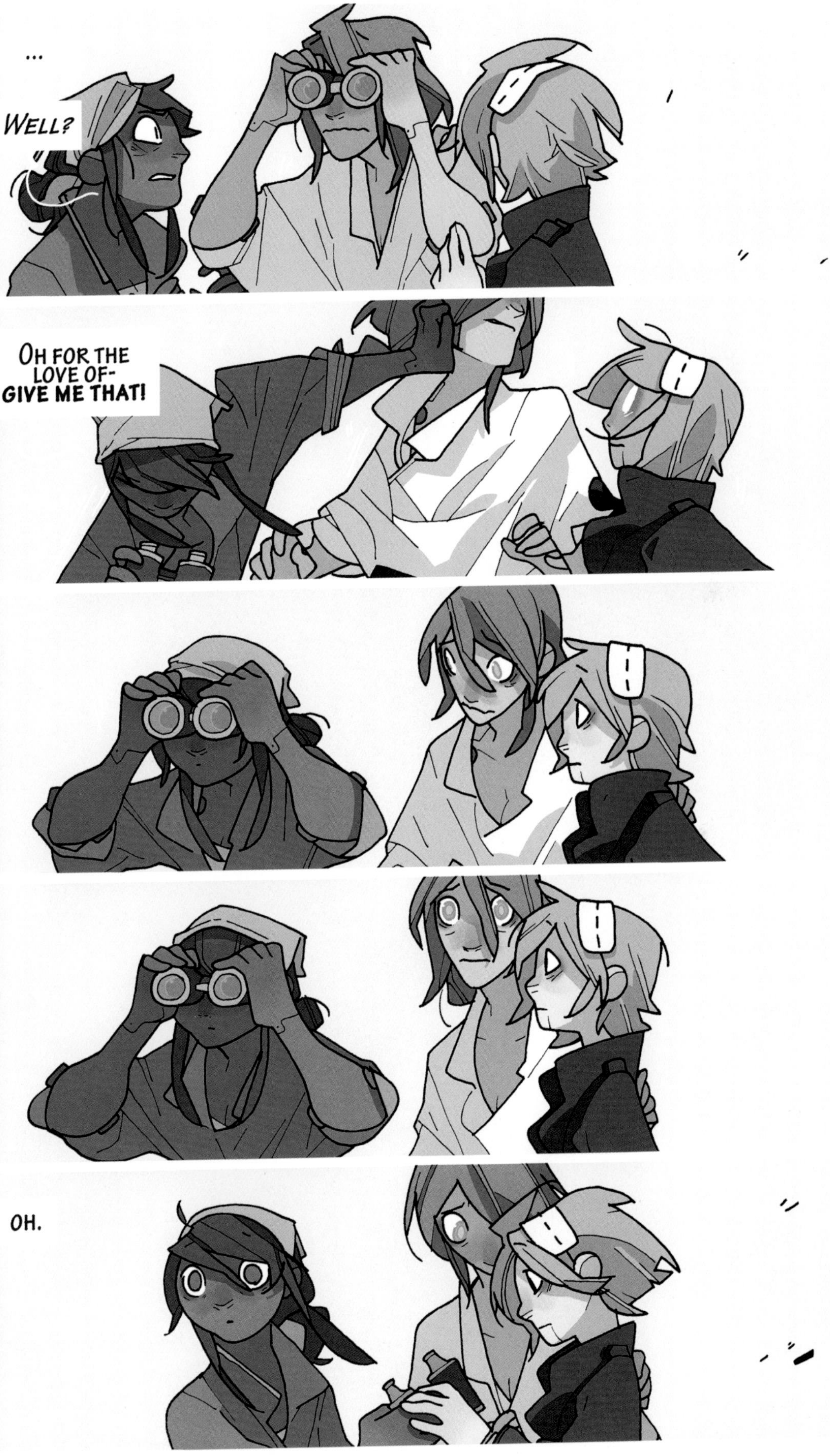
...
WELL?
OH FOR THE LOVE OF-
GIVE ME THAT!
OH.

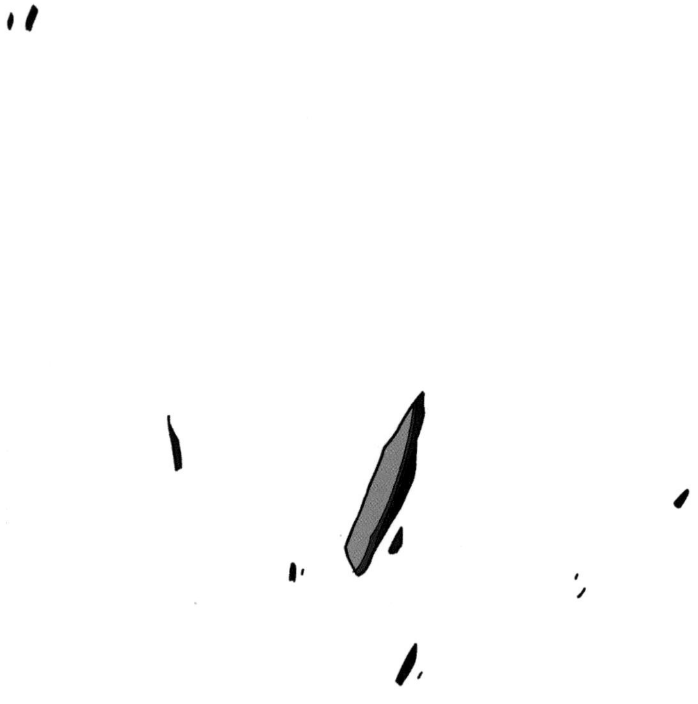

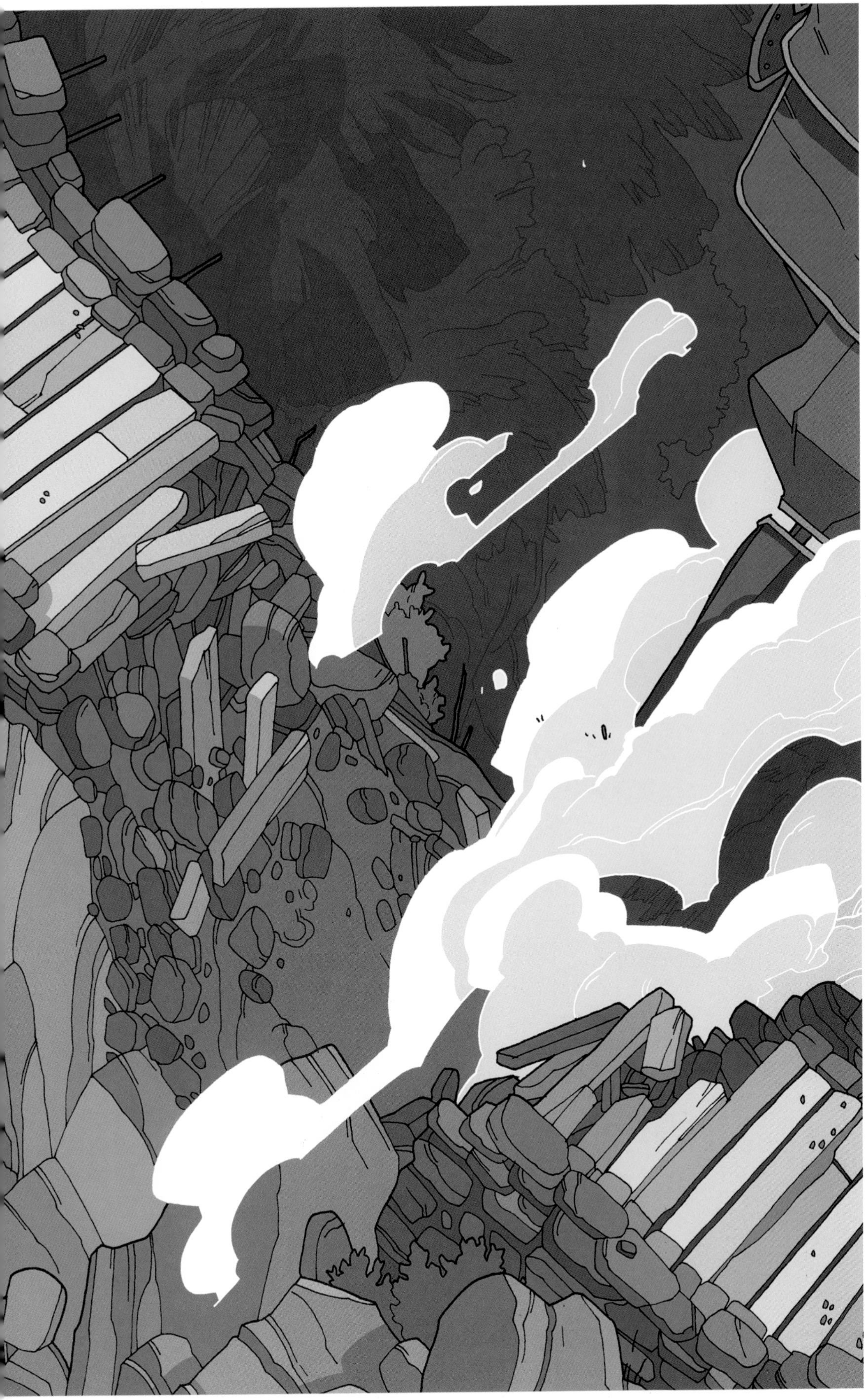

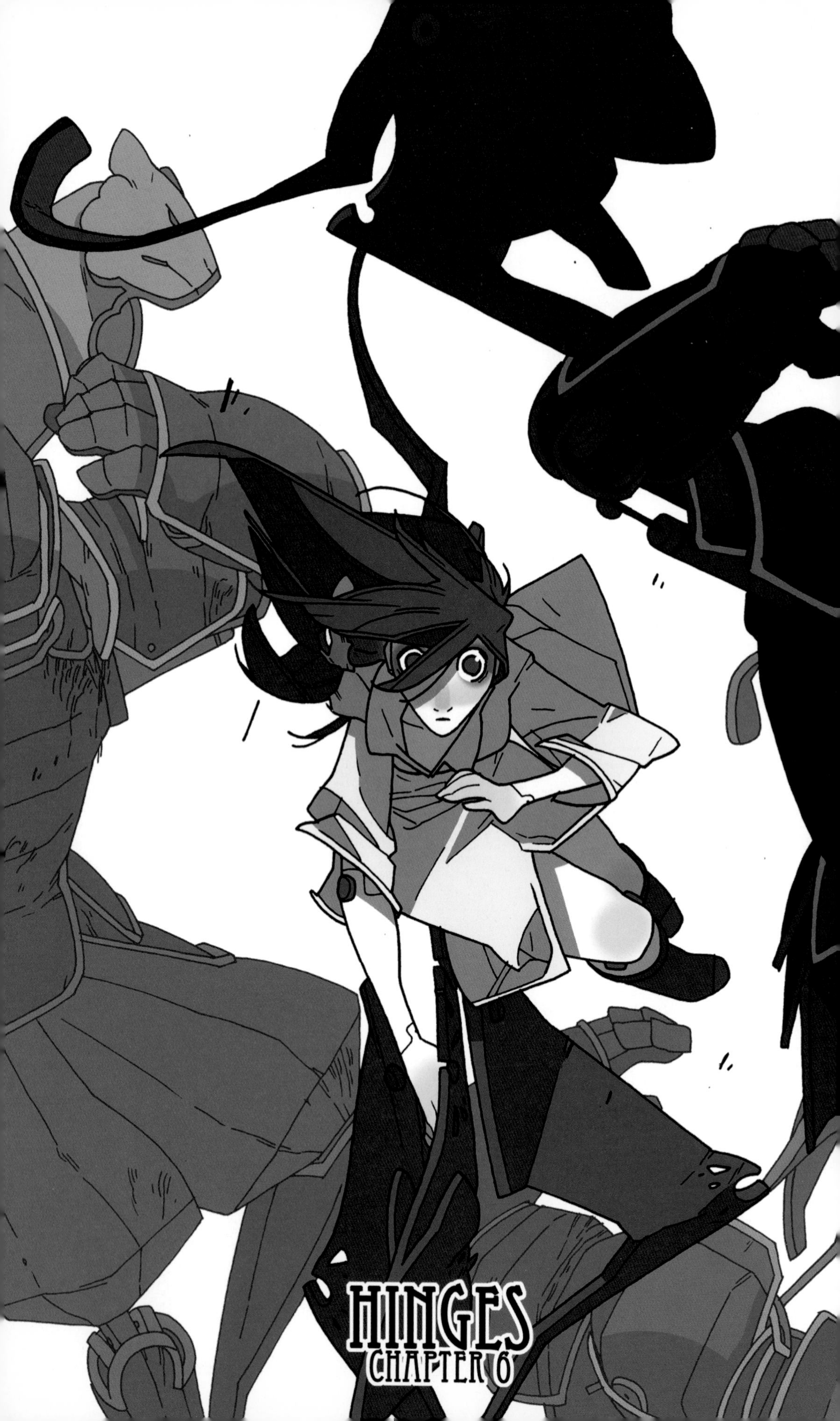
HINGES
CHAPTER 6

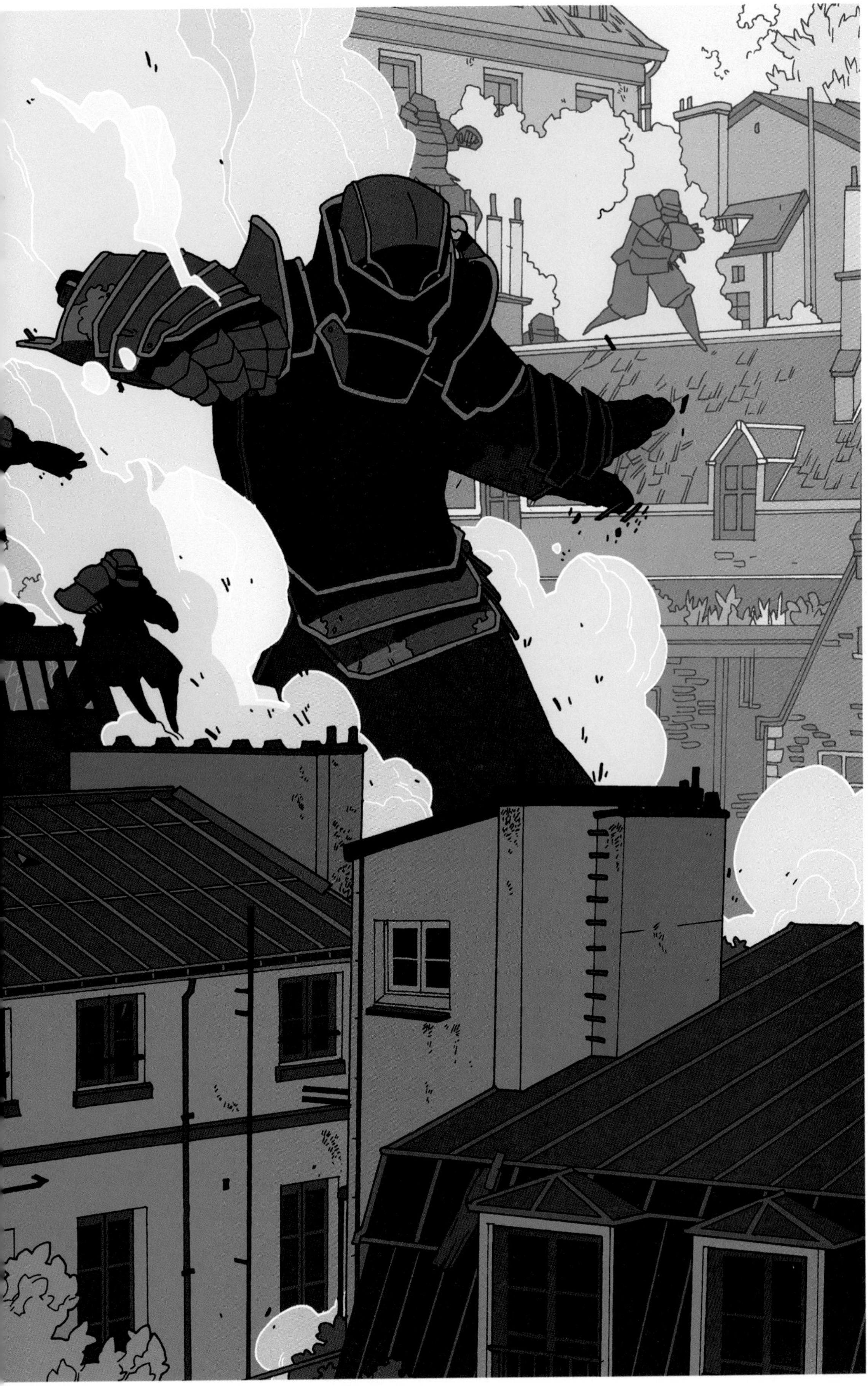

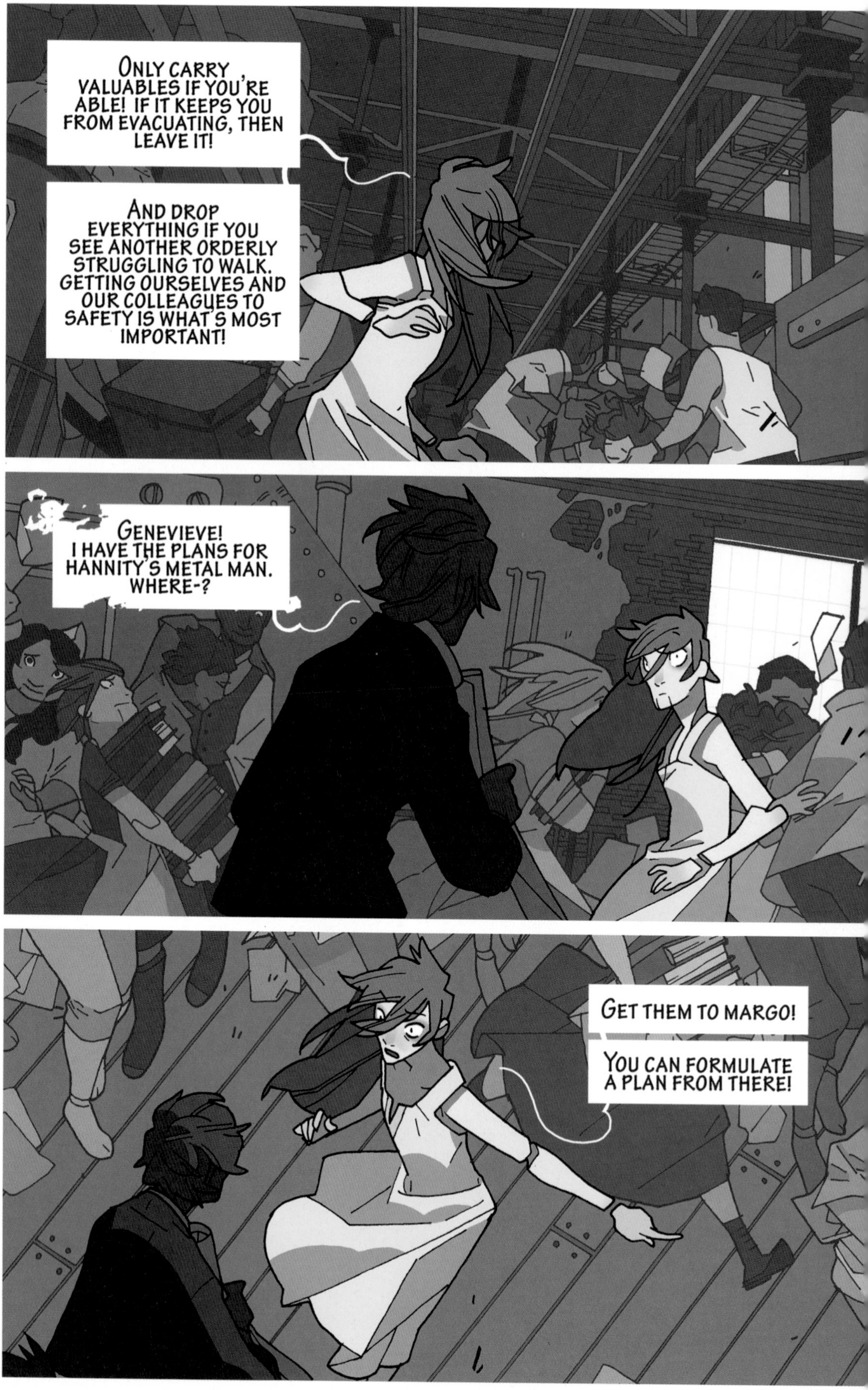
ONLY CARRY VALUABLES IF YOU'RE ABLE! IF IT KEEPS YOU FROM EVACUATING, THEN LEAVE IT!
AND DROP EVERYTHING IF YOU SEE ANOTHER ORDERLY STRUGGLING TO WALK. GETTING OURSELVES AND OUR COLLEAGUES TO SAFETY IS WHAT'S MOST IMPORTANT!
GENEVIEVE! I HAVE THE PLANS FOR HANNITY'S METAL MAN. WHERE-?
GET THEM TO MARGO!
YOU CAN FORMULATE A PLAN FROM THERE!

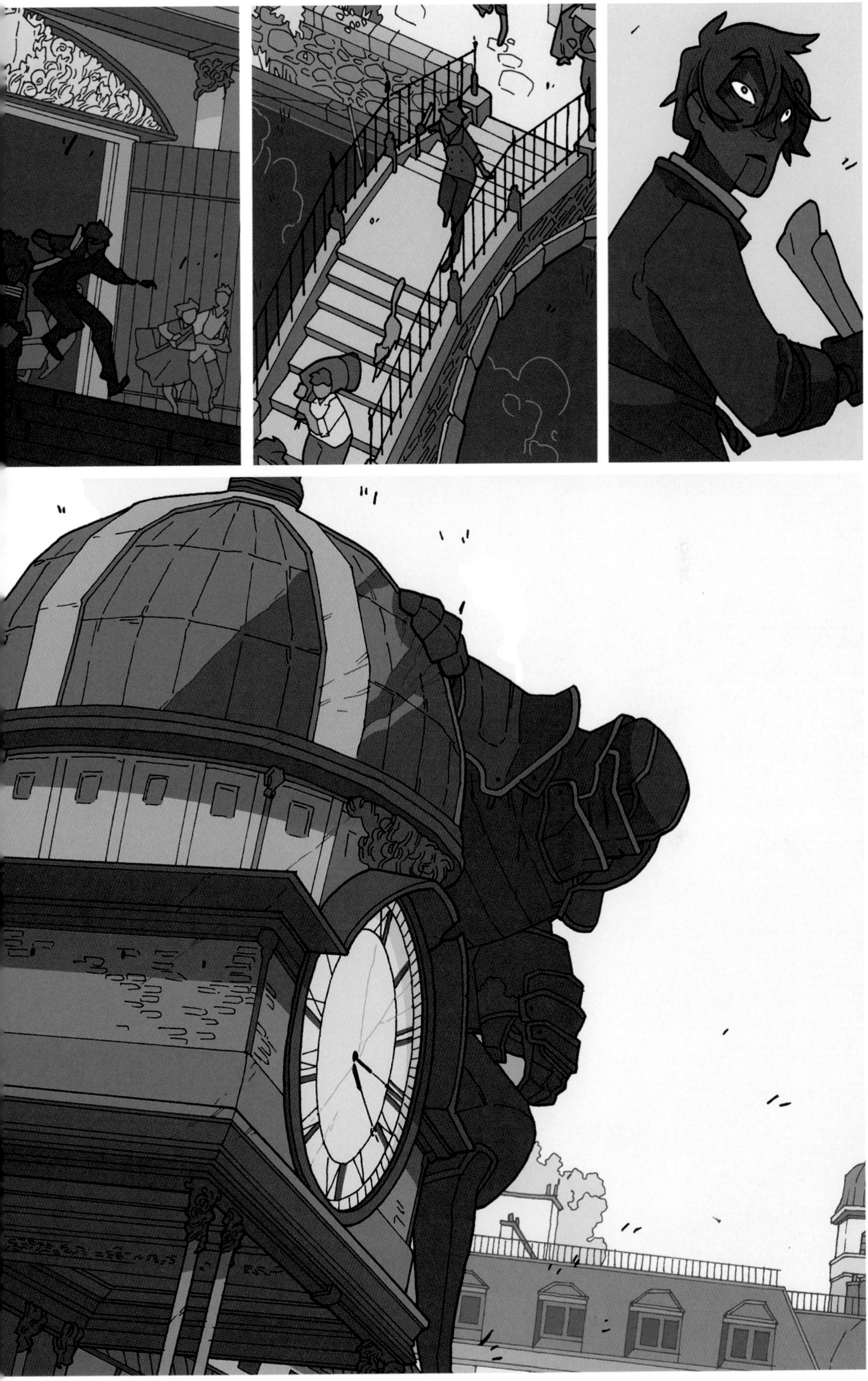

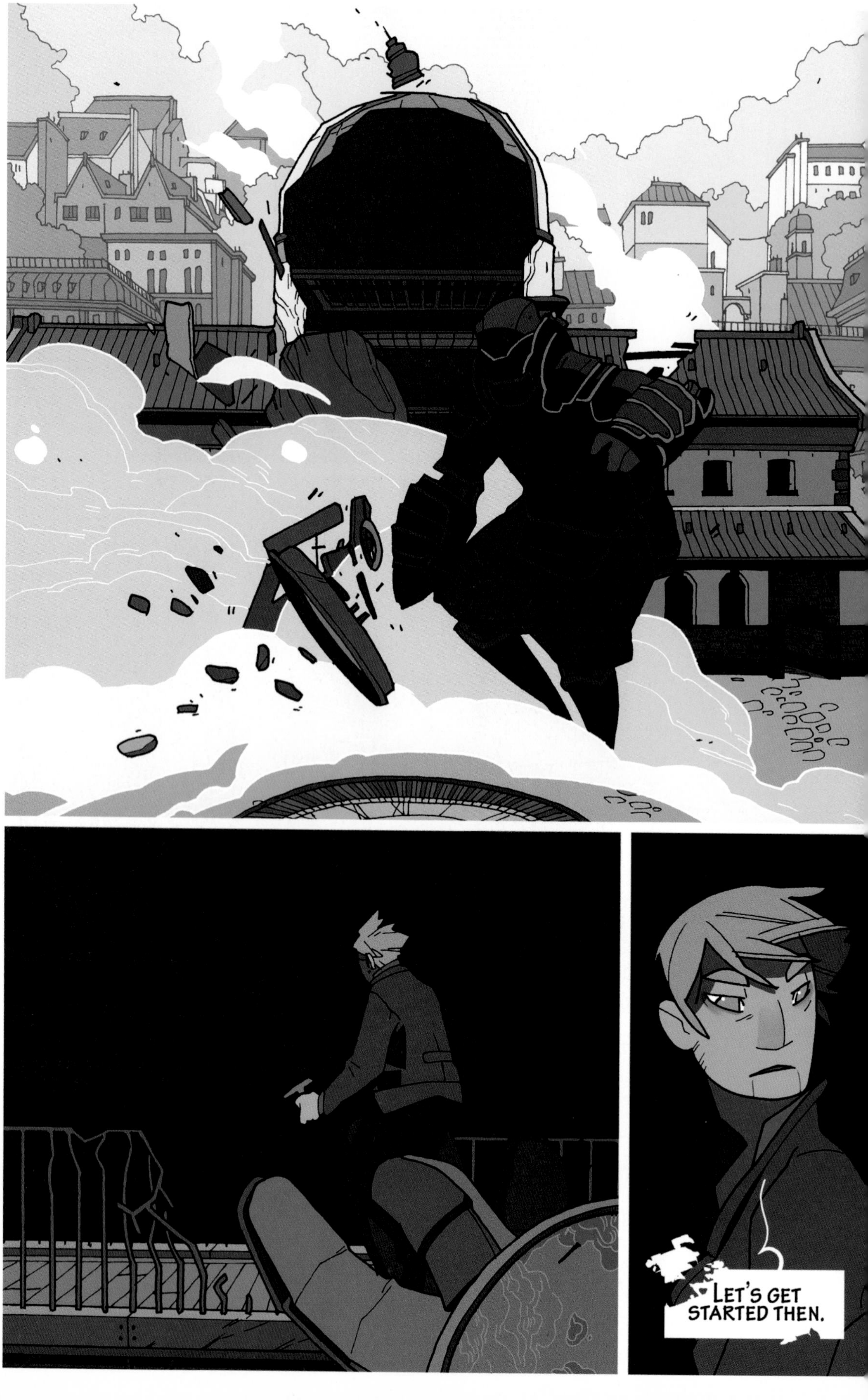
LET'S GET
STARTED THEN.

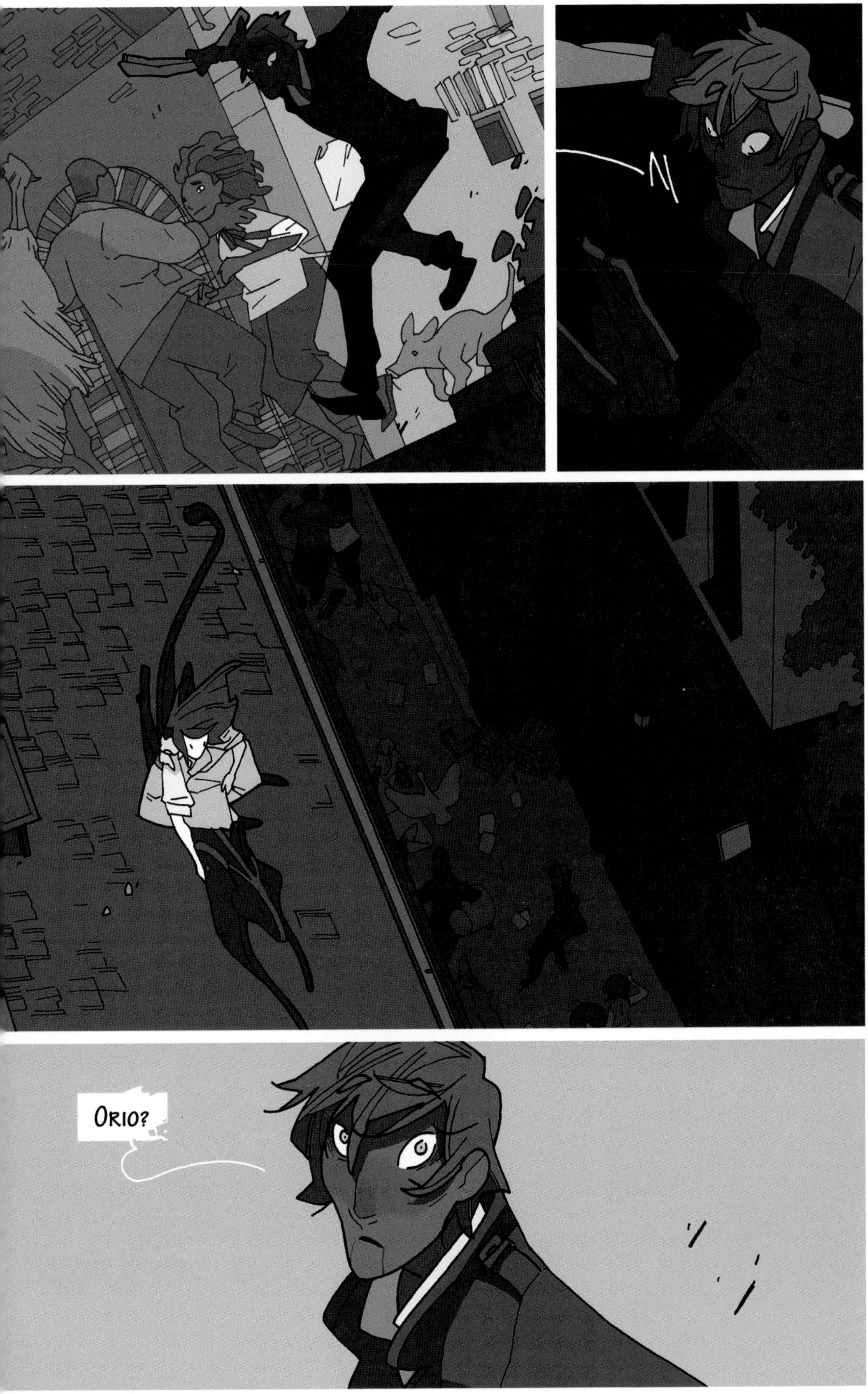
Orio?

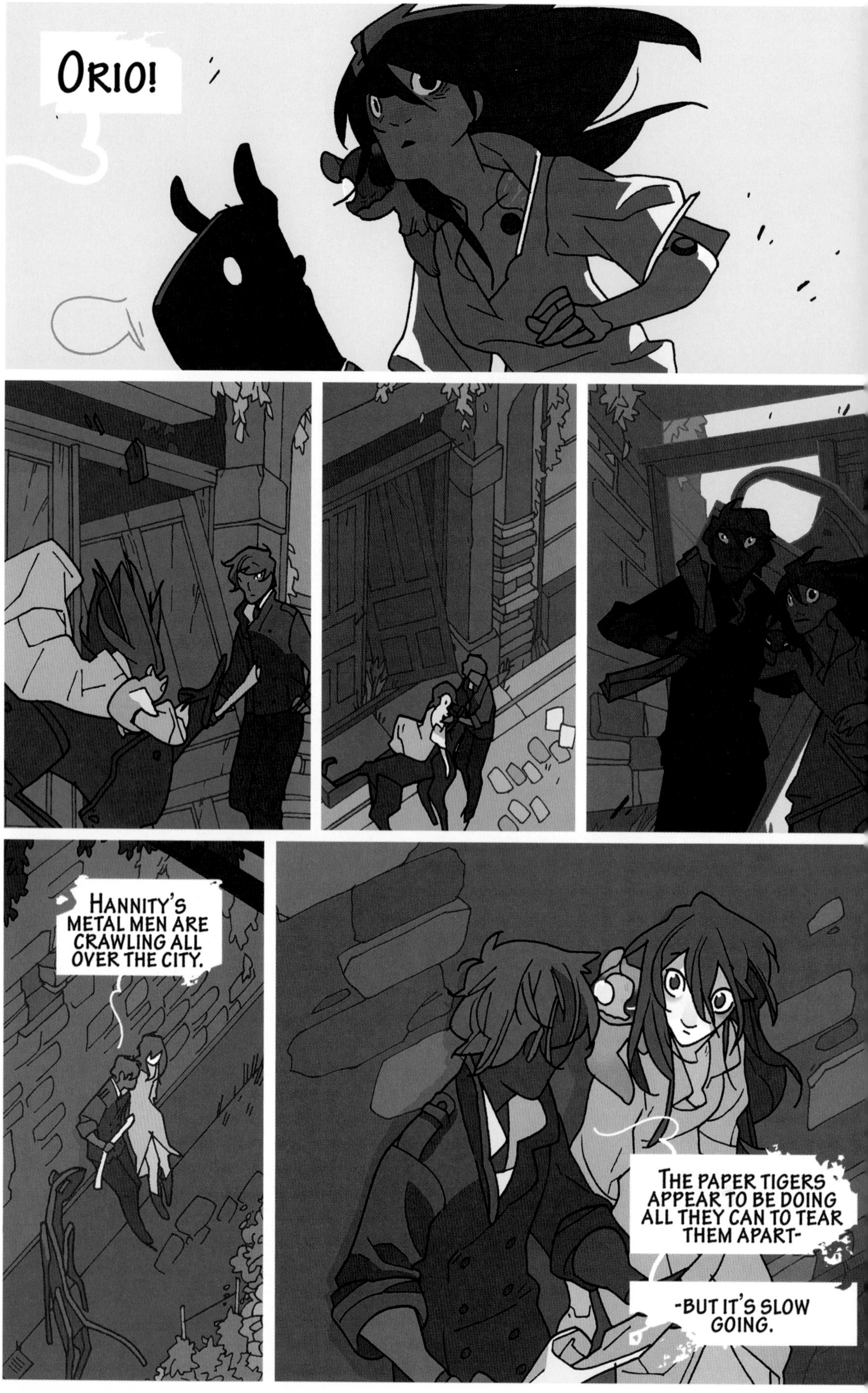
ORIO!
HANNITY'S METAL MEN ARE CRAWLING ALL OVER THE CITY.
THE PAPER TIGERS APPEAR TO BE DOING ALL THEY CAN TO TEAR THEM APART-
-BUT IT'S SLOW GOING.

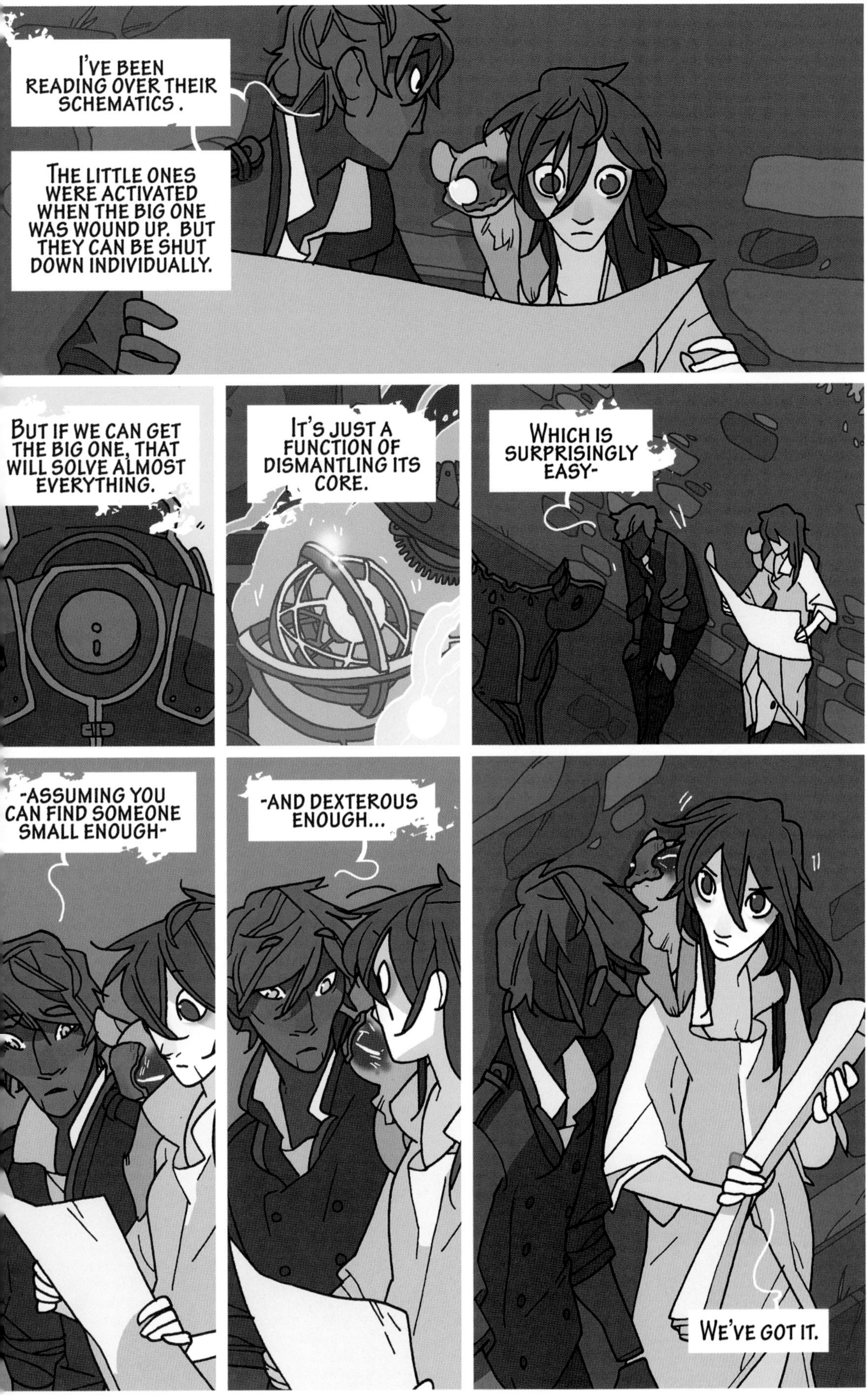
I'VE BEEN READING OVER THEIR SCHEMATICS.
THE LITTLE ONES WERE ACTIVATED WHEN THE BIG ONE WAS WOUND UP. BUT THEY CAN BE SHUT DOWN INDIVIDUALLY.
BUT IF WE CAN GET THE BIG ONE, THAT WILL SOLVE ALMOST EVERYTHING.
IT'S JUST A FUNCTION OF DISMANTLING ITS CORE.
WHICH IS SURPRISINGLY EASY-
-ASSUMING YOU CAN FIND SOMEONE SMALL ENOUGH-
-AND DEXTEROUS ENOUGH...
WE'VE GOT IT.

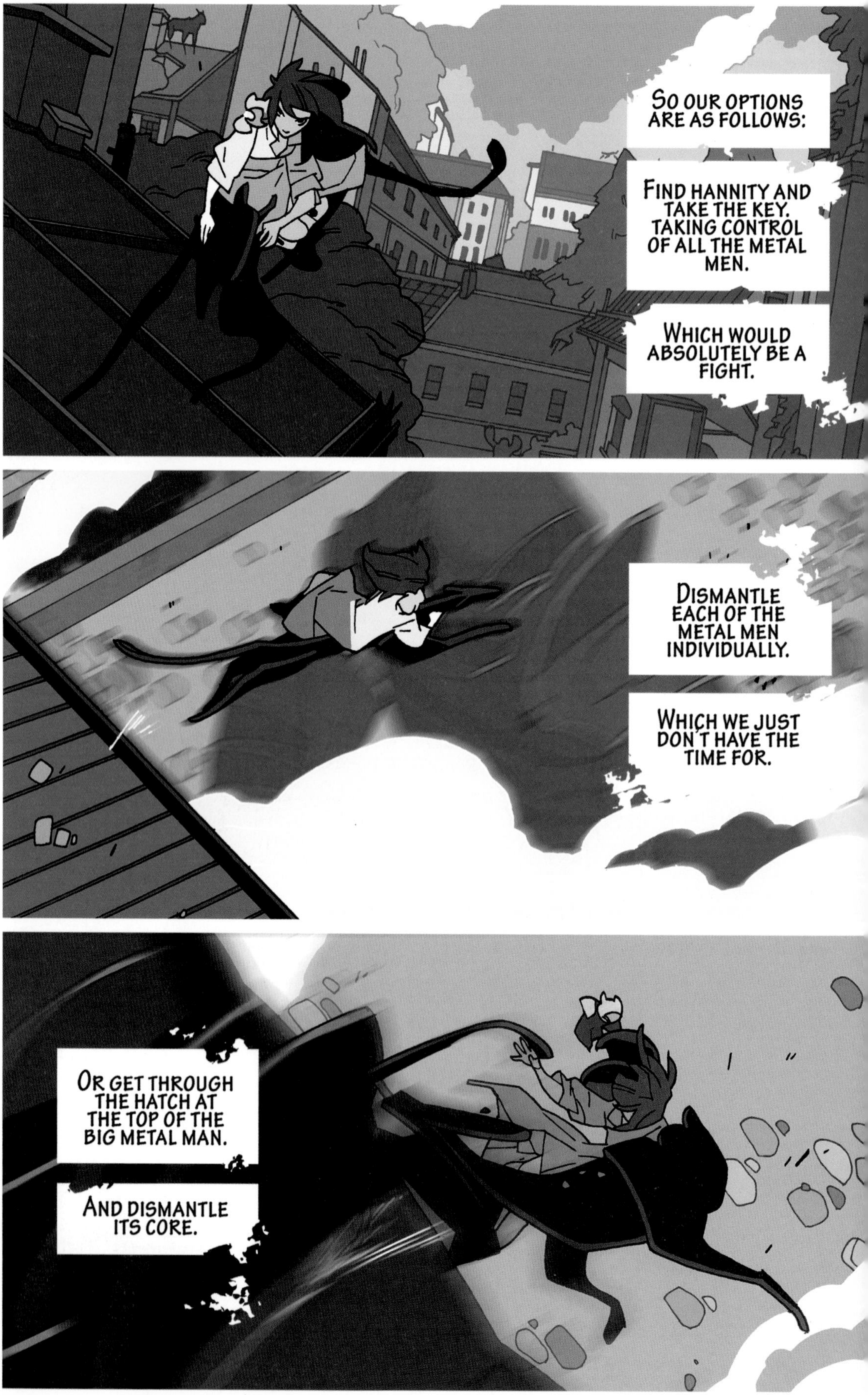

So our options are as follows:
Find Hannity and take the key. Taking control of all the metal men.
Which would absolutely be a fight.
Dismantle each of the metal men individually.
Which we just don't have the time for.
Or get through the hatch at the top of the big metal man.
And dismantle its core.

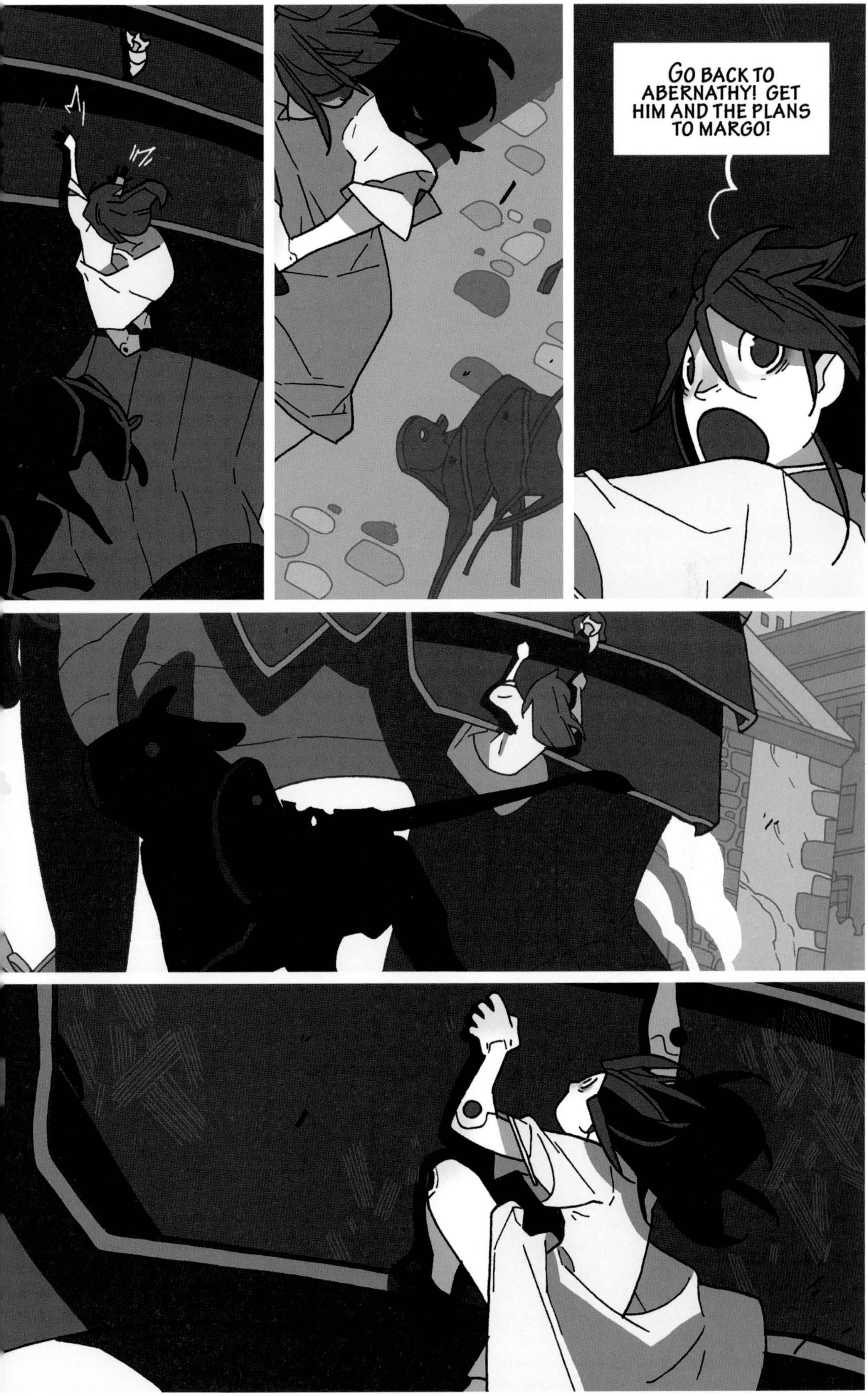
GO BACK TO ABERNATHY! GET HIM AND THE PLANS TO MARGO!

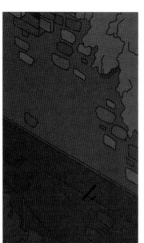

THIS.

THIS IS NOT A GOOD LONG-TERM STRATEGY.

WE CAN'T PUSH BACK LONG ENOUGH TO KEEP THEM FROM GAINING GROUND.

WHEN SOMEONE HAS A BETTER PLAN, WE CAN USE IT.

UNTIL THEN, THIS IS THE ONLY PROBLEM WE CAN FOCUS ON—

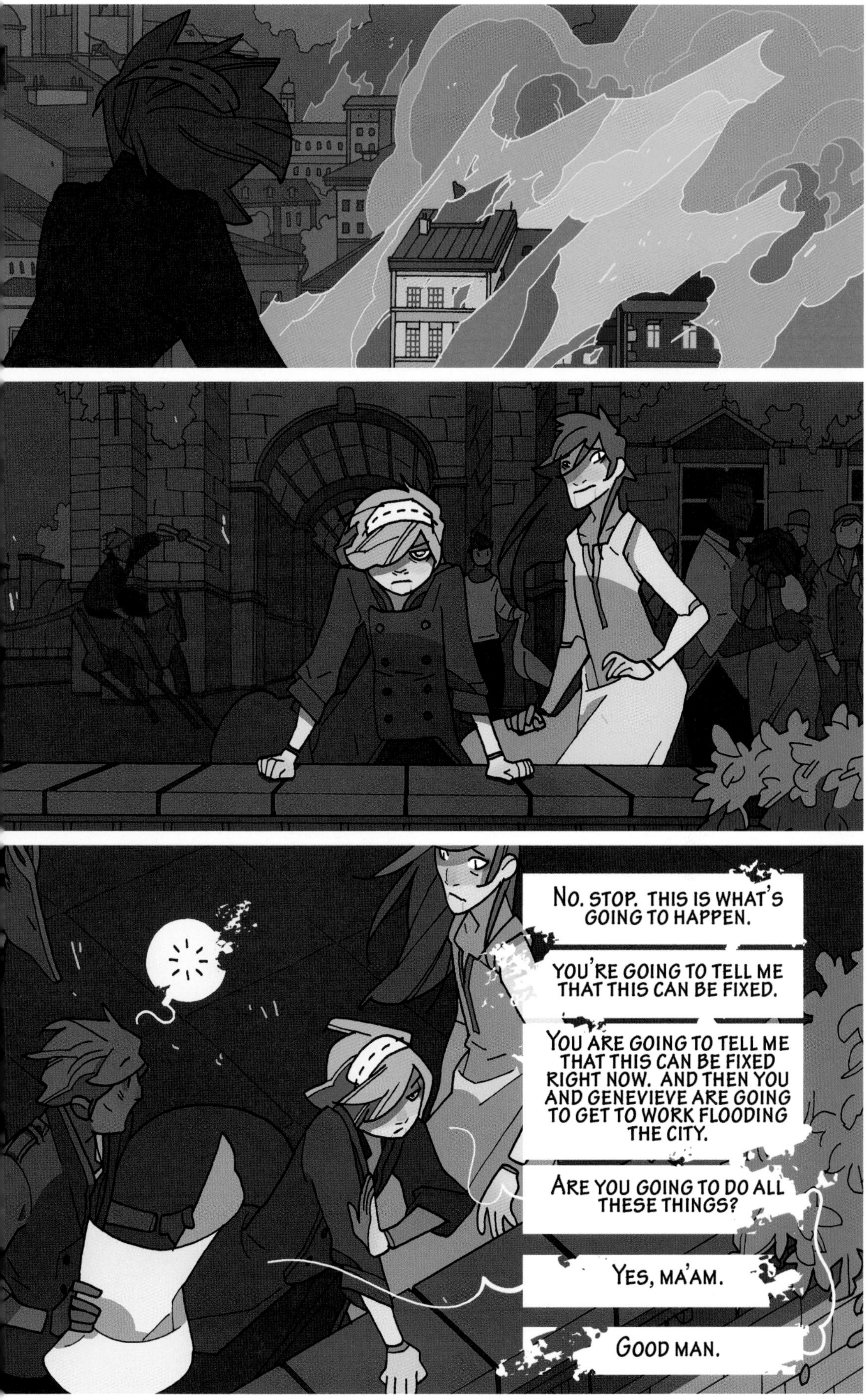
No. STOP. THIS IS WHAT'S GOING TO HAPPEN.
YOU'RE GOING TO TELL ME THAT THIS CAN BE FIXED.
YOU ARE GOING TO TELL ME THAT THIS CAN BE FIXED RIGHT NOW. AND THEN YOU AND GENEVIEVE ARE GOING TO GET TO WORK FLOODING THE CITY.
ARE YOU GOING TO DO ALL THESE THINGS?
YES, MA'AM.
GOOD MAN.

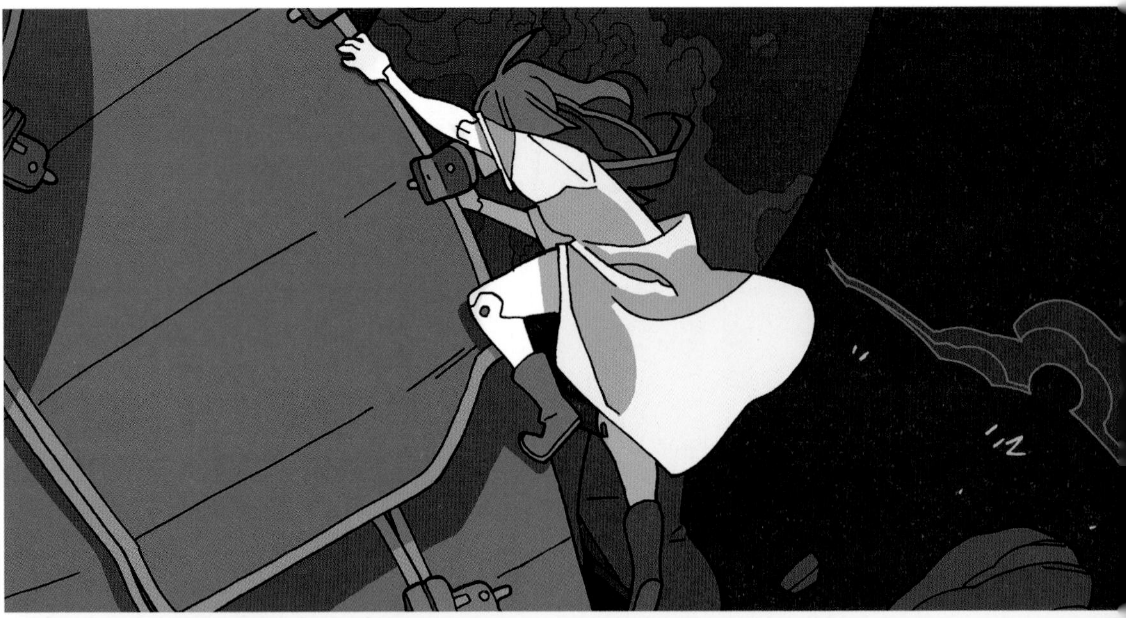

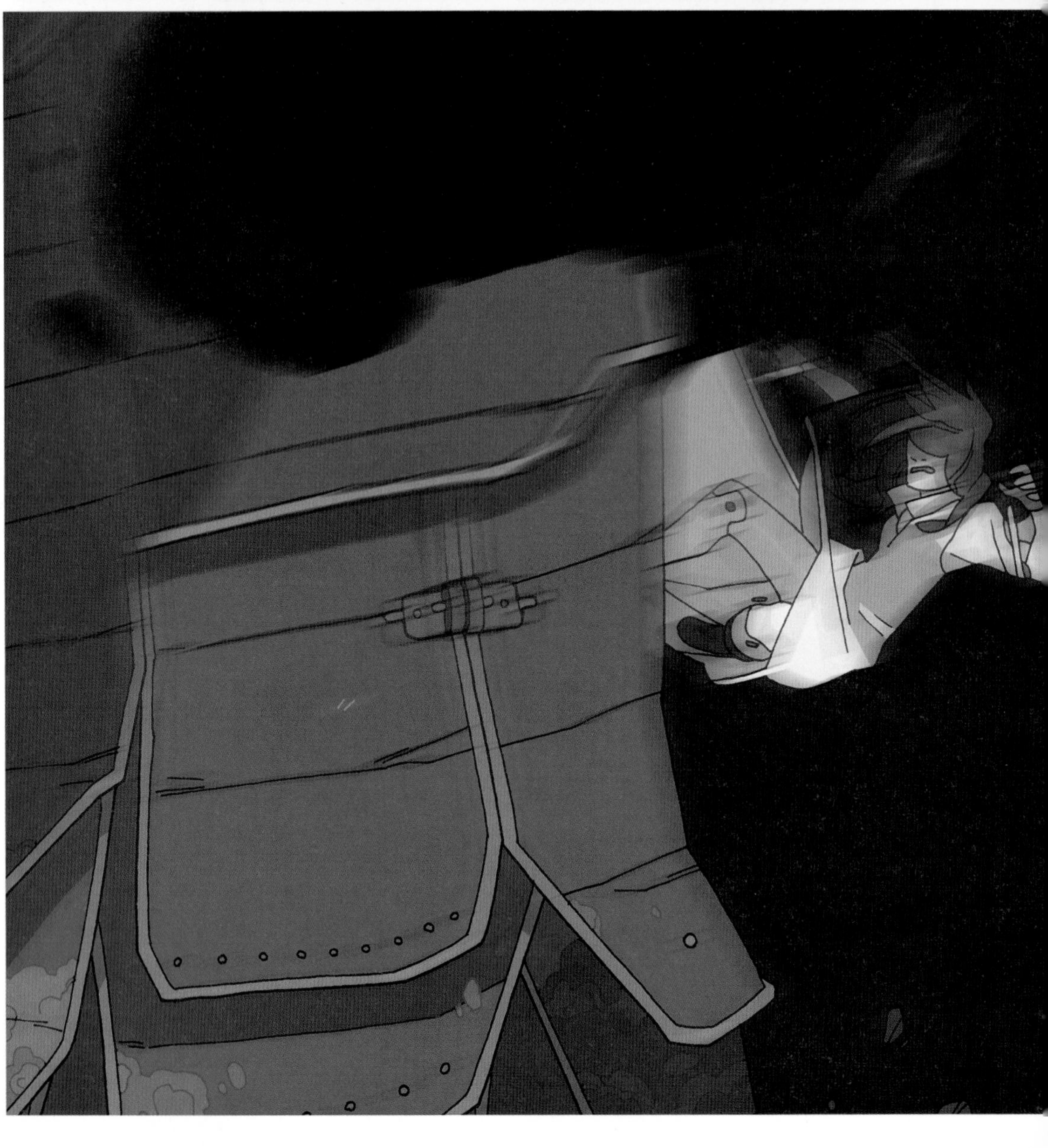

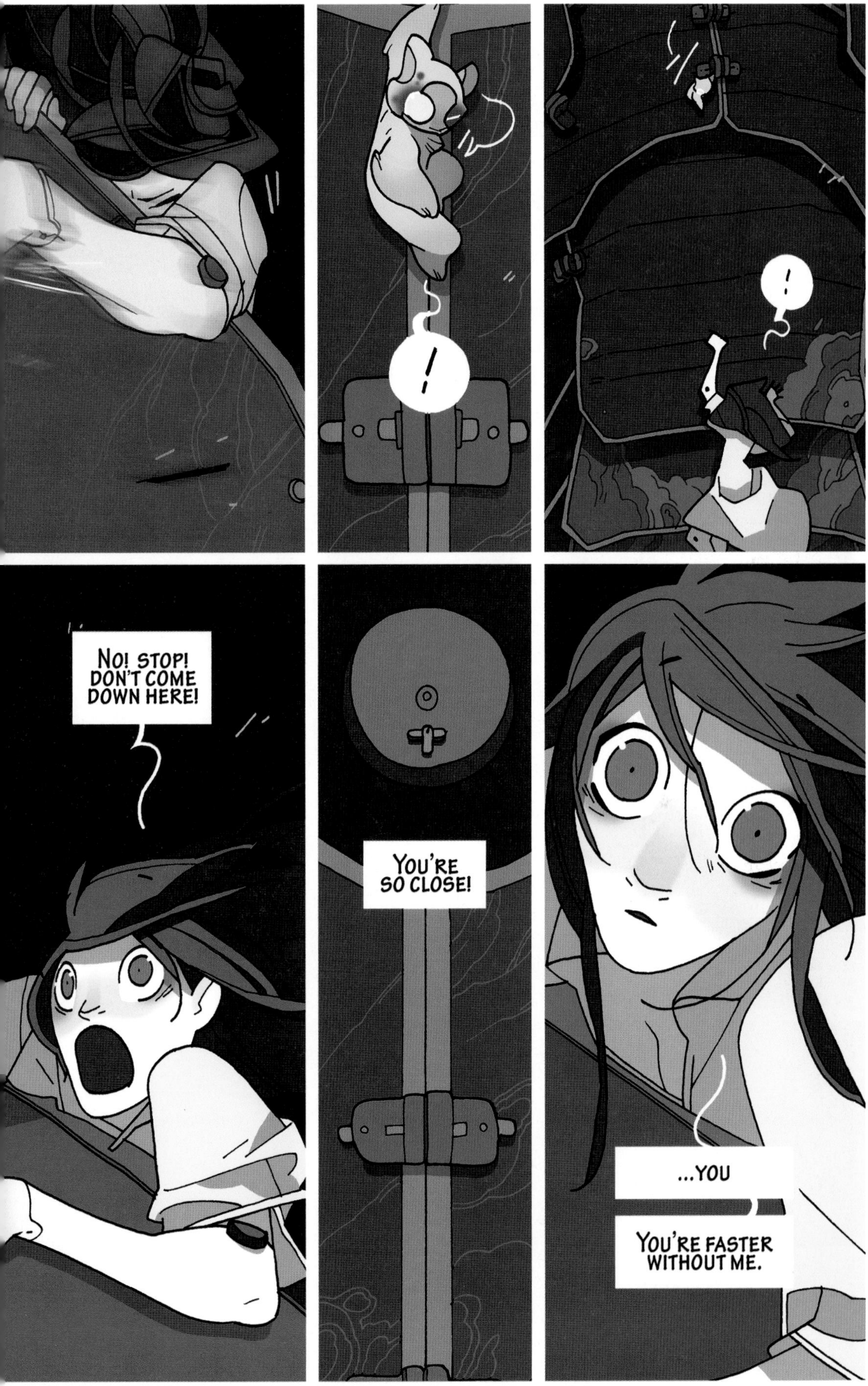
!
!
No! stop! don't come down here!
You're so close!
...you
You're faster without me.

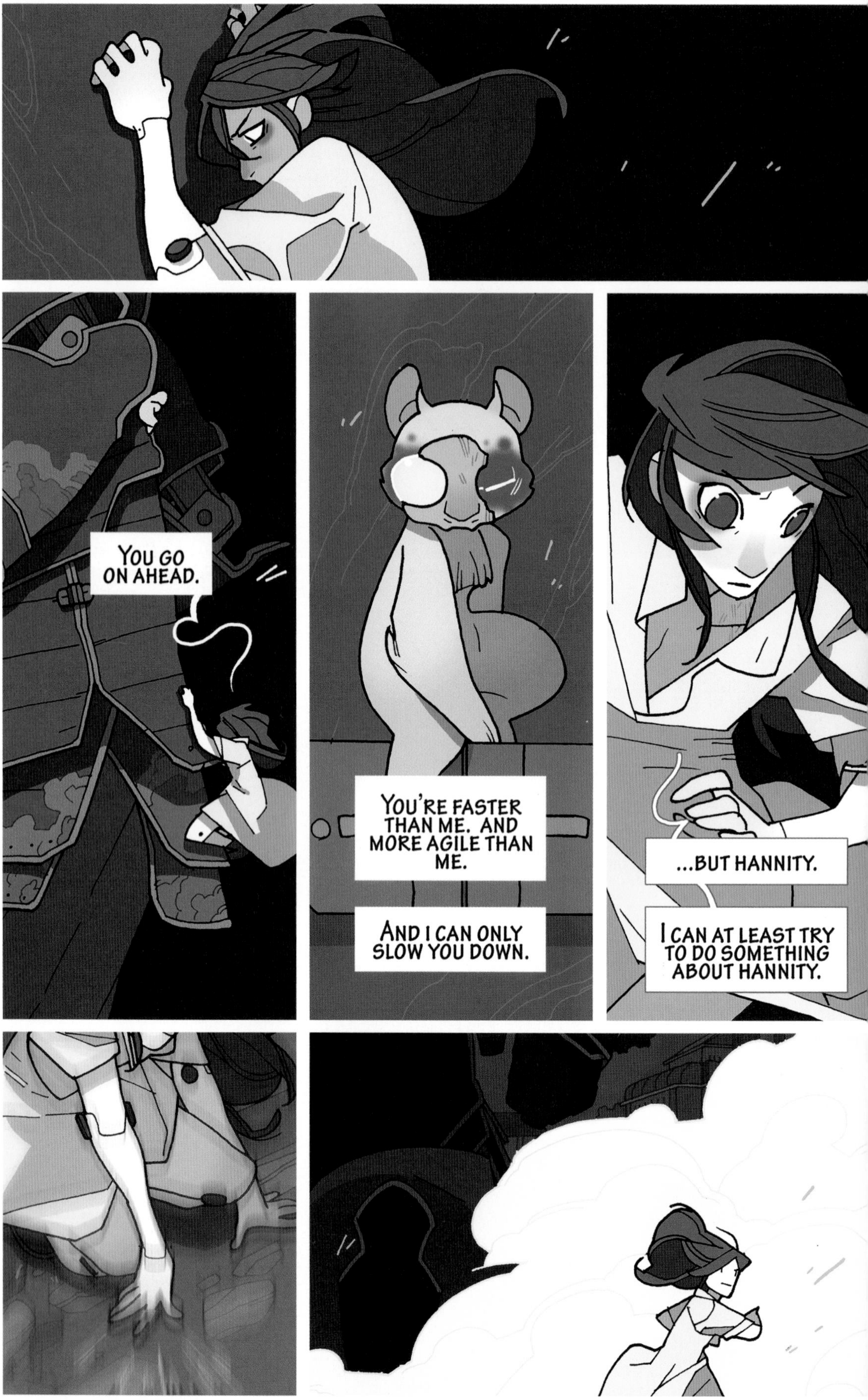
YOU GO ON AHEAD.
YOU'RE FASTER THAN ME. AND MORE AGILE THAN ME.
AND I CAN ONLY SLOW YOU DOWN.
...BUT HANNITY.
I CAN AT LEAST TRY TO DO SOMETHING ABOUT HANNITY.

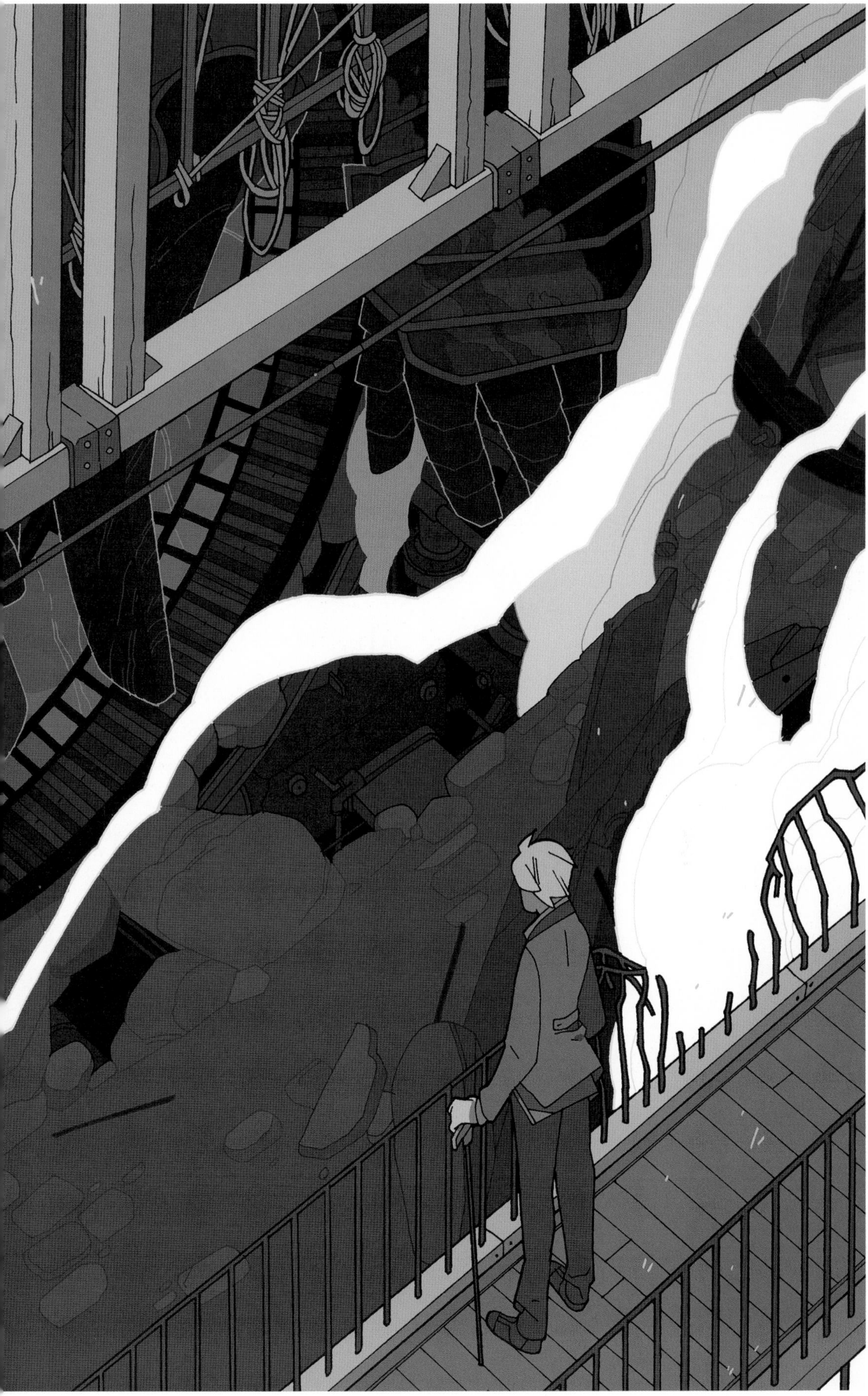

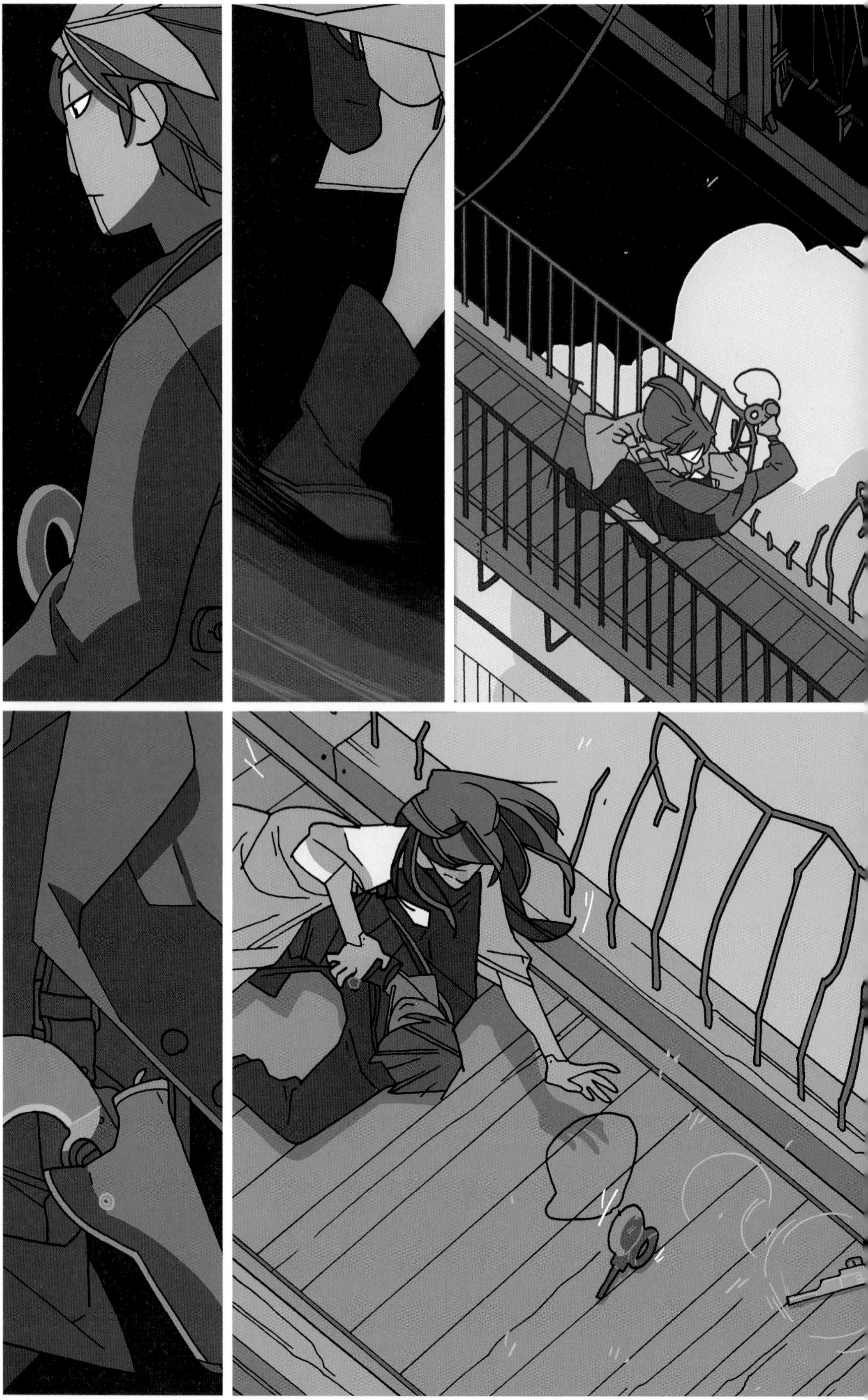

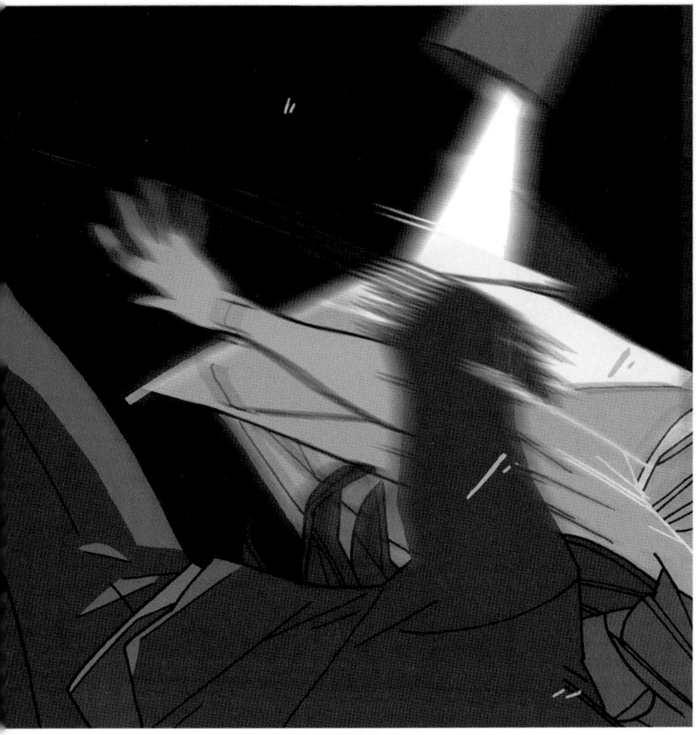

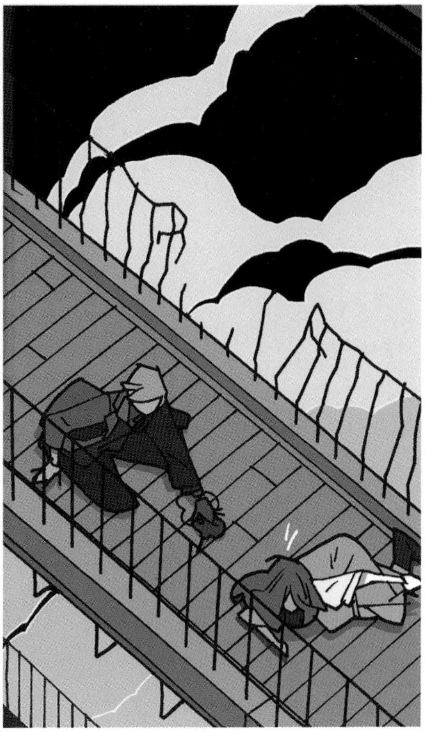

click

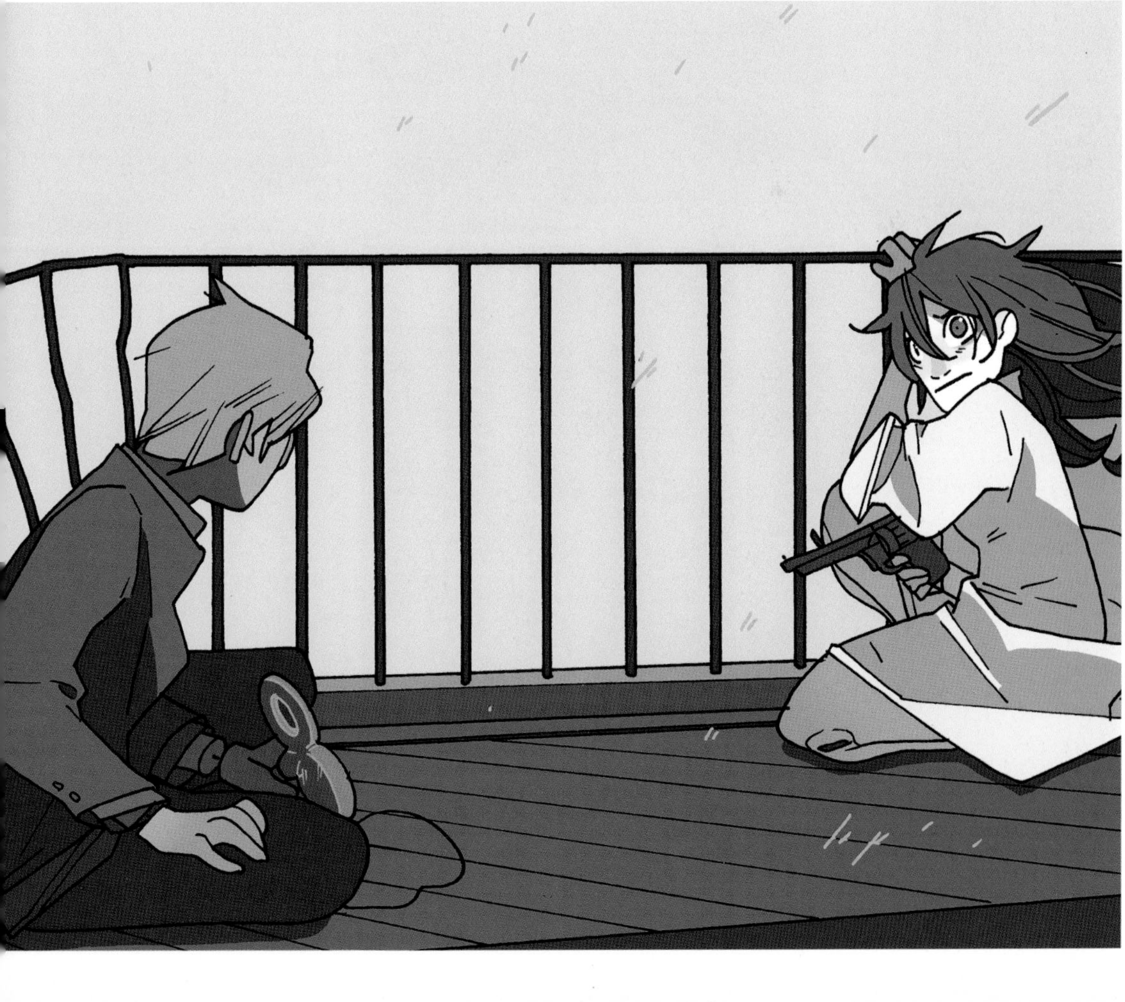

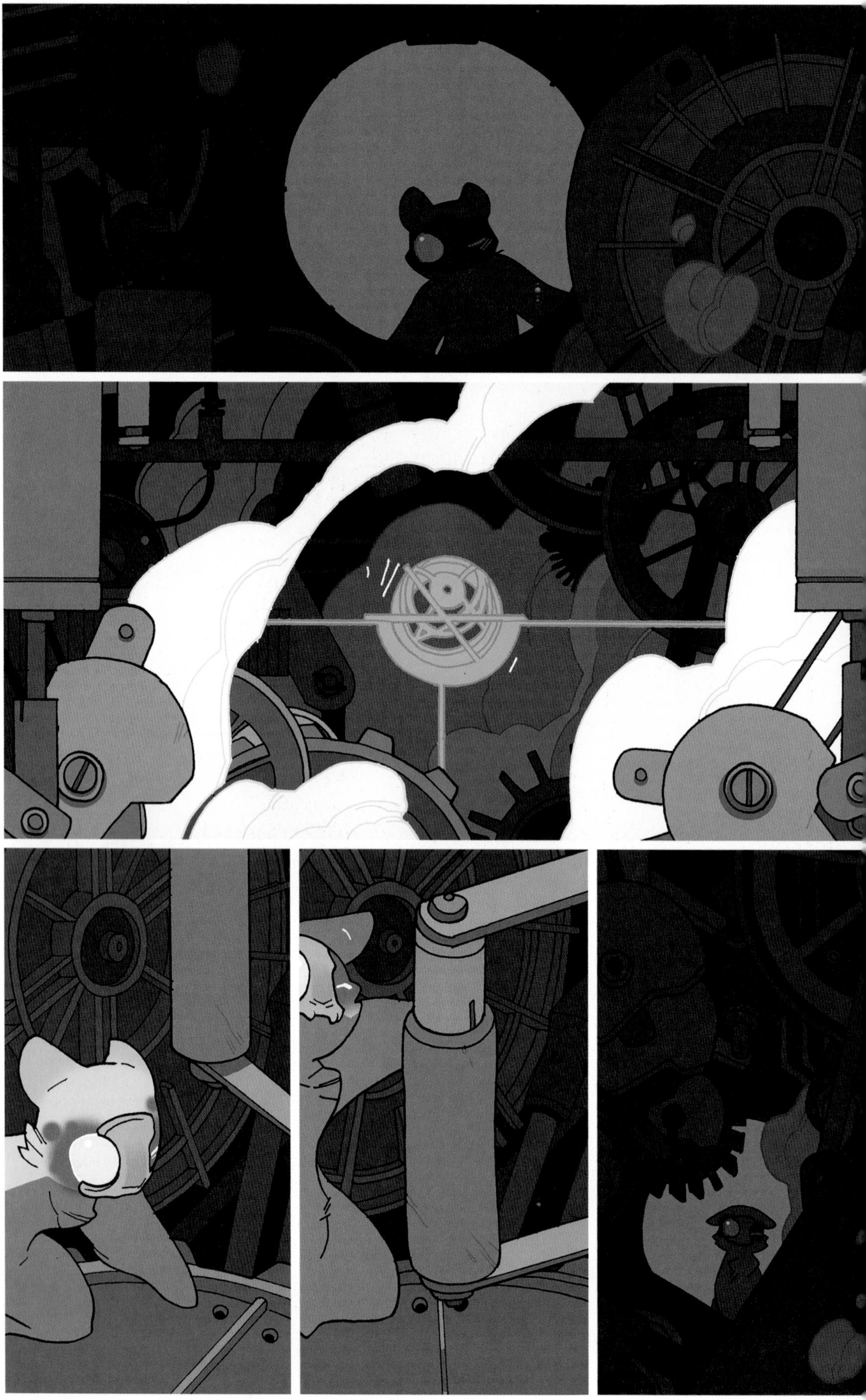

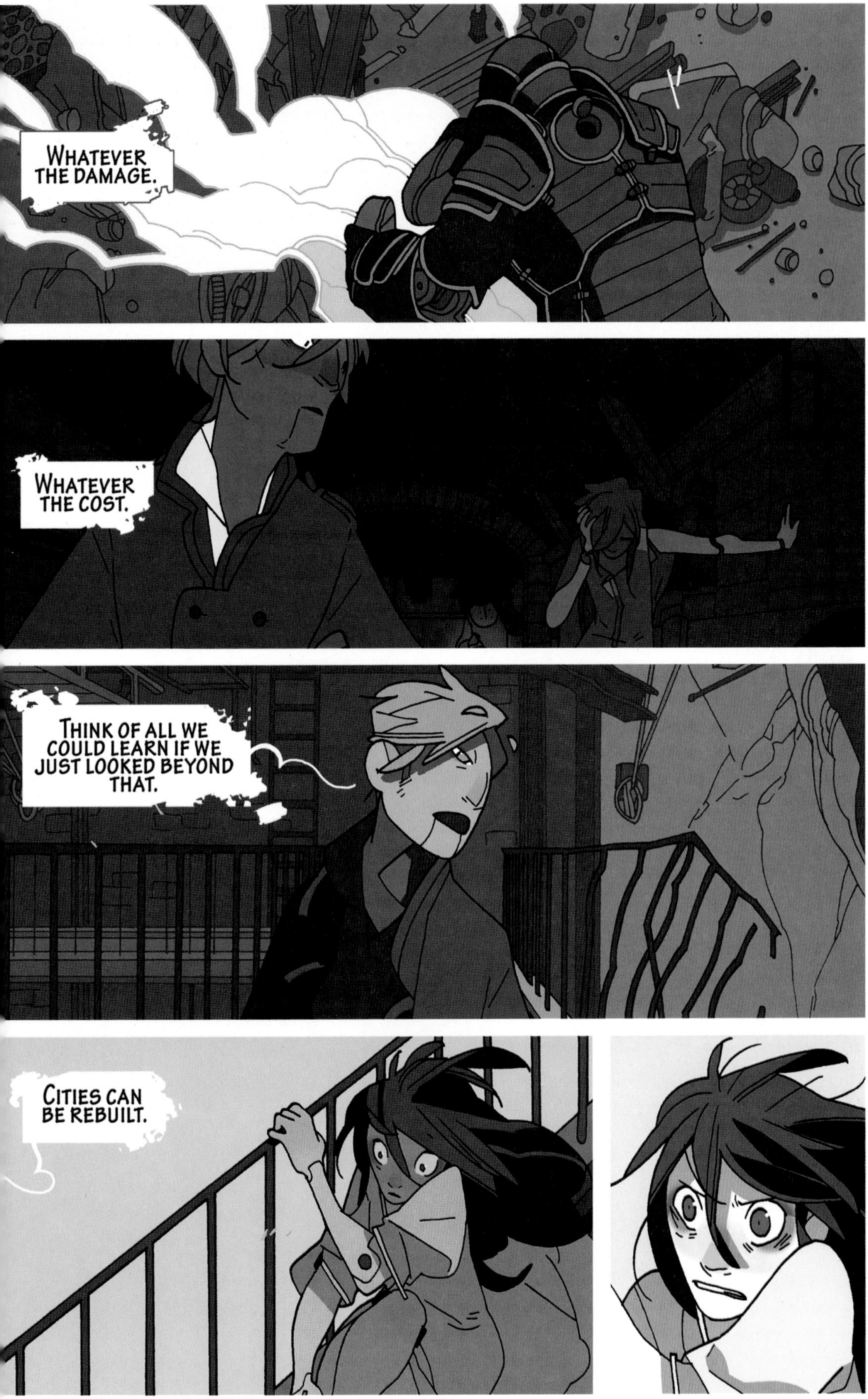
Whatever the damage.
Whatever the cost.
Think of all we could learn if we just looked beyond that.
Cities can be rebuilt.

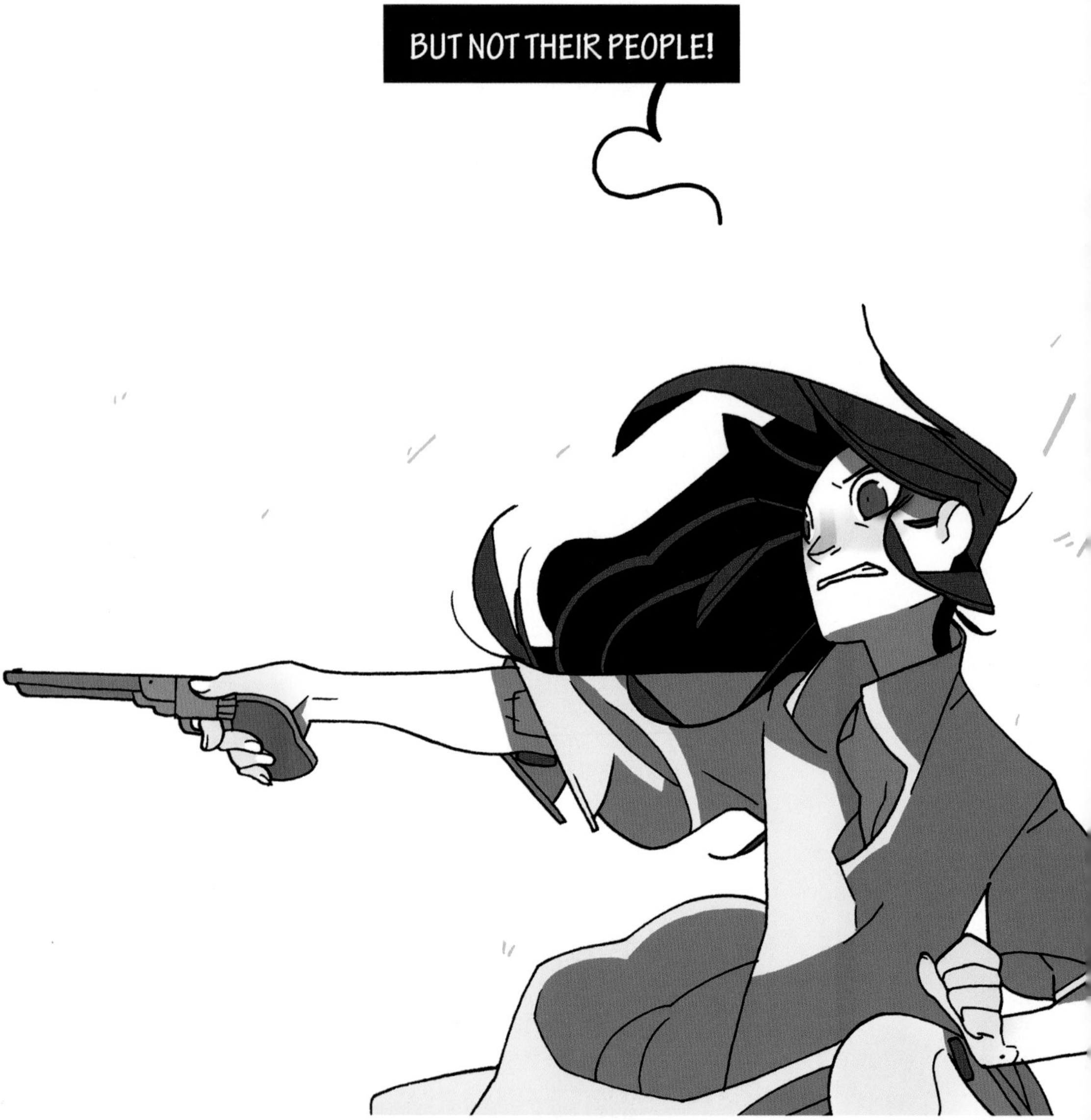
BUT NOT THEIR PEOPLE!

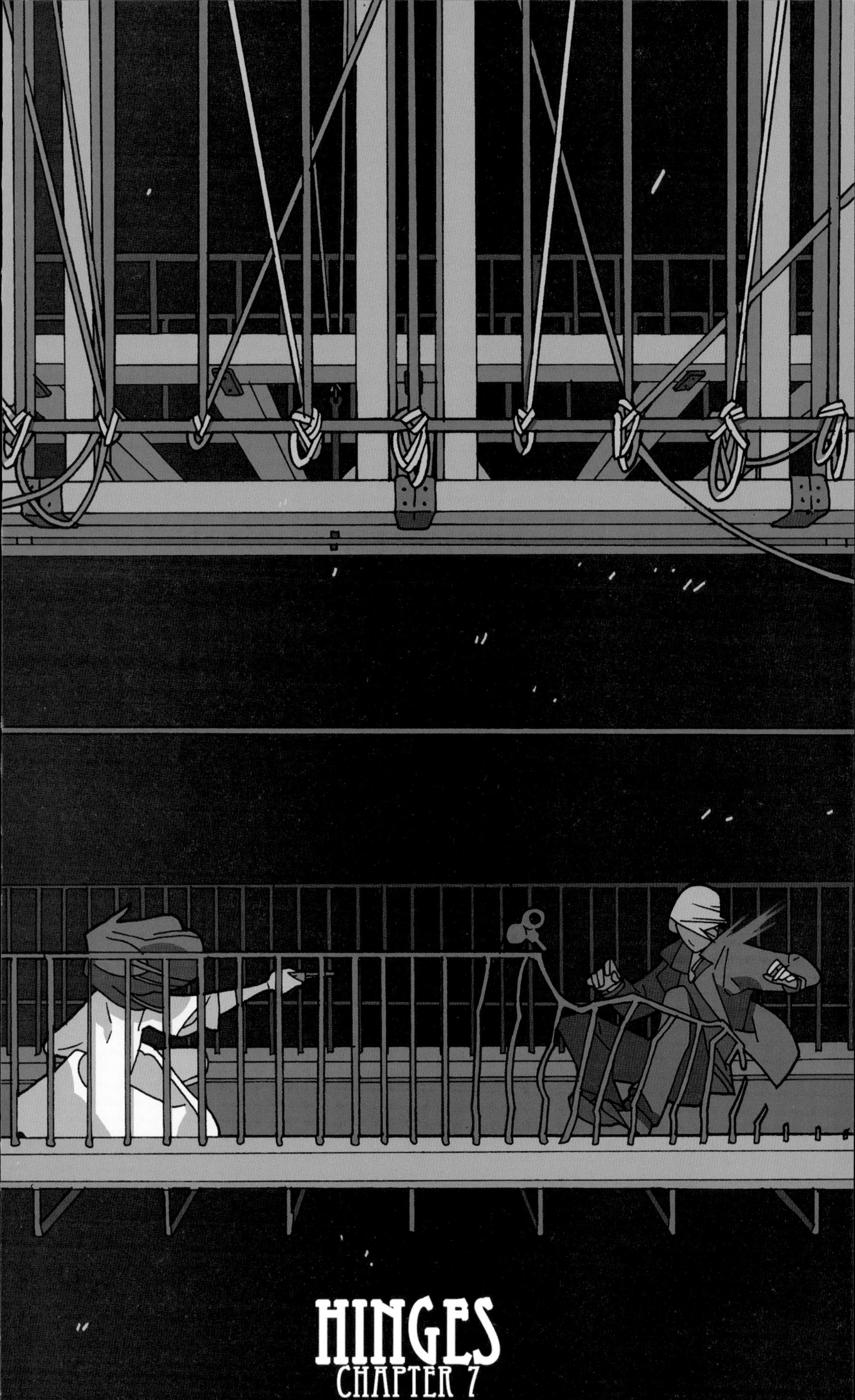
HINGES
CHAPTER 7

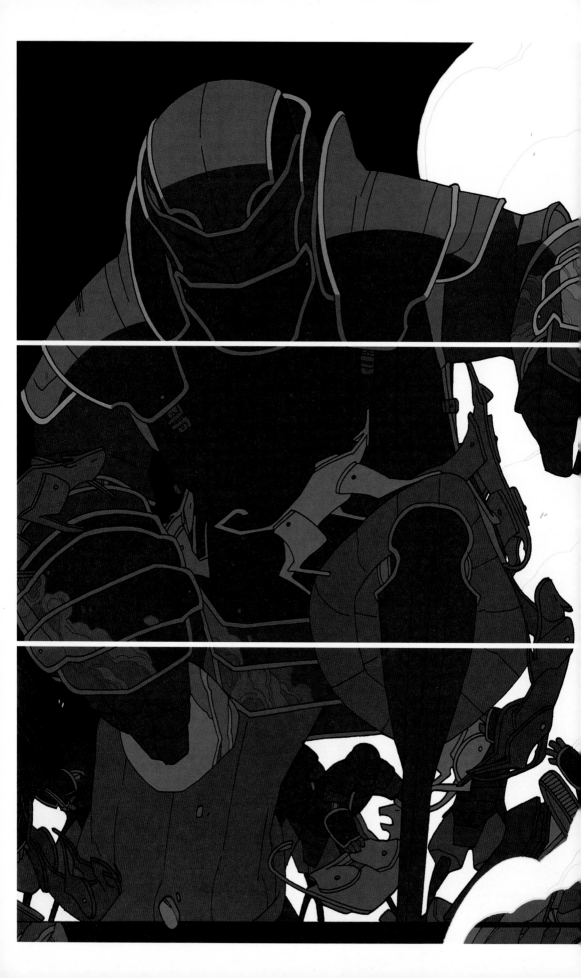

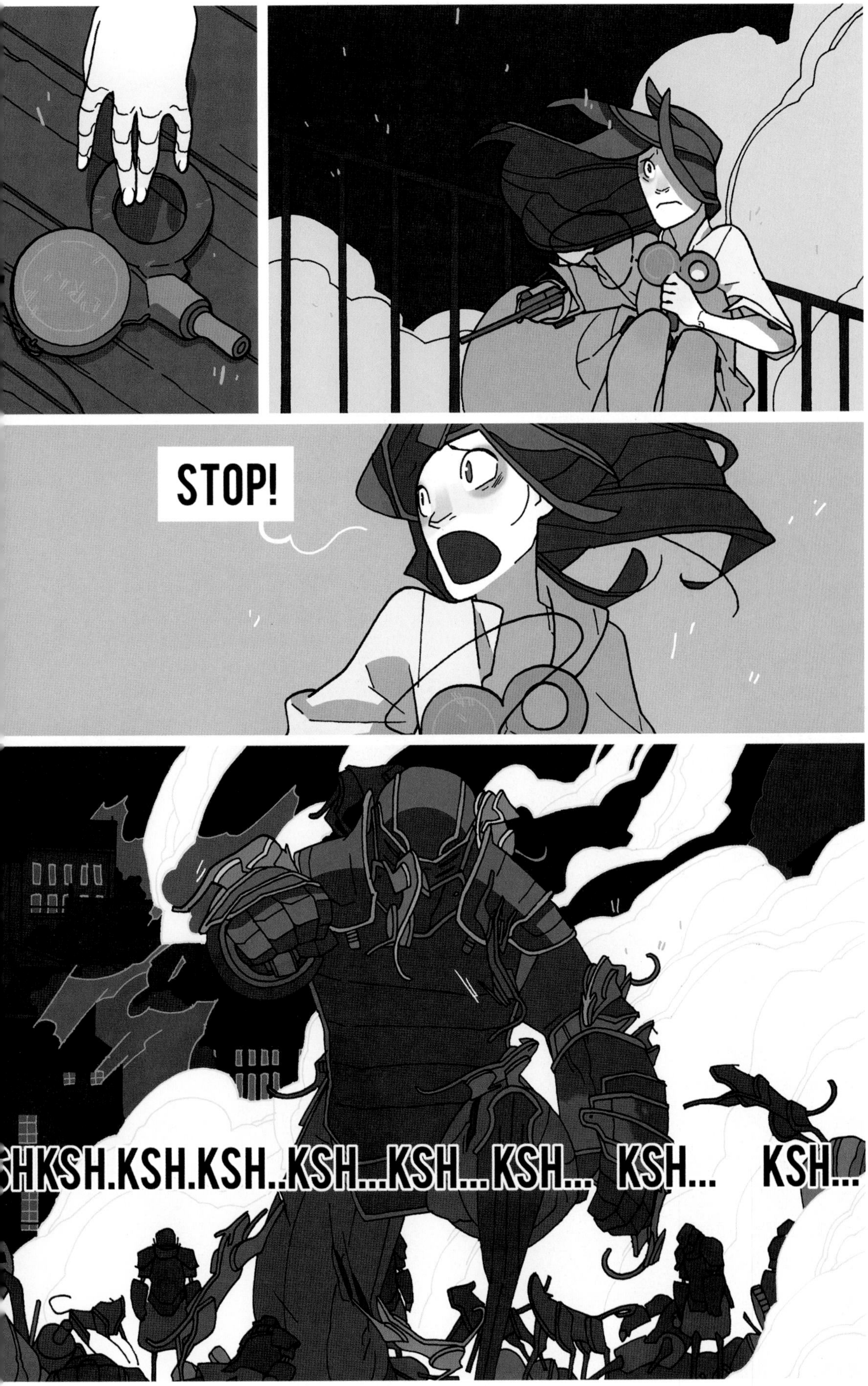
STOP!
SHKSH.KSH.KSH..KSH...KSH...KSH... KSH... KSH...

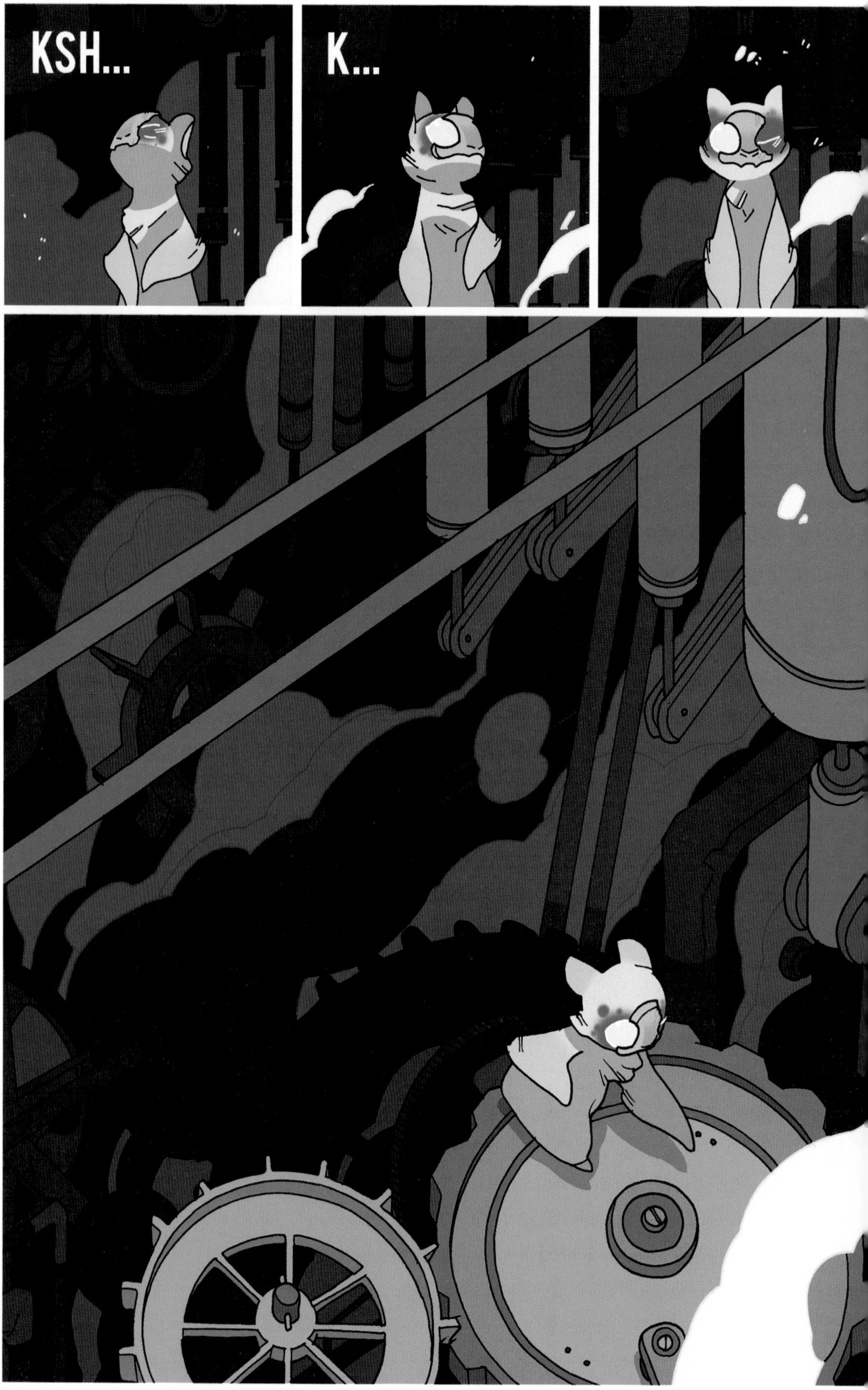
KSH...
K...

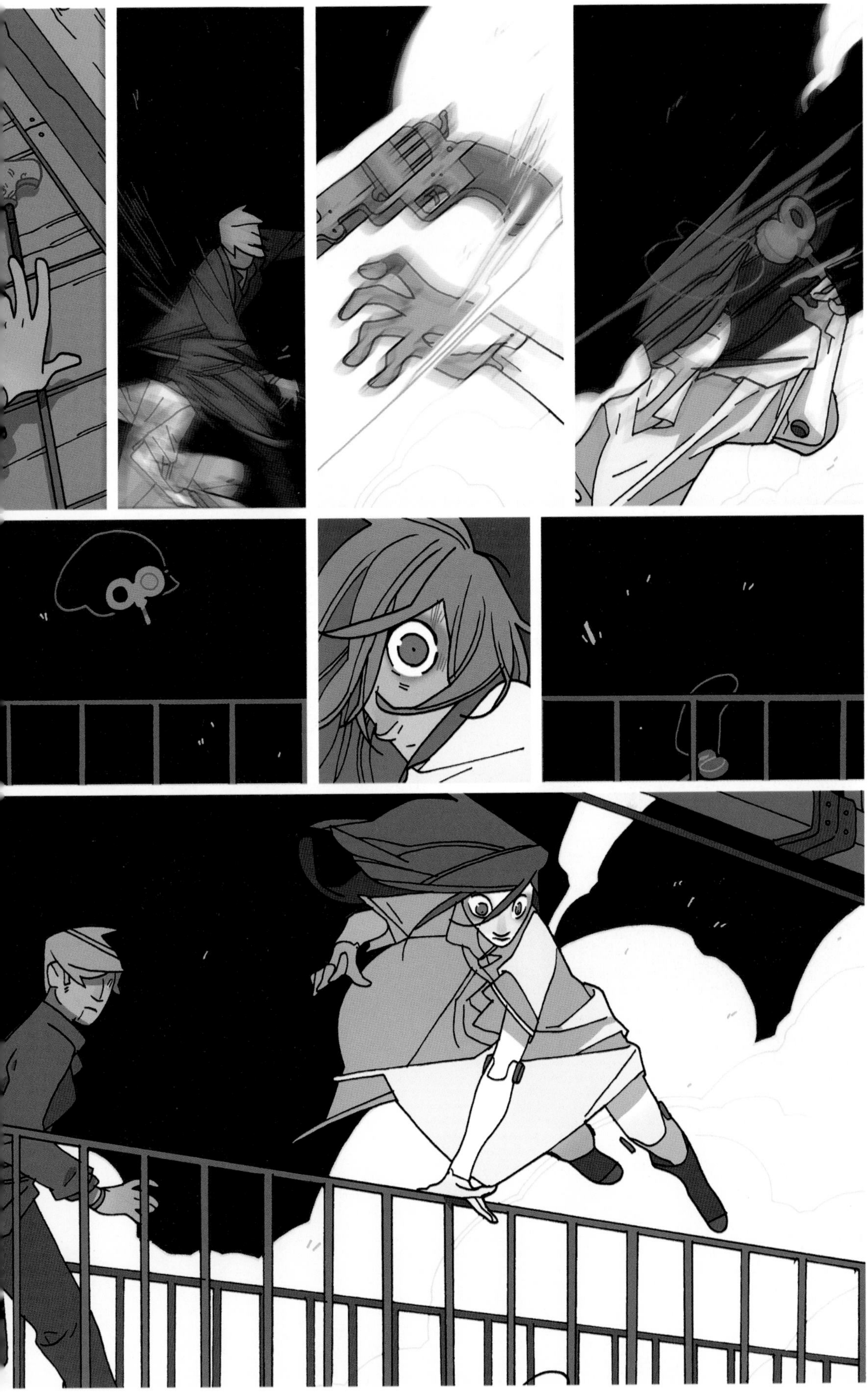

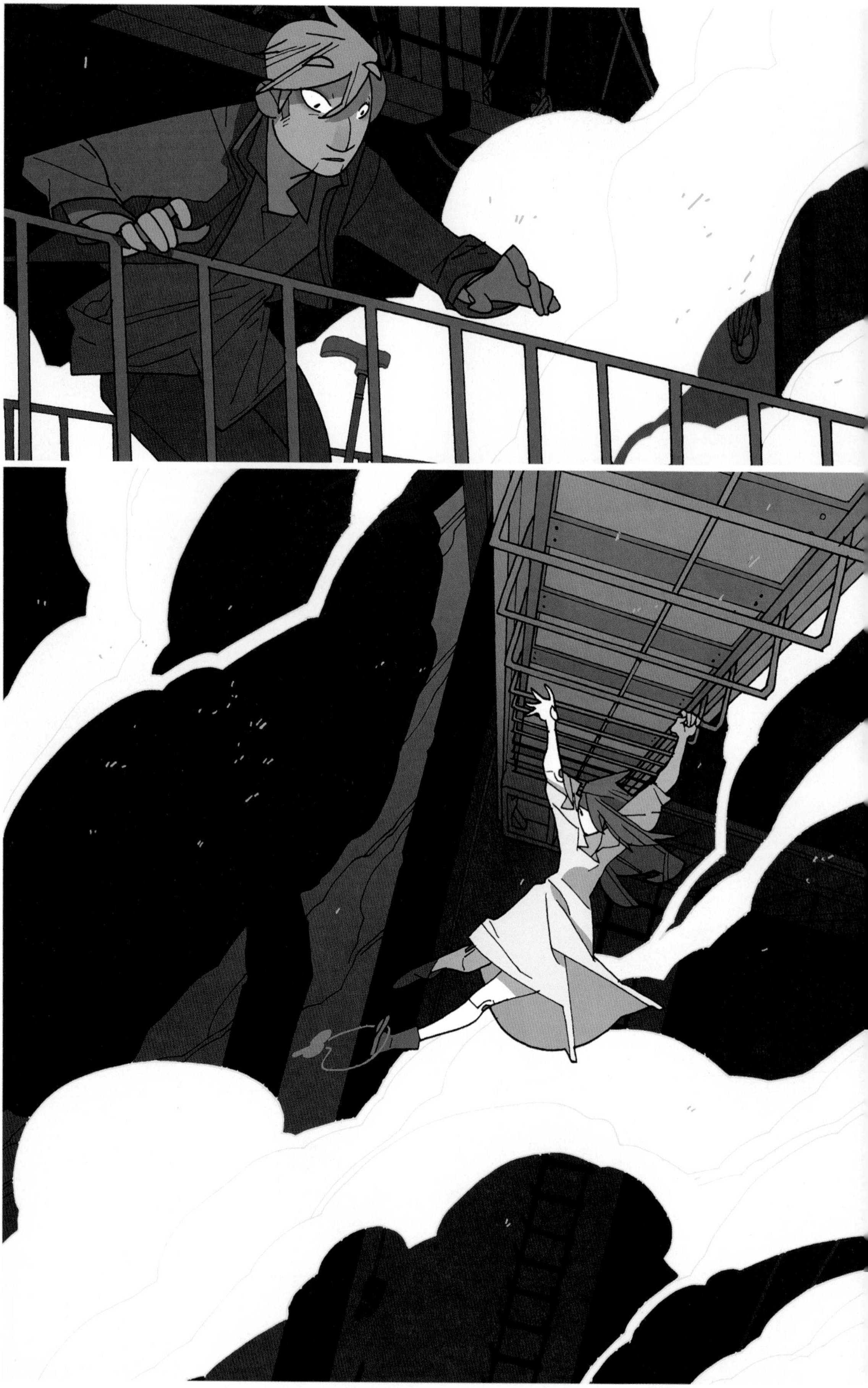

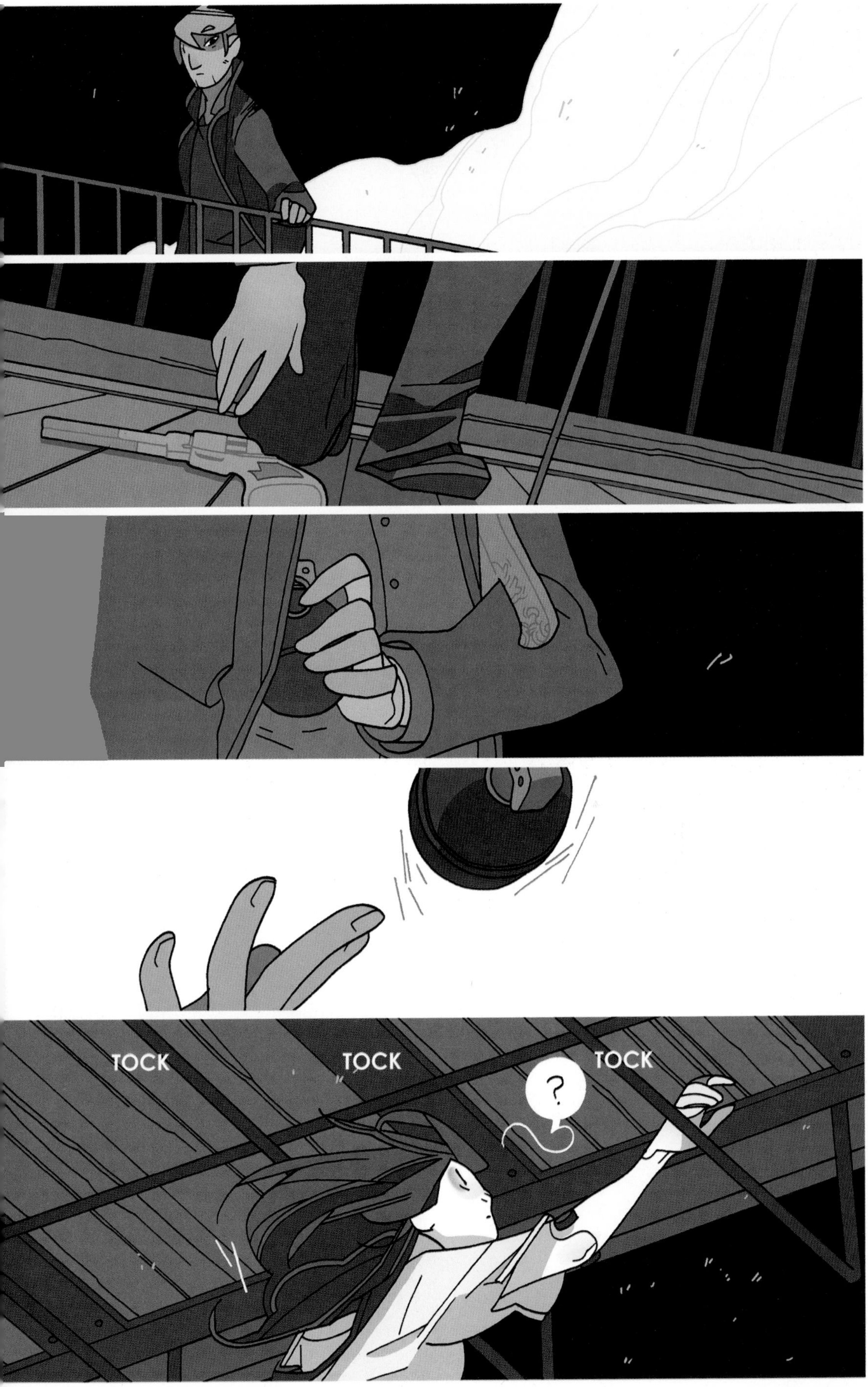
TOCK
TOCK
TOCK
?

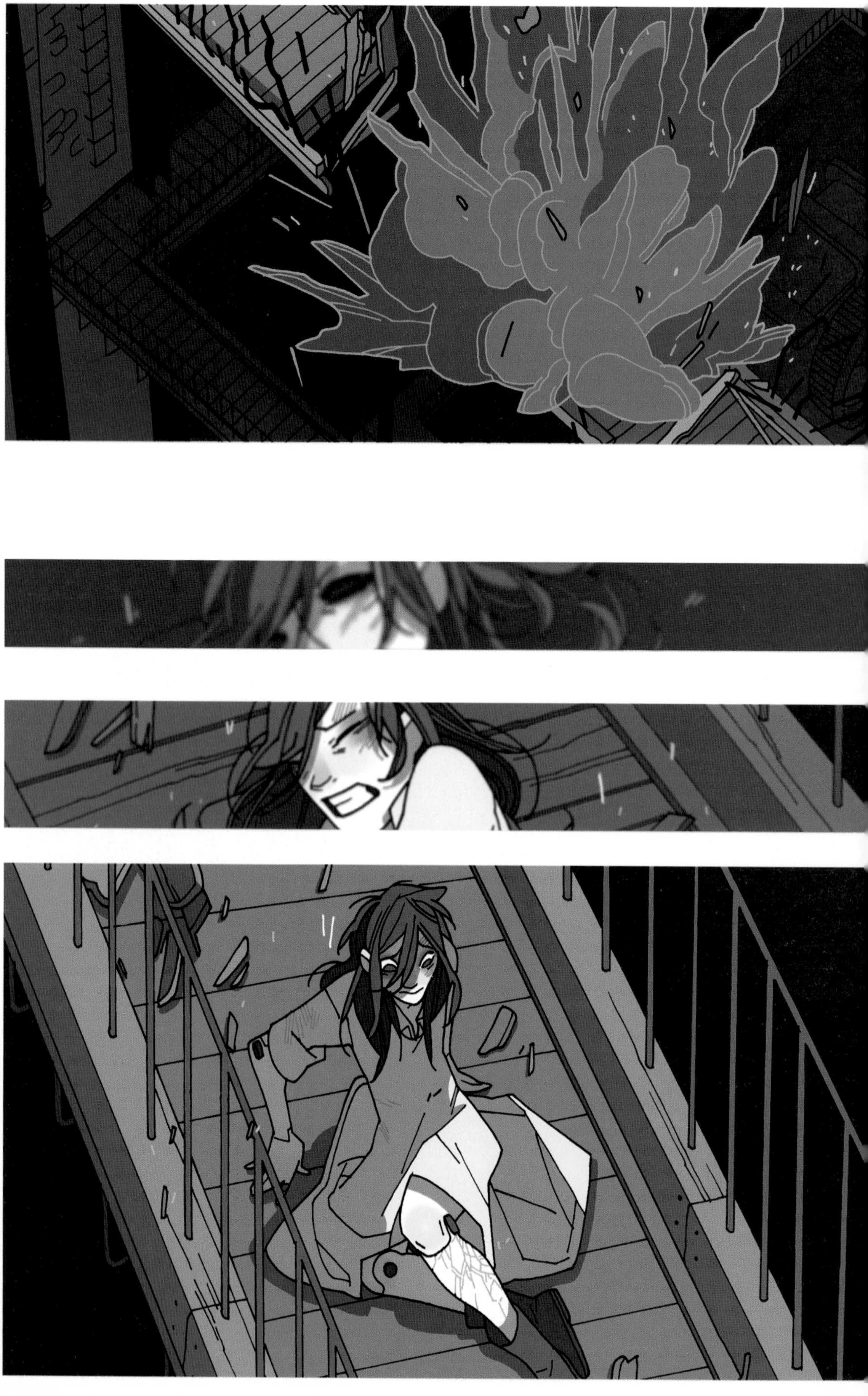

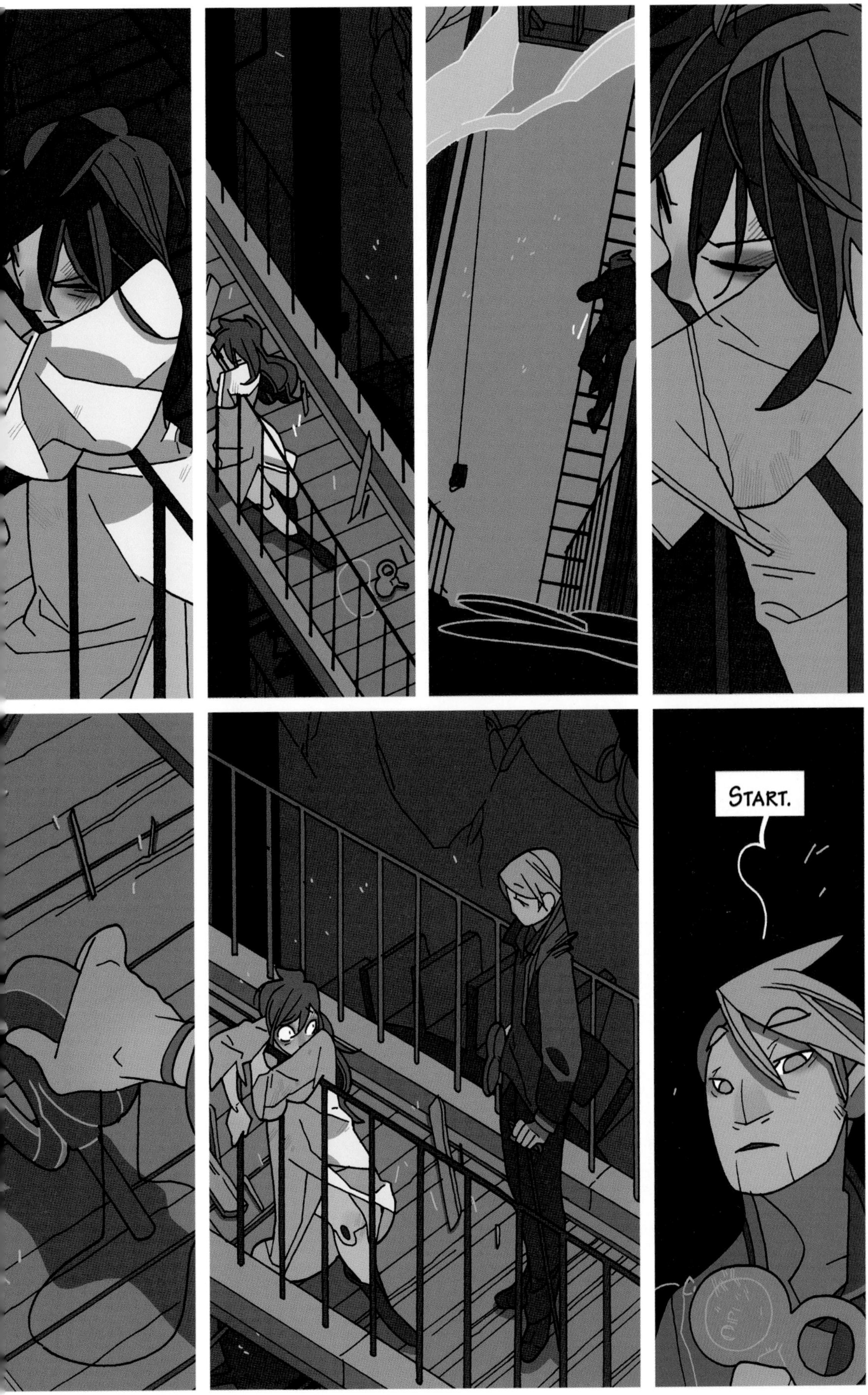
START.

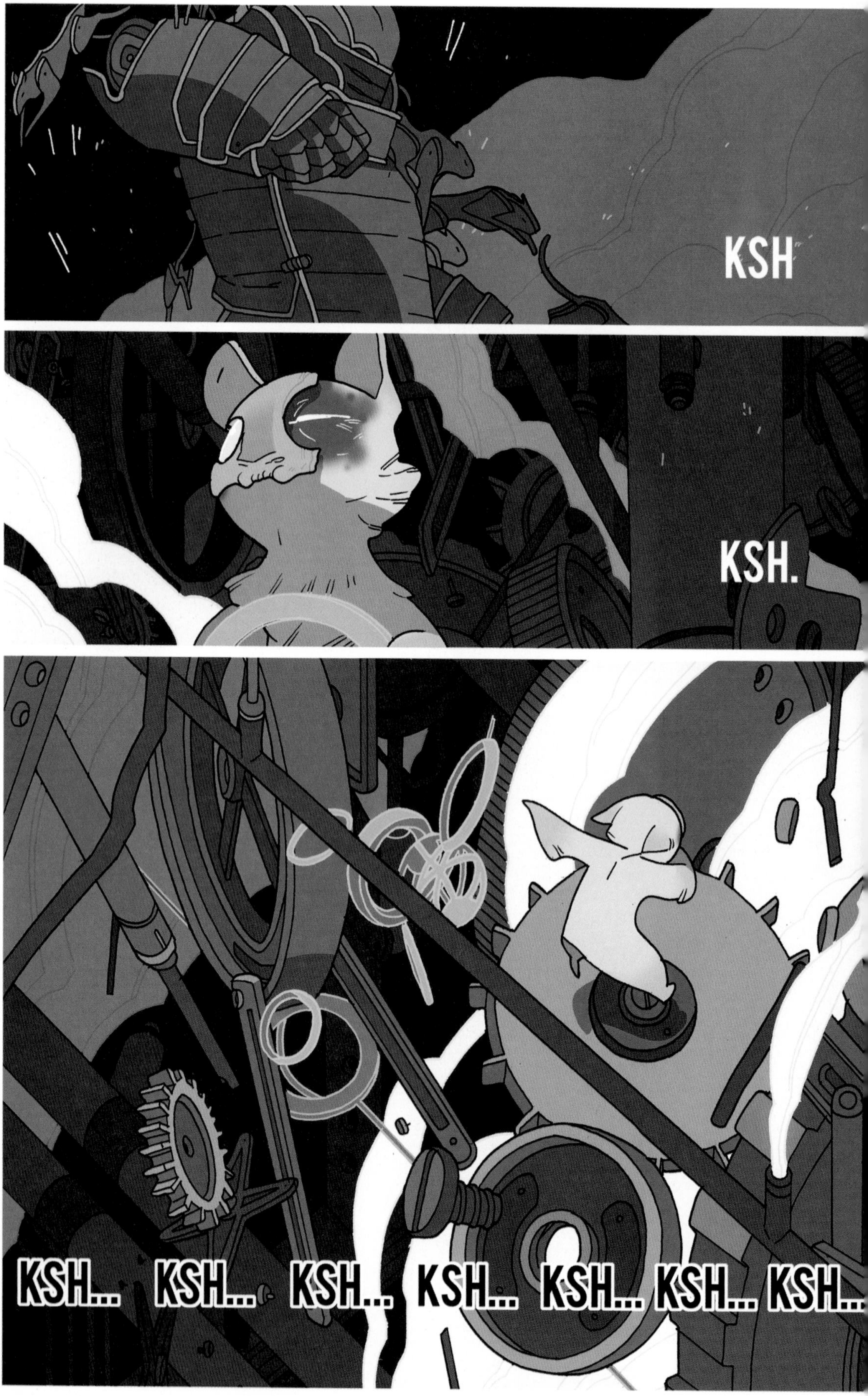
KSH
KSH.
KSH... KSH... KSH... KSH... KSH... KSH... KSH...

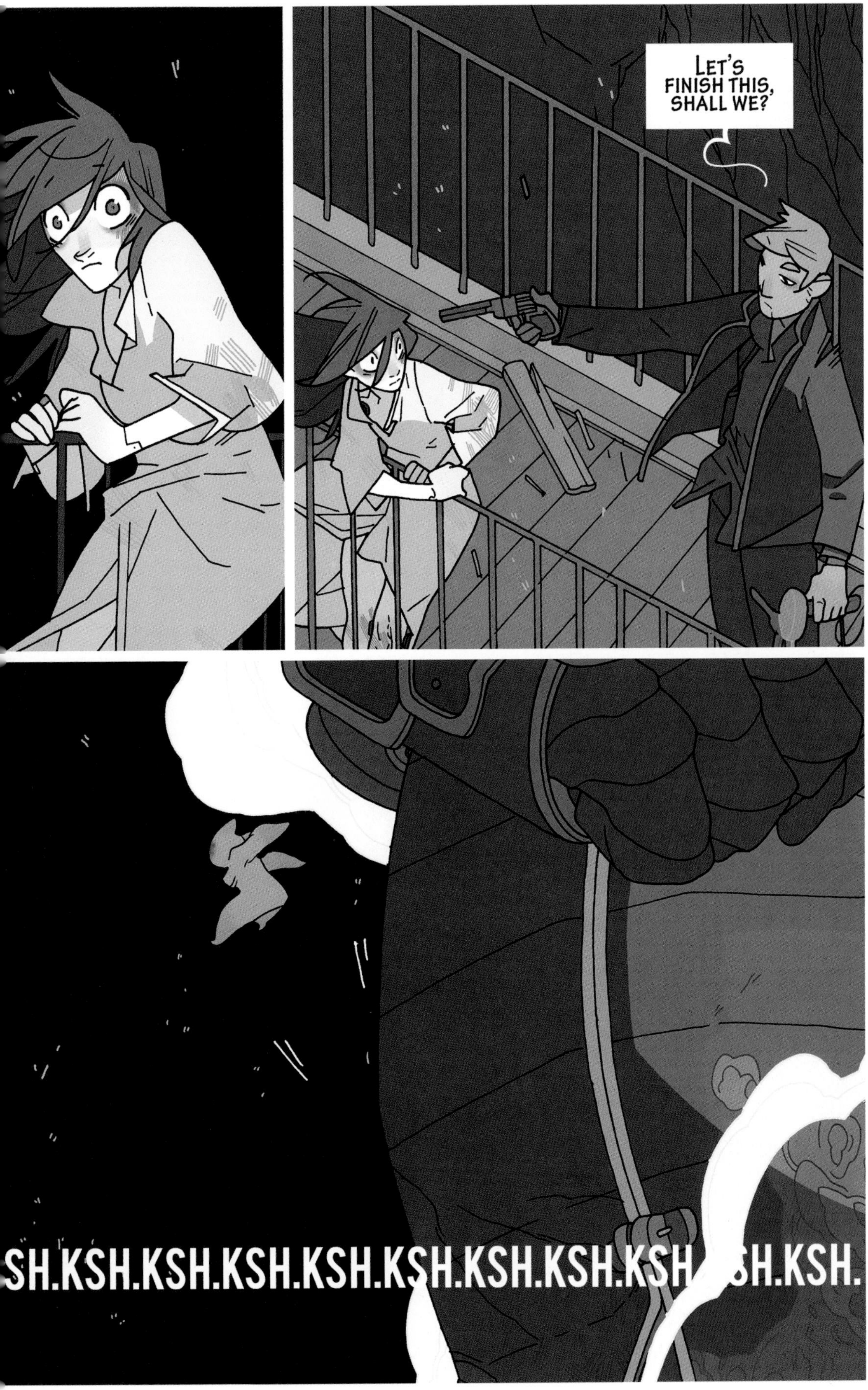
LET'S FINISH THIS, SHALL WE?
SH.KSH.KSH.KSH.KSH.KSH.KSH.KSH.KSH.KSH.KSH.

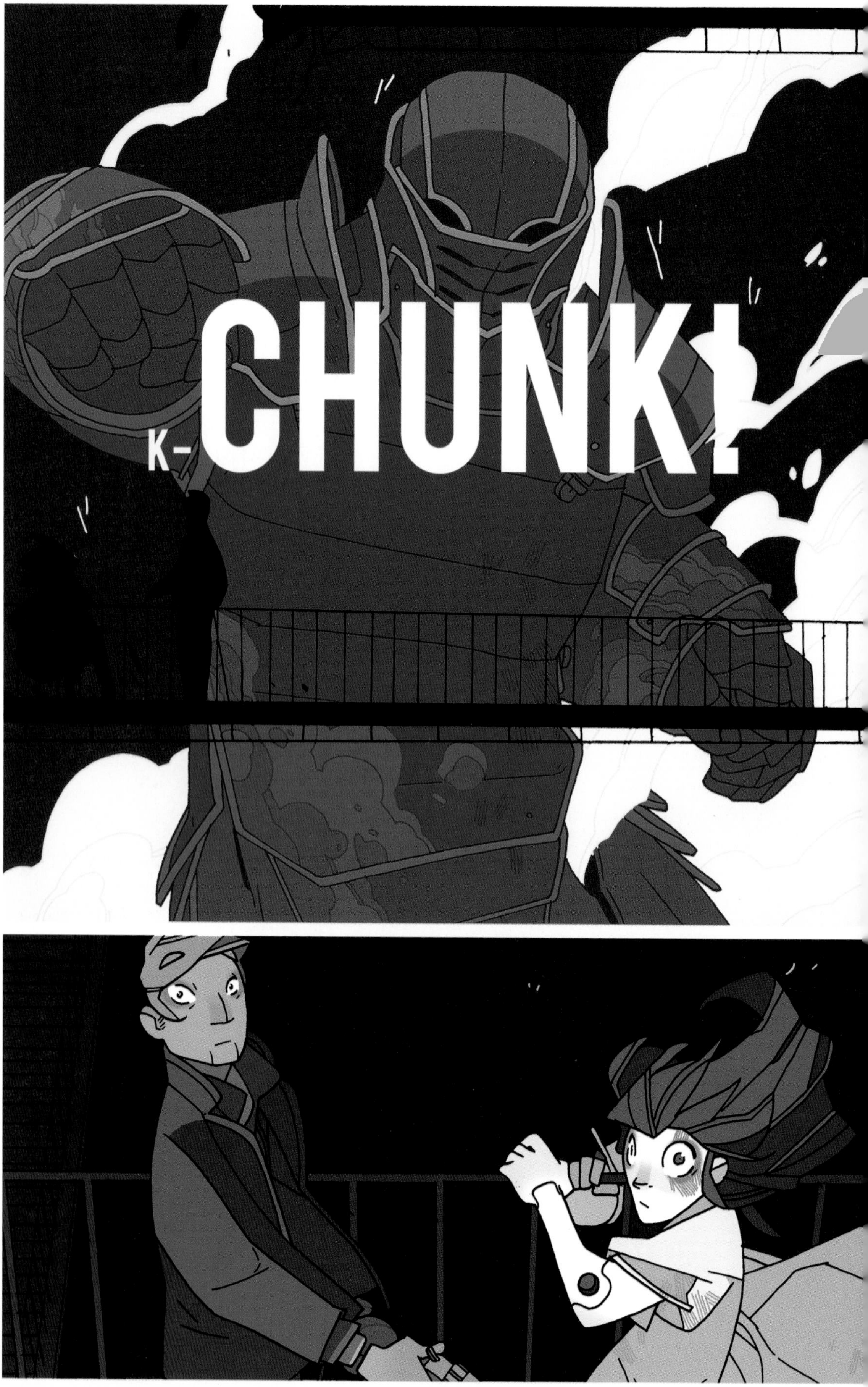
K-CHUNK!

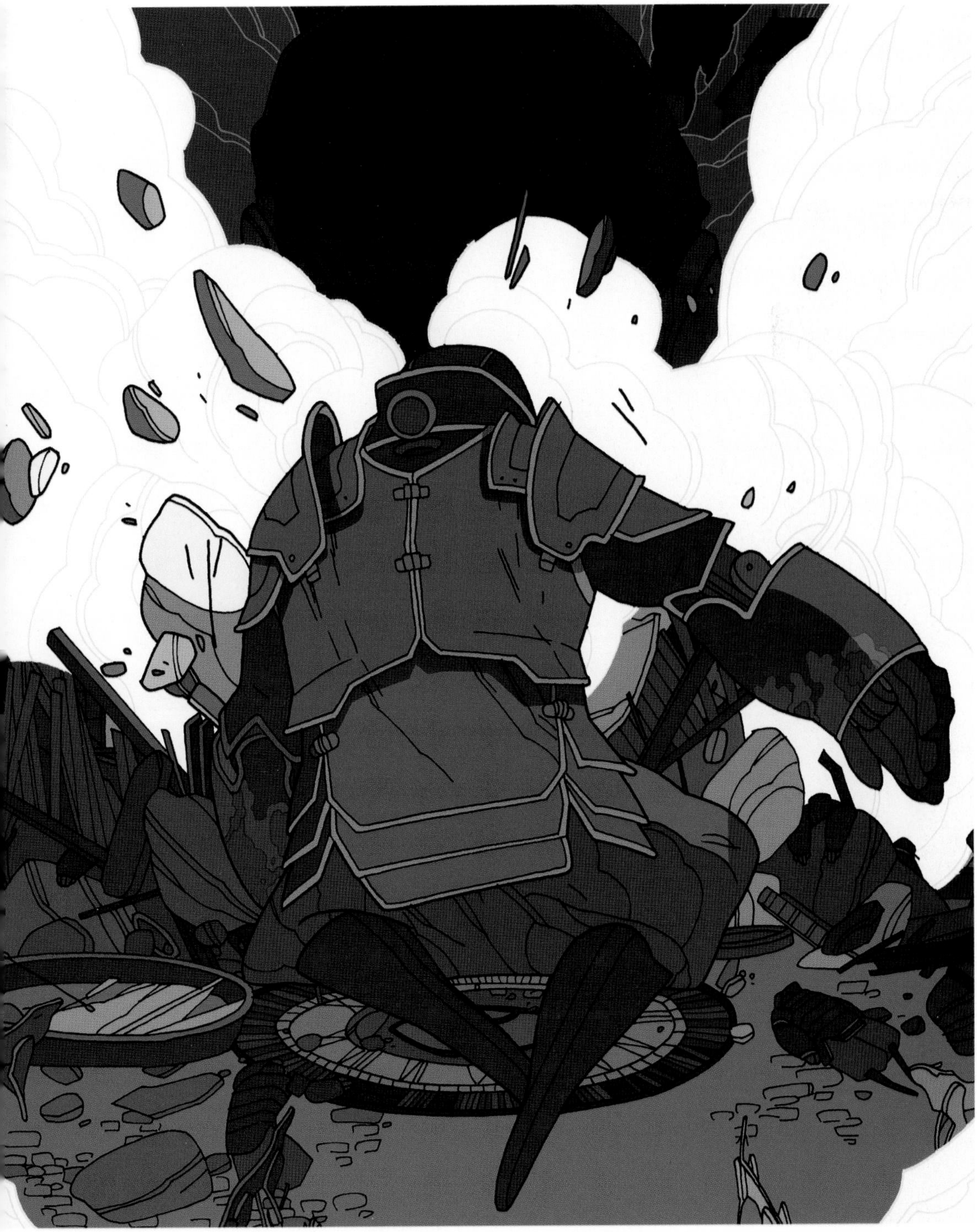

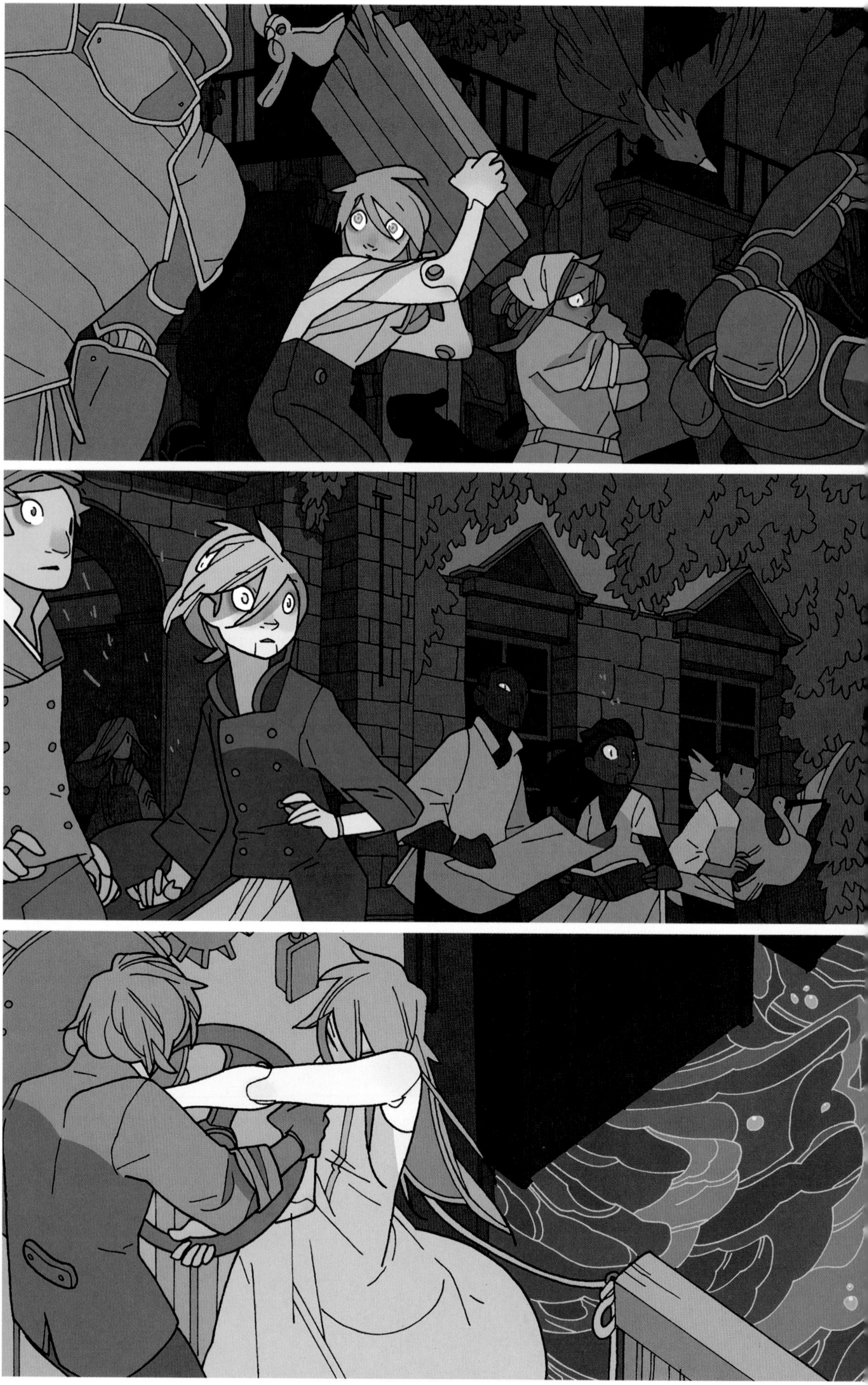

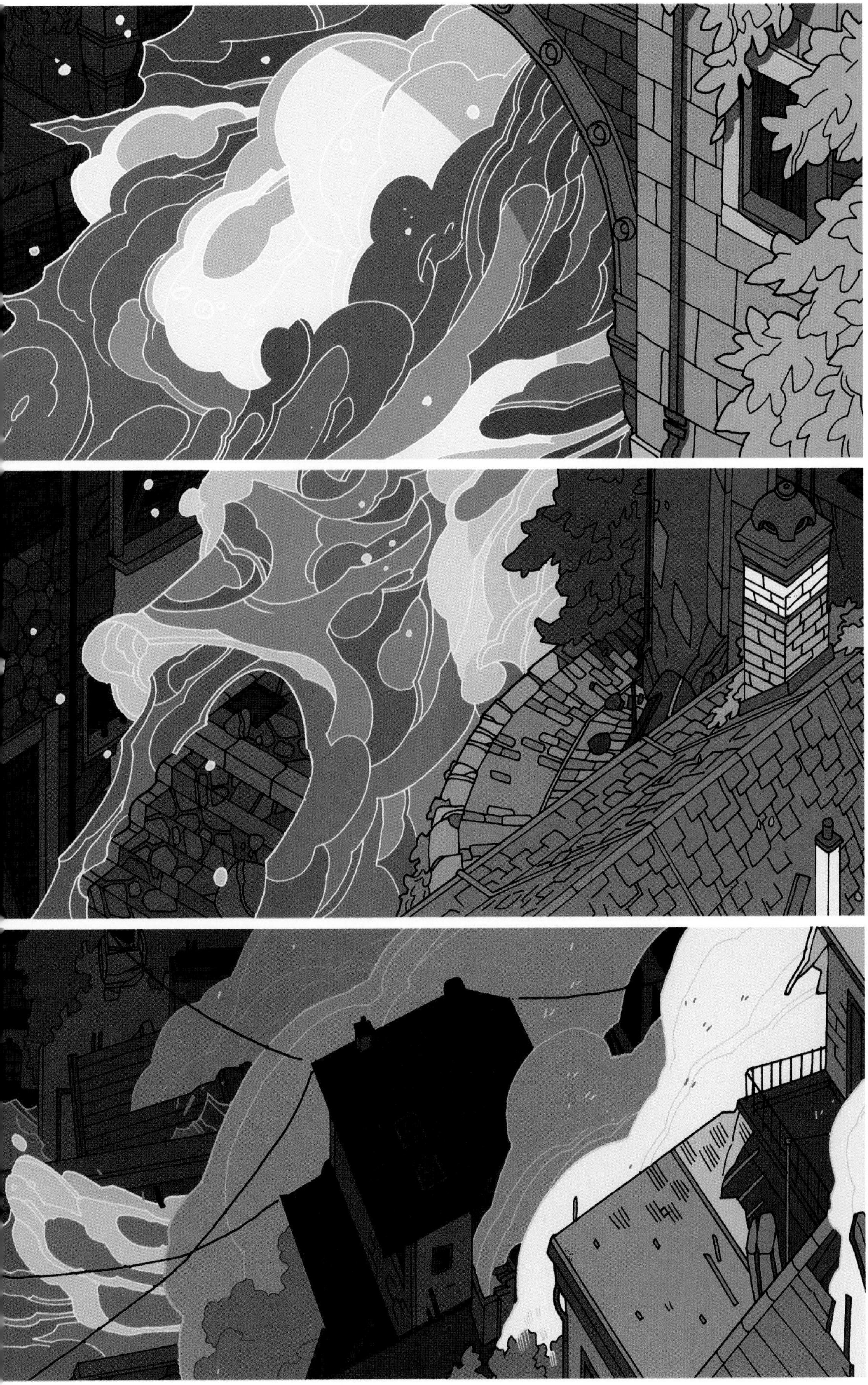

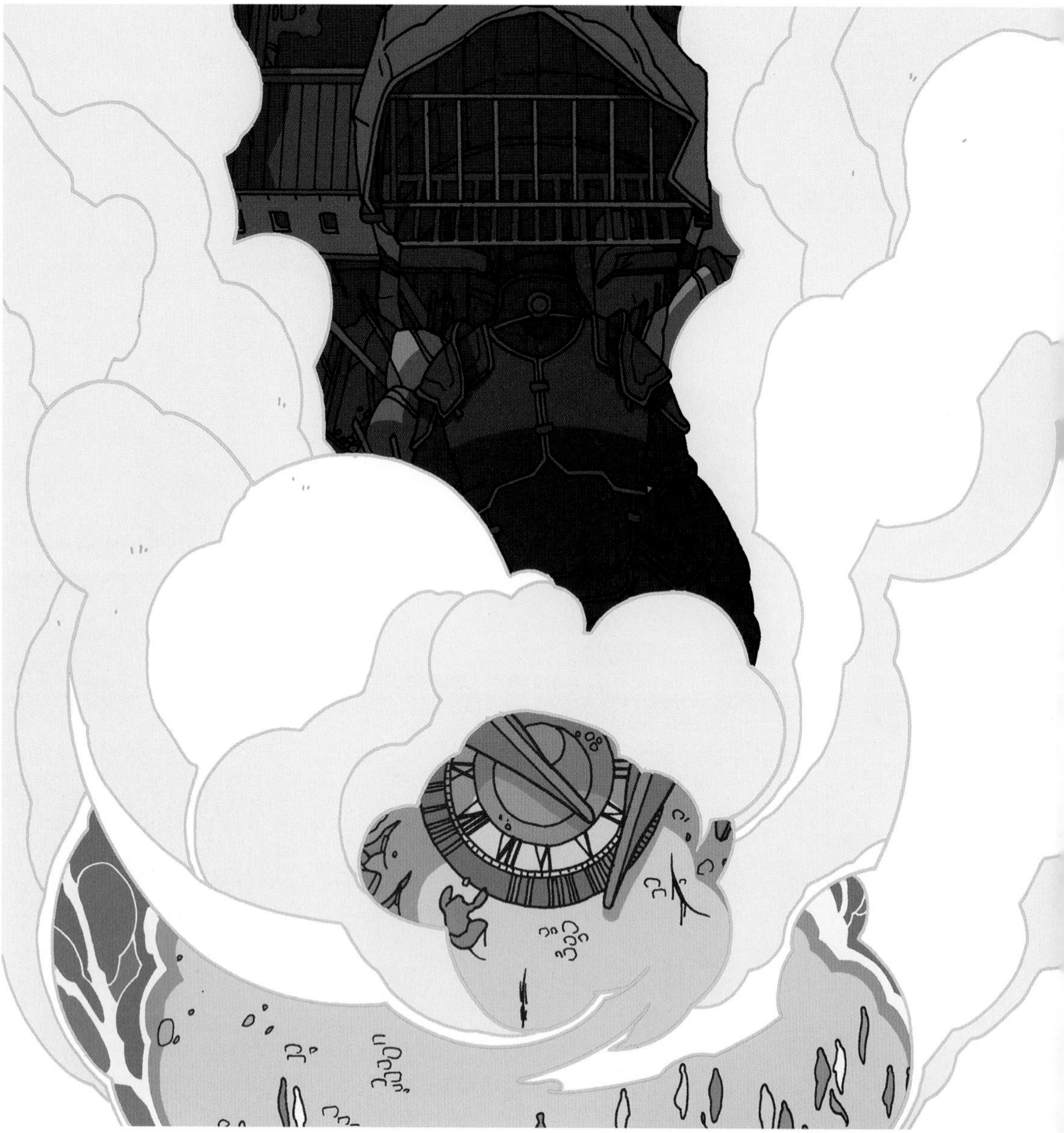
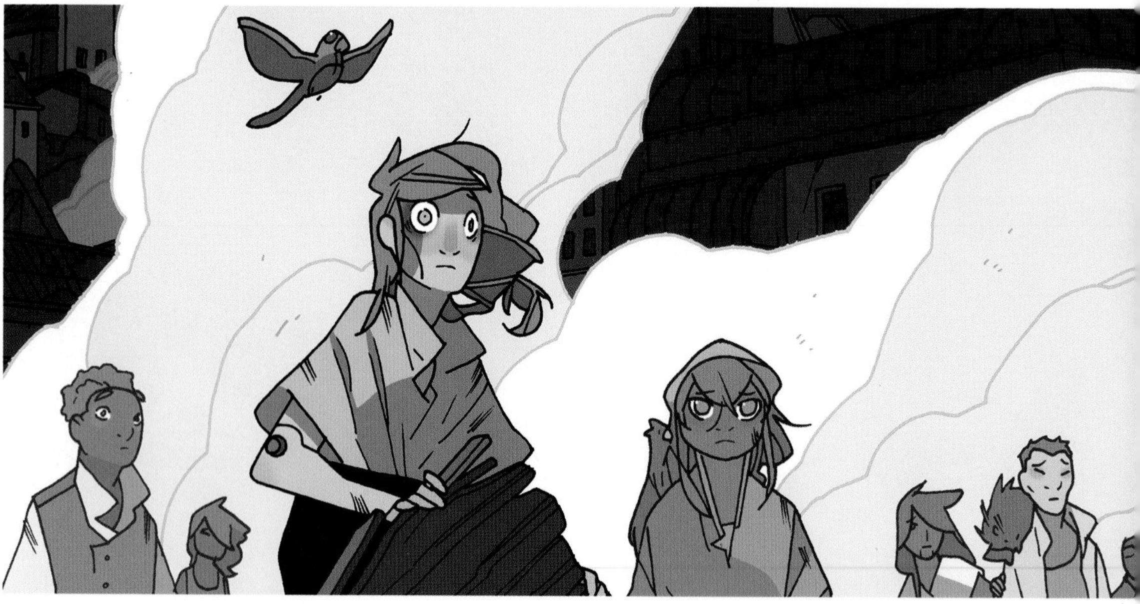

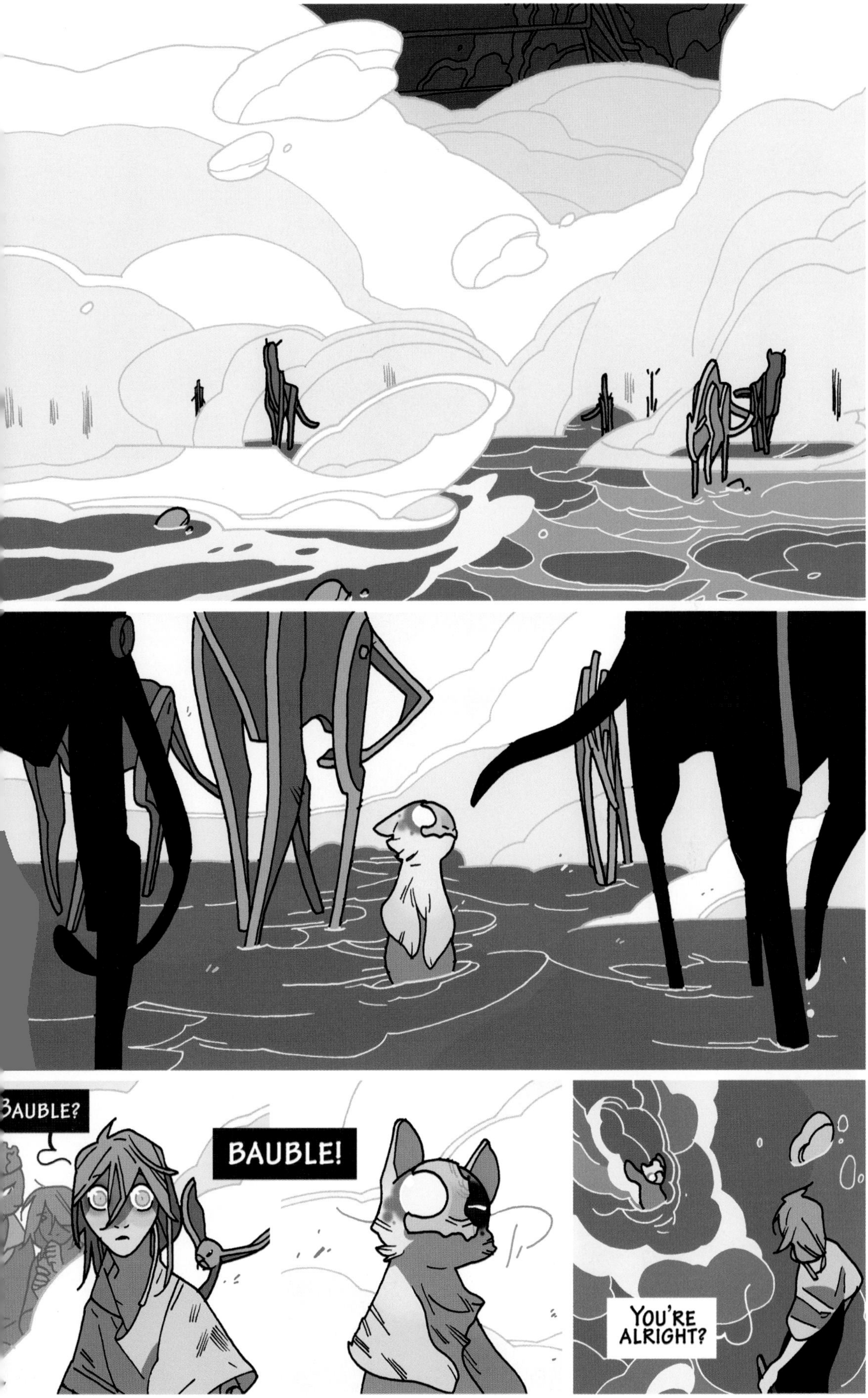
BAUBLE?
BAUBLE!
YOU'RE ALRIGHT?

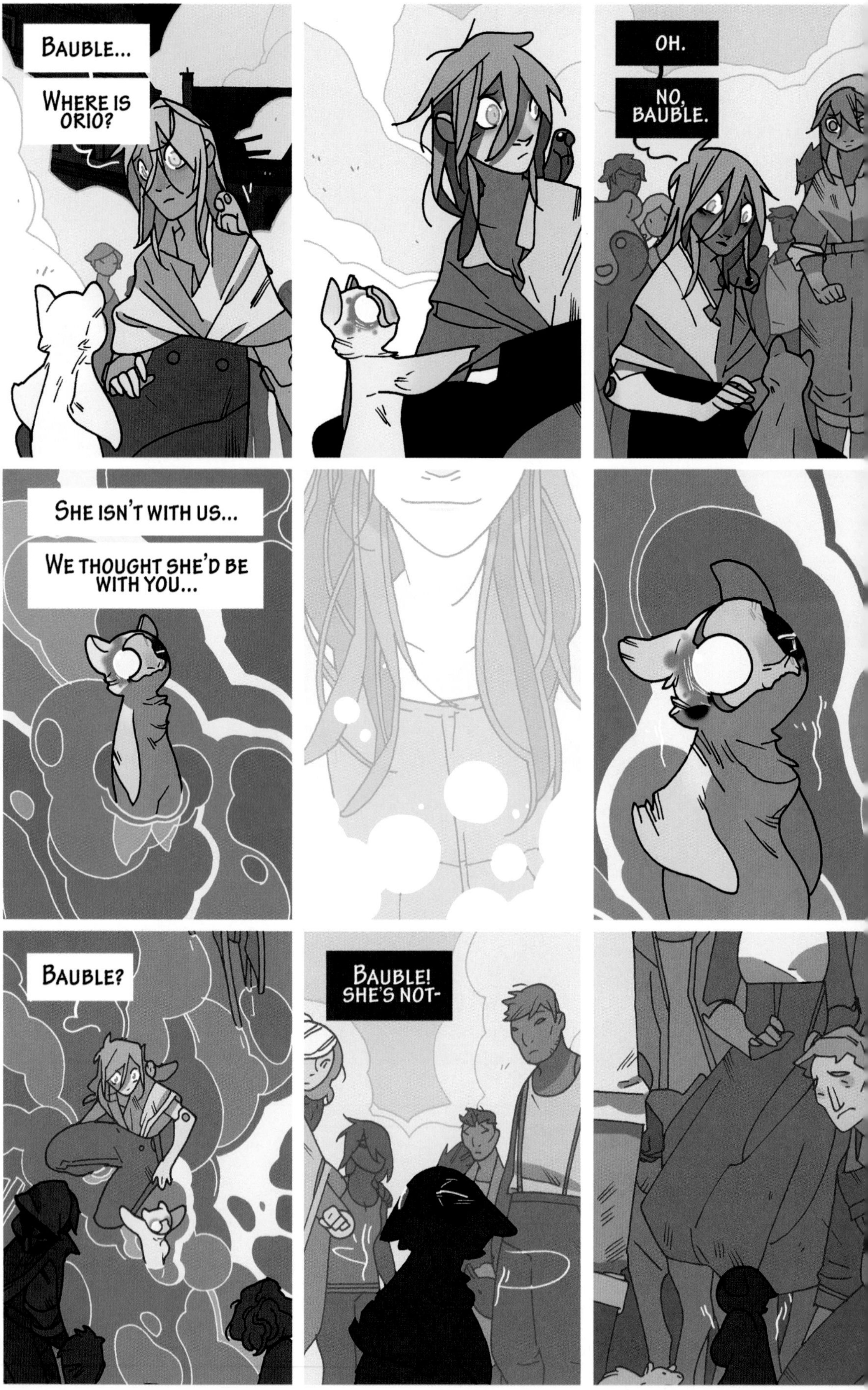
BAUBLE...
WHERE IS ORIO?
OH.
NO, BAUBLE.
SHE ISN'T WITH US...
WE THOUGHT SHE'D BE WITH YOU...
BAUBLE?
BAUBLE! SHE'S NOT-

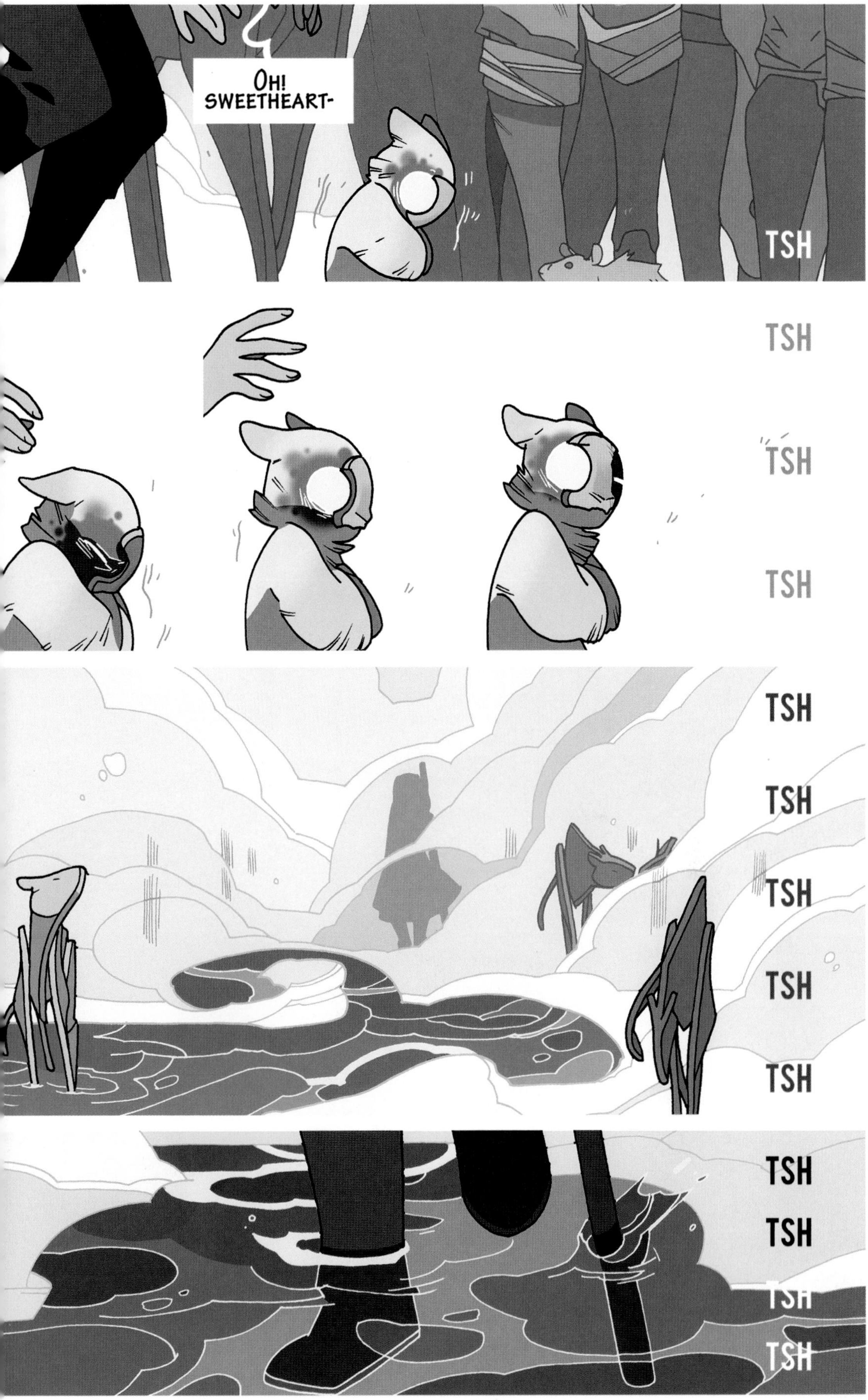
OH!
SWEETHEART-
TSH
TSH
TSH
TSH
TSH
TSH
TSH
TSH
TSH
TSH
TSH
TSH
TSH

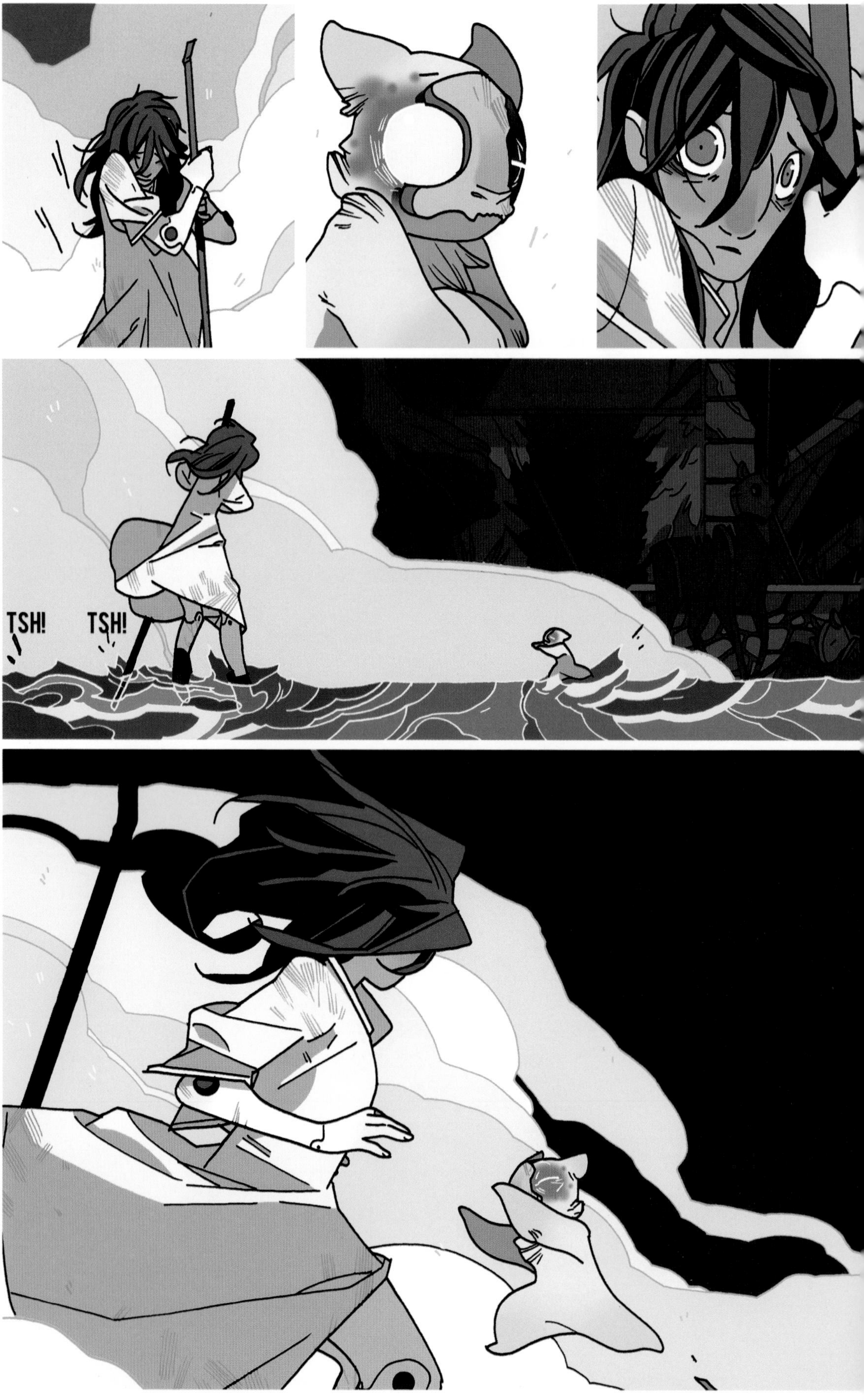
TSH!
TSH!

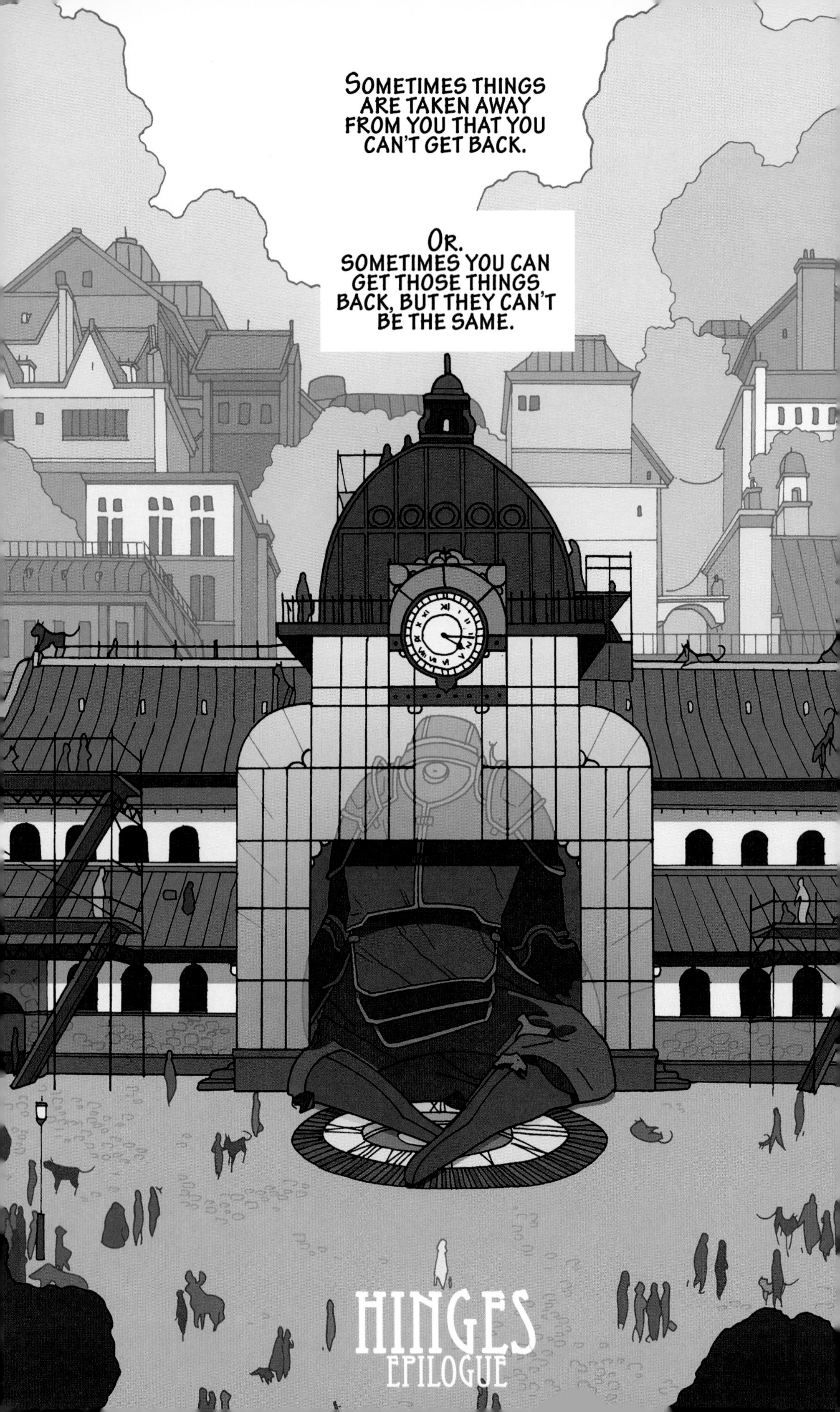
SOMETIMES THINGS ARE TAKEN AWAY FROM YOU THAT YOU CAN'T GET BACK.
OR. SOMETIMES YOU CAN GET THOSE THINGS BACK, BUT THEY CAN'T BE THE SAME.
HINGES
EPILOGUE

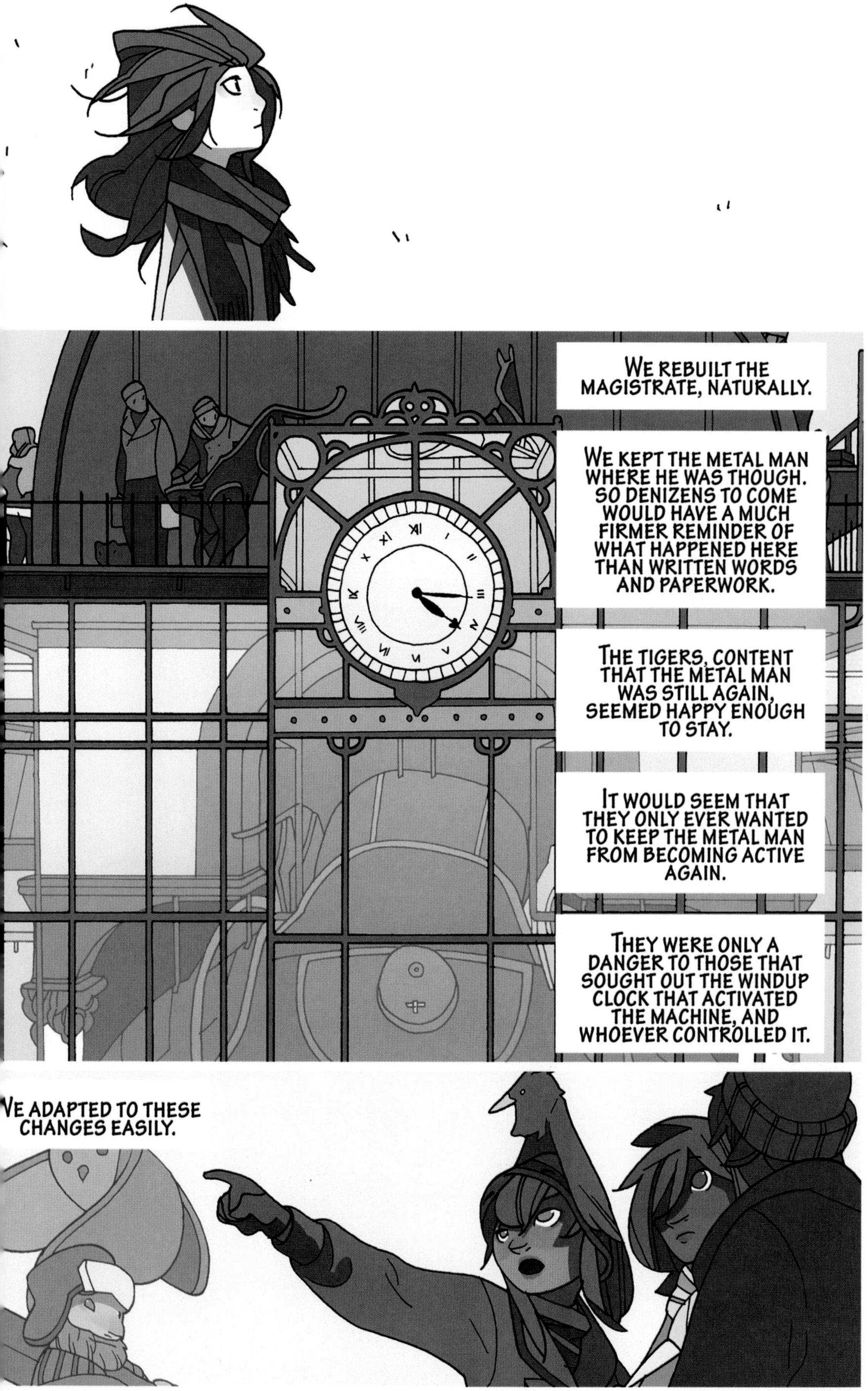
WE REBUILT THE MAGISTRATE, NATURALLY.
WE KEPT THE METAL MAN WHERE HE WAS THOUGH. SO DENIZENS TO COME WOULD HAVE A MUCH FIRMER REMINDER OF WHAT HAPPENED HERE THAN WRITTEN WORDS AND PAPERWORK.
THE TIGERS, CONTENT THAT THE METAL MAN WAS STILL AGAIN, SEEMED HAPPY ENOUGH TO STAY.
IT WOULD SEEM THAT THEY ONLY EVER WANTED TO KEEP THE METAL MAN FROM BECOMING ACTIVE AGAIN.
THEY WERE ONLY A DANGER TO THOSE THAT SOUGHT OUT THE WINDUP CLOCK THAT ACTIVATED THE MACHINE, AND WHOEVER CONTROLLED IT.
VE ADAPTED TO THESE CHANGES EASILY.

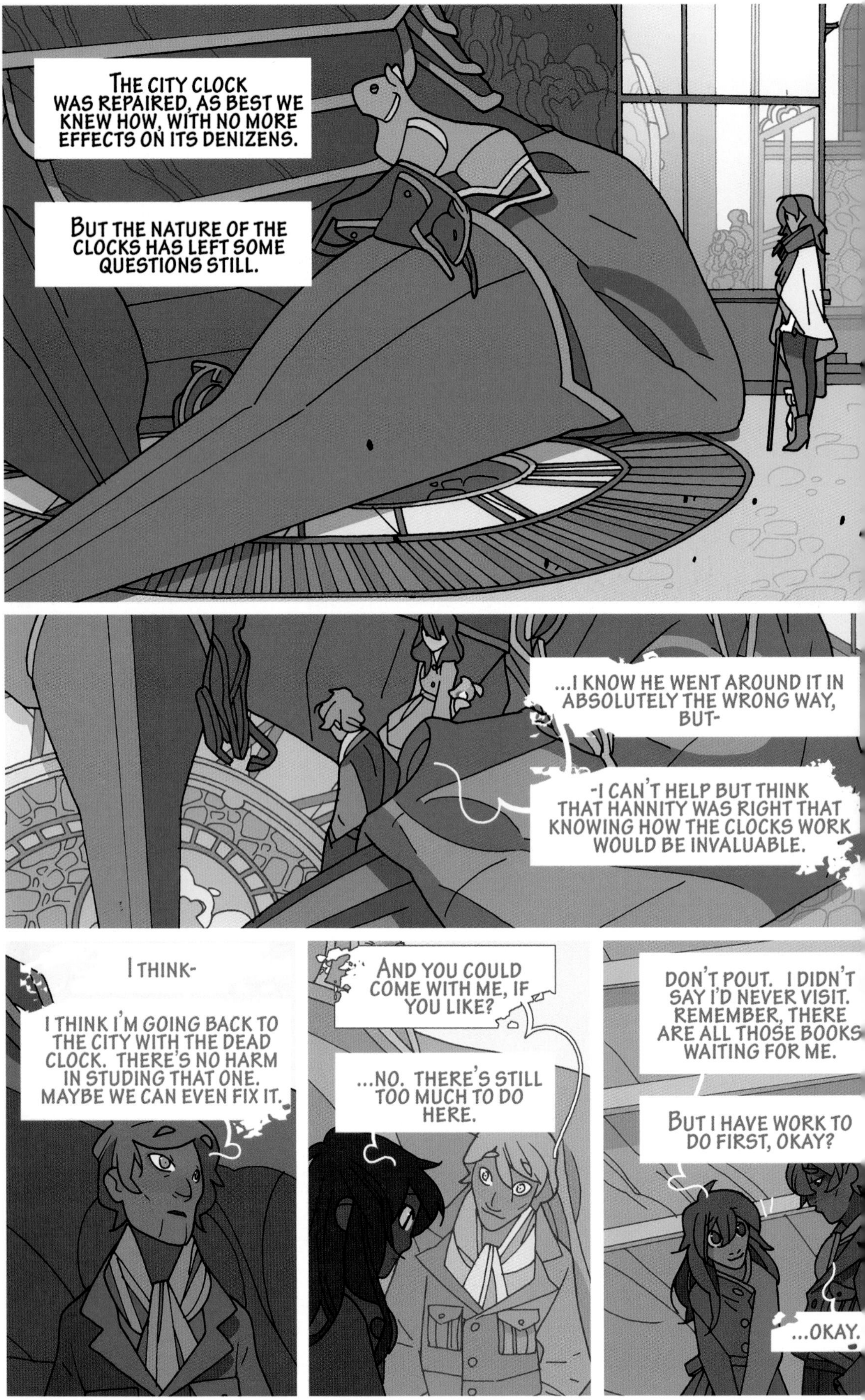
The city clock was repaired, as best we knew how, with no more effects on its denizens.
But the nature of the clocks has left some questions still.
...I know he went around it in absolutely the wrong way, but-
-I can't help but think that Hannity was right that knowing how the clocks work would be invaluable.
I think-
I think I'm going back to the city with the dead clock. There's no harm in studing that one. Maybe we can even fix it.
And you could come with me, if you like?
...No. There's still too much to do here.
Don't pout. I didn't say I'd never visit. Remember, there are all those books waiting for me.
But I have work to do first, okay?
...Okay.

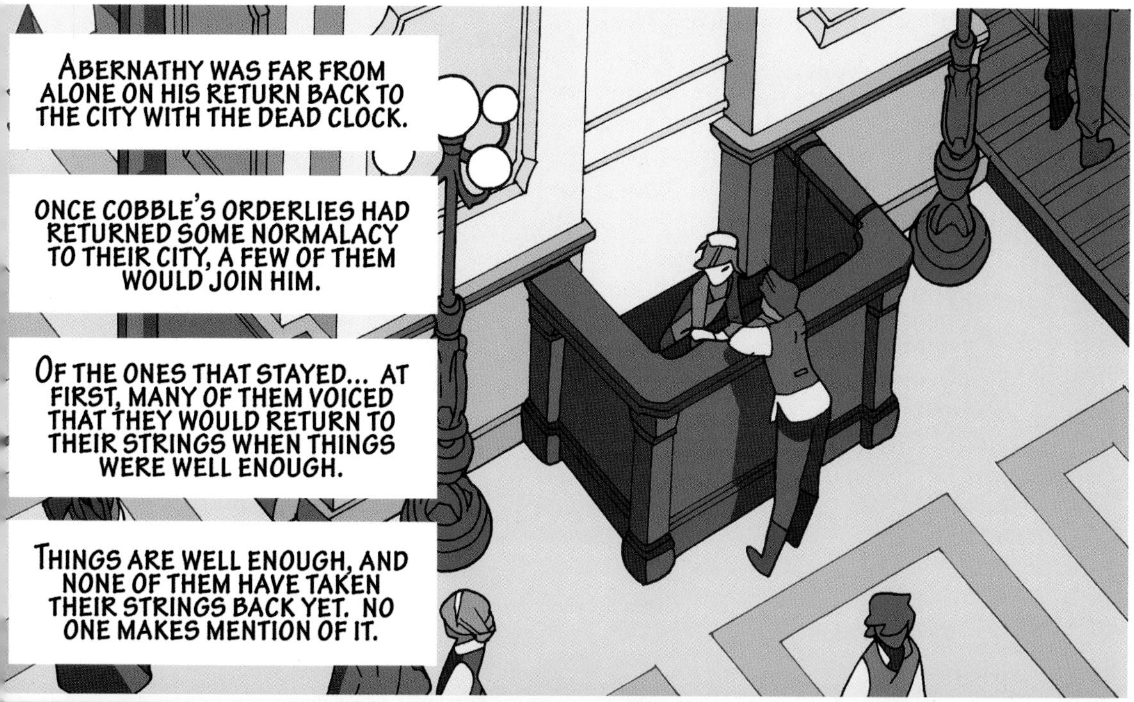
ABERNATHY WAS FAR FROM ALONE ON HIS RETURN BACK TO THE CITY WITH THE DEAD CLOCK.
ONCE COBBLE'S ORDERLIES HAD RETURNED SOME NORMALACY TO THEIR CITY, A FEW OF THEM WOULD JOIN HIM.
OF THE ONES THAT STAYED... AT FIRST, MANY OF THEM VOICED THAT THEY WOULD RETURN TO THEIR STRINGS WHEN THINGS WERE WELL ENOUGH.
THINGS ARE WELL ENOUGH, AND NONE OF THEM HAVE TAKEN THEIR STRINGS BACK YET. NO ONE MAKES MENTION OF IT.

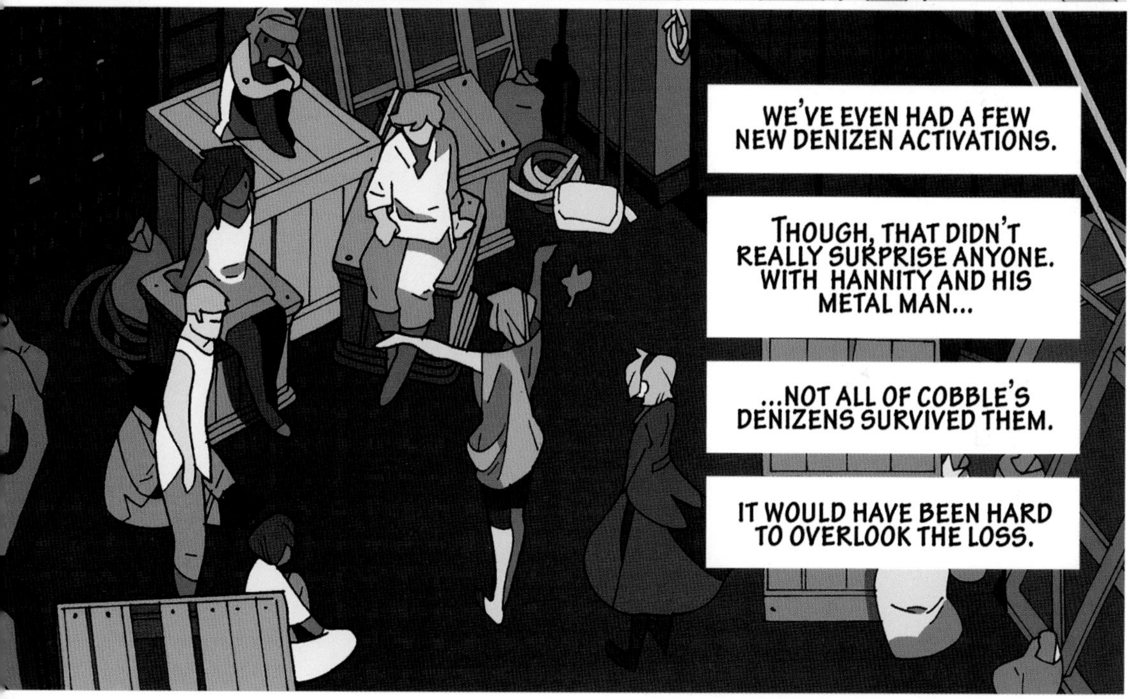
WE'VE EVEN HAD A FEW NEW DENIZEN ACTIVATIONS.
THOUGH, THAT DIDN'T REALLY SURPRISE ANYONE. WITH HANNITY AND HIS METAL MAN...
...NOT ALL OF COBBLE'S DENIZENS SURVIVED THEM.
IT WOULD HAVE BEEN HARD TO OVERLOOK THE LOSS.

WE NEVER FOUND ALL OF HANNITY.

EVERTHING THAT HAPPENED-
EVERYTHING THAT HAPPENS-

-HAS ITS COSTS.

NO.

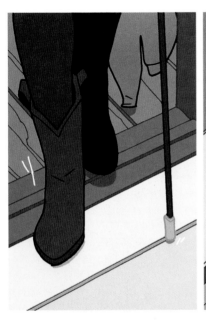

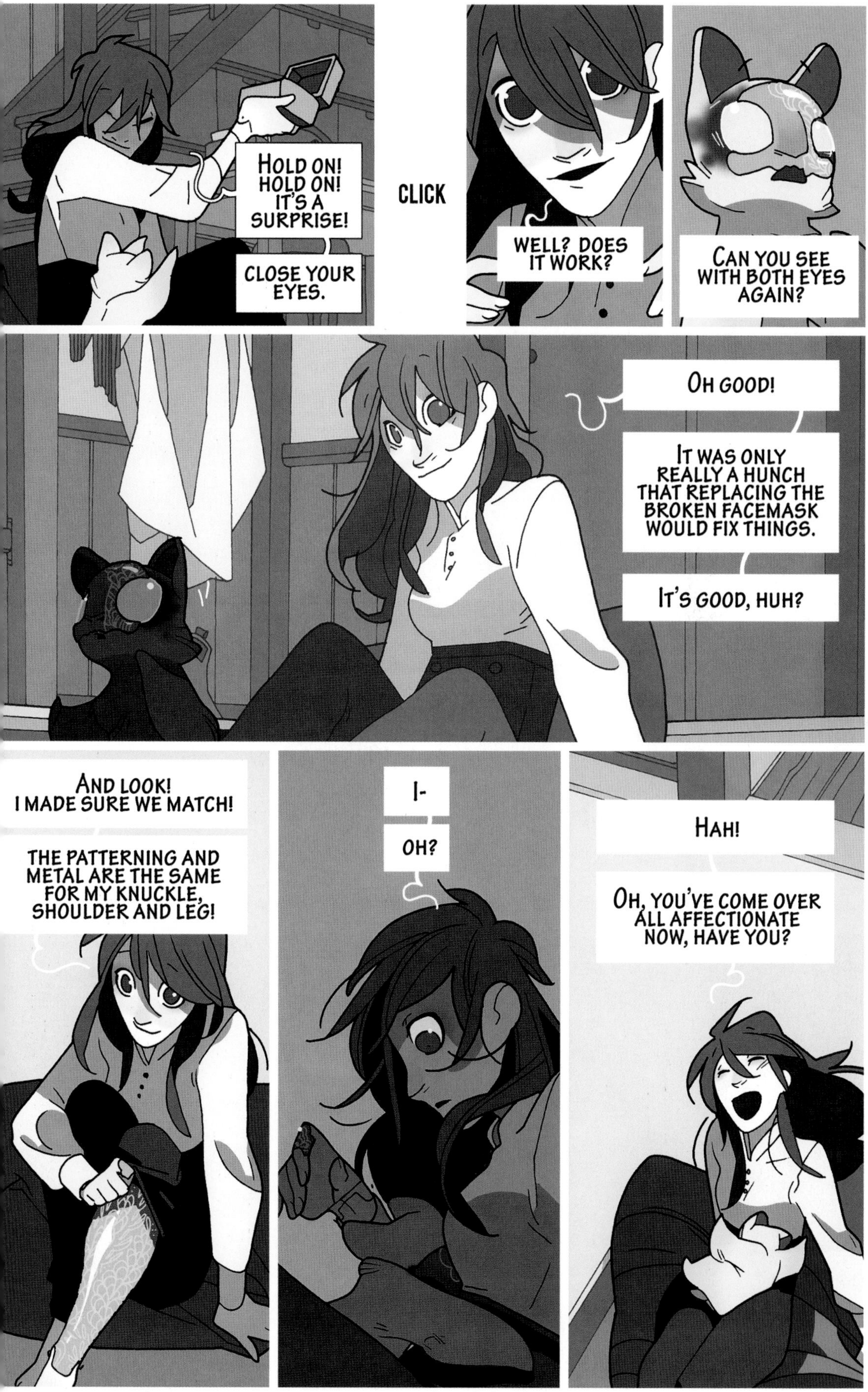
HOLD ON!
HOLD ON!
IT'S A SURPRISE!
CLOSE YOUR EYES.
CLICK
WELL? DOES IT WORK?
CAN YOU SEE WITH BOTH EYES AGAIN?
OH GOOD!
IT WAS ONLY REALLY A HUNCH THAT REPLACING THE BROKEN FACEMASK WOULD FIX THINGS.
IT'S GOOD, HUH?
AND LOOK! I MADE SURE WE MATCH!
THE PATTERNING AND METAL ARE THE SAME FOR MY KNUCKLE, SHOULDER AND LEG!
I-
OH?
HAH!
OH, YOU'VE COME OVER ALL AFFECTIONATE NOW, HAVE YOU?

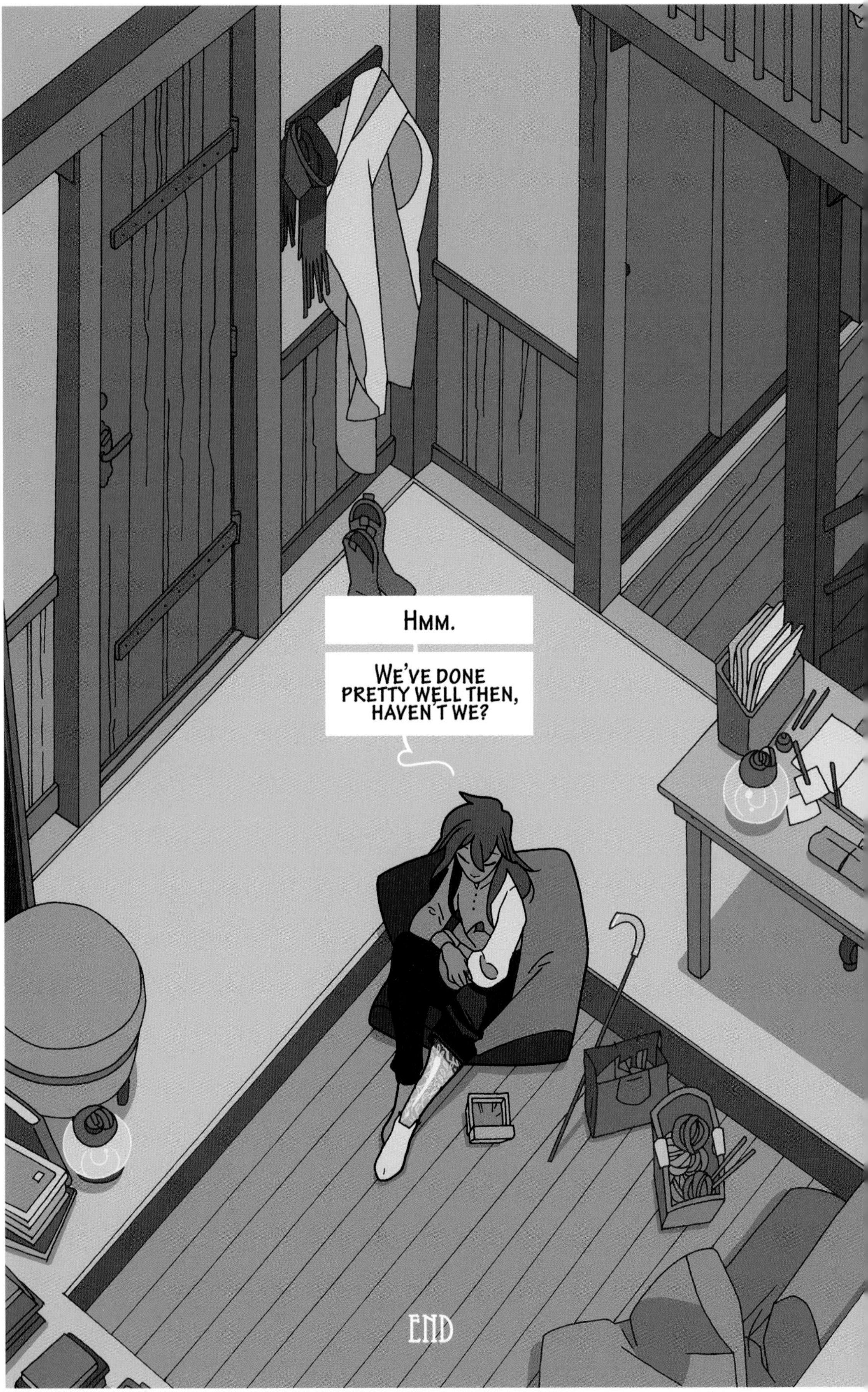
Hmm.
We've done pretty well then, haven't we?
END